LYD

OR

A WEB UNWOVEN

BY

CATHERINE BOWNESS

ACKNOWLEDGMENTS

With love and gratitude to:

Sophy and Ben for invaluable technical and emotional support
as always

and to

Janis and Lyn for their endless patience, helpful advice and
continuing encouragement.

Previous Books by Catherine Bowness

The Lost Palace
Christmas at Great Madden

For Children
The Adventure to the Lost Palace

Regency
Alethea or A Solemn Vow
Cynthia or A Short Stretch of Road
Euphemia or The Secret Widow
Sylvia or the High Moral Ground
Mary or The Perils of Imprudence
Honoria or The Safety of the Frying Pan
Agnes or The Art of Friendship
Letitia or The Convalescent Heart
Cecilia or Flight from a Shadow

Contents

Chapter 1

It was Lydia's seventeenth birthday when she was delivered to her guardian's house for the first time. Peering through the windows of the coach as it swept up to the front door, she tried not to remember her sixteenth birthday, which had been spent with her father in what she must now think of as her 'old' home. It was no longer hers – or her papa's - because, now that he was dead, Melway Hall had gone to his heir, an odious cousin who had been waiting with a singular lack of patience for the prize to fall into his lap.

Lord Melway had been ill for some time before he died so that the heir had been obliged to kick his heels for what he evidently considered an unconscionable length of time. In his impatience, he had taken a house nearby from which he insisted on calling upon them at frequent intervals, almost licking his lips as he gazed around what would be his as soon as Papa conceded defeat to the Grim Reaper.

"I never felt so bitterly my lack of a son until Cousin Richard began to hover over us," her father had said.

"Oh, Papa, perhaps he will not turn out to be so bad after all," she had replied, trying to comfort him.

"On the contrary, I am afraid he will be worse," the sick man said with a sad smile. "And his wife is dreadful. She has not, at least in my presence, gone so far as to take out a tape measure, but she has undoubtedly been assessing the size of the rooms and the length required for what I daresay will be perfectly hideous new curtains."

"Well, thank goodness we will not have to look at them," Lydia said with a shudder.

They both knew that it would not be long before he left her and, aware that her father's greatest anxiety concerned her and how she would manage without him, she had done her best to appear cheerful – and indeed humorous – in the face of the shadow darkening their lives. He had done his best to prepare for what was to come.

The new Viscount would turn her out of the house almost before the old one was cold and she must have somewhere to go because, although the usual arrangement would probably have been for her to remain until she married, it seemed likely that this heir – and his wife – would wish to be rid of her long before she had had a chance to find a husband.

The guardian to whom he had consigned her was an old friend from school, university and the army. They had fought together on the battlefields of France until Lord Melway had been wounded at Waterloo and sent home to die – a task which, in the event, had taken longer than expected. Lydia had never met her future guardian. All she knew of him was that he was Earl of Maresfield and that he had not only a wife but a number of children.

Her father had seen this as an advantage. "It will give you a chance at a family, which I am afraid your mother and I have denied you," he had said.

Lydia supposed he must know of what he spoke but, for herself, she had never felt the lack of siblings although she had felt the lack of a mother. Lady Melway had died when Lydia was six years old so that, although she could remember the presence of a mother, she had little recall of her particular one.

After she died, her father had – eventually – married again, Lydia believed in an attempt to provide her – and perhaps his estate – with more children. Neither the marriage nor its purpose had been a success; her new mother had, while showing tenderness to the small girl when her husband was present, never warmed to her and had indeed positively rejected her when her own attempts at childbearing had proved unsuccessful. Like the previous Lady Melway, she had suffered a number of miscarriages and stillbirths, the last of which had carried her off.

Maresfield Hall came into view, revealed in all its medieval glory as they rounded a bend. It was, Lydia was sure, a handsome edifice and had clearly been well maintained, its brick walls now a faded pink adorned with an extensive creeper positively dripping with long, drooping mauve flowers, but to Lydia it was hideous. Her home, built some two hundred years later, had been long and rambling and a deal less intimidating.

"My! Isn't that beautiful?" her companion exclaimed. "You'll like living in a castle, will you not, Miss Lydia?"

"I suppose I shall grow used to it," she replied without much hope.

"Of course you will, my love," the other woman said

comfortably, patting her hand. "It's bound to feel a bit strange at first, but I'm persuaded everyone will welcome you just as though you were one of the family."

Lydia doubted it and the truth was that she was not sure whether she wished to be one of this family or whether she would prefer to remain the sole representative of her own.

"Chin up!" Sarah said in a firmer tone. She was not a governess, nor yet a companion; Lydia was too old for a governess – and in any event orphans did not generally bring their own governesses when being absorbed into another family – and too young for a companion. Sarah was a maid; she had, when she was young, been the little girl's nursery maid and had been employed by the Viscount almost from the moment of his only living child's birth. There had been a proper nurse in charge of the nursery when she was born but she had been quite old at the time, having been his lordship's when he was a boy, and had long since, along with Papa, Mama and all the little brothers and sisters who had never once drawn breath, gone to a better place. Sarah had looked after Lydia all her life and both hoped that she would be allowed to remain with the girl in her new home. It all depended, Sarah knew, on how ready the new family was to allow the poor little orphan to keep her own servant.

Lydia, although by no means an heiress, was not poor and was perfectly capable of paying Sarah's wages herself out of the allowance which she had always enjoyed. But, now that she had a new guardian, it would be he who administered her inheritance and he who would decide whether Sarah should be kept or laid off. They both knew this although neither could bear to discuss it.

When the carriage came to a halt outside the door, the groom let down the steps and assisted them to alight. As he was doing so, the great oak door opened to reveal an inscrutable male retainer and a frowning female, who was presumably the housekeeper.

This person's first words were not encouraging. "You're late," she said, frowning. "We were expecting you hours ago."

Lydia, who had not known that a time had been fixed for their arrival, apologised.

The housekeeper nodded and stood back to allow the girl to enter. "Well, you'd better come in; her ladyship is waiting for you. Who is this person?"

"My maid, Sarah."

"Indeed? I do not remember being told to expect a maid as well.

You had better go round the back; servants do not come in this way," she added to Sarah.

Lydia, blinking back tears at this unpromising start, kissed her maid, and said, "I will send for you as soon as I can."

"Don't you worry, Miss," Sarah said, her own eyes beginning to water.

The heavy door was shut behind Lydia, who shuddered as though she had been admitted to prison.

"Come this way, Miss," the housekeeper said, primming her lips and leading the way through a hall whose walls were adorned with what seemed to Lydia to be a vast number of heads of dead creatures – not only stags, but also tigers.

As she was led across the hall, she enquired what would happen to Sarah.

"She'll be found a room for the time being, but I don't know whether her ladyship will allow her to remain."

Lydia nodded. "I have some money of my own," she said. "I can pay her myself."

"We'll see," the housekeeper said and, after knocking upon a door at the back of the house, ushered the girl into a large, sunny room where a surprisingly young woman was sitting with a baby on her lap.

"I've brought Miss Lydia, my lady," the housekeeper said by way of introduction.

Lydia dropped a little curtsey to the woman who, in spite of her extreme youth, she took to be the Countess. Her hostess stared at her fixedly from a pair of large blue eyes.

"Oh, yes; you were supposed to arrive at three," she said, looking pointedly at the clock on the mantelpiece which registered ten to four.

"I am sorry, my lady; it was a long journey."

"I know that; I am not entirely ignorant."

Lydia did not reply to this curiously defensive comment for she could think of nothing useful to say, but she wondered why her ladyship should think she was being accused of ignorance.

"You may go, Black," the Countess said coldly. The housekeeper bobbed a respectful curtsey and retreated, shutting the door behind her.

"Come here then," her ladyship commanded.

Lydia approached warily, feeling a little like a new dog invited on approval and determined to refrain from displaying her teeth, at least in

10

the first instance. She was afraid that her decision to appear conciliatory meant that she was not displaying a great deal of spirit which, from the Countess's hostile manner, she felt was required.

She received confirmation of this suspicion a moment later when the Countess said, "Well, there's no need to creep about like that. I won't beat you, although I daresay my lord might. What have you got to say for yourself?"

"Thank you for taking me in," Lydia muttered feebly.

"I don't want your gratitude any more than I wanted you," the Countess said flatly. "Your father must have been all about in the head to leave you to my lord. He already has far too many children."

"He was a friend of Papa's," Lydia explained, finding a wisp of spirit to defend her father's choice, which she was rapidly becoming convinced had indeed been poor.

"A school friend," the Countess said. "Their school days were a long time ago and my lord, if he was ever amiable enough to have any friends, has long since lost that ability."

Lydia wondered why the lady had taken him to husband if he was so disagreeable. She was quite a young lady and could not have been married for more than a few years.

"He can be quite charming when he puts his mind to it," the Countess explained, answering the unspoken question. "But, beyond that, he is neither a good father nor a good husband – and I should know about the latter. He is not here at present – indeed he is not often here, which is a good thing for everyone. Come and sit down by me and I will endeavour to explain the household to you."

"Thank you, my lady."

Lydia sat down obediently on the footstool to which her hostess directed her. This put her at an even graver disadvantage for now she was sitting more or less at the feet of the autocratic young woman.

Before any explanations could be given, however, the baby began to cry. The Countess, an expression almost of pain passing across her delicate features, began to jiggle the baby up and down, an action which did not appear to have a soothing effect upon the infant, whose tears increased. In a few moments both mother and baby had become very red in the face; the Countess's blue eyes began to snap and the baby's screwed up into narrow slits as it directed all its energy into increasing the volume of its protest.

"Do you know anything about babies?" the Countess asked.

"No, my lady, I am an only child."

"Well, now is the time to learn," her ladyship said and thrust the bundle at Lydia.

It was fortunate she was already sitting because the child proved to be much heavier than she had expected and, wrapped as it was in innumerable shawls, was so hot that it put Lydia in mind of a large piece of meat summarily removed from the oven.

"Oh!" she said, shocked and frightened. She had never seen a baby before, much less held one. "Is it a boy or a girl?"

"A boy – but much use that is because my lord already has several sons. I don't know why he married me – he doesn't seem to like me, and he didn't need a son."

"What is his name?" Lydia asked, staring, horrified, at the shrieking infant on her lap.

"My husband or the baby? Baby's name is Jasper."

"How do you do, Jasper?" Lydia said, supporting the infant with one arm and holding out the other hand.

The child grasped it; his little fingers were hot and sticky so that Lydia wondered if she would ever be able to detach her hand from his. He stopped screaming and stared at her with his mouth open; his face was still red and his cheeks were wet with tears but there was something about the expression in his eyes, some dawning understanding that this might be someone who had no expectations which he could not fulfil, which completely threw her. From thinking him a horrid, noisy, hot bundle and wishing that his mother had not seen fit to hand him over, she quite suddenly felt as interested in him as he clearly was in her. Both smiled beatifically at the same moment and Lydia was sufficiently inspired to kiss his damp cheek.

He gurgled and took hold of a portion of her hair with such force that she could not move her head without hurting herself.

"I am delighted to make your acquaintance, Jasper," she said gravely. "My name is Lydia and I hope we will become friends."

"He seems to like you," his mother said in a disapproving tone. "You're the first person he has shown any affection for in the whole of the time he has been on this earth. He does not like me above half, and I am sure he does not like Nanny Macintosh much more – although he always looks quite pleased when she collects him. She is very strict so that I should imagine they are always at loggerheads. She puts him in his crib and leaves him to scream – and he *will* scream and scream until, in the end, she is forced to pick him up again – or, more often, to send the nursemaid to do so. That is why he is sitting with

12

me – she is at the end of her tether, although of course she doesn't like to say so in case we lay her off. Do you think we should?"

"I've no notion," Lydia admitted. "I've never met a baby before. Why do you think he does cry so much?"

"I cannot tell; like you, I have never met a baby before," the Countess said.

Chapter 2

From this more promising development, Lydia and the Countess found a certain accommodation between them.

Nanny Macintosh, when she came to fetch Jasper and found him, several of his shawls discarded, sitting happily on Lydia's lap, looked displeased. She was quite an old woman and could not resist pointing out that she had been his lordship's nurse when he was a baby.

"He was a little angel," she said with a fond, reminiscent smile. "I can't think where Master Jasper gets his nature from."

Judging by the Countess's ill-concealed squirming in response to this observation, Lydia thought the nurse must be implying that any lack of agreeability in the infant had clearly been inherited from his mother.

"Perhaps he has a pain in his tummy," Lydia suggested for one of the baby's least attractive habits, which he had already displayed a number of times, was a tendency to vomit with alarming frequency over whomever he was sitting upon at the time.

"Has he been sick?" Nanny Macintosh asked.

"Yes, several times."

"Very likely it's the wet nurse," Nanny said. "I've told her not to eat onions. It is high time, in any event, that he was properly weaned."

Lydia, not considering herself qualified to comment upon this diagnosis of the problem, said that she thought he had been too hot as well. "He seemed happier when I took off some of his shawls."

"I only hope exposing him like that will not lead to an inflammation of the lung," Nanny said disapprovingly. She considered herself to be the expert and, while only partially successful at concealing her impatience with the mother, was outraged to receive suggestions from a slip of a girl who had not been in the house above five minutes.

She snatched the baby from Lydia's lap and began once more to swaddle him in the discarded shawls. Jasper, who had been enjoying himself with a young woman who was apparently interested in what he had to say, screwed up his face and recommenced shrieking.

Lydia glanced anxiously at the Countess whose face bore a look of unmistakeable disgust. "Pray take him away, Macintosh!" she said, averting her gaze from her infant.

"Come along then, Master Jasper," Nanny said and bore the

screaming infant from the room.

Silence fell between the two women until Lydia asked, "Has he many brothers and sisters?"

"Yes, a great many, but they are none of them mine. He is my first – and, I sincerely hope, my last."

"Do the others all live here?"

"Most of 'em, most of the time; the only person who doesn't live here – and hardly ever visits us – is my husband."

"Is he still in the army?" This was Lydia's seventeenth birthday and she did not have a great deal of experience of people, but her extensive reading had led her to believe that most mothers liked – nay, were devoted to – their children – and sometimes even had a fondness for their husbands.

"No; he was wounded at Waterloo – I understand it was after that that your father decided to leave you to him. He has barely darkened the doors of his ancestral home since, although I suppose I should be glad about this. At least it makes it less likely that I will have another."

Lydia nodded, not trusting herself to find the right words to express sympathy for a confession which she thought had been made too early in their acquaintance and whose subject matter caused her embarrassment.

"Papa and Lord Maresfield knew each other at school," she murmured, trying to find an innocuous and far from intimate connection between her and her hostess.

"When did your mother die?" the Countess asked abruptly.

"A long time ago – when I was quite a little girl."

"Why did your papa not marry again?"

"He did - twice - but they died too."

"Oh dear – and both without having any children?"

"No; or at least, one died along with her son when he was born. The other died of an inflammation of the lung after she had been riding in the rain."

"He seems to have been very unfortunate. Maresfield has nine children, including the baby. They are all, apart of course from Jasper, the progeny of his first wife. I can't think why he married me – we have only been married a year and a half and yet he already avoids me. I am beginning to think he simply wanted a mother for his children because he is always away in London and they are always here with me – except of course when they are at school."

15

"Are any of them here at present?" Lydia asked after a long pause while she wracked her brain for something to say to this strange, abrupt woman who seemed inclined to give voice to what most people would consider better left unspoken.

"Oh, yes, most of them; it's the holidays, you see – although fortunately nearly the end. You will meet them later, I suppose. How old are you?"

"Seventeen – today – my lady."

"Good Gracious – I thought you much younger. You are very small. Did your father not feed you properly even though you had no competition?"

"I think I am probably made that way; my mama was like me, I understand."

"I see. I suppose your papa married her for her money, did he?"

Lydia thought that this conclusion must have been arrived at because she was not pretty and, having already claimed a strong likeness to her mother, had thus damned her mama as a plain woman possessed of a fortune. She would have been more annoyed if she had not already decided that the Countess – who was excessively pretty – was perhaps missing one or two essential components in the upper storey.

She said, "She was not an heiress but she did have a substantial portion. It is this, which is not part of the entail and which my father did not touch during her lifetime, which has been bequeathed to me. I am not, as I am sure you are aware, my lady, entirely without funds of my own."

"I see; how do you mean to use them? Are you intending to offer to pay for your bed and board?"

"I own I had not thought of that; I supposed that all that sort of thing would already have been arranged between the lawyers."

"No doubt it has, but my lord has not seen fit to inform me of the result."

"Nor me, my lady."

"Well, I don't suppose he would since you are by way of being on the other side; I would, however, have expected your lawyers to have informed you of the basis on which you are coming to live here. For instance, since you are older than you look, or than I took you for, am I to suppose that you no longer need to avail yourself of the services of the governess who sees to my lord's daughters and his younger sons?"

16

"I do not believe so, my lady."

"So how will you occupy yourself all day? Do you expect me to accompany you to the assembly rooms?"

"I suppose I could help to look after the younger children. How old are they?"

"Oh, lord, I don't know. The eldest, Lord Chalvington, is one-and-twenty; he has two sisters, one of whom is nearly eighteen and the other not much more than a year younger; the others are, so far as I can recall, fifteen, fourteen, ten, eight and nearly four. My predecessor, as you can see, gave birth to a great many children in quick succession; I am sure I do not know how she managed it – Jasper very nearly killed me. The eldest girl is agitating for a Season and the younger is still nominally under the control of Miss Westmacott, the governess, although in truth she has never been under anyone's control; neither of them has."

"Are they all girls except for Lord Chalvington?"

"Oh no, which is why I cannot conceive what led his lordship to marry me – he has plenty of sons."

"Perhaps he fell in love with you, my lady."

The Countess laughed at this although there was little amusement in the sound. She drew back her lips, opened her mouth and emitted a sort of titter.

"I own I thought so too at the outset, but I have been proved mistaken. I can only suppose he wanted me to manage his children, as I said, in particular the two older girls, who are extraordinarily difficult. Unfortunately, as they are not much younger than I – and I have been dreadfully ill since Jasper was born – I am afraid I have not fulfilled that particular purpose. I have sometimes wondered if that is why he is so exceedingly displeased with me. The younger of the two big girls – and they are big - is Anthea; her elder sister, who is not much of an improvement so far as conduct is concerned, is Alicia. All their names begin with the same letter, which I have always thought absurd and confusing, but understand that was my predecessor's conceit. Lord Chalvington rejoices in the name of Ambrose and his brothers are Amos, Adrian, Albert and Amory. The youngest girl, who is ten, is Amabel."

Lydia thought it unlikely she would be able to remember any of these names, let alone assign them to the correct people.

Her ladyship, perhaps divining something of this or, more likely, simply growing tired of entertaining the orphan, rang the bell and requested Miss Westmacott's attendance.

The governess, when she eventually appeared – and it was some considerable time before she did - looked exhausted. She was a youngish woman, probably not much more than five and thirty, although she might have been much younger. Her face was pale and prematurely lined as though her skin were criss-crossed by a ghostly spider's web and yet, in spite of this sign of advancing age, her lips were voluptuously full, although to Lydia's mind, spoiled by a tragic droop at the corners. Her hair was what is popularly described as red – a sort of burnt sienna in fact – and her eyes were brown and excessively large so that, apart from the fragility of her skin and the discontent of her expression, she might have been a beauty. She was wearing a plain grey dress which showed signs of having been much darned; the stitches were very neat and small but, although it was clear that a good deal of trouble had been taken to match the mending thread to the original, it was nevertheless not quite exact. The effect of this was to provide a surprising degree of embellishment to an otherwise exceedingly dull garment; further ornament was amply provided by the figure of the woman wearing it, whose shape seemed more suited to a dancer than a governess for she was neither tall nor short, was slender but curved and possessed of an innate grace which no amount of dull clothes nor dissatisfaction with her life could altogether stifle. Every effort seemed to have been made to hide her beauty for her hair was pulled straight back from her face and fastened in the most uncompromising knot Lydia had ever seen. No doubt at the beginning of the day she would present as neat, although possibly rather startled, but by this time of the afternoon her rich curls were beginning to escape from their confinement and a number clustered around her face, softening its lines and imparting a degree of quite sensual promise. Lydia was both too young and the wrong sex to appreciate this picture but, later, she understood better the curious despair she felt in the young woman's presence. It seemed to her then that Miss Westmacott served as a sort of pictorial example of the many reasons why no young woman would want to take up such a profession.

"Ah, Miss Westmacott," the Countess said, making an effort to sit upright for she had begun to subside in her chair as the day wore on.

"My lady," Miss Westmacott murmured, dropping a small curtsey.

18

"This young woman is Lydia Melway, whose father has left her to my husband in his will. She has been delivered today but, as his lordship is not on the premises, we must do our best to find her a place in the house. It is her birthday today," Lydia was surprised and rather touched that the Countess had remembered this. "She is seventeen so possibly a little old for your classes but it's my belief that she would benefit from them – and indeed that you and the children will benefit even more from her joining them. She has requested a role where she can be of assistance in the household and it seems to me that helping you would be of enormous benefit to everyone. She has already proved her ability in the handling of children by soothing my son almost the moment she took him upon her lap."

"Certainly, my lady," Miss Westmacott said with a noticeable absence of enthusiasm for the promised assistance. "Will you come with me, Miss Melway?"

Lydia rose, bobbed a small obeisance in the direction of the Countess, who nodded benevolently, and followed the other woman out of the room.

"Have you been shown to your chamber?" the governess asked as they made their way across the hall towards the stairs.

"No."

"Am I to assume that you do not know where it is?"

"Yes."

"In that case, we will need Mrs Black's assistance."

Miss Westmacott addressed one of the two footmen standing in the hall, requesting him to fetch the housekeeper.

"We will wait here." Miss Westmacott sat down on one of the elegant upright chairs ranged against the wall and Lydia sat down beside her.

"I believe she met me on the doorstep," Lydia said. "She took me straight to her ladyship because she seemed to think I was late."

"Of course. Everyone is always late here. You will find us a busy household," she went on, although, in spite of the vast number of children whose names the Countess had reeled off, there was no sign of busyness anywhere. The house was quiet, the remaining footman motionless.

"Yes; his lordship has a great many children," Lydia murmured; a pointless remark for clearly Miss Westmacott knew, probably more precisely than anyone else, how many children the Earl had – at least in this house. She felt her exchanges with the governess had so far been

19

distinguished by what she feared was a want, not only of enthusiasm, but also of originality, nicely matched by Miss Westmacott's manner ever since they had been introduced.

"Indeed; your help in managing them will be of enormous assistance," Miss Westmacott said graciously but without much evidence of conviction.

They were still sitting there awaiting the arrival of Mrs Black when the front door burst open and a young man strode into the house. He was probably not yet quite fully grown but was already tall, although slender as a sapling. He was dressed for riding and, throwing his whip, gloves and hat upon a table, was about to run up the stairs when he noticed that, of the two women seated in the hall, one was unfamiliar.

"Didn't see you sitting there so quietly - how do you do?" He held out his hand to Lydia, who took it. He had a firm clasp and, close to, could be seen to be more than usually handsome: his hair was a very dark chestnut brown and cut rather long – most likely it had not been cut for some time – and his eyes were that mixture of colours known as hazel, large and sparkling. Everything about him seemed to be fairly pulsing with energy so that the quietness of the hall, the sobriety of the footman and the patience of the governess were immediately altered and infused with liveliness.

"Chalvington," he said.

"How do you do, my lord?" Lydia responded politely.

"Ambrose, this is Miss Melway. She has come to live with us," Miss Westmacott explained in anything but delighted tones.

"Really? I hope you won't come to regret it," he said, bestowing upon her a brilliant smile, which revealed a set of perfectly white and even teeth.

"I'm sure I shan't," she said, although her tone lacked certainty.

He took her remark in the spirit in which it was meant, saying, "We'll try to make that the case. To what do we owe your presence?"

"Your father - Lord Maresfield - is my guardian."

"Good Lord! I am his eldest son so let me, on behalf of us all, welcome you to our family. Why are you sitting in the hall as though waiting to be summoned before a judge?"

Lydia was prevented from answering by the appearance of Mrs Black, who, upon receiving instructions from the governess, led the way to the stairs.

Lord Chalvington bade her a friendly farewell, assuring her he would look forward to their next meeting.

The three women went up the stairs and some way along a corridor before Mrs Black opened a door and stood back to allow Lydia to enter her chamber. It was a small room but appeared to be equipped with everything that anyone could possibly require; it looked out upon a *parterre* and, beyond that into a meadow. Sarah was already there and engaged in unpacking her trunk.

"Who are you?" Miss Westmacott asked sharply.

"I am Miss Melway's maid, ma'am," Sarah replied, bobbing a curtsey whose height was carefully calculated to the recipient's perceived status.

"You have a maid?" the governess asked.

"Yes."

"I don't know whether you will be permitted to have a servant of your own," Miss Westmacott said doubtfully; it was the first hint of uncertainty Lydia had perceived in the governess.

"I will speak to her ladyship later," Lydia said, raising her chin and looking down her nose, although the governess was several inches taller.

"If you like to come with me, I will show you the schoolroom," Miss Westmacott said in a colder but, Lydia could not help noticing, less patronising tone.

The schoolroom was almost bursting with people and looked at first sight to contain more than seven children and a nursemaid. They were all there except for Lord Chalvington, who had presumably taken himself off to his own apartments to change out of his riding dress.

If Lydia had thought the previous Countess's conceit of giving them all names beginning with A would be confusing, she realised, as soon as she saw them, that that would be a minor detail for it seemed to her that they looked as alike as a litter of puppies, the only major differences between them being their sex and size. She would, she thought, have to try to remember their birth order and attach that to their names if she were to have any hope of distinguishing one from another.

Nobody seemed to notice the return of the governess so that, drawing a breath the better to project her voice into the *mêlée*, Miss Westmacott was forced to raise her voice.

"Children! Be quiet!"

There was neither a noticeable diminution in noise nor many

heads turned towards their preceptress, but the governess did not allow that to deter her from imparting her information. "I have brought you a new sister," she said. "Her name is Lydia Melway and she is your papa's ward."

Chapter 3

Lady Maresfield heaved a sigh when the door shut upon the governess and her husband's new ward.

She had been dreading the arrival of the girl and had, so to speak, armed herself with her baby upon her lap in preparation. Because she had expected her nearly an hour before she walked in, she had been forced to spend a more than usually prolonged period with her son, trying, with increasing desperation, to entertain him. The result of this was a feeling of despair for it seemed to her to be perfectly clear, not only that her son disliked her, but that he preferred the new arrival. This was hardly surprising considering that she herself was vastly more taken with Lydia Melway than with any of the other Maresfield children, except of course for Lord Chalvington, who could no longer be described as a child with any degree of accuracy.

The only bright point on which she tried to focus her mind was that the girl did not in any way resemble her husband. She had been much afraid, when first told of her, that one of his by-blows was to be foisted upon her and, already wilting under the burden of his legitimate children – who, she was convinced, all hated her – did not know how she was to support the humiliation of enduring the presence of an illegitimate child of his. Sometimes she wondered if her indifference towards her own was related to her growing enmity towards his father and her despair as she observed that, with every passing day, the child grew to look more and more like his half-siblings. He seemed to have a horridly similar personality too: noisy, selfish, demanding and hostile.

As for her husband: she did not know what he felt, either for her or for Jasper. He had been gone for so long that she wondered, half humorously, whether she would recognise him if he walked through the door. He had remained in the house for a few days after the baby's birth and had, she gathered – for she had not been in a position to judge - evinced a proper degree of pride in the infant.

She had done her best to behave – and feel – as she believed a mother should but was aware that it had not been enough. She barely knew one end of her son from the other – both were equally off-putting, to tell the truth – and, by the time Nature had decided that she would not after all die this time, she had grown thin and pale with dull hair and darkly-circled eyes. She was not surprised – indeed she was almost relieved – when her husband returned to the battlefields of France.

23

Her head ached and she reverted, as so often, to dwelling upon her secret wish that she had died after – or preferably before – the birth. Everything had been utterly miserable since. Her body was unrecognisable, her looks and spirit damaged apparently beyond repair. Was this all there was now? And was it thus for most women? She began to think it might be. All that preening and giggling and flirting, all that careful deploying of oneself in the best possible light to attract the finest husband Society could provide, led inevitably to this: pain, misery and loneliness. At least the Earl had plenty of children already, several of whom were sons, so that the only ray of hope penetrating her wretchedness was the thought that, now that she had lost her looks, he would be unlikely to wish to father another child with her.

Nanny Macintosh was another member of the household whom she disliked and whose disapproval had a withering effect upon her. She had not been the Countess's nurse; she had been the Earl's and made a point of the superiority of her position in the household on this account. She had overseen his lordship's first smiles, first steps, first mashed food and had, in addition, applied the first – and, the Countess strongly suspected, the only - discipline he had ever received. It was generally supposed that he must have undergone some later from his first tutor and, no doubt, a deal more when he was packed off to school, although she could discern no evidence that he had. However, no one supposed that, since leaving Eton and Oxford, anyone had seen fit to correct the smallest portion of his behaviour.

Nanny Macintosh held fast to her belief that she was the only person on Earth whose strictures he heeded. Privately, Lady Maresfield wondered if it was the old woman who was responsible for his selfish, demanding nature and, whilst hoping that her son would not be led in the same direction, could think of no means to prevent it. Nanny Macintosh ruled the household.

The Countess shook herself – a mistake because it only exacerbated her headache - rose and went to her little desk in the corner of the room. There was a pile of correspondence through which she knew she must wade; she could not go on delaying replying to all these letters for ever.

The subject of the letters was similar in every case, although the approach made by each writer – and they were all female - differed according to character. The reason all these women had felt inspired to put pen to paper was that Lady Alicia, the Earl's eldest daughter, had reached an age when everyone expected her to be launched upon the

Marriage Mart. The Countess was surprised that they remembered this fact for she would have expected them to be more concerned about their own daughters, nieces and granddaughters, but so it was; everyone seemed to know that the Earl of Maresfield's eldest daughter was less than two years younger than his wife and were perhaps curious to know how well she, Emmeline Fetcham, was coping with stepchildren so close to herself in age. As the Season was already more or less upon them, they were engaged in making up their lists for luncheons, picnics, routs and balls.

Emmeline was expected to bring her newly acquired daughter to London and accompany her on the endless round of social engagements which she had herself undergone such a short time ago. She knew that this was necessary; indeed, if she had not been so mired in despondency, the prospect of finding a husband for the girl, and thus removing her from the household, ought to have been a sufficiently attractive carrot to prompt her to dip her pen in the ink.

Unfortunately, she had by no means recovered her spirits since the dreadful ordeal of giving birth and the dashing of all her romantic hopes regarding her marriage. She found it difficult to do anything at all and the idea of returning to London, where she had been happy and where she had met her husband and indulged in what she now realised had been a ridiculous belief that she would live happily ever after, was disheartening

She realised too that dragging tiresome girls around London would be a part of her life for some considerable time for, following Alicia, there would be Anthea. She had hoped that she could have delayed that for a year, giving her two years to recover before launching another difficult girl, but, now that Lydia had arrived, she was afraid she would have to introduce her to the *ton* next year – and Anthea the one after. There would be no respite.

Neither of her stepdaughters could by any stretch of the imagination be described as amiable but both were at least handsome; Lydia, who appeared to be more agreeable, was a plain little thing who looked at least five years younger than she was. While taking Alicia around would be painful and would very likely involve frequent tantrums, she did not suppose that it would be difficult to find her a husband so long as the girl was prepared to conceal her character for long enough to reach the altar; finding one for Lydia might be more problematic.

She drew a piece of paper towards her, dipped her pen in the ink and began a reply to Lady Trowbridge, whose letter was on the top of the pile. She remembered the woman from her own come-out, and did not like her but comforted herself with the thought that that might have been largely due to her own success – or perhaps more properly her mama's - in bringing Lord Maresfield up to scratch. Lady Trowbridge's elder daughter had languished, unsought, for two Seasons. She had now been placed with an obscure baronet who lived in the north, only just in time to permit her mama to bring the next one out.

There was also the fact that, since her own marriage and the disillusion which had followed, she did not know how she could bear to return to London, this time as a chaperone, and endeavour to show enthusiasm for the whole tragi-comedy which was the Marriage Mart. Girls, she thought, were displayed like horses, put through their paces and then, not to put too fine a point upon it, sold to the highest bidder – although of course no money was received from the buyer; rather the seller sweetened his offering with a dowry. She had foolishly believed Maresfield had fallen in love with her and, although the prospect of being obliged to become mother to eight children had been something of a fly in the ointment, she had been delighted, flattered, even ecstatic, when he made his offer.

The ink had dried on her pen by the time she lowered it to the paper; she dipped it again and began to write, saying all that was expected of her – she was nothing if not well brought up even if there were moments when she indulged herself by being rude. She signed it, not with a flourish but with determination. She had done it: she had committed herself and Alicia to a trip to London. Having begun, she continued and wrote three more letters in a similar style before taking a fresh piece of paper and applying herself to making a list – several lists.

This proved to be difficult so that she began to wonder if her reluctance to face another Season was not so much to do with her fear of returning to London as with her ignorance of how to proceed.

In the end she wrote another letter, this time to her mother, begging her for help in arranging all the parties and introductions which would be required. When she had done, she rang the bell and instructed the butler, Pelmartin, to see that it was posted to Lady Fetcham as soon as possible. Someone would be obliged to take it to the post office and pay for its transmission; the others would have to wait for his lordship to frank them when he next visited – an event which might not take place for weeks – or even months. In any event, since she had decided to throw herself upon her mother's support, that doughty matron could be asked to cast an eye over her daughter's first efforts at behaving like a proper countess with a grown-up daughter.

By the time she had done this, the afternoon was well advanced and there was barely time to go out for a walk before she must change for dinner, a meal that was eaten early since his lordship had decreed that they must keep country hours – whether he was there or not.

It was a fine afternoon and she found, as always, that going out lifted her mood. She was not accompanied by any other member of the household; indeed, although she spent most of her time alone, it was only when she was outside that she could be certain that no one would disturb her.

This afternoon, her spirits rose slightly at the prospect of the new ward's presence at dinner for she had found the girl unexpectedly pleasing once she had got over the usual shameful feeling of jealousy at observing how much her child preferred almost anyone else to his mother; she wondered if this was because the girl had shown no disposition to set herself above her ladyship – unlike the odious Nanny Macintosh, whose manner never failed to make the Countess feel inadequate.

Chapter 4

Silence did not fall upon the schoolroom when Miss Westmacott spoke but there was a diminution in the cacophony. The smaller children continued to shout and cuff each other but both Alicia and Anthea ceased their chatter and directed their gaze upon the new arrival.

"Hasn't my father got enough children without acquiring a ward as well?" Alicia asked, directing a look of scorn at Lydia.

"There is no need to be uncivil," Miss Westmacott said coldly. "Please greet your new sister in a proper manner. This," she added to Lydia, "is my lord's eldest daughter, Lady Alicia."

"How do you do?" Lydia said politely.

"I am very well, thank you," Alicia responded. "I suppose you have lost your papa," she went on, her eye moving over Lydia's black dress. "Is that why you have come?"

"Yes."

"I am sorry for your loss."

"Were you attached to him?" the next girl, Anthea, enquired rudely.

Both were well-grown females with the familial chestnut hair; Alicia's had been put up – not very well and, by this time in the afternoon, it was beginning to escape its bonds - but Anthea's was tumbling down her back in luxurious waves, ineffectively anchored by a blue ribbon.

"Yes." Lydia was conscious that her contributions had so far been woefully inadequate but this stark – and unfeeling - question concerning her beloved papa could not properly be answered on account of its having triggered the hateful, and only too frequent, response of the pricking behind the eyes which she had learned presaged tears. She could not – would not – cry in front of these people.

"And I suppose you have no mother either," Anthea went on, as though having somehow shed both parents was a character flaw.

"No; she died some time ago."

"Mine died three years ago, after Amory was born." Anthea pointed at the smallest child, who was engaged in a fight for a toy horse with a slightly larger boy. "I don't think we'd notice much if Papa died for he is hardly ever here," she added in what was perhaps meant as a conciliatory gesture.

There was no proper answer Lydia could think of to this depressing statement so she nodded in what she hoped was a sympathetic manner.

"Are you related to us?" the largest boy asked. He had stopped what he was doing as soon as he noticed her.

This was easier to answer. "No; my papa and yours were at school together and then in the army – in France."

"Papa was wounded at Waterloo," the boy went on. "Was that when yours died?"

"No, he died afterwards, but it was on account of the wounds he received then."

He nodded and Miss Westmacott, who had been standing beside Lydia during this interrogation, interrupted to introduce him as Lord Amos.

"My brother, Chalvington, was in that battle too," Amos went on, ignoring the governess, "but, luckily, he wasn't hurt – or only a very little."

"You must have been relieved. Is he still in the army?"

"No; Papa never wanted him to join up but Ambrose – that's Chalvington – made such a fuss that he gave in, but only on the condition that he resign his commission when Boney was finally done for; he said he would be better to go back to Oxford, which he had begun before he persuaded Papa to allow him to fight. I think Papa made sure he wasn't in the front line because otherwise it's pretty amazing that he wasn't killed, or at least hurt. Ambrose gets quite miffed if you say that, so I advise you to keep your lips closed."

Lydia could not conceive it likely that the subject would come up between her and the lively young man she had met in the hall. "My lips will remain sealed," she said gravely.

"Good! Have you got any brothers?"

"No, I am afraid not; I have neither brothers nor sisters."

"Lord! Lucky you – there are far too many of us!"

She laughed. "But I don't suppose you're ever lonely."

"No, but I wish I could be alone sometimes."

"Have you met Baby Jasper?" a small girl enquired, sidling up to Lydia.

"Yes; he was with his mama when I arrived."

"I like him much better than Amory," the girl said so that Lydia wondered if she had only asked the question in order to be able to remind her brothers how much she disliked them. "He never stops

29

talking, and I don't like Albert much either because he pulls my hair; I'm Amabel, by the way."

"How do you do, Amabel? I believe you're ten, aren't you?" Lydia asked, after a painful moment of wracking her brains to remember the list of names and their order which the Countess had reeled off.

"Yes! How old are you?"

"Seventeen today."

"Goodness! I thought you were younger than that – you're between Anthea and Alicia then."

"Yes. How old did you think I was?"

"About twelve," the girl said after contemplating Lydia with her head on one side for at least a minute.

"I am little undersized," Lydia admitted with a rueful grin.

"We're all quite big," Amabel confided with a sideways glance at her sisters. "They don't like that – they would prefer to be like little dolls – but we can't help it, can we? Papa is very tall and Mama was not one of those little dabs."

"As I am."

"Oh!" Amabel had the grace to blush. "But I wish I looked like you," she added in a small voice.

"Gracious! Why in the world would you want to look like me?" Lydia asked, astonished.

"Because you're like a little pixie – and I think that's sweet."

"I see; well, I would rather be an amazon."

"Oh, don't say that in front of Alicia or Anthea – they would be bound to think you were mocking them. That's what Ambrose calls them."

It began to seem to Lydia that there were a great many things she could not say in front of one or another of the Maresfields and she had almost decided to open her mouth as infrequently as possible when there was a knock upon the door.

Invited to enter, Mrs Black came in with the news that it was time for those who took dinner in the dining room to change. Lydia looked at her interrogatively and received a nod.

"Yes, you, Miss Lydia; her ladyship said I was to tell you particularly that you are to take dinner downstairs."

This announcement was met with fury by Anthea.

"Why should she go downstairs? She's probably younger than I! It's monstrous!"

30

"I daresay she can be more relied upon to conduct herself appropriately," Alicia replied, making no attempt to conceal a malicious smile.

"No, I think it is because, in spite of my being so small and thin, I am in point of fact seventeen," Lydia explained, claiming her new advanced age as a *fait accompli* rather than just a birthday and, at the same time, making her first attempt at a soothing intervention. Being her parents' only child, she had never suffered the biting blast of a sibling's cruelty nor the demeaning sense of inadequacy that she somehow divined in Anthea.

"Seventeen?" Alicia turned her venom upon the new girl. "Will you be expecting to be launched too? Nobody would believe you're grown up! It would be ludicrous!"

"I don't think I'm quite ready for that," she replied mildly. "In any event, my papa has only recently died."

Alicia looked both deflated and embarrassed by this explanation and Amos said, "He was wounded at Waterloo — and then died of his wounds."

"So was ours!" another, smaller, boy said, approaching her for the first time.

"Yes, but he didn't die, stupid!" a slightly larger one reminded his sibling.

"Not yet!" the first one, who looked to be about eight and must therefore be Albert, reminded him.

"Oh, how can you even think he might?" Anthea exclaimed, apparently forgetting that, five minutes earlier, she had claimed she would barely notice her father's demise, "or mention it? You might tempt Fate!"

Miss Westmacott took a hand. "It was some time ago now and your father is more or less recovered," she reminded the children. "I don't think there is any need for anxiety on that score."

"No, he's far more likely to die in a riding accident or be killed in a duel," Alicia said bitterly.

"I think we've had enough of this sort of speculation," Miss Westmacott said sharply. "Miss Lydia, can you find your way back to your room to change for dinner? I am needed here to oversee the children's supper."

"I'll take you," Alicia surprisingly offered.

As they went out, Lydia asked whether Alicia knew to which room she had been assigned.

31

"No, I've not the least idea, but I daresay we'll find it eventually. Mama – of course she is not my mama, but I am obliged to call her that – goes into a pet if we are not downstairs at what she considers to be the proper time. Did you ever have a step-mama?" she added, as they walked down the corridor.

"Yes, I had two, but they both died and neither of them gave birth to any living children so that I am quite inexperienced when it comes to brothers and sisters."

"How fortunate you are! They are the most frightful burden. Anthea is always wanting to push herself forward and the boys are just silly – always fighting and shouting. I own I dislike them all intensely."

"Does Lord Chalvington fight and shout?"

Alicia laughed. "No; he thinks he's above such things – and in any event, he's not here very often. I quite like him as a matter of fact, but I don't think he likes me; he prefers Anthea."

Lydia, having no idea of the truth or otherwise of this claim and realising that a sense of inadequacy was not confined to the younger siblings, said nothing.

It did not take them long to find her chamber because she knew it was on the same corridor as the schoolroom. As they traversed the length of it, Alicia pointed out other people's rooms, including her own, and it was she who eventually paused outside a door, saying, "I should think it must be this one. Shall we see?"

Lydia nodded and Alicia turned the knob, revealing that the room was presently occupied by an elderly servant, who was carefully aligning hairbrushes on the dressing table.

"Who's that?" Alicia asked suspiciously.

"Sarah – my maid."

"You brought a maid with you?"

"Yes; I was not permitted to travel alone."

"Of course not, but I suppose she could be sent back."

"I don't believe she could; there is no 'back' to go to; our house has been taken over by Papa's heir and, since Sarah has always been my maid, there is no place for her now."

"She will have to find another position," Alicia said.

"Shall I go straight downstairs when I have changed?" Lydia asked, ignoring this.

"Yes, if you can find your way. Once you get downstairs, one of the footmen will direct you."

"Thank you."

Alicia nodded and withdrew.

"I hope I will not have to send you away," Lydia told Sarah, shutting the door. "Have you been provided with accommodation?"

"Yes, Miss. That Mrs Black has put me in a small room by myself – 'for the time being', she said. I am not hopeful that I will be permitted to stay."

"I will speak to her ladyship," Lydia promised. "She is not half so terrifying as Mrs Black made her out to be."

"Perhaps she liked you, Miss."

"I can't think why, but I believe she did, in the end." Lydia did not say, for she did not consider it proper to share confidences of such a nature with the maid, but she rather thought it had something to do with the way she had soothed the child – which might have worked in quite the opposite fashion – as well as the fact that she and the Countess were both interlopers – and the Maresfields, with their size and loudness, were an intimidating pack.

"You always were too modest," Sarah said with a smile. "A person would have to be very odd not to like you."

As she spoke, she was unbuttoning her mistress's dress, took it off and threw an almost identical one over her head. The new one differed not at all in colour, being unremittingly black, but had a lower neck and was made of crepe rather than cotton.

"Now, sit down, Miss, and I'll do your hair."

Lydia was slight and pale with very dark hair so that, dressed all in black, she seemed part of the shadows from a distance but the Countess, who was a yellow-haired beauty, had been wrong in her initial assessment of the girl as 'not particularly pretty'. Lydia was, in fact, exceedingly pretty: her features were unusually symmetrical, small and exquisite, although her eyes were rather larger than entirely necessary. They, like her hair, were very dark and so shadowed by eyelashes that it was sometimes hard to read her expression.

Her hair arranged to her and Sarah's mutual satisfaction and tied with a black ribbon, she set off for dinner.

"Will you be able to find the way, Miss Lydia?" Sarah asked.

"I don't know precisely where they meet but I can find my way downstairs and will then seek directions from one of the footmen."

In the end she did not have to go to such lengths for she met Lord Chalvington as she began to descend the stairs. He came bouncing up behind her and hailed her with a cheery, "Wait for me, O new sister!"

She stopped, turned and met his smile with one of her own. Apart from the baby, Ambrose was the only member of the family so far who had greeted her with anything approaching pleasure; she did not suppose that was related to her character but had rather more to do with his own; all the same, even the boys in the schoolroom who had questioned her about her papa had not shown such friendliness and most of the females – including the Countess at first – had been as wary as cats.

"Have you been introduced to my brothers and sisters?" he enquired, slowing his progress and matching it to hers.

"Yes; Miss Westmacott took me to the schoolroom."

"Lord, one of the circles of hell," he said lightly. "Did you meet Alicia there? She's the only one who is permitted to dine with us, thank Heaven, for it would be past endurance if we had to put up with Anthea as well."

"Yes, she was there. She helped me to find my room afterwards."

"And left you to get lost on the way downstairs!"

"No; she enquired if I would be able to manage and suggested I ask one of the footmen if I became lost."

"Oh, that was unusually considerate of her. Perhaps her animosity is not so much universal as directed at Anthea – and of course Mama - and she will be amiable towards you."

Lydia did not reply for it seemed to her that whatever she said she might be seen to be taking sides.

Lord Chalvington grinned. "I take it you are without siblings?"

"Yes."

"Is that why your father left you to us – in the hope of expanding your experience of family life? It seems a trifle excessive!"

"I own he did mention it; he thought I would benefit from the family he had failed to provide. But I think the main reason why he chose your father was because they had been friends at school and then later fought beside each other. He explained that none of our relatives were the sort of people he wished me to live with; I don't think there are very many of them, in any event."

"Really? I suppose there must be at least one – the fellow who's turned you out?"

"Yes, but I had not met him until just before my father died – and, when I did, I could quite see why Papa did not want me to live with him. He is perfectly odious. My family has not, recently, been

34

much good at producing sons."

"Should have married into ours; we don't seem to be deficient in that respect, although there are a good many other talents, as well as virtues, conspicuous by their absence."

Chapter 5

Lady Maresfield, who had set out on her walk in such a hurry that she had neglected to put on her bonnet – almost as though she were bent on escaping from something or other - slowed to a more thoughtful pace as she thought of Lydia Melway. She had not been looking forward to her arrival with anything approaching enthusiasm and had been determined, before she saw the girl, to behave in her most intimidating manner in order to impose the discipline upon her husband's unknown ward which she had so signally failed to achieve with his children. She was aware that her stepchildren had no opinion of her for they flouted her wishes at every opportunity. It did not seem that she had the natural authority to impose her will; the harder she tried to stiffen her resolve – and her manner – the less they liked her.

She had been married for less than two years and was very unhappy. Her husband, who had seemed to admire – nay, perhaps even love – her when they married, had quickly become bored or irritated – she was not sure which – and removed himself from the house in which he had installed her. She had not seen him almost from the moment she had begun to increase and put this down to her having been extraordinarily unwell, although it was true that it also coincided with the last months of Bonaparte's reign and Lord Maresfield's active role in defeating the tyrant. He had not, then, been dallying in London with his mistresses but fighting for his country.

She had, in spite of fancying herself still in love with him at that point, been glad when he had gone for her suffering could at least be borne without the additional burden of trying to retain her looks, which seemed to have fled as soon as she began to increase. He had returned immediately after Jasper's birth but had not stayed more than a few days because Bonaparte, apparently determined to cause disruption on the domestic front if he could not have his way on the battlefield, had escaped from Elba and posed a sufficient threat for Wellington to have recalled his troops, including all officers. She had not seen him since.

From some of the stories she had heard from other wives, she supposed she should be thankful she was neglected rather than abused but her heart drooped within her all the same for, not only had she believed herself in love with him, but his apparent distaste for her had wounded her deeply.

And then there was his horrid family with whom she must contend. The youngest, Amory, had clung to her at first. Her heart had warmed to the little boy but, as the months passed, he too had turned away, clinging instead to his eldest brother, Lord Chalvington. She was not surprised that his instinct warned him against trying to adhere to either of his oldest sisters. The youngest, Amabel, had been seven when their mother died and was undoubtedly the least unappealing of the three girls, but she had been too heartbroken herself to take much interest in the motherless boy at first.

Lord Chalvington, on the other hand, although he looked much like his younger siblings, seemed to have been fashioned from a different emotional mould. She had not met him before her marriage for he had been in France so that, when he returned, lively and triumphant, she had suffered a pang as she saw how like he was to his father and yet how beguilingly different! While she wondered at Lord Maresfield's leaving them in charge – as it were – of the household together, she soon became convinced that the parent was very likely indifferent to the possibility of his eldest son and his new – ridiculously young – wife falling in love with each other.

The Viscount had not remained long in residence before recommencing his studies at Oxford but was now at Maresfield again for a few days before the start of the summer term. He brought a feeling of renewed life and joy to her pitifully lonely existence but, along with this, there was a good deal of uneasiness for she found herself embarrassingly attracted to him and suspected he felt the same way. If he were ever to attempt to make love to her, she was afraid she would be unable to resist him – and where, in God's name, would that lead?

The thought of Ambrose made her walk more quickly again, and even at one point pick up her skirts and run as though she were hoping to leave her sentiments behind. Her pleasure in the outdoors was clouded by the knowledge that she could not stay out for long but must return and face the usual disagreeable dinner with Alicia sniping at her.

She wondered what Ambrose would make of Lydia, a girl whose slight and insubstantial appearance belied what she had so far seen of her character.

It was late when she got back, out of breath and wilting under the usual anxiety which enveloped her as soon as she came within a stone's throw of the house. She was afraid that, if she did not change rapidly, she would be down later than the others, which, since she had been at pains to promote the idea of herself as a stickler for punctuality, would give Alicia further ammunition to attack her and cause the new ward to lose any respect which she might still retain.

She hurried upstairs where she found her maid, Streeter, awaiting her.

"Oh, my lady, what lovely roses in your cheeks!" the woman exclaimed.

"I went too far," she explained breathlessly, "and realised that I would be late for dinner if I did not run back; but I do feel better for the exercise."

"I'm sure you do, my lady. Will you wear the yellow tonight?"

"Whatever you have put out; it is unimportant."

Streeter nodded but did not comment. She helped her mistress to change into the jonquil crepe and then attended to her hair, brushing out the tangles which had formed as she ran, hatless, through the wind.

She arrived in the saloon only minutes before Alicia but had been able to seat herself and assume an expression of impatience by the time the girl entered.

"I understand we are to be joined by Papa's new ward," the girl said, elevating her chin, a pose she frequently adopted with her stepmother, believing, correctly, that it made the other woman feel small.

Alicia was a tall and well-proportioned young woman, but it would not be accurate to describe her as 'adorable' or even 'taking'. She was too big, in every aspect: her figure, although excellent, was of the 'full' type rather than the slender; her eyes were large and very dark and, set in a face more round than oval, were divided one from the other by a formidable nose. This evening she was wearing a pale blue silk with a matching ribbon threaded through her luxuriant chestnut curls.

"Yes; I hope she will be able to find her way here."

"She assured me she could; in any event, I suppose it will not be beyond her to ask one of the footmen." This was spoken with contempt but generally, although she was never friendly or loving, Alicia was pleasanter when they were alone; her acidity seemed to be mainly deployed for the gallery.

They had not been in the room for many minutes and had only just been served drinks when the door opened again to admit Lord Chalvington and Lydia.

38

"We met at the top of the stairs," he said, ushering his companion inside. "At least, that is not altogether true for in point of fact we met earlier in the hall. But I came upon Lydia making her way downstairs and have been able to escort her."

"I told her to consult a footman," Alicia snapped.

"The advice proved unnecessary," he pointed out amiably. "Mama …"

Emmeline wished he would not call her 'mama'; none of the others did, which, she was convinced, was because they thought her an unworthy substitute; in his case, she suspected he addressed her thus in order to emphasise the relationship and remind them both that he was her husband's son.

"We have already met," the Countess said. "I hope your chamber is to your taste, Lydia."

"Oh, yes, thank you; it will be more than adequate."

"Will it? It is a very small room," Alicia said. "Are you a poor relation – although extravagantly accompanied by a maid?"

"I am not a relation at all, so far as I know."

"Oh, yes, I heard you had brought your maid," the Countess said. "I don't know whether his lordship will be prepared to pay her wages."

"I am perfectly willing to pay them myself."

"Indeed? Have you so much money at your disposal, and have you already discussed your allowance with his lordship?" the Countess asked, raising her brows.

"He's not over-generous to the rest of us," Alicia put in with a scowl.

Lydia stared, swallowed and shook her head. It had not occurred to her that the Earl might not continue to pay the generous allowance her own father had made her. She was beginning to see that living with the Maresfields might not only be noisy and lacking in privacy but might also curb her liberty. She spent very little; what would she have bought and where would she have found it? She had always lived in the depths of the country, far from even the most unsophisticated local shop. Spending it on Sarah, who did not deserve to be cast out without a job at her age, and who was in any event a much-loved connexion from a past now forever vanished, had seemed like a good idea.

"But whatever he chooses to advance Lydia will surely come from her own money?" Lord Chalvington said. "It doesn't sound as if she is expecting him to pay her maid's wages himself, although he could perfectly well afford it."

"I don't doubt it," Alicia said, "but it's my belief he likes to keep us on short commons so that we are under his thumb."

"I don't believe it," her brother said. "If he wanted to keep us under his thumb, he would surely hang around a bit more. If I were you," he added to Lydia, "I wouldn't worry about it. You can ask him when he next turns up."

She nodded.

"My brother," Alicia said, "has his own funds, left directly to him by our grandfather who, Papa maintains, positively wanted to encourage him to be extravagant."

Lord Chalvington shrugged but said, "He told me that he wished me to be independent at an early age because he remembered with such bitterness the arguments he had with Papa when he was a young man and wanted to save us both from a similar experience. My father," he added to Lydia, "was excessively extravagant in his youth and, if he seems a trifle purse-pinched lately, it is on account of his having embarked upon the common practice of turning into his father as he ages."

"Grandpapa," Alicia said, "did not have a round dozen children – Papa has at least three born the wrong side of the blanket," she added in an aside to Lydia, "nor did he marry in almost indecent haste the minute Mama died. I do not think Papa resembles him in the least."

"Grandpapa was not widowed until a few years before his death," Chalvington reminded her, "and Grandmama only had two children so that you are right that there is little similarity in that respect. All the same, Papa is growing increasingly like Grandpapa in other ways."

"Papa doesn't confine himself to his wife though, does he?" Alicia asked spitefully.

"My sister has very little time for Papa just at present," Chalvington explained, refraining from comment on his grandfather's marital fidelity or otherwise. His stepmother was stony-faced, and Lydia thought that the girl's spite was directed more at her than at the absent Earl. "She is annoyed because he has not permitted her to flaunt herself in London until she is eighteen – which she will be very soon."

"It's all very well for you," Alicia retorted. "You can go where you please and do please; I am forced to remain here with the children and …" She stopped abruptly, even her bad manners seeming to prevent her from naming her stepmother outright.

"I have begun the preparations for your come-out," Lady Maresfield said in a cold voice.

40

"Have you? Have you truly? Oh, that is something! Will *she* be coming-out at the same time?" she asked with a malevolent glance at Lydia.

"I told you upstairs that I will not," Lydia said quietly. "My father died very recently."

Alicia threw up her head and glared at the new arrival, clearly outraged by this intervention. "But it will not be your decision, will it? If Mama *wants* to get rid of us both at one fell swoop, she will not hesitate to force you to lay aside your mourning and come with us. I should not be surprised if we were to take Anthea too."

Lydia said nothing and it was left to Lord Chalvington to apply the balm of his amiability to his stepmother, whose expression had grown increasingly frosty, but who disdained to open her mouth in her own defence.

"Well, now that you have insulted us all, I daresay you feel better," he said. "I don't think it likely that Mama will decide to bring you and Anthea out at the same time but, if she does, you can be sure she will have good reason. Not everyone has such base motives as you, dear sister, and I am persuaded whatever Mama decides will be for the best."

"It will probably be put off because she'll no doubt be increasing again soon," Alicia muttered, determined to have the last word.

Nobody replied to this, perhaps thinking that, if Lord Maresfield continued to spend so little time in the same house as his wife, there was little chance of that.

Dinner was a tense affair, the Countess silent and cold, Alicia looking for every opportunity to insult both her and Lydia, and Ambrose endeavouring to control them as though they were a particularly difficult set of horses.

Afterwards, they retired to the saloon again, initially leaving Lord Chalvington to drink his port on his own.

"When my brother comes in, we are generally expected to play something – or sing something – or perhaps both," Alicia warned. "Apparently it is useful to practise doing these things although there is no pleasure in it for either performer or listener, but we are obliged to follow the conventions. Were you used to play for your papa? And was it only you and he in your house?"

"Yes, latterly we were alone. I did play for him – and sometimes sang, as you say. He insisted that he enjoyed it, but he may only have been trying to be polite."

"Perhaps you play well; I do not – and I cannot sing. I don't know why, but I seem to be unable to hit the right notes – at least I think that is the case for people generally look pained when I open my mouth; the truth is that I cannot, myself, tell one way or the other."

"Perhaps you could play, Alicia, while Lydia sings?" the Countess suggested.

"Would you like to look through the music to see if you can find something you know?" Alicia asked. "I have tried them all – endlessly."

Lydia rose obediently and went to the *pianoforte*, on top of which was a pile of sheets of music. She was still sorting through it when Chalvington came in.

"Are you going to entertain us?" he asked. "Would you like me to turn the pages?"

"It is your sister who is going to play while I essay a song," she explained. "I am presently looking for something with which I am familiar."

"Do you like to sing?"

"Not particularly, but I understand your sister prefers to play and I daresay you don't any of you wish to sit here all night while we go through our paces one after the other."

He laughed. "I own I am not eager to listen to my sister sing, but I am looking forward to hearing you."

"I would caution you against too much optimism," she said lightly, choosing a piece of music and waving it at Alicia. "This one was a particular favourite of my mother's, Papa used to say."

"You had better sit down, Ambrose," Alicia said, rising and glancing at the sheet of paper. "Yes, it is a pleasant little tune and not too long; let us by all means try that."

She seated herself at the instrument, propped the music on the stand and looked interrogatively at Lydia who nodded.

With a great show of reluctance bravely overcome, almost as though she were forcing her way into a lion's den, Alicia commenced. She did not play well; her touch was heavy and unsympathetic so that Lydia wondered why in the world she had been so foolish as to suggest they embark upon a piece that she loved, and which brought back all sorts of painful memories of happier times. She sang as best she could, matching her timing to the somewhat erratic progress of her accompanist. She had a sweet, pure voice entirely in keeping with her unsophisticated appearance. When they came, much to the relief of everyone in the room, to the end, her ladyship and Ambrose applauded politely.

"Not one of my best efforts," Alicia acknowledged, rising from the stool and inviting Lydia to take her place.

Chapter 6

Lydia looked interrogatively at her ladyship, who said. "Yes, I would like to hear you play; you have a pleasant voice and are no doubt proficient at the keyboard as well."

Lydia, aware that this remark implied a degree of criticism of Alicia's performance, stood up again and began to search amongst the pile of sheet music once more. Wilting under the weight of attention concentrated upon her back, she chose something almost at random, sat down again and attempted to focus her eyes upon the music. Before she had touched the first note, Lord Chalvington was beside her.

"I don't suppose you need my help," he said breezily, "but I will be honoured if you will allow me to turn the pages."

"Thank you."

She squinted at the music and realised that she had picked up something she had never played before; it was a sonata by Haydn, but not the one she had supposed it to be when she chose it. She would have to do her best, although sight-reading Haydn was always difficult on account of the quantity of notes which must, generally, be played fast. She peered at it anxiously before commencing.

She could play well – and she supposed that Lady Maresfield had guessed this to be the case from the way she had sung. Her skill had been something which she knew had given her father pleasure and for that reason she had practised assiduously and had, locked in her memory, a number of pieces. She was tempted to ignore the written notes and play the sonata she knew by heart but, conscious of Chalvington's presence beside her, feared that he might notice the disparity between her performance and the printed sheet and, with his easy insouciance, comment upon it. She began with a sort of desperate confidence but soon found that her attempt to keep the rhythm going was much hampered by the slowness with which she was able to decipher the notation.

"I don't believe you've ever seen the piece before," he said quietly when she came to the end.

"No; I own I did not look at it properly and mistook it for one I know well."

"Well, you made a pretty good fist of it."

"I will practise later so that I will do a bit better next time."

"Why do you not play something you know now – show off your prowess?"

"I should think the audience will have had quite enough of being obliged to listen to a succession of indifferent performances."

"By no means; I suspect you have a not inconsiderable talent. In fact, if you play something to which I know the words, we can perform together. That might be a little less intimidating. In any event, I will enjoy it."

"Do you sing, my lord?"

"I do, although not outstandingly well. Shall we essay something together?"

"Perhaps you should make sure your mama and sister are prepared to endure another song?"

"Mama, Alicia," he said at once, "Lydia and I are going to perform together."

"He only wants to show off," Alicia muttered.

"We will enjoy that," the Countess murmured and received a furious look from Alicia.

Lord Chalvington ignored it, found the music for the piece he favoured and arranged it on the stand.

"Oh, this one!" she said.

"Yes; do you dislike it?"

"Not at all. Are you ready, my lord?"

"Champing at the bit," he replied.

She launched into the introduction and was pleasantly surprised when he joined her in a light baritone. This time she was able to keep up with the rhythm of the piece and he was able to match it so that they skipped along pleasantly enough. At the end, he bowed, she curtseyed and the Countess clapped, joined after a moment by Alicia putting her hands together with a show of reluctance.

"My brother," she said, when the performers joined her and her ladyship, "thinks he is quite the musician. See how he is preening himself!"

Lydia smiled. "He sings very agreeably," she said.

"I must warn you not to praise him too much; he is already far too full of himself. In my opinion, he needs taking down a peg or two."

"You're as sour as lemons," the Viscount told her lightly. "We all look eagerly for something my sister does well, but it has so far proved almost impossible to find anything. No, no, Alicia, don't fire up, you know I'm teasing."

"But you are not!"

"I'm only trying to give you a taste of your own medicine. You criticise everyone else but do not like it when you receive the same treatment."

"I don't think anyone likes to be criticised," Lydia said mildly.

"Oh!" Alicia exclaimed, becoming red in the face with vexation. "What I do *not* like at all is to be defended by a poor relation!"

"I am neither poor nor a relation," Lydia reminded her.

"Oh! Are you going to put on airs and look down on us? If you're so rich, why have you come to batten on us?"

"Not through choice!" Lydia retorted, becoming irritated in her turn. "My father left me to yours so that I have been obliged to come here! I can assure you I have no more wish to be in this house than you have to welcome me."

"I am delighted you have come," Lord Chalvington said, "but I feel I should warn you that my sister hates everyone so that the best advice I can give you is to avoid her as much as possible."

Alicia jumped up and ran out of the room, slamming the door behind her.

"Oh dear," the Countess said. "I have today begun to write letters to people about arranging her come-out but, when she behaves like that, I fear that she is not old enough – not mature enough – to be trusted to conduct herself with propriety in public. How would it be if she rushed headlong out of the room in London? We would never live it down."

"She will not," Chalvington said. "She is bored but I am certain she can – and will - behave perfectly well in Society. She will not wish to be disliked."

"She seems to do everything possible to make people hate her," the Countess said.

"That is only because we are her family and she is already convinced of our antipathy."

This discussion was brought to a close by the arrival of the butler with the tea and it was not long after this that Lydia, pleading fatigue on account of her long journey and the excitement of coming to a new house, withdrew.

"Shall I take you up to your room – we don't want you getting lost?" Chalvington asked.

"Oh, you need not go to so much trouble," she replied. "I am sure I will be able to find it."

"Eventually, but we don't want you inadvertently disturbing Alicia."

She bowed her head obediently and took her leave of the Countess, who wished her a good night and begged that, if anything was amiss, she should not hesitate to ring the bell.

"I hope you will be happy here," she said, "although I daresay you are wondering if that will be possible after tonight's exhibition."

"You are very kind, my lady," Lydia replied but did not comment on the likelihood of contentment beneath the Maresfield roof.

Chalvington, when they set off up the stairs, did not hesitate to point this out. "I notice you gave my mama no assurance regarding happiness."

"That was not on account of your sister's petulance but because I am myself somewhat sunk in gloom at present."

"Oh, I am sorry! Of course you are! Forgive me!"

"I am persuaded I will soon become accustomed to my new life," she said without much conviction.

"I should think it might take some time though; you were used to a much smaller household and this one is in any event disordered and joyless. Even the children, whose natural childish high spirits you might think would inoculate them against grown-up tensions, feel it and display their own version of misery in their behaviour."

"I suppose they miss their mother; it is not so very long since she died, is it?"

"No – and Papa's extended absences do not help. When we were still fighting, he had every reason to be away and, while naturally they were all anxious on his behalf, they did not feel abandoned, so to speak. Now, I think they do."

"I am sure her ladyship does her best to comfort them," she said tritely.

They had by this time reached the corridor on which Lydia believed her room to be located and Lord Chalvington paused. He said, "That remark is unworthy of the person I believe you to be."

"What do you mean?"

"My stepmama is not a woman much enamoured of children and you cannot have failed to notice that, even in the short time you have been here."

"You just accused me of vapidity; I will accuse you of insensibility," she retorted.

"*Touché!* She is not happy either. She is only a couple of years older than Alicia and married my father, I think, because she fancied herself in love with him. Since then she has suffered a positive torrent of disillusionment – and is as bored as Alicia but with less hope of any alleviation in her situation."

"I suppose your father fell in love with her too – or was she an heiress?"

"Oh no, she was not; she had a modest portion but no fortune. She was – is – very beautiful and Papa has always been inclined to be swayed by a woman's appearance. I suppose he may have thought himself in love – I can't conceive it likely that he was looking for a mother substitute for his children when he chose Emmeline Fetcham."

There did not seem to be a suitable reply to this for Lydia subscribed to the general opinion that maternally-minded females presented rather differently from the Countess, but she found herself almost overcome with pity for the poor, despised woman downstairs. Fortunately, they had by this time arrived at a closed door which Lord Chalvington seemed to think might be hers.

"Is this your room?" he asked, putting his hand on the knob preparatory to opening it.

"I am by no means certain."

"There, you see, that's why you needed me as an escort. If it turns out to be Alicia's, I'll be able to defend you."

He turned the knob and flung back the door, revealing Sarah apparently still folding clothes.

"If I were you, I'd tie a ribbon or something round the doorknob," he advised, "so that you'll be able to recognise it in future. Is this your maid?"

"Yes. You did not have to wait up for me, Sarah."

"Have they provided you with a bed?" his lordship asked practically.

"Oh, yes, thank you, my lord – although I don't know that I'll be permitted to stay more than one night."

"Of course you will," he replied expansively. "I'll make sure of it. Miss Melway cannot be left without you."

"Oh, thank you, sir," Sarah said, tears starting to her eyes.

"Can you do that?" Lydia asked, doubting.

"Of course I can! I'm the master of this house while Papa is away and, as he's away most of the time, there will be no difficulty. There will not be any even when he returns because he won't, begging your pardon, Sarah, be in the least interested one way or the other. So, when you've finished unpacking your mistress's effects, you had better unpack your own. Good night, Lydia; I hope you sleep well. If you find anything not to your liking, simply ring the bell and request whatever it is you require. I shall issue instructions below for your most minute orders to be carried out at once."

When he had gone, Sarah helped her young mistress undress and tucked her into bed.

Chapter 7

The Countess, left to herself, picked up her book and began, idly, to turn the pages. She thought it very dull although her great friend, Lottie Colebourne, had raved about it in the letter accompanying the gift.

Lydia had retired to bed exceedingly early and Emmeline wondered if that was a sign of her dissatisfaction with her new lodgings or whether she always scuttled off soon after dinner. She reflected that the girl had not had an encouraging first evening and hoped that she would not be too unhappy, although it seemed to her that everyone in the house was miserable except for Ambrose – and she supposed he kept his spirits up by not spending a great deal of time there. The pair had made a charming picture at the *pianoforte*; indeed, she suspected that, if she and Alicia had not been there, they would have spent the entire evening playing and singing together.

She rose and went to look out of the window at the wide sweep of the garden. The sun had set and twilight was well advanced, rendering the scene almost grey as though sketched in pencil. She felt her future weighing upon her, equally colourless and ghostly and wished that she could escape. What, in Heaven's name, was the point of any of it? Her baby liked her no more than her husband or stepchildren did; she wondered if she should run away and whether they would even notice her absence.

She was standing there, unaware that her shoulders were drooping in despair, and did not know that Chalvington had returned until he spoke.

"You look despondent, Mama," he said.

She almost jumped. "No, not at all," she replied in an unnecessarily loud voice as though she hoped thus to dispel the ghosts. "It is a beautiful time of day – twilight – is it not?"

"Yes, but melancholy. Come and sit down by the fire – the evenings are still chilly. We can play a game of piquet if you like."

She turned and saw him, bright and bursting with life; he threw another log on the fire and straightened to give her a smile. She felt her heart turn over. She had known her husband for a bare six months before they married; now, whenever she felt the familiar – and unwelcome - thud in her chest at the sight of her stepson, she found herself thinking of how she had believed herself in love with his father. Her husband was more than twenty years her senior so that she found herself wondering if she had in fact fallen out of love with him and into love with his son. The boy, so like his father in appearance, was a mere two years her senior.

She watched him as he fetched the card table and set it up.

"Would you like a drink?" he asked.

She shook her head and then thought better of it. Why not?

"Yes," she said. "Do you know, I think I would?"

"Good. What will you have?" He tugged the bell.

"Orgeat, I suppose."

"You don't sound exactly enthusiastic and, to my mind, it is a revolting concoction. Why do you not join me in a brandy?"

"What will Pelmartin think?" she asked, drawing her brows together anxiously.

"He is not paid to have an opinion on what you decide to drink after dinner," he said, grinning.

The door opened and the butler, a man on the brink of leaving middle-age, bowed in anticipation of his orders. When he received them from Lord Chalvington, his face remained impassive and he withdrew.

"He does not approve," Emmeline surmised.

"I cannot conceive what makes you think that; he never shows emotion. I believe he has spent near thirty years removing it from his character; there is no speck remaining."

"He did though; I saw him swallow."

"I daresay he had a mouth full of spit and did not want it to drip from the corners of his lips."

"He wanted to say something but decided not to; he swallowed his words."

"Nonsense! You refine too much upon what you believe other people think. In any event, what Pelmartin thinks is of no interest to anyone – unless he has a brother or a sister – or perhaps some nephews and nieces."

"It will make him spy on me even more than he does already."

"If he was really spying upon you, I daresay he would conceal it more carefully. His impassivity is part of his job; he would soon find himself laid off if he made a practice of passing judgment on his employer's orders."

"I wish I could send him away. I do not like him."

"You don't like many people," he pointed out, but softened his observation with a smile.

"They don't like me."

"It is a vicious circle: you perceive them as not liking you and respond by taking against them and in no time everyone is convinced that their wariness – and that, in my opinion, is the origin of the difficulty – is justified. You cannot expect children to greet a new mother with joy, particularly if it is not long since the old one died."

If she had been about to reply, she did not for the door opened to admit Pelmartin with the brandy. He put the tray down on the table in the window, bowed and withdrew.

"He dislikes me," Emmeline said.

"Again, it's clearly mutual."

Lord Chalvington was engaged in pouring the brandy and now brought a glass to his stepmother.

"I don't want it!" she said pettishly, pushing his hand away.

"It'll do you good."

He did not move but remained beside her, the glass held out. Emmeline's face screwed up and for a moment she was tempted to knock the glass and spill the wine but, looking at the steady young hand, she rather doubted that she would be able to achieve such a childish action. She took the brandy.

He picked up his own and returned to his chair opposite.

"Shall we drink to the arrival of Lydia Melway who, it's my belief, will change a great many things in this house?" he asked, raising his glass.

"Do you think her so powerful? She is very small and slight – and young - to have such an effect."

"She is resolute."

She stared at him, startled by this assessment. She wished she could be described thus but knew that she could not; on the rare occasions when she managed to stand her ground, she rather thought that her determination would be more accurately described as 'stubborn'. Mesmerised by his gaze and resolved not to show petulance, she took a cautious sip of the brandy and began to cough.

He jumped up, took the glass from her hand and patted and rubbed her back until she ceased to convulse.

"You see, you were wrong to insist," she said when she was able to speak.

"I deny that. It's always difficult to do or try something new. Have you ever drunk brandy before?"

"Of course not; women don't drink strong liquor."

"Now that's where I definitely know better than you, Mama. They do – sometimes in large quantities."

"Do you wish to turn me into a tosspot?"

"Good lord, no! If you think one glass of brandy will have such a long-lasting effect, you had much better go back to the orgeat. Shall I summon Pelmartin?"

"No, pray do not," she cried, almost panic-stricken as she saw him rise and approach the bell again.

"What else do you think about the girl?" she asked, more for something to say than because she wished to hear his opinion.

"Which girl? The house is full of them."

"The new one, of course – my husband's ward – the one you just described as resolute."

"I like her."

"So does Jasper – and he likes hardly anybody."

"I daresay he takes his cue from you, Mama. I had the impression you liked her too."

"She is well-mannered and respectful," she explained. "I cannot conceive it likely that she will make a practice of going into a miff."

He laughed. "You cannot be certain of that yet; she was on her best behaviour tonight and, from what I could see, the effort exhausted her; that was why she wanted to retire."

"Yes," she agreed with feeling. "It is fatiguing going to a new house and meeting new people – and more particularly so when you know that you cannot leave."

"Would you like to? Leave?"

"I don't know; where would I go? I have nowhere to which I can flee, but I do not like being here. I own I have not become accustomed to it."

"Would you be happier, do you think, if you had no stepchildren?"

She thought about this with her head on one side, her butter-yellow curls catching a beam of candlelight.

"I suppose I would be lonely," she said at last.

"There! That is the first positive thing I have heard you say about us."

"I am sorry; I think the trouble is that there are so many of them and they are so undisciplined. I suppose you will say that that is my job, but I do not know how to get through to them, particularly Alicia and Anthea, who, I am certain, positively detest me."

"So many of them?" he asked, raising an eyebrow. "Why do you not say 'you'? I am one of them."

"I know, but you do not seem like them. You are much older – grown-up in truth - and you have been to London, which everyone says broadens the mind."

"And the battlefields of Europe."

"Indeed – them too. You are a comfort to me," she went on.

"I am glad. I suspect little Lydia will comfort you too. She was not intimidated by Alicia. In any event, with any luck, my sister will soon be married."

She nodded. "Do you ever see your father in London?"

"Of course; I lodge in his house, but we are not really in the same set."

For the first time she thought he had an evasive look.

"Has he …? Does he ever mention me?"

"Not to me; I don't suppose he would think it appropriate to ask his son how his stepmama did."

"But how is he? Does he have a riotous life in London?"

"Not so far as I am aware, but, Mama, I must beg you not to quiz me on my father's conduct. It would be wholly improper for me to comment upon it – and it is improper for you to ask me."

She flushed and picked up her embroidery. It was through a haze of tears that she jabbed the needle viciously into the material and pulled it through as though she almost wished she was eviscerating either her husband or Lord Chalvington.

"You will see when you bring Alicia to London for her come-out," he said in a softened tone.

"Will I? I would not put it past him to leave the metropolis as soon as I arrive. Very likely he will go to Paris or somewhere."

"I shouldn't think he would choose Paris just at present. I understand life is very unsettled there."

"I daresay it is more peaceful than this house," she muttered, her head still bent over her work.

"But is it peace you seek? I am not convinced that it is not amusement which you lack so demonstrably. It's all very well taking refuge in the country but there is not a great deal to occupy you here except for the children – whom you dislike."

"Am I such an unnatural female?"

"Not to feel affection for someone else's progeny? No, I don't think so. I can't imagine that anyone, other than a fond parent, would be much taken with my brothers and sisters."

"You are young."

"Older than you."

She looked up suddenly, sharply, and met his eyes.

"I'm going to bed," he said abruptly, throwing the rest of his brandy down his throat and rising. "Good night, Mama."

When he had left the room, she threw her embroidery aside and picked up her book instead but, after staring at a few pages, realised that she was still thinking of Lord Chalvington in a way that she knew was both wrong and silly. She told herself that the way his eyes rested on her face was nothing in the least special and that he could not be held responsible either for their melting quality or the way they appeared to communicate something which she could not bear to name even in her own mind. She was, she told herself severely, imagining the whole and the sooner she took Alicia to London the better. There, she was bound to find any number of men with whom she could flirt – or perhaps even embark upon an *affaire* with 0now that she had produced a completely unnecessary sixth son for her husband.

She wondered if he, Maresfield, would be annoyed by her turning up in London, where he was no doubt enjoying himself in a manner ill-befitting a husband, but decided that she did not care what he thought so long as he did not resort to curtailing her activities, either by physical or emotional restraint. She had, ever since he had brought her to Maresfield, felt almost imprisoned by the house and its extensive grounds, but had meekly accepted her place there. But, really, why should she? He had not ordered her to remain – had merely left her there – and she had been too spiritless to move.

Well, she would; she would go to London at once. She would take Alicia with her – that would be a penance in itself – and see what would transpire; Chalvington would in any event soon be returning to Oxford for the summer term.

But what of the new ward? Should she take her too? It would no doubt annoy Alicia if she did, but she rather thought that it would be unkind to abandon her in Kent almost the minute she had arrived. She would not, of course, want to attend parties or go anywhere where she might be seen on account of being in deep mourning, but she might, all the same, prefer to be in London than abandoned in the country with the rowdy Maresfield children. In any event, she was the Earl's ward and should surely be handed over to him.

She wondered what had possessed Lord Melway to leave his daughter to her husband – a man who already had a vast number of children of his own, in none of whom he took the least interest. For the first time, she pondered on her husband's conduct and considered whether it might be related to what he had undergone during the numerous battles in which he had been engaged. Could his apparent falling out of love with her have anything to do with what he had suffered? And had he once been a fond father? Was his indifference only recent and, if so, was his children's behaviour related to their disappointment and sense of abandonment, just as hers was?

Instead of taking umbrage, thinking she was to blame and – if the truth for once be admitted – transferring her sentiments improperly to his son – she should perhaps be thinking less of herself and more of him. Her heart lifted – briefly – as she thought of how she would bring him comfort, how they would rediscover their original passion and all would be well.

Fired with enthusiasm for this new project, she went back to her writing desk, amended the letter to Lady Trowbridge signed and sealed it, and wrote another to her mother, suggesting she travel directly to London. She signed and sealed this one too and, still full of resolution, placed both on the hall table for Pelmartin to take to the post.

Chapter 8

Lydia, reassured that Lord Chalvington had given permission for her maid to remain, got into her bed with a clear conscience and a sense of relief that one of her anxieties had been laid to rest.

It was, however, a long time before she slept. Having been brought up by herself, without either brothers or sisters, or indeed even a cousin to call her own - or not one with whom she was acquainted in any event - she had no experience either of children or of people forced to live together who did not like each other.

The atmosphere in the saloon after dinner had been tense, not unlike sharing quarters with a couple of animals, each of whom resented and feared the other but, knowing they were incarcerated together with little hope of escape, had come to some sort of accommodation whereby they scratched each other from time to time, hissed frequently but refrained from engaging in such a serious conflict that one or both might have sustained unrecoverable-from injuries.

Amongst the people she had so far encountered, only Lord Chalvington and the two little boys had seemed pleased to meet her. The Countess had been wary, initially disapproving but eventually accepting – if not precisely with warmth – of her presence. Alicia was openly hostile.

She rather suspected that she was to be deployed, without pay, to assist the governess in managing the children and, while it might prove both interesting and satisfying to get to know the juveniles, she did not think the same would be true of the governess, whose hostility seemed to go deeper than the Countess's and to involve a degree of inflexibility which was almost repellent.

In spite of these drawbacks, she told herself firmly that her new home and the people in it might have been a great deal worse for, however vexatious Miss Westmacott proved, it was not she who would have the ordering of her but her ladyship and she, unless Lydia was much mistaken, was suffering more from thwarted love than deficiency of character.

When she rose in the morning, the sun was shining and she could see Lord Chalvington cantering across the fields at the back, accompanied by an eager dog.

She washed, dressed – this took little time as her choice was restricted to one or two almost interchangeable black gowns - and sat down at the small dressing table in her chamber while Sarah arranged her hair.

She enquired whether her maid had been comfortably accommodated and received confirmation that she had been provided with a room of her own.

"That is good – or would you prefer to share?"

"No, I don't think so, Miss. It's a very small room but the bed was comfortable and the window looks out on this same side. It's always cheering to have the morning sun come into one's chamber."

"Indeed."

When Lydia went downstairs, she met the butler, Pelmartin, in the hall and was shown into the breakfast parlour, a charming room also facing east, which was painted pale green. Nobody was there so she sat down and was almost immediately served coffee by the butler himself.

"Am I very early?" she asked.

"Oh no, Miss; his lordship has already gone out riding and will probably be back soon. Her ladyship usually comes down at about nine. Lady Alicia is accustomed to eat her breakfast in the schoolroom."

"Perhaps I should have gone there."

"I don't think her ladyship expected that, Miss. She'll be down herself directly. I don't know whether you're interested in current affairs, Miss, but his lordship always has a newspaper delivered." As he spoke, the butler picked it up and passed it to her.

"Thank you."

She was still reading the headlines and drinking her coffee when the door opened to admit her ladyship.

"Oh, you are up early!" she said with a brightness that seemed startlingly at variance with her depressed mood the night before.

"Yes; I hope I am not too early."

"Goodness, no! You can get up whenever you like. Did you sleep well?"

"Yes, thank you, my lady."

"Good. After you had gone to bed last night, I decided to go up to London within the next few days. It's time Alicia was presented and, as the Season has already begun, there is no time to be lost. Amongst other things, she will need to be suitably outfitted without delay. I am hoping she will like that," she added with the first hint of uncertainty.

"I am certain she will; most people like new clothes."

The Countess, with a sympathetic expression, said, "I will buy some for you too."

"Thank you; that is very kind, but I do not need any."

"Not many of us need any," her ladyship said with a little smile, "but that doesn't by any means prevent most of us from purchasing them. Oh, I know that you cannot wear anything but black for months and months, but I am persuaded we can find something in a sombre hue."

It was Lydia's turn to smile, sadly. "I do not know when I would wear such a thing, my lady."

"Oh, pray do not call me 'my lady'; I am not much older than you. My name is Emmeline."

"Thank you."

"No, it is I who will thank you for it will make me feel more like myself – the person I used to be. Here, everyone calls me 'my lady' or 'Mama' – and I am not their mama, nor anything like old enough to be. Why, Ambrose, Chalvington, is older than I!"

"You are Jasper's mama."

"Yes, but he cannot talk yet. In any event, I have by no means become accustomed to being a mother."

"I am sure it must be a shocking thing – to become a mother – even though, of course, you knew it was going to happen and it no doubt brought you great joy," Lydia said sympathetically. "But I am persuaded it must take some getting used to, as it were."

"Yes, it was – shocking. I have discovered that I do not find it easy to adapt to new situations. It must be shocking for you to come here," she added, betraying for the first time a degree of empathy.

"Yes, in a way it is, but I did not expect it not to be – and neither was I looking forward to it. I know I will have to get used to it and you have been very kind and welcoming."

"Have I? I am sure Ambrose has; he is such an agreeable person."

"He said I could keep my maid, Sarah, last night. Does that meet with your approval, ma'am?" She could not quite manage to address her hostess as 'Emmeline' just yet; clearly, she was still suffering from the after-effects of shock.

"Yes, of course. If having your maid with you makes you happy, you shall certainly keep her."

Lydia thought that her ladyship's manner had changed so markedly from that which she had at first displayed that she wondered whether she had imagined the wariness the night before – or whether the Countess was given to sudden changes of mood. This morning she was all smiles and, indeed, almost overpoweringly affectionate.

"Thank you," she murmured and was relieved when Lord Chalvington came into the room.

"Good morning," he said in his bright, pleasant manner. "Did you sleep well in your strange new bed, Lydia?"

"Yes, thank you, and I saw you riding across the fields earlier this morning. Your dog seemed to be enjoying himself."

"Oh, Bruno! Yes, he is still very young – scarcely six months – so greets everything as though it were not only entirely new but specifically put on Earth to entertain him. Do you ride?"

"Yes, although I have not done so recently."

"In that case, would you like to come out with me after breakfast? I don't suppose you brought any horses with you, but I am sure we can find one to suit. Do you prefer them spirited or calm?"

"Oh, I believe I would prefer calm, my lord."

"A calm one will be carefully picked out for you. Will you come too, Mama?"

"No; I have decided to go up to London within the next few days and will be busy arranging our departure."

"Good Lord! That's a sudden decision. Will you take Alicia?"

"Of course; that is the main reason for going."

He laughed. "If you plan to leave her there, I can save you the trouble and deliver her to Papa myself. I was thinking of returning to London before the beginning of term."

"I was intending to present her. Is Papa in the London house?"

"Yes."

This admission was greeted with an uncomfortable silence while the Countess recruited her forces to deal with the prospect of sharing a house with her husband again, and Ambrose waited for her response. Lydia buttered another roll and avoided looking at either of them.

"I believe that is something else I must do as soon as possible: write to ask if he would find it inconvenient for us to arrive just now," Emmeline said at last.

"I suppose he knows how old his daughter is," Ambrose hazarded.

"But we cannot turn up on the doorstep without warning," she argued. Her voice had lost its brightness.

"No, probably best to let him know, but do you really think you must ask permission? I do not; I simply appear, and he always seems quite pleased to see me."

"You are his son."

"Indeed; but it is not unknown for fathers to find their sons' presence annoying. I should think he would be delighted to see you, Mama."

"If you think that, you know nothing about it!" she snapped, her voice rising abruptly from the despair into which it had sunk and hovering instead on the edge of hysteria.

"It's my belief you refine too much upon his absence from this house and jump to the – I am certain – erroneous conclusion that he remains in London to avoid you. I am sure he does not. He is not much of a countryman and has never spent much time here – even when my mama was alive. He has always preferred the bright lights of the metropolis."

"Do you think so?" she asked, apparently surprised.

"Yes; always. And, what is more, he never took much interest in us either. Begat us, greeted us with a perhaps less than satisfactory degree of pride when we first arrived, and then left us here to grow up without much interference from him. I have always thought he considers us more in the manner of vegetables than people with whom he might find he had something in common."

Lydia, still buttering rolls and swallowing them slowly but steadily, found she had eaten a good deal more than she usually did at breakfast but, the conversation having taken such an intimate turn, she considered it imperative not to draw attention to herself.

"I cannot conceive why he married me," the Countess muttered, apparently addressing her coffee cup.

"That is an absurd thing to say," her stepson said. "No one – no man, in any event – would have the least difficulty in understanding his motivation for marrying you, Mama. Pray don't tell me, because it is none of my business, but, if he has said aught to make you take that view, I am certain he did not mean it. He has not been himself since he returned from France. He was very badly wounded, you know, and is by no means recovered. I have noticed an increased irritability in his manner, possibly due to lingering pain from his injuries."

"I will write while you and Lydia go out," Emmeline said, ignoring the explanation for her husband's defection and making an effort to compose herself. "Unfortunately, I have already invited Mama to visit – I thought it would be useful to have her with me when I launch Alicia; indeed, I suggested she go directly to London; I hope she will not arrive before we do for whatever would Maresfield say if she turned up on the doorstep? Do you think Papa will object?"

61

"I don't suppose so; it's a big house and no doubt he will be able to take refuge in the library if he finds her too overpowering. Are you expecting Papa to frank the letter?"

"No; I was afraid it might be waiting for years if I kept it until he came again. I put it on the hall table."

"It may not have gone yet; would you prefer not to have Grandmama's company after all? Shall I go and see if it's still there?"

"It is not; I already looked. I wrote it last night after you retired and put it out before I went to bed. It was not there this morning – when I put out some more – to other people."

"Oh, well, in that case I daresay she will soon be packing her effects to go to London." He pushed back his chair and asked Lydia if she was ready to go out.

"No, not precisely. I will have to change," Lydia said, relieved that she could at last stop eating pieces of buttered roll.

"I'll wait for you in the hall and show you the way to the stables. Then you can choose your own horse."

"Is this arrangement acceptable to you, my lady?" Lydia asked. "If you have anything you wish me to do, I am very willing to defer my ride."

"Are you indeed?" Chalvington asked. "What if I say that it would not suit me if you were to keep me hanging about while you do something or other with my siblings? I suppose that's what you mean. You're not a nursery maid, are you?"

"No, but I thought your mama might wish me to do something to help," Lydia said, blushing.

"The most helpful thing you can do is come riding with me," he said. "I am one of his lordship's children, I suppose, and I need entertaining. Also, before you decide you cannot bear to live here, I would like to show you the stables and something of the estate."

"I don't think I'm in a position to decide whether I like it here or not," Lydia said. "I've been willed to your papa and it's my understanding that I'm not free to leave until I reach my majority."

"Or get married, I suppose. In any event, you have certainly not been indentured to Mama to act as an unpaid drudge."

"I don't require anything," the Countess said. "But I am immensely touched that you thought to ask. I hope you'll enjoy your ride."

Sarah was somewhat put out when Lydia requested help to change into her riding habit. It had been unpacked but, not having been worn for some considerable time, the maid was of the opinion that it needed cleaning and airing; she had not been expecting her mistress to go riding so soon after arriving.

"Oh, pray don't worry about that, Sarah," Lydia said. "I daresay any disagreeable mouldy smell will soon dissipate once I am outside."

Sarah wrinkled her nose but fetched the garment, thrust it out of the open window and shook it vigorously before helping Lydia into it. It was not fashionable – indeed it was several years old – but it still fitted. It had not, however, been dyed black for nobody had anticipated Lydia getting upon a horse so soon.

"Do you think it is disrespectful to Papa to wear a colour?" she asked, startled to see herself clad in the deep, forest green, a colour which became her well.

"No, of course not, Miss; he'd be pleased to know you were getting out into the sunshine. It's a very dark green, in any event – almost black in the shade."

"Yes."

Lydia, once her hat was placed rakishly upon her dark curls, thought that she looked very different to the little creeping ghost in black that had been delivered like a parcel the day before and wondered if Lord Chalvington would recognise her when she went downstairs.

He, standing at the window when she descended, heard the crisp clip of her boots on the stairs and turned to watch her come down the last few steps.

"I'm sorry to have kept you," she said, meeting him halfway across the hall.

"Not at all; it was worth it. I take it you're wearing your own habit for surely none of my sisters' would fit so well; they are all giantesses and you resemble a little elf – especially dressed in green."

"It's not quite proper, but I have nothing else at present."

He looked her up and down in a way that might have been unsettling if he had not been so exceedingly pleasant.

"I know what you could do next time," he said at last. "You could change those beautiful green feathers for some black ones. Would you like me to see if I can obtain some?"

"Could you – and do you really think that would be enough? I own I'm reluctant to dye my habit for I'm excessively fond of this colour and, in any event, dyeing often has a disagreeable effect upon the quality of the material."

"Of course I could. Leave it with me and I will have found something by the end of the day so that you'll be able to swap them in time for our ride tomorrow morning."

She smiled. "You may regret saying that when we've been out. It's a long time she I was in the saddle and I may fall out of it and embarrass you hugely."

"You will do no such thing. Now let us go to the stables and choose you a suitable mount."

Half an hour later the pair set out across the fields, following the same path that he had taken earlier; this time he did not have the dog although Lydia expressed disappointment on the animal's behalf.

"He's too ill-mannered to trust with a lady mounted on a strange horse and riding across unknown territory," his lordship said.

"I believe you're expecting me to fall off and fear that Bruno's antics might tip me off even more quickly than I can achieve all by myself," she said.

"I am expecting no such thing; it is you who has warned me of your uncertainty about remaining securely in the saddle; it would not do if I were to ignore that. We will take him next time if all goes well."

"Now I feel as if I'm undergoing a test," she complained.

"If you are, it is not one where I am about to judge you. All I wish to make my mind up upon is whether you and Nerys suit each other."

Lydia did not argue any further for she suspected she had brought the Viscount's over-protection upon herself.

Nerys was a dainty little mare who seemed as gentle as a lamb and made no fuss about the new rider being placed upon her back.

Chalvington dispensed with the groom's attendance, swearing to keep a close eye on Miss Melway himself.

Chapter 9

The Countess, left alone, returned to her writing desk and began a letter to her husband.

She had written to him once or twice during the time when they were affianced and again, after they were married, when he was in France, but she had not done so since he had resigned his commission. He had not written to her either. She had seen nothing of him – and heard nothing from him – for several months except a brief note to warn her of Lydia Melway's imminent arrival. He had stayed at Maresfield Hall for only a few days before returning to the front after their honeymoon and had visited again for an even shorter period after their son was born, a sojourn of which she knew little for she had been delirious most of the time. Recalled to the army when Bonaparte landed in France after his escape from Elba, she had not seen him since, only hearing from his sister that he had been badly injured and was remaining in London under the care of the most eminent physicians who could be found. Apparently, he was still there.

She wondered, as she drew a sheet of paper towards her and picked up her pen, whether he would remember a prior engagement somewhere outside London as soon as he received her letter. She did not believe her stepson's assurance that he had not grown tired of her; indeed, she was convinced that he was doing his best to avoid her. She had not originally intended to write before going to the metropolis but had thought simply to arrive. She realised now that it would be unwise to surprise him. If she appeared unexpectedly, with Alicia in tow as well as Lydia, she was afraid that the blame for any ensuing scenes would be laid squarely upon her shoulders. In addition to whatever humiliation she might suffer at his hands, the young women's contempt would be insupportable and the servants would spread pernicious gossip throughout London, which would ruin Alicia's chances of making a good match, perhaps of making any match. The upshot would be that they would all be forced to return to Kent with their tails between their legs and – worst of all – little prospect of being rid of Alicia.

But what should she say? Should she begin by enquiring how he did, whether his injuries were improved? Or should she simply state baldly that she had decided to escort Alicia to London – and would bring his lordship's new ward at the same time – and hoped that this would not inconvenience him?

She spent some time mending her pen, dipped it in the ink and addressed her husband thus:

"My lord, I hope this finds you in good health. Jasper and I are well.

"As the start of the Season is upon us and Alicia is now almost eighteen, I have decided to bring her to London within the next few days. Mama will probably accompany us.

"Your new ward, Lydia Melway, arrived here yesterday. She is, of course in deep mourning, having, as you know, lost her father only a few weeks ago. She seems a pretty-behaved girl. I will bring her too as I understand you have not met her."

She paused. Had she said too much? Or not enough? And was her tone too critical or, alternatively, too abject? It was no use asking Ambrose for his opinion – really, he should not be asked to give one on how his stepmama should address his father – and, in any event, she rather thought he would be breezily dismissive of her uncertainty.

She shrugged, bent over the paper again, discovered that the ink had dried upon her nib, dipped it once more and affixed her signature with such resolution that she almost expected the paper to tear. She sprinkled sand over her missive, although by this time only the signature was wet, folded and sealed it and rang the bell.

Satisfied with her actions, she went up to the nursery where she found her small son sitting on the floor surrounded by toys and watched indulgently by Ann, the nursery maid. The baby had finished his breakfast some time before and all trace of whatever revolting substance was generally spooned into his mouth had been cleaned off his face – she had gone in too early on one occasion and found him smeared in what she took to be porridge and engaged in throwing quantities of the stuff across the room, employing his spoon with admirable expertise to increase his reach.

He looked up as she came in and favoured her with a smile, such a rare greeting from anyone in the house except Lord Chalvington, that she felt her heart turn over with pleasure.

"Good morning, my treasure," she said with unusual enthusiasm, bending down to pick him up.

But Jasper took exception to this for he was enjoying himself knocking over the tower of bricks which Ann patiently built up for him time after time. He struggled and, in doing so, hit her in the face with one of his flailing arms.

66

Mother and child both burst into tears, Jasper with a good deal of accompanying noise and his mother with a sort of partially suppressed gasp. She put him down again, but the pleasant mood was broken, and he flung himself backwards with a screech.

Emmeline, who might have complained in a lachrymose fashion about the fact that her son disliked her if Lydia had been beside her, said nothing but clamped her lips together for she was afraid that Ann, an inexperienced girl of barely sixteen, would retail the whole episode to Nanny Macintosh.

The girl knelt down, righted the baby and wiped his nose. As she was doing so, Nanny Macintosh came in, no doubt alerted by Jasper's outraged screams. He stopped crying but continued to gasp and hiccough so that she was forced to remonstrate with him, telling him that brave boys did not make a fuss about toppling over; after all, at his age, this was only to be expected. Jasper seemed to find this lecture comforting, in spite of its being delivered in a stern tone, for he brightened, picked up a brick and threw it with some force in his mother's direction.

"I am going to London soon," Emmeline said, adding impulsively, "and I intend to take my son with me." She had had no such intention when she entered the room and, having once more been repulsed by the baby, had no wish to have him with her; she did, however, have a burning desire to defy the nurse's expectations.

"Do you think that wise, my lady?" the old woman asked, dismissing the nursery maid and retrieving the scattered bricks.

"I suppose I may do what I like with my own son – and his father will wish to see him."

"Oh, indeed," Nanny replied at once, softening. "He will notice a great change in the little man."

"Yes."

The Countess sat down and watched her child as he waited for his nurse to finish piling the bricks carefully one on top of the other until there was a tall tower, rising above his head. She saw how patiently he waited, how he resisted the urge to push the edifice over at once and saw too how Nanny held his eyes while she completed her task.

"There," the old woman said at last, sitting back on her heels and smiling at the child. "What are you going to do with that, young man?"

He raised his arm, held it for a moment while his wide dark eyes teased her and then, with a triumphant whoop, he sent the bricks flying again.

"Will he learn to build them up himself one day?" Emmeline asked.

"Oh yes, my lady. See how carefully he watches me."

"Yes; I do, and I see too that he waits for you to tell him when he can knock them over."

Nanny laughed comfortably. "Oh, he doesn't always do that. He was probably showing off to you, my lady."

"I'm sure he wasn't. I don't think he cares what I think."

"He doesn't care what anyone else thinks yet; indeed, I'm not sure he knows he's thinking himself. Will you take Ann to London with you, my lady?"

"Yes, but I think Jasper would like you to come too, Nanny. Would you do that?"

"Oh, my lady!" The old woman's joy was shaming. "I'm sure Ann could manage," she added, trying to suppress her pleasure.

"Very likely, but I don't think Jasper would want to come without you."

"He's used to me. I'm a bit possessive of him, because I love him so much, so I suppose Ann doesn't get much of a look-in."

"I imagine it was like that when my husband was a baby: you were the nursery maid then, weren't you?"

"Yes; that's when I came. He was such a lovely baby too – just like this one." Nanny seemed to have forgotten her animadversions on the baby's nature the previous day; Emmeline had not, having taken them as a direct criticism of her character more than of her son's, to whom she knew the old woman was devoted.

"And Ambrose? Was he like Jasper too?"

"Oh, he was always such a happy little lad. Lord Jasper can be irritable at times, as was Lord Maresfield, but Lord Ambrose – he was the sunniest baby I ever met!"

Emmeline smiled. "He still is. Do you think babies display the characteristics they will have when they are grown-up?"

"Oh yes, my lady, undoubtedly. Jasper could be his father, you know – more than any of the others. Lord Ambrose was much sunnier, as I told you; Lady Alicia was more irritable; I always thought she wished she had been the first and she was annoyed that everyone liked her brother so much. Of course, that can't really be true because she cried more than any of the others right from the moment she arrived on Earth – before she even knew she had a brother. I don't know why. We used to send for the doctor all the time when she was an infant, but he could never find anything wrong with her – I think it's just her character."

"Oh dear! Poor Alicia! Do you think she is unhappy?"

"Yes, I do, my lady."

"Perhaps she will be happier in London."

"I never heard of anyone that was happier in London, my lady; people are more likely to be unhappy there, but she may be more contented once she's married. Many women are."

Emmeline thought that she was not; she had, so far as she could recall, been a perfectly contented girl; she had been positively wild with happiness when she was first married but, sadly, that had all drained away and left her with the most dispiriting hole where happiness and contentment had once resided.

"But you will not mind coming to London with Jasper?"

"Oh, no, my lady; I could not be unhappy when I am with him."

Emmeline wondered, not for the first time, whether poor Nanny Macintosh felt bitter that she had not been able to have children of her own. She had herself discovered that motherhood was by no means the fulfilment that it was made out to be, but she suspected that a woman who liked babies might feel differently.

"Good. Well, I will leave you now because I have a number of letters I must write."

"Of course, my lady. Will you give Jasper a kiss before you go? Look, he is waiting for one!"

"I am sure he is not – not from me, in any event."

Emmeline looked at the baby; he sat upon the floor with his legs stretched out before him and stared at her. She was not overly fond of the boy, but she had to acknowledge that this morning, freshly dressed in white with a blue sash encircling his little body and his golden hair neatly brushed, he was a beautiful sight. So often he was not: when he was red in the face with screaming, his mouth was open in an ugly square and his chin was adorned with spittle, he was not at all pretty.

"Goodbye for the time being," she said, kneeling down and bending to kiss his soft face.

He gurgled quite happily as his mother's scented cheek touched his and her silken hair brushed his face. He put up one hand and clamped the fingers around a portion of her hair so that, when she tried to withdraw, she was held fast.

"Do you like my hair?" she asked. "If you pull it much harder it will fall down, like the bricks. I expect you would like that, would you not?"

She did not suppose that he had understood but he did pull harder and several curls escaped from their pins to dangle invitingly before him. He seemed delighted by this result and put up both hands the better to grasp this shining new toy.

"Now, now," Nanny said, seeing the tears start to her mistress's eyes and aware that having one's hair pulled, even by a person who meant no ill, could be exceedingly painful. "You must let Mama go, you know. See, you're hurting her. You must uncurl his fingers, my lady," she added to the Countess.

Emmeline tried but every time she succeeded in freeing one curl, he snatched at another until most of her hair had fallen down around her shoulders. Jasper was transfixed by the possibilities stretching before him and positively rocked up and down in his excitement.

To her surprise, this painful way of playing with her son began to give the Countess a certain amount of pleasure. The baby was enjoying himself, gurgling happily and fully engaged with this new game so that Emmeline, for the first time, began to see that he was a human being with whom it was possible to have an affinity; until now he had been plonked upon her lap in the late afternoon – a time when babies are often irritable – and she had been ignorant of how to engage with him. He, wanting his supper and his bed, had been frustrated by being abandoned a long way from where he knew what he wanted was to be found, and had reacted accordingly, with the result that she had grown irritable too and they had, together, worked themselves up into quite a temper. Nanny Macintosh's arrival after half an hour seemed to the child to be exactly what he wanted because he associated her with both supper and bed. His smiles warmed Nanny's heart and filled his mother's with despair.

Now, playing with him in his own room at a time of day when he was more ready to be amused and focussed on neither his empty stomach nor his increasing exhaustion, she discovered a different child – a child whose dark eyes had begun to dance teasingly, a look which put her in mind of Lord Chalvington.

"Oh, you naughty, wicked boy!" she exclaimed. "Will you let me go?"

She abandoned her attempts to unfasten his fingers from her hair and instead began to tickle him. He let go at once, squirming and wriggling with delight and, moved beyond either her or Nanny's expectation, she caught him in her arms, pulled him on to her lap – there on the floor – and began to cover his face with kisses.

While the Countess was discovering her son's appeal, Lydia was discovering the delights of the Maresfield estate and the joy of being once more on horseback.

She and Lord Chalvington rode out across the fields, skirted a small wood and made their way down to a riverbank.

"Do you like to swim?" he asked.

"I have not the least notion; I never have. Do you swim in this river?"

"Oh yes, often in the summer. It is not too deep and not too wide so that there is little danger of getting into difficulties. Also, as you see, there is not a great deal of vegetation at the edge, which makes it easier to get in and out. Shall we dismount?"

"If you like, but I will not swim – or attempt to – if that is what you are suggesting."

"Certainly not; the weather is not yet warm enough, but the water is quite shallow here so that, if one takes off one's boots, one can walk in a little way and join the fish."

"Do they not object?"

He laughed. "I haven't asked them, but they don't seem to; they're very friendly. I daresay it would be a different story if one were to go in lower down in the village, where I daresay they're more accustomed to people trying to catch them. Shall we go and look? I won't ask you to take off your boots and go in."

When she assented, he dismounted and lifted her down.

"You're light as a feather," he remarked, setting her upon her feet.

"There is not very much of me," she agreed, smiling. "I mean, I am not very tall."

"No, not like my sisters who are veritable amazons."

"They are very handsome."

"Indeed; that is just it – handsome but not pretty. Alicia will find that she overtops a number of men and that will make her self-conscious and them nervous."

"I am persuaded she will have many admirers."

"Not many," he said. "A few, I don't doubt. She is inclined to be a trifle abrasive which, together with her size, will frighten them off, I should think."

She thought that, while he was very likely correct in his assessment both of his sister's character and of her likely success on the Marriage Mart, he was perhaps judging her effect on men by his own criteria. She wondered if he liked short women but, having already acknowledged that she was not tall, did not like to ask the question.

He led her to the water's edge and they sat down. She could see that it was indeed very shallow just there although further out she thought it took a noticeable step down. The water ran clear and fast, almost singing as it went, and she was soon mesmerised by the little ripples and the way the portion she had been watching flowed past and disappeared, its place immediately taken by more of the same.

"You can see how fast it is if you throw something in," he said, apparently divining her thoughts.

He leaned over and picked up a twig, which he threw in. It was borne off on the current at once and was soon out of sight.

"It will find itself in another place in no time," she said. "Imagine if that were a person! When it comes to itself it will not recognise anything around it."

"No," he agreed, smiling at her. "It's not unlike you, is it? You have been thrown into the Maresfield river and are being carried off in a direction I'm sure you never expected before you entered the water, as it were. Do you feel as though Fate has decided to throw you into a river?"

"I own I had not thought of it in quite that way," she said thoughtfully. "But, yes, I suppose so."

"That twig cannot control where it ends up," Chalvington said. "It's at the mercy of anything and everything it meets on its way – the wind, the current, whatever it comes across as it's carried down the river, in addition to its own weight and resistance to both rotting and sinking – and my throwing it in in the first place. You have more say in what happens to you."

Chapter 10

"I don't know that I do. Papa did tell me to whom he had willed me, but he didn't precisely ask my opinion – and I would not have been able to give it in any event because I had not met your father. I believe he was looking for certain things and intending to avoid others, but perhaps there were a good many obstacles – traps - whatever you choose to call them, that he did not take into account. I confess it does seem odd that he chose a man who already has so many children that he cannot possibly want any more! Sorry, that was perhaps a tactless thing to say."

"Not to me, it wasn't. I'm the eldest, the heir, and therefore I suppose, more desired in the first place than some of the subsequent ones, although my importance has been diminished by the others – there are plenty to take my place if I break my neck – but I would advise against saying the same thing to my mama; she might take umbrage on Jasper's behalf."

"Was it," she asked after a pause while she thought about the Countess and her apparent indifference to her baby, and wondered whether in point of fact implying that her child was of no importance to his father would strike her as insulting, "your father who arranged when and by what means I would arrive here?"

"I don't know," he admitted. "I suppose it must have been – unless it was Mama."

"She was clearly expecting me – indeed Mrs Black, who greeted me, complained that I was late. Had she not told you I was coming? You must have been startled to meet me in the hall, although you concealed it well."

"No, but I had only just arrived myself. I got here late the night before, after she had retired."

"Do you think the twig will reach the sea?" she asked, abandoning her attempt to understand the intricacies of her new family by any means other than analogy. She had been watching its progress until it disappeared when the river took a turn.

"It might, but I should think it will more likely become snagged on something first. One doesn't see many twigs in the sea, does one?"

"That's another thing of which I am almost wholly ignorant. I have been to the seaside but have never been on a boat. I own, when we did make trips to the beach, I was not thinking of twigs!"

"No, I expect you were thinking more of pebbles – and perhaps sand."

"And shells."

"Yes. Did you live near the sea?"

"We were not a very great distance so that, when I was a child, Papa used to take me sometimes."

"Did your mama die when you were very young?"

"Yes; I don't remember her well; I was six when she died. Sarah, the maid I've brought with me, was my nursery maid and has been with me for as long as I can remember. When she came, I'm told I had a starched sort of nanny in charge of me – a little like Nanny Macintosh, I suppose."

"Nanny Macintosh's starch is very shallow; she has been with us since Papa was born."

"I daresay she's devoted to you all."

"Yes – and we to her. I think Mama is a little frightened of her, but she's far less terrifying than she seems."

"To you, because you know and love her, but I suspect she makes Lady Maresfield feel like an interloper; she not only has to deal with all the children, who are openly hostile, but also with their nurse."

"Yes, it's very hard for her. She was barely eighteen when she married Papa. We were still at war with France and Papa was in the army so that they had only a brief honeymoon, after which he returned to his regiment. She gave birth to Jasper while he was away although he did manage to take a few days' leave in order to meet his latest son soon after he was born. He could not stay long for it was only a couple of months after Bonaparte escaped from Elba and everyone who could be fighting was needed. I was out there too and did not meet my new mama until after Waterloo – when I sold my commission at Papa's insistence. He only consented to buy me one on the understanding that I would sell out as soon as the war was over. I did, having in any event discovered that I did not particularly enjoy being a soldier in peacetime."

"I don't think I would like to be one in wartime," Lydia said, staring at him.

"Well, no, there are obvious disadvantages, but it's quite stimulating and makes one feel very alive – no doubt on account of being a whisker away from death all the time. On the other hand, the army in peacetime is quite dull: there is nothing much to do except ride up and down and pretend to fight; the way people bear it is to spend a lot of time drinking and carousing. They do that on the eve of battle

74

too, but then there's the added excitement of it being perhaps the last time one will ever do such a thing."

Lydia, finding a good deal in this summary which horrified her, said, "Were you wounded?"

"No – or not seriously. I received a scratch of two and a few bruises, but I was lucky. Papa was badly hurt – and so, I believe, was your father."

"Yes; Papa died of his injuries, although not for some time. He had leisure to plan for my future. He would have liked me to have married but I am only just seventeen and, although I thought I had an admirer, we had not known each other long enough for him to feel entirely convinced that I was the right bride."

"Were you – would you have married him if he had made an offer?"

"Yes, I think I would, in the circumstances, for it would have set Papa's mind at rest."

"Does this gentleman know where you are now?"

"Yes; at least I told him my guardian was to be Lord Maresfield so I don't suppose he would find it difficult to trace me."

"In that case I don't doubt he will write to you. Would he have been a good match?"

"He is Lord Dorman."

"Oh, I have met him; I don't know anything to his detriment, but he's far too old for you. You cannot marry a man past forty."

"I suppose your stepmama did. How old is your papa?"

"Two-and-forty; you are right: he is too old for her and I fear that may be part of the difficulty between them. She is very young to be abandoned here in the country with a baby and a parcel of stepchildren. I think he's forgotten how much the young crave entertainment."

"She'll enjoy launching Alicia."

He laughed without much amusement. "I don't think she will – there's not much affection between them and Alicia will be difficult to control, especially for Mama, who has no influence over her."

"Oh dear; but they will be in your papa's house, will they not? Cannot he exercise some degree of authority over her?"

"Over whom? Alicia?"

"Yes."

"I daresay he could but whether he will is another matter. Come, it must be nearly time for nuncheon? Shall we go back?"

Lydia, gaining the impression that he was as unfamiliar with this subject as she was with battles, said, "Yes, of course."

But they did not go back immediately.

"Would you like to see the house Papa gave me when I reached my majority?"

"Yes. Is it nearby?"

"Oh, yes, it's on the estate. I think he gave it to me because he wants me to be fixed here and run this place. Now that I've sold out, he believes I must be at a loose end – or will be when I've finished at Oxford - and wishes to have me gainfully employed while he – well, in point of fact, I do not know what he intends to get up to once he's recovered from his injuries – which are still excessively troubling."

"Do you wish to take over?"

"Not particularly. It is not that I mind becoming a country bumpkin or running the estate – I have known that that would be my future all my life – it is more that it's not at present mine so that all I can do is act as a sort of manager."

"But if your papa wishes you to run it?"

"He won't want me to make major decisions about it without consulting him – and at present it is difficult to speak to him about anything serious. He has a tendency to bark at one if one asks him to do anything. I think he says, 'For God's sake, get on with it!' more often than he says anything else."

"Oh! But, if he has asked you to stand in for him and he doesn't wish to discuss it, can you not take that as *carte blanche* and do what you think best?"

"I suppose so, but the truth is that I don't know anything about it; I'm afraid of making the wrong decisions."

"Do you have a land manager or someone of that kind? When you were both away fighting there must have been someone attending to it?"

"Yes, there is; he's part of the difficulty. He holds strong opinions which don't chime well with mine but, as I said, I don't feel comfortable with contradicting him on account of his long experience, not only of estate management, but of this estate in particular."

"Does your father trust him?"

"He calls him an old woman."

"Perhaps you could persuade your father to lay him off and replace him with someone with whom you are more in sympathy."

"Yes, but Papa will not discuss it!"

"I see."

It did not seem to Lydia that there was any more harmony outside than there was inside. If she were to liken them both to twigs thrown into a river, she thought that Ambrose's route was almost as strewn with impediments as hers. It would, she reflected, be a miracle if she did not find herself entangled in something or other before many more days had passed, and she could see that he, in spite of his insouciant manner, had a tricky course to steer.

They rode on for another half-hour until they saw between a band of trees a handsome house, probably built more than a hundred years before at the beginning of the eighteenth century. It sat in its setting as though it had grown there and Lydia thought it much prettier than Maresfield Hall, which was not only too big but had had a number of wings added at different periods so that it presented almost as a village more than a house.

"There it is!" Ambrose said, gesturing grandly towards it.

"It is enchanting!" Lydia responded. "Do you live there most of the time when you're not in London or Oxford?"

"I don't live there at all yet. It does indeed look enchanting from here but, close to, you will see that it has been much neglected. At present, it's positively overrun with builders, mending and painting and generally making the place habitable."

As he spoke, he rode forward and Lydia followed, a step or two behind. Somehow it seemed right that he should lead the way to his property. Close to, it was apparent that it did need a good deal of work for the faded pink of the brickwork was pitted and in places not supported by an adequate degree of mortar. The windows needed painting and one or two lacked glass.

As they rode up, a man detached himself from the several who were up ladders and carrying buckets and implements of various kinds and presented himself to the Viscount.

"My lord: you can see we are hard at work restoring your house."

"I can see that everyone is bustling about with a great sense of purpose; I hope you're doing what needs to be done."

"Indeed, my lord. We'll soon have it habitable." The man looked curiously at Lydia, perhaps wondering if this girl were to be the house's new mistress.

"Is it safe for us to come in?" Chalvington asked.

"Mostly, my lord. Will you let me escort you so that I can be sure neither you nor the lady steps in a hole?"

"Would you like to have a look?" Ambrose asked Lydia.

"Oh, yes, if it will not cause too much trouble to the workmen."

"Not a bit of it. I daresay they like to show off their work."

Lord Chalvington helped her to dismount again and, passing the reins to an exceedingly youthful boy who ran up apparently with the express purpose of looking after the horses, led her towards the door.

Inside, the house appeared to be even more dilapidated than it was outside but, again, there were a number of men working.

"Nobody has lived here for more than fifty years," Ambrose told her as he led her through rooms whose plaster was either falling off in chunks or being chipped off by men with chisels. "I am told it was built – a stone's throw from the main house – for my great-great-grandmother, who, legend has it, took against my great-great-grandfather and ran away. When he caught up with her, she told him she would throw herself in the river if she had to come back to Maresfield – history is not altogether clear on whether it was *Lord* Maresfield or Maresfield Hall towards which she had developed such an antipathy - but he, apparently still devoted to her, promised to build her a new house, untainted by anything from the past. This is the result."

"Which river was she thinking of casting herself into?" Lydia asked, having become stuck at a point in the story which was exercising her considerably.

"I suppose the one into which we threw the twig; we stopped at a shallow section, but it is quite deep in places."

"Oh, of course, I had forgotten that. My mind became fixed upon her throwing herself into less than two feet of water and how embarrassing it would have been to have been obliged to climb out again and go home wet through."

"Two feet would be enough to drown. In any event, she did not do it."

"No; did she come and live here then?"

"Well, no, sadly she didn't. By the time it was finished, my great-great-grandfather had died and she – apparently – refused to leave Maresfield again."

"Goodness! That is a very sad story! Has anyone lived here since?"

"I gather one of the subsequent heirs, although not her son, stayed here for a bit until he inherited. But the truly dismal thing is that it has almost never been lived in for long and yet it is, as you say, enchanting."

"Yes, it is – or could be. Do you intend to spend most of your time here?"

"I don't know about *most* of my time but, when I am not abroad or in London or Oxford, yes. I have no more than a term left at Oxford as I had already completed most of my degree when I begged Papa to let me join up. I hope my father will live for years so that I daresay I will get married eventually and then I will hope to bring my bride here."

"I should think she will love it."

"The only drawback from her point of view might be that it is so inconveniently close to Maresfield, but we will have to be firm with my brothers and sisters and not allow them to overrun the place."

"Are you thinking of marrying soon?" she asked, rather startled for he was very young.

"No, but it will be some years before they all go their own way."

It was not long after this - and Lydia had admired the vista stretching out before the drawing room windows - at present a somewhat disordered pile of stone – and been told that a *parterre* was planned - that his lordship recalled the time and said, if they were not to be unconscionably late for nuncheon, they had better not delay any longer.

The boy who had been holding their horses was rewarded with a couple of coins and they remounted.

"Would you object to a canter?" Ambrose asked. "We are so very late that Mama may send out a search party if we do not show our faces soon."

Lydia, already feeling more comfortable upon her mare and by now convinced that she could trust the creature, assented and they took to their heels as soon as they had left what would one day be the garden of his lordship's house. It was an invigorating ride and, by the time they arrived at the stables, her cheeks were pink and her eyes shining.

They met the governess, Miss Westmacott, in the hall. Lydia wondered what she was doing there for it seemed to her that she stepped out of the shadows the moment the door was opened.

"Where are all your charges?" Chalvington asked her teasingly.

She flushed but raised her chin and retorted, "They are eating their nuncheon. I am about to go for a walk."

"Should you not be speaking French or something to them over their meal?"

"I own I had hoped Miss Melway might do that," she replied with a haughty look at Lydia, who, after the canter, looked somewhat dishevelled, her dark curls beginning to make their way down her neck beneath a hat that was a trifle askew.

"Was I supposed to be doing that?" Lydia asked, taking off the hat and causing her hair to fall down in earnest in a tumbling cloud.

"I was under the impression you were supposed to be helping me in the schoolroom," Miss Westmacott returned with a sour look.

"Indeed? I had not supposed it to be a fixed arrangement," Lydia admitted pleasantly, sure of her ground because the Countess had expressly given her permission to go out with Chalvington.

"I fear you may have the wrong idea about Miss Melway," Lord Chalvington said. "She does not occupy a *position*; she is my new sister."

This defence clearly irritated the governess. Her face grew red and her tone sharpened as she said, "What a lot of 'relatives' you have, my lord: a mother and now a sister, neither of whom share your blood."

"No; am I not fortunate to be so blessed? Come, Lydia, it is time we changed our apparel and presented ourselves for nuncheon; Mama will be in the small dining room."

"And where will I find it – and shall I be obliged to compare dining rooms before I can be certain I have gone to the right one?" she asked, amused.

"If neither I nor Miss Westmacott is here when you come down, one of the footmen will show you."

"Thank you."

Lydia bobbed her head at the governess and ran up the stairs, her hair tumbling down her back and her hat swinging from her fingers.

Chapter 11

The Countess, setting her son once more upon the floor after her avalanche of kisses, rose to her feet and smoothed her skirts.

"I must go now and speak to Alicia," she told him. "We are going to London soon."

He received this piece of news with apparent astonishment, staring fixedly at her face.

"There are some pretty parks in London, and I am sure you will like being taken to them," she said. "You must not worry that Nanny will be left behind; she will come too; and it will be good to see Papa, will it not?"

Jasper did not react to this promised treat with any noticeable degree of pleasure, but he could not tear his eyes from his mother's face. She kissed him again on his smooth, broad forehead and made for the door. She wondered, as she closed it behind her, whether she would have been flattered if he had tried to detain her in any way – or indeed cried when she left.

Her next port of call was the schoolroom for, although Alicia was no longer a pupil, she spent most of her time there on account of there being nothing much to do anywhere else; annoying her brothers and sisters – and Miss Westmacott – was not such bad sport.

With her hair dangling around her face after her son's ministrations, she was forced to return to her chamber to pin it up again before she felt equal to braving the schoolroom. She found everyone sitting at their desks except Alicia, who lounged in the window seat with an open book in her hands and a sullen expression upon her face.

"Good morning, children." The Countess's *bonhomie* was so patently false that several made faces and one or two snorted openly.

"Stand up and say good morning to your mama, children," the governess instructed in a tone that indicated her opinion of her ladyship as well as her lack of surprise that they had not performed this simple mark of respect without being prompted.

They all stood up and murmured the greeting except Alicia, who remained where she was but began to twirl one of her curls derisively. She had not yet completed her morning *toilette* and was still very much *en déshabille*, her hair tumbling unrestrained down her back.

"What is your lesson this morning?" the Countess enquired with an assumption of interest.

"History," Amos replied. "It's very boring and I've already learned it all at school."

"I daresay you have, but it will be new to your younger brothers and sisters; perhaps you could help Miss Westmacott by explaining some of the more difficult aspects."

"I might if I could concentrate for long enough," he said, "or if she would stop talking. It's no good us both speaking at once."

"No, of course not; I did not mean that you should set up as a rival teacher, only that perhaps you could speak quietly – whisper even – if one of your brothers or sisters does not understand quite exactly."

The boy yawned in an exaggerated manner, putting one hand partially in front of his mouth as he did so. Emmeline felt a strong desire to hit him and wondered if the governess felt the same. She looked at the other woman and surprised a peculiar – and unsettling – expression upon her face.

"I really came in here because I would like a word with Alicia," she said, abruptly abandoning the attempt to take an interest in her stepchildren's studies.

The governess had been in her position for considerably longer than Lady Maresfield had been in hers and appeared to suffer from the same degree of hostility and resentment towards her mistress as the children.

Overnight, a germ of an idea of such startling daring that it almost made her tremble to engage with it had entered Emmeline's brain: since her lord was never there and hardly ever saw his children, she had begun to wonder if it might not be possible for her to sack the governess and engage a new one of her own choosing. She suspected that the schoolroom was a hotbed of – unspoken – conspiracy with Miss Westmacott's hostility feeding the children's. If she were to lay off the haughty governess, surely the children would mellow towards her eventually.

In fact, now that both Amos and Adrian were at school, would it not be possible to send Anthea to some sort of select seminary, where she might – with determination and dedication on the part of her teachers - be taught some manners? That would leave only the youngest three - and Amabel could no doubt follow her sister to the seminary in due course, perhaps even as early as next year.

The two smallest boys, Albert and Amory, had some years to go before they would attend Eton like their older brothers, but surely a tutor would be more appropriate for them. They, particularly the youngest, Amory, were not yet so entrenched in their dislike as to recoil whenever they saw her. Indeed, Amory occasionally made an attempt to climb upon her lap until told off by Miss Westmacott.

"Yes?" Alicia said discouragingly.

"I am going to take you to London," Emmeline announced. She had toyed with the idea of sending for Alicia to impart this news downstairs but then, as she was up here after visiting her own child and was buoyed by her unexpected success with him, had decided to waste no time in alerting the girl to what she believed would be a delightful prospect.

Initially, at least, she seemed to be mistaken in this assumption. Alicia tugged at the curl that was already wound around her finger and glared at her stepmother.

"Why?" she asked.

"To present you to Her Majesty."

There was a moment's silence as this sank in and the first person to comment upon it was Anthea, who was always ready to find injustice and fault wherever she could.

"What? You're taking her to London? What about me?"

"That was what I said," Emmeline returned coldly, her skin beginning to prickle with anxiety. "It will be your turn next, but not for another couple of years. In the meantime," she added, suddenly almost drunk with the power of her position which she perceived, perhaps for the first time, revealed upon the upturned faces of her audience, "I am looking around for a suitable school for you."

"What? You'll send me to school? Now? I'm much too old for school!" Anthea shouted, jumping up and stamping her foot.

"You will have two years there," Emmeline said into the silence which had engulfed everyone else. "It's my belief that it will do you a great deal of good – and you will make new friends there."

"I don't want any friends!"

"That is only because you have never had any; I can assure you that you will enjoy your time there. I am thinking of my old school, which is in Bath and where I made a great many friends, to whom I am still close. You are," she went on boldly, "a clever girl and will enjoy being taught a variety of subjects by expert teachers."

"Who wants to be clever? I don't want to be a blue-stocking! Nobody will marry me then!"

"A clever man might be delighted to meet a young woman who could discuss books and art with him – even science. Do you suppose men are only interested in simpering ninnies? It is at present only a suggestion, but I intend to discuss it with your father."

"Ha! Ha! That'll put your nose out of joint," Alicia said unkindly to her sister. You'll have to study Latin and Greek, I expect, and stay up all night to catch up with what you've missed under Miss Westmacott's direction!"

"I won't! I won't go!" Anthea shouted, bursting into tears. "Why should I?"

"Because it will be good for you," the Countess said, adding more gently, "You'll see, you'll enjoy it – and Latin and Greek will not be part of the curriculum for girls."

"And what are you planning to do with Amabel?" Alicia asked.

"Nothing at present, but she will go to school too, probably in a year or two's time. Now, Alicia, would you like to come downstairs with me where we can discuss your come-out?"

It was only as she turned to go that she saw the governess's expression and wondered what she could have said to paint such a look of horror upon the other woman's face. She had no particular desire to please Miss Westmacott, whom she cordially disliked and whose pernicious influence with the children she suspected of causing most of her difficulties, but she had certainly not expected the removal of the two most tiresome pupils to have so shocked or saddened their preceptress that her complexion had whitened and her eyes had a look which must have been commonplace in those approaching the scaffold.

She stalked down the corridor, descended the stairs and led the way into the morning room without looking round but certain that Alicia was behind her.

"Sit down; would you like a cup of coffee?" she enquired, turning at last to see the girl, her mouth open, entering the room behind her.

Alicia nodded and the Countess pulled the bell.

"Where is Lydia?" Alicia asked.

"She has gone riding with Ambrose. Why? Do you wish her to be present? We can defer our talk if you prefer."

"No; why should I want her here? What are you going to do with her? Are you going to sack Miss Westmacott and install her as governess instead?"

The Countess raised her brows. She had not thought of that; in any event, Lydia had not come to them as a governess but as an equal.

"Certainly not; I intend to take her to London to meet your papa."

"Oh! Am I expected to share my come-out with her?"

"Certainly not," Emmeline repeated. "She has just lost her father and will not wish to make her come-out this year. I had thought that she could be presented next year and Anthea the year after."

"You'll be busy! Or is that what you want - to be darting about London going to parties all the time? I expect it is, for you certainly don't fit into country life, do you?"

"It is not your place to decide where I fit in or where I don't," Emmeline retorted, closing her lips as Pelmartin brought in the coffee.

She poured it and invited Alicia to take her cup. Alicia, who had begun to shake for some reason, succeeded in spilling a quantity of the hot liquid into the saucer as she returned to her seat.

"One of the things you had better practise before we go to London is managing a cup and saucer without spilling the contents," Lady Maresfield said unkindly. "My mama will be joining us and will, I am sure, pay close attention to your manners and mannerisms. We cannot have you blundering about like a bull in a china shop when you get to London."

"I don't want to go to London."

Emmeline blinked. She guessed that the girl simply wanted to defy her but suddenly realised that the defiance might extend far enough for her to, as it were, cut off her nose to spite her face.

"I thought it was your dearest desire," she said in a different tone.

"Well, it is not – not if you are going to humiliate me. I would prefer to stay here. Nobody will like me in any event."

"I'm persuaded that's not true. Why in the world would people not like you?"

Emmeline tried to ask the question in a spirit of astonishment while in point of fact she had no difficulty in imagining her stepdaughter's unpopularity. She was too tall, too big in every direction, spoke too loudly, smiled too little and was, in addition, *gauche* and lacking in accomplishments. She held Miss Westmacott responsible for this last; she had listened to both Alicia and Anthea playing and singing with a quite remarkable lack of harmony ever since she had acquired them as stepdaughters, but it was not until the previous evening, when she had been treated to a performance by another young woman, that the reality had been borne in upon her: neither girl had been taught to play or sing to an acceptable level. She did not think that Lydia was anything more than a competent, perhaps somewhat above average, player but the difference between her performance and Alicia's was too marked to be due only to absence of talent on Alicia's part.

"Nobody likes me."

"Not many people know you. There are not, unfortunately, a vast number of other girls your age in the neighbourhood – and perhaps it is also on account of having so many brothers and sisters – but in any event you have not had the benefit of meeting many people. You will see, when you get to London, that there will be any number who will like you and wish to be your friend."

"Isn't the purpose of going there to find a husband? I can't conceive that anyone would feel that strongly about me."

"Of course you cannot; it is all very new and different to even contemplate the possibility of such a thing. I assure you, I felt just the same before my come-out."

"But you are beautiful!" Alicia exclaimed unguardedly.

"Do you think so?"

"I don't like you," the girl responded sullenly, clearly regretting her remark, "but no one could deny that you are excessively pretty. I suppose that's why my father snapped you up. Did you have a lot of suitors?"

"I don't really remember. The thing is, you see, that as soon as I met your father, I had eyes for no one else."

Alicia looked up, startled, possibly for the first time in her life acknowledging that other people did not necessarily think exactly the same way as she.

For a moment Emmeline thought she detected a shaft of pity in the girl's eyes for a woman who had been abandoned and must, if she had thought herself in love, have been wounded.

"I suppose Lydia has the right sort of accomplishments," Alicia hazarded, clearly still suffering from Emmeline's earlier criticism.

"I do not know her well," the Countess replied. "Certainly, she can play the *pianoforte* and has a pleasing voice. I do not know what else she can or cannot do, but it is of no importance at present since she will not be accompanying us to any entertainments being, as she is, in deep mourning."

"So what will she do to occupy herself while we are gallivanting around Town?"

"I own I had not thought of that, but I suppose she can read, practise her playing, which it's my belief she enjoys, perhaps walk in the park. What, after all, would she do here?"

86

"Go riding with my brother, I suppose. Do you think he has conceived a *tendre* for her?"

"I have no notion; if such a thing exercises you, I suggest you ask him."

"Perhaps I will. She strikes me as just the sort of girl men find appealing: small and quiet."

Emmeline, who had her own reasons for hoping that Lord Chalvington had not developed an attachment to the new ward, understood her stepdaughter's anxiety on this score immediately. She said, "Not all men like the same women and there will be any number who will admire your looks and spirit more than hers."

"But not many who would not choose you above either of us," Alicia said sharply.

Emmeline, once again understanding Alicia's meaning, flushed uncomfortably but said, "I am persuaded you are mistaken. I would strongly advise you not to compare yourself with other women; just try to be yourself."

"A moment ago you advised me not to behave like a bull in a china shop! That is me – and I do not see how I can change."

"I apologise for that. In truth, I am convinced there will be any number of gentlemen who will like you for who you are. I don't think you should be concerned about whether or not you will have any suitors. You are bound to have a vast number. In any event, although I suppose one cannot pretend that being launched into Society is not primarily concerned with the Marriage Mart, there is no need for you to feel you have to find a husband. There truly is no hurry."

"I am persuaded you wish to be rid of me as soon as possible," Alicia said sullenly. "Why, you seem bent on sending us all away with your plans to despatch Anthea to school."

"I think school would be of benefit to her. And taking you to London and sending her to school do not, to my mind, constitute evidence of my desire to send you *all* away."

Chapter 12

After nuncheon, determined to show herself willing to pull her weight in the household, Lydia took herself to the schoolroom and discovered that early afternoon was a time when the children put on coats and boots and went for a walk in the grounds, escorted by Miss Westmacott.

The day had clouded over since her ride with Lord Chalvington and she was glad of her own pelisse and bonnet; the coat had been dyed black but the hat, whose style and material did not lend themselves to dyeing, had been adapted by the addition of a portion of black silk wrapped around the crown and allowed to fall from the brim, partially covering her face, not unlike a short veil. This rather peculiar arrangement had the useful effect of providing a topic for comment, although, in the usual Maresfield manner, this was not much restrained by consideration for its object. Fortunately, Lydia, never having been subject to criticism in her own small family and lacking vanity, was not in the least distressed by this; indeed, she was glad to be able to prompt what she hoped might turn out to be an innocuous discussion of the fine art of contrivance.

Whether Miss Westmacott considered it rude or unbecoming to discuss a person's millinery in such detail remained a mystery for she said nothing, and her habitual withdrawn expression did not change.

"It's much prettier without the veil," Amabel said. "I like that green and it suits your complexion."

"Thank you, but, unfortunately, it's the wrong colour," Lydia told her.

"I think it's silly to have to wear black all the time just because someone's died," Albert said, pushing his sister out of the way.

"It's a mark of respect," Lydia explained.

"Didn't you respect your papa enough when he was alive that you are obliged to make such a point of it when he's dead?" Adrian asked. "I don't respect mine much and I don't think I'd even notice if he died, but I suppose I'll still be expected to wear black, practically for ever."

"That is quite enough," Miss Westmacott intervened. "Making derogatory remarks about your father is ill-bred."

"I don't see what it's got to do with breeding," Amos said, unexpectedly coming to the defence of his brother.

"What is ill-bred?" Amory asked. "Does it mean mouldy?"

"Or perhaps just badly-made," Amabel suggested, beginning to laugh. "It's a horrid thought."

"It'll make you ill if you eat it," Albert explained, joining in this doom-laden scenario with enthusiasm and launching into a description of the ghastly symptoms which would result, inevitably, in death.

"And then everyone who hadn't eaten the ill bread would have to wear black for years and years!" Adrian concluded, neatly bringing the conversation full circle.

Lydia, thinking that, when they egged each other on in this manner, they were quite appealing even if the subject matter was gruesome, said, "I believe Miss Westmacott meant that it was improper to speak rudely of your father."

"I suppose you mean because of course we're all well-bred, in the sense that Papa is a nobleman and Mama was the daughter of a Duke, but we don't always behave well," Amos said. He had somehow wormed his way between his smaller brothers and sister to walk close beside Lydia.

"Yes. Breeding refers to both lineage and upbringing – it is generally assumed to be a combination of the two."

"We were better bred when Mama was alive," Anthea said, casting a look of dislike at Miss Westmacott.

There was a brief silence while everyone paid a silent tribute to the dead woman, which provided the additional benefit of casting an aspersion upon the governess, until Amory said, "I didn't know Mama."

"Of course you did; you are her son and she didn't die until you were about six months old," Albert said impatiently.

"I don't remember her."

"No; one can't remember anything much before one is about three," Lydia said.

"I remember when Miss Westmacott came," Anthea said.

"You can't – you were only one!" Adrian reminded her.

"I do though – and so does Alicia. Mama never liked her, you know," she added in a loud whisper to Lydia. "It was Papa who employed her; apparently he found her in London and brought her down with him one day."

"And she's never left from that day to this!" Amos said.

"That will do!" the governess exclaimed, coming to life as suddenly as though she had been a doll animated by intervention from the gods, and casting the boy a furious glance.

"Well, I think you're very lucky to have such a faithful governess," Lydia said pacifically. "Lots of children are so horrid to their governesses that they do not stay more than a few months. Miss Westmacott has been outstandingly loyal to you all."

"I wish she would go!" Anthea said, not quite beneath her breath. "But it doesn't seem to matter what we do – she won't leave. We tried begging Mama to send her away soon after she came – well, I don't remember that, of course, but Alicia tells me she and Ambrose did their best. And then, when Mama wouldn't listen, they played all sorts of tricks on her, but she still wouldn't go."

"I think you should be ashamed of yourselves," Lydia told them. She glanced at the governess, who had put on speed and was now walking as though leading a march through enemy territory and expecting to be shot at any minute. Her head was held high and her shoulders were rigid.

"Our new mama doesn't like her either," Anthea went on. "I expect that's why she's going to send me to school."

"Is she?"

"Yes, she told me so this morning – and she's going to take Alicia to London to find her a husband."

"I'm sure she'll be pleased about that," Lydia said weakly.

"Yes. And then I think she'll probably sack Miss Westmacott and ask you to be our governess instead."

"I think you're jumping to conclusions without much evidence. I am not a governess."

"I don't think it's very difficult; I'm sure you could be one – and we'd like you. Amos thinks you're excessively pretty," she added in an even more confiding whisper, this one not meant to be heard by anyone, particularly Amos, who was still walking very close on the other side.

"I should imagine it would be well-nigh impossible," Lydia said. "You strike me as an exceedingly unruly lot. I should not like to have the disciplining of you."

"Oh, don't worry; we'll do whatever you tell us to," Amos said. He was fifteen and already several inches taller than Lydia.

"I hope you would, but I would not be *your* governess in any event; you already go to school. Why do you not look – all of you – to see if you can find a wildflower you've not seen before?"

She raised her voice as she made this suggestion and they all, even Amos, ran off and started poking about amongst the undergrowth.

"You won't find flowers hiding under leaves," she said. "They like the sun."

"Oh! Look, this is a new one!" Amabel cried, picking a white flower and bringing it to Lydia.

"Well done! That's an anemone," Lydia informed her. "They do like to be in shady places, but not right underneath big leaves. There are usually lots of them together."

"Like us," Albert said. "We're always together."

"No, we're not, stupid," Amos said scornfully. "Adrian and I go away to school for weeks at a time, and now Alicia and Anthea are leaving too."

"We're together now," Albert said stubbornly.

"Yes, but that's not *always*, is it? Do you know what 'always' means?"

"Yes, of course I do: you're always horrid to me."

Pleased with this incontrovertible truth, he ran off and began to pick anemones with enthusiasm.

Lydia followed and said gently, "They like to be picked with stalks so that you can put them in water when you get home. They won't live long if they can't drink – and they do that through their stalks. As a matter of fact, anemones don't live long *in* water – they don't really like to be picked at all so it would be kinder to leave them alone and simply admire them whenever you come this way."

The little boy stopped at once and looked up at her with an anguished face.

"I don't want to kill them," he said.

"Of course you don't, but the plants won't miss a few."

He nodded, stood up and made to drop the ones he had picked.

"No, you need not abandon those. Why don't you bring them home and we'll press them between two pieces of paper and then they'll be there for ever."

"But they won't be alive, will they?"

"No."

"I don't think I'll want to look at dead flowers." But he didn't drop them; he looked at them sadly, now somewhat crushed in his palm.

"Shall we see if we can find any more that you haven't seen before?" Lydia asked. "It's just the right time of year to find lots of flowers coming out."

91

He nodded and, to her surprise, put his other, free, hand into hers and walked beside her, chastened but confiding.

Amos, still on her other side, said, "You see, you've already proved what an excellent governess you would make. Our present one never does that sort of thing."

"I don't suppose she has time – and there must be lots of things she does that I don't know how to do."

"She's very good at screaming at us."

"I am not at all surprised! You are an excessively disorderly family and you all talk and argue at once; how in the world is she to make herself heard if she doesn't raise her voice?"

"She has favourites too." This was Amabel, crowding in beside Albert.

Lydia did not think it would be politic to enquire as to their identities, although she was surprised that the complaint came from Amabel, who seemed to her to be a pleasant child, less given to either sullenness or aggression than her older siblings.

"She thinks I'm her favourite. She's always saying so, but I can't see it myself. She gets very angry with me – angrier than with any of the rest of you," Amos said.

"Yes, but she always lets you have what you want in the end and she's much more interested in what you've got to say."

"That's because I *am* more interesting."

Lydia and her companions had fallen some way behind Miss Westmacott by this time, possibly because they had lingered over the anemones. The governess was still striding along, looking, so far as Lydia could see, to neither right nor left. She was accompanied by Adrian and Amory, whose little hand she held so firmly that she seemed to be almost dragging him along.

They walked some way and Lydia thought Amory must be exhausted by the time the advance party turned round and met the dawdling one.

"You have picked a lot of flowers," Miss Westmacott observed.

"Yes; that was my suggestion," Lydia said. "I thought it would be educational for them to learn about how plants grow and so on."

"They have already learned that," the governess snapped.

"They don't seem to have taken it in very well," Amos muttered. "Lydia is going to help Albert press some."

"I don't think you should call her 'Lydia'. She is Miss Melway."

"I don't think she is," Amos corrected. "She isn't a governess, as she keeps telling us, or an assistant governess; she's by way of being a sister – a very charming one too. I don't call my sisters 'Lady Alicia' or anything like that."

"Do you object to being addressed by your Christian name?" It was the first time that day that Miss Westmacott had spoken directly to Lydia.

"No, not in the least; I don't think, in any event, that it would be appropriate for me to object when I am delighted – flattered indeed – to be thought of as a sister."

"Well, only a sort of sister," Amos said quickly. "Because you aren't related to us."

"I understand you've been here a long time," Lydia said to Miss Westmacott, addressing her in an attempt to shake off Amos, whose closeness was beginning to irk.

"Yes; I came when Alicia was a very small child – too small really to need a governess, but Lord Maresfield wished her to have one from the start."

"I am persuaded you must have grown fond of the family," Lydia suggested, although she had not seen much evidence for this assumption.

"Of course. And now there is another, Lord Jasper."

"I suppose you miss the boys when they go to school."

"I own I do, although the schoolroom is much quieter when they are away. In any event, there seems to be a constant supply of children. I daresay it will not be long before Lord Jasper has a brother or sister."

"She writes to us at school," Amos told Lydia.

"They don't often write back," the governess admitted. "It will be a wrench if Anthea is sent away too," she added.

"She will be home in the holidays," Lydia said.

"Did you go away to school?"

"No; I had a governess, but there was only one of me so that I daresay she had an easier task."

"It is not easy teaching every subject to a number of children of differing ages at the same time," Miss Westmacott admitted, climbing down a step or two from her high horse. "I am sometimes afraid that I have neglected certain aspects of their education. I am aware, for example, that neither of the girls plays competently – I do not myself, you see - and hope it will not impede their chances of making good marriages."

"Oh, I shouldn't think so," Lydia replied, although in truth she had no idea. "I can't imagine that most gentlemen care tuppence about whether their wives can play or not."

"Were you used to play to your papa?"

"Yes – and he said he liked it, but very likely he was simply being polite. Would you like me to help instruct Amabel in the instrument? I was fortunate enough to have a governess who was particularly talented on the *pianoforte*. She was not so well-informed on all subjects; for example, my French is abominable."

"Mine is quite good," Amos said at once. "Shall I teach you, Lydia?"

"I daresay your father might not agree with that," she said weakly.

"Why not? I don't think he cares what we do, and I expect he'd rather I did that than bait Miss Westmacott and fight Adrian."

"I suppose it is not an absolute choice between the two," she returned.

He laughed. "No; I own I would find it difficult to stop fighting Adrian – he is very annoying – and I only tease you, Miss Westmacott, do I not? I think you quite like it."

Miss Westmacott disdained to answer this and, since they had reached the house by this time, was able to lead the way inside and up the stairs, still holding Amory's hand, without giving the boy a chance to pursue the point.

Lydia retired to her chamber to take off her hat and coat. She found Sarah there, busily engaged in exchanging the green feathers in her mistress's riding hat for black ones.

On enquiry, it turned out that Lord Chalvington had already been out, purchased the black ones and given them to Sarah.

"He's an agreeable young man, that one," Sarah said. "Approved of in the servants' hall."

"Goodness! I suppose they have opinions on everyone." Lydia, to her shame, longed to know what they were but did not like to ask.

Sarah, however, knew her mistress – and loved her – so she said, "They don't have much opinion of Lady Alicia or Lady Anthea – and I wouldn't like to tell you what they have to say about the younger boys."

"Albert and Amory? Little Amory is not much more than a baby and really can't be held responsible if he has not been properly disciplined. I thought Albert perfectly pleasant. He took a great interest in the wildflowers I encouraged him to pick."

"I don't mean those two; I mean Lord Amos and Lord Adrian. Apparently, they're always fighting when they're home; the general opinion is that everyone's much happier when they're away at school."

"They're very close in age," Lydia said. "I daresay that makes them more rivalrous and – don't boys fight all the time in any event?"

Sarah laughed. "Yes, but that's playfighting. Those two fight quite seriously."

"I wonder if Miss Westmacott favours Amos over Adrian. The other children apparently believe him to be her favourite."

Chapter 13

Two days later Lady Fetcham, the Countess's mother, arrived shortly before nuncheon.

Emmeline was once more at her writing desk, trying to compose a number of letters to acquaintances who she hoped might be able to help her launch her stepdaughter into London Society.

Lydia was out, as seemed to be becoming a habit, riding with Lord Chalvington, and the children, including Lady Alicia, were in the schoolroom. In spite of the fact that it was the school holidays, lessons continued in the usual chaotic manner, not helped by the presence of the two schoolboys. Lydia had suggested that she could perhaps help Miss Westmacott in the mornings as well as the afternoons, but Lord Chalvington cast a damper upon this laudable aim by saying that she was not a servant, nor even a poor relation; if she really wished to spend the afternoon in a madhouse, he would not stand in her way, but he did not think it appropriate for her to pass the mornings there as well as the afternoons.

Lydia, who had by this time been informed by her ladyship that it was her intention to take her to London, had allowed herself to be persuaded to abandon Miss Westmacott in the morning. She did not enjoy her afternoons with the children, mainly because she could no longer pretend that Amos had not conceived an absurd passion for her. She wanted to assist the governess, in spite of not feeling particularly warmly towards her, as she perceived her as much put-upon and probably lonely, marooned as she was between the servants and her employer.

It was clear that her presence in the schoolroom had an excellent effect, Amabel and Albert being particularly keen for her to help them with whatever project they had in hand. She knew too that, because of his infatuation, Amos behaved much better when she was there; he refrained both from bullying Adrian and 'rising' to his barbs – most likely because she had expressed disapproval of this sort of conduct – and was trying, not very successfully, to behave in a manly way. He even tried to calm the irritable relations between Alicia and Anthea.

In any event, when Lady Fetcham's cavalcade swept up the drive and debouched her and her myriad attendants in front of the steps, nobody, except perhaps one of the footmen who were always on duty in the hall, was there to witness her arrival. The footman must, however, have conveyed the news to Pelmartin – probably when he saw the carriages rounding the corner of the drive and making their final approach — because her ladyship had no sooner placed her foot upon the ground than the door opened and the venerable butler descended the steps to welcome her.

Lady Fetcham greeted him graciously and sailed into the hall where she paused while Pelmartin caught up with her and suggested she might wish to be shown to her chamber before being conducted into the presence of her daughter. By not so much as the tremor of an eyebrow did he disclose that she had not been expected.

Lady Fetcham was a woman in her mid-forties. She had, like her daughter, been a beauty in her youth and retained enough of her looks for it not to be altogether inaccurate to describe her thus even now. Her yellow hair was fading and gradually changing from gold to silver and, as it was still very abundant, she wore it in the most fashionable style. Just now, of course, a large and very becoming hat with a number of feathers was perched upon it, shadowing her face and drawing attention to the exquisite cheekbones which, now that her bloom had faded, were perhaps her chief claim to enduring beauty.

Knowing her daughter and alerted by her most recent letter to the strain under which she appeared to be wilting, she chose — as Pelmartin had intended - to be shown to her chamber where she planned to recruit her forces for the confrontation with a glass of sweet sherry wine — a concoction despised by many but which she found reviving — a change of apparel from her travel-stained garments and a few minutes of soothing chatter with her maid, a woman who had been with her for so long that neither could remember a time when they had not faced the world together.

Lady Maresfield, sitting at her desk and chewing her pen, a habit from which her mother had failed to wean her in spite of admirable perseverance, was informed of her parent's arrival. At once horrified that she had come to Maresfield and relieved that she had not followed her instructions and gone directly to London, she did her best to reconcile both herself and Pelmartin - whose extreme lack of expression alerted her to his own shock - to the presence of the matriarch. While she acknowledged that she needed support, she had, since writing the letter requesting Lady Fetcham's presence in London, had cause to lament her hastiness; sober reflection had reminded her that her ladyship's presence in the household would be unlikely to provide unmitigated comfort and might indeed provoke further disagreement.

Indeed, since the evening she had spent writing a quite ridiculous number of letters to an absurd variety of persons, for most of whom she felt little fondness, she had had time to regret her decision to take the girl to London. She thought now that it would have been better if she had gone alone to beard her errant husband, although she rather thought she might have taken Lydia, if only to remove her from Lord Chalvington's presence.

The pair were getting along famously and, although there was no sign that Ambrose saw the girl as anything more than a rather more agreeable sister than the ones he already possessed, she found herself eaten up with jealousy. This disagreeable humour had forced her to acknowledge that her sentiments towards her stepson were inappropriate and to convince her that either he must leave or she must. The obvious place for her to flee was to her husband's side where she might find herself even more unhappy, but where she would at least be in the right and where, if it proved he no longer wanted aught to do with her, she could seek a more suitable lover than his eldest son. The fact that she, hitherto renowned for her moral rectitude, found herself thinking in this improper fashion made her wonder if she was further on the road to insanity than she had hitherto allowed herself to consider.

The usual hour for nuncheon approached and Ambrose and Lydia, rosy-cheeked and full of energy, had returned from their ride, changed out of their riding dress and presented themselves in the saloon before there was any sign of Lady Fetcham emerging from her chamber.

"I saw signs of arrival in the hall," Chalvington said.

"It is Mama; she evidently misunderstood my request for her to join me in London and has come here instead. Pelmartin sent her upstairs and I have not yet seen her."

"Good Lord! I suppose we must pretend we were expecting her? Shall we have to wait for our nuncheon? I own I am famished – and so no doubt is Lydia."

"I daresay it is already laid out so that, if you cannot bear to wait another minute, I see no reason why you should not commence without us. I will of course await Mama."

"Oh, I should think we had better wait for her too," he said lightly, "if we are not to start off upon the wrong foot. Lady Fetcham is a stickler for proper conduct," he explained to Lydia.

Lydia did not altogether believe this since she had been given the same information regarding Lady Maresfield but had not found it to be at all accurate.

"Where did you go this morning?" Emmeline enquired, trying to subdue the monstrous jealousy by appearing to take an interest in their outing.

"Oh, the usual way: to inspect my house and see how the repairs are coming along, via the river where we indulged in a little childish play of throwing sticks into the water in a sort of race."

"Who won?"

"I did, but Lydia said it was not a fair contest since mine was bigger than hers. I don't believe that had anything to do with it; the fact was that mine got caught in a more energetic current and hers slammed into a water lily, which put an end to its engaging in the race any further."

"So it was a question of luck?"

"More or less, although I own I did succeed in launching mine further down; all the same, it might have evened out in the end if there had not been such an extensive clump of waterlilies on Lydia's side."

"Who chose the sides?" the Countess asked, clearly convinced that there had been a certain amount of skulduggery on Chalvington's part.

"Oh, we did not precisely choose a side," Lydia explained, smiling. "We were standing together, on the same side of the river, and tried to throw them in at the same time but the truth is that Ambrose was able to throw further than I could so that he already had an advantage when his landed some four or five feet ahead of mine. And then mine, possibly in a fit of umbrage, turned round in circles a few times before drifting off into the waterlilies. It's my belief it took refuge in indecision."

The Countess laughed. Whatever her sentiments regarding the obvious pleasure these two took in each other's company, she could not help being amused by their, clearly perfectly innocent, antics on the riverbank.

It was on to this scene of light-hearted merriment that Lady Fetcham made her entrance. She was surprised to see her daughter apparently so happy, particularly in view of the desperate and somewhat disjointed letter which had propelled her from her own house to this one.

"I am glad you are feeling so much better, my dear," she said in a voice that sounded anything but pleased.

"Oh, Mama! Chalvington and Lydia have been playing silly games on the riverbank and are entertaining me with a description of the way their sticks behaved. Let me introduce you to Lydia Melway, Maresfield's ward."

"Sticks? Riverbank? It sounds irresponsible. How do you do, Miss Melway? I see that you are in mourning."

Lydia, instantly rendered ashamed of her levity, dropped a respectful curtsey and enquired politely how her ladyship did.

"Very well, thank you. I have come at my daughter's request to advise on and assist with Alicia's introduction to the *ton*. Where is she?" she asked her daughter with a glance around the room as though she suspected the girl might be hiding somewhere.

"Upstairs in the schoolroom. She prefers to be there," the Countess answered.

"If that is the case, I cannot conceive how you can suppose that she is ready to be introduced to Society. Why did you not take her out on this riverbank expedition?" she added to Lord Chalvington.

"I did not think of it," he admitted.

"I see." Lady Fetcham looked meaningfully between her step-grandson and the new ward.

Emmeline, whose mind had turned to her mother in her hour of need, as so many people's do in spite of any number of experiences to the contrary, remembered why she had not invited her mama to visit for some considerable time. She had, recently, tried to model herself upon her parent, hoping that her ladyship's cold, haughty manner might establish her authority more readily in the household than her own, much feebler, approach. Now she also – how in the world could she have forgotten – recalled her mother's disagreeable habit of putting two and two together and unerringly arriving at the correct answer.

"Shall we go in to nuncheon?" she asked. "We have been awaiting your arrival, Mama."

"Have you? I can't think why; you know I never take nuncheon."

"I know there have been times – recently – where you have declined to eat even the merest morsel, but I thought that, after such a long journey, you might feel the need of a little sustenance," Emmeline suggested.

There was no reply to this other than a faint lift of an eyebrow, but her ladyship conceded that she would not be averse to a glass of wine after the journey, which had indeed been long.

"Will you take my arm, Grandmama?" Ambrose enquired, offering it with his easy smile.

Even Lady Fetcham was not entirely immune to the young man's agreeable manner and consented to place her hand upon his arm, enquiring as she did so what he was doing these days. Was he on furlough?

"Oh no; I have sold out."

"Whatever for?" she asked, quite shocked and forgetting to phrase her question in the usual sarcastic manner.

"Papa wanted me to go back to Oxford; when I joined up, he made that a condition of buying me the commission."

"Indeed? How exceedingly odd! Are you telling me he permitted you to put yourself in danger during the war but sees no point in your remaining there when you would be perfectly safe?"

"It does seem illogical if you assume he cares about whether his eldest lives or dies. I am not myself convinced that is the case; after all, he has a great many sons; how is he to find occupation for them all if he cannot be rid of one or two?"

Lady Fetcham said, "I remember now that you always were inclined to inappropriate levity – no doubt you are encouraging the young woman – I forget her name – to engage in merriment at a time when it would be more usual for her to maintain strict sobriety."

"Oh, I don't think I am doing that precisely – and it would be wholly inaccurate to say that Miss *Melway*," he placed heavy emphasis upon her name, "has been merrymaking. I believe it is good for her to be out in the fresh air and I suppose we have to do something other than recite prayers."

"How old is the girl? Should she, in any event, be galloping about the country alone with you? I hope you take a groom."

"She is seventeen."

"Indeed? She does not look it – she is very small."

"My blood sisters are quite large," he said apologetically. "Would you like me to carve the ham, Mama?"

"Yes, please." Lady Maresfield rang the bell, requested wine and lemonade together with the presence of Lady Alicia.

It was some time before Alicia deigned to join the party and they had almost finished their repast. Not a morsel of food had passed

101

Lady Fetcham's lips, but she had not been so abstemious with the wine and had managed to drink several glasses. As a consequence, her complexion was rosier than when she had first arrived and her temper, always inclined more to the icy than the fiery, was not improved. Lord Chalvington had taken it upon himself to entertain her, no doubt in a charitable attempt to save his stepmother and Lydia from being the butts of her criticism.

Lydia, thankful that she was such a dull little thing and naturally inclined to fade into the background, watched the growing discomfort between mother and daughter with trepidation. Neither the Countess nor her mother were related, so far as she knew, to the Maresfield children – apart from Jasper who was too young to manifest the familial irritability – so that she marvelled at the similarity between the visiting Baroness and the resident family.

When Alicia did appear, she seemed to have made every effort to annoy the two women. She was dressed in an outgrown gown which accentuated her figure in a manner guaranteed to disgust the Baroness, wore her hair down, although tied back with a huge bright red ribbon, and bore an expression of boredom mingled with irritation – as though, Lydia thought, she had been disturbed wrestling with a ticklish piece of research.

"Well!" the Baroness exclaimed, looking her up and down as though determined to miss no detail of her failings.

"Good afternoon, Grandmama!" Alicia said sweetly, dropping the older woman a curtsey.

"Have you no gowns which fit you?" the older lady predictably asked.

"Not to speak of," Alicia replied, her face revealing her pleasure at this aspect of her appearance having drawn a comment so swiftly. "Mama has promised me some new ones when we go to London."

The Baroness nodded. She had fired her dart and, although it had not had quite the result she had hoped, she decided to move on with her interrogation.

"Are you looking forward to meeting the Queen?"

"Not particularly, but I suppose that is a necessary part of the process."

"What then are you looking forward to?"

"Oh, going to Astley's Circus!" Alicia replied with an assumption of guilelessness.

102

"I have been wondering," the Baroness said thoughtfully, putting her head on one side and gazing at her step-granddaughter in an assessing manner, "whether you are in point of fact mature enough to be introduced to Society. Do you understand that being presented to the Queen is only a small – although of course the most important – part of being launched? There will be a great many balls and routs and so on which you will be expected to attend – and you may find yourself besieged by suitors for your hand." This last was uttered in a doubtful tone.

Alicia, displaying more maturity than Lydia had seen before, did not react to the provocation and the Countess, pulling herself together, came to her defence, saying, "It is all rather daunting, not least going to the metropolis for the first time. There are any number of things to do, places to see and so on without bothering one's head about the balls."

"Possibly," the Baroness agreed in a bored tone, "but most young ladies are only interested in the balls."

"Alicia is not most young ladies," her brother said, amused. "She has never much liked what everyone else enjoys."

"London," the Baroness opined, "is given over to providing what most people do enjoy. If she does not care for that sort of thing, I should think she might be well advised to remain here. You could try taking her to the local assembly rooms," she added to her daughter.

"Now that is not such a bad idea," Ambrose said enthusiastically. "I'll squire you there, Alicia. We could go tonight, and you'll see whether you like that sort of thing. No point in going to London if you don't – you'd be miserable. There are a huge number of entertainments in the metropolis, but you will most likely only attend Astley's once, whereas you'll be obliged to go to balls all the time."

Even Alicia brightened at this so that Lydia wondered if in fact a good deal of her sullenness related to a lack of confidence.

"Have you a gown that fits you?" the Baroness enquired.

"The assembly rooms are only open on Fridays in any event," the Countess said, "so that we will have to wait until tomorrow, which gives us plenty of time to purchase a gown. Would you like that, Alicia?"

"I'm not certain," the girl replied, either unnerved or unwilling to climb down from her high horse.

"You take her out this afternoon and find her one," Ambrose said. "Grandmama must be excessively fatigued after her long journey and will, I daresay, be delighted to be able to spend the afternoon in peace and quiet."

Chapter 14

And so it was that Lady Maresfield took her stepdaughter out for the first time to buy a new gown. Lydia declined to accompany them, saying that she had promised to help in the schoolroom that afternoon. Lord Chalvington managed to deter the Baroness from accompanying her daughter and granddaughter and ushered her into a quiet saloon where, after drinking a cup of coffee with her, he left her to read her book in tranquillity.

The pair in the carriage did not find a great deal to say to one another. In point of fact they had hardly spent any time alone together since Emmeline had joined the family. Alicia had rarely – and not at all for several years – been to Tunbridge Wells for any purpose whatsoever and, as they reached the outskirts, was struck by the number of buildings cheek by jowl with one another and, even more, by the vast number of people scurrying hither and thither upon the pavements.

Emmeline, perceiving this and desirous of avoiding any kind of verbal disagreement with the girl, did not comment upon the crowds, not wishing to add to the girl's anxieties or give her any fuel with which to make a scene. She pointed out the assembly rooms when they drove past them and, shortly after, the carriage drew to a halt in front of a row of shops.

Neither woman had ever graced the ladies' outfitters which they entered. Emmeline, equipped with an enormous number of clothes for her own presentation a scant two years previously and another vast quantity as a *trousseau* when she married, had seen no reason to buy any more since she had been living in the country and doing nothing. In any event, she had spent most of the time either suffering from the ill effects of her interesting condition or the after-effects of a difficult birth.

However, in spite of her outfit being two years out of date, the proprietress of the shop recognised a grand lady when she saw one and hurried up, curtseying and begging to be permitted to assist *Madame*. She probably knew the mission which had sent the two women forth for, although they were much of an age, it was immediately apparent that one was a grand married lady with a good deal of money while the other was a somewhat clodhopping young person let out of the schoolroom for the first time.

The Countess, adopting her grandest manner, announced that they were looking for a gown suitable for her daughter to attend the assembly rooms the very next evening.

Whatever the proprietress thought of such a hasty decision – clearly having been taken without preparing suitable apparel beforehand – or of the claim that one was the mother of the other when it was clear there were a paltry number of months between them, she gave no indication of her thoughts but expressed herself delighted and honoured to be offered the outfitting of such a charming young lady.

Both Emmeline and Alicia, although they rarely saw eye to eye, were completely in agreement with the erroneousness of the proprietress's assessment of Alicia. Many adjectives could have been applied aptly to the girl, but 'charming' was not one of them.

Gowns were withdrawn from hanging rails, discussion was entered into on what colour the young lady favoured – and which ones were likely to flatter a female blessed with such natural beauty – and so on – and on – until both ladyships were not only confused but irritated and, together, fairly longed to complete a purchase as soon as possible in order to be able to escape from the onslaught.

"I suppose," the Countess managed to say at last, "that for a first appearance it is usual to wear white – or some variation upon it."

"Indeed," the proprietress agreed at once. "With her autumnal colouring, I think cream might be a flattering colour for the young lady."

"Autumnal colouring?" Alicia queried with contempt. She had, before they set out, determined not to misbehave or to say anything which might not be quite *comme il faut* but, brought up in a household bursting with irreverent young males, she had little patience for absurd descriptions of a person's appearance.

"Oh, yes, Miss; your hair resembles a horse chestnut."

"Or a chestnut horse," Alicia snapped.

"Oh, Miss, I didn't mean to be disrespectful; it's a beautiful colour."

"Thank you; and I am not a miss; I am a lady."

"Oh, beg pardon, my lady! I meant no harm! Will you try this gown, my lady? I venture to think it will suit you exceedingly."

"Indeed? What do you think, Mama?"

"I believe it is worth trying it on. It is a pretty colour and I particularly like the lace on the bosom and sleeves."

Emmeline, seeing the turn matters had taken, had been about to abort the whole expedition – or, at the very least, try a different shop - and was relieved when Alicia consented to be guided into a back room where the proprietress helped her to take off the dress she had been wearing and put on the other. This was not easy as Alicia was unusually tall and the proprietress exceptionally short.

However, the change was eventually effected and Alicia encouraged to return to the main room where her stepmother was sitting on a damask-covered chair and wondering how she was to deal with the irate girl – which was what she fully expected her to be when she emerged from the back.

She was therefore astonished when a very goddess stepped forward. The gown fitted her to perfection, its high waist accentuating a bosom that was well-formed, and falling gracefully to finish at the girl's toes. She was surprised that it was long enough for Alicia was certainly taller than the average but the proprietress had chosen well.

"Oh, that is lovely!" she exclaimed. "Have you seen how very well you look?"

"I have not looked in a mirror, if that is what you mean, but I can see you're quite surprised that I've turned out less repulsive than you had expected!"

"I'm astonished that the dress is long enough," Emmeline returned, not wanting to encourage Alicia in her hostile manner for fear of shocking the shopkeeper. "I'm not in the least surprised that you look beautiful – you are beautiful. I have always said so."

"Not in my hearing!"

"Look at yourself in the mirror!" the Countess advised, "and tell me that the woman you see there is not ravishing."

Alicia allowed herself to be steered towards the mirror and looked in wonder at her own image. It was perfectly true that she did look gratifyingly handsome, but she wished she were not so tall. The little proprietress barely reached her shoulder.

"I am too tall," she murmured.

"You are all tall," Emmeline said, "as well as exceedingly handsome. I am struck by how strong the likeness is to your father!"

"I know! I wish I looked like Mama – or like little Lydia. She is pretty."

"Yes, she is, but you are beautiful. Be proud of what you are, Alicia!"

"Do you think I should?"

"Yes, without a doubt."

The dress was purchased, and the Countess and her stepdaughter returned to Maresfield in a more amicable mood than on the outward journey.

Alicia went straight upstairs to the schoolroom where she found all her brothers and sisters, including Lord Chalvington, as well as Lydia and Miss Westmacott.

When questioned by her brother on the success of the expedition, she said, "The shopkeeper praised my 'autumnal' colouring!"

"Did she, by Jove? I suppose we are all inclined that way. I wonder why none of us looks much like Mama."

Lydia, looking round the myriad heads of hair, noticed that everyone in the room, excepting her, had more than a touch of what could be described as an autumnal hue for even Miss Westmacott's burnt sienna locks were, although redder than most of the Maresfields', undoubtedly on the same spectrum.

"What did your mama look like?" she asked Chalvington for Alicia was describing her new gown in glorious detail to Anthea.

"There is a portrait of her above the mantelpiece in the blue saloon," he said. "I will point it out to you next time we are in there. She was dark, like you, which may explain why none of us has been blessed – or cursed – with flaming Titian hair. The reddest is probably Amos, and I think Jasper may turn out to be fair – like his mother."

"I don't think he looks much like her in other respects," she said. "Except of course that he has blue eyes. He has the same nose as you."

"That is true, but I still think he may turn out fairer than the rest of us. He's a handsome boy, do you not think?"

"Oh, exceedingly," she replied, laughing. "He has the most speaking eyes – even if they are blue!"

"Ah, that is definitely a family feature!"

While Alicia was retailing her exciting afternoon with more enthusiasm than anyone could recall seeing her display before, Lady Maresfield, after taking some time removing her hat and pelisse, made her way to the saloon where her mother was still recumbent upon a *chaise longue* with a book in her hand.

"Ah, there you are!" Lady Fetcham exclaimed as though she had been searching for her daughter for several hours and was surprised to find her at last.

"Yes. We had a successful trip; Alicia has a lovely gown, with which she seems delighted, so I suppose we will go to the assembly rooms tomorrow if Ambrose will take us."

"I assume the little ward will not accompany you."

"No; as you know, her father died recently. I am sure she will not. Will you come, Mama?"

"Do you know, I think I will? I have not been to a ball for a very long time – not I think since your Season – so that it will be a useful reintroduction to dancing and partners and social chit-chat. But will Chalvington want to come if the ward is to remain here?"

"I don't see why not." The Countess was aware that her tone was a trifle snappish and added, "It was he who suggested we go in the first place."

"Oh, yes, but you know what young men are like: they don't think very coherently and I daresay he forgot the little ward's situation. After all, he did not think of it when he engaged in childish games on the riverbank."

The Countess grew quite red with vexation. "If you are implying what I think you are, you are not being precisely coherent, Mama. If they were playing childish games, it follows, does it not, that they were not doing what I think you suspect?"

Lady Fetcham tittered. "You must know that childish games played by people who are not children frequently end in all sorts of quite grown-up games. I suppose he is bound to come to London with us; why do you not leave the ward behind to help the governess?"

"Because she is not an employee, my husband is her guardian and they have not, so far as I know, ever met. If there is what you seem determined to think of as some sort of *tendre* between her and Ambrose, I daresay he will decide to stay here if we leave her behind. In any event, he will have to go back to Oxford soon."

"True; and it will be much better to have them under our eye in London where they will not be able to wander off to the river and loll about on the bank by themselves. Where are they now?"

"I have no notion where he is; she went up to the schoolroom with Alicia when we came in."

"Then I'll wager that's where he is."

109

Emmeline was much afraid that her mother was right and was beginning to wish, quite violently, that she had not invited her to accompany them to London. She had done so in a fit of uncertainty and lack of confidence in her own ability to launch Alicia but had discovered on the shopping trip that the girl was by no means unmanageable, particularly if one were kind to her.

The following evening, after the early dinner which seemed to be *de rigueur* in the country, the four who were to visit the assembly rooms changed into their finery and set off.

"I am sorry you are not coming with us," Chalvington said to Lydia. They were alone together in the hall while they waited for the other three women to finish their preparations.

"I own I am sorry too," Lydia said, "but it would be quite improper for me to be dancing so soon after Papa's death."

"I know, but I daresay you could in a private house."

"Possibly, but I cannot imagine when I am likely to find myself in a private house where there is dancing as I will not be accepting invitations in London."

"I expect Mama will give a ball in our own house; you will be able to dance there. I will be sure to come up for it!"

"Oh, not at a ball; I don't think I could. What," she added with, for her, an unusual degree of feminine anxiety "in the world could I wear? I cannot be seen in anything but black and that would look very odd at a ball!"

"That's true, but I'm sure something can be done. Lavender – you could wear that, could you not?"

"Not for another five months."

"I know what we can do: presumably Miss Westmacott gives a few lessons in dancing from time to time; why do we not encourage her to do that and you and I can show the children how it should be done?"

She laughed. "I'm not sure I know."

It was, of course, at this very moment that Lady Fetcham descended the stairs.

"What a deal of amusement you find in each other's company," she observed, raising her eyebrows.

"Indeed! We see eye to eye on a number of subjects," Chalvington responded, unabashed.

Alicia appeared a few minutes later, walking carefully in her new dress. Lydia exclaimed in a gratifying manner and wished the girl an enjoyable evening.

"You'll take Tunbridge Wells by storm," her brother said teasingly.

"I suppose you mean everyone will run for cover," she said sullenly.

"If you take that attitude, I daresay they will," Lady Fetcham interrupted. "This is a precursor to your appearance in London, Alicia, and I hope you will use it wisely."

The girl flushed angrily and was clearly searching for a suitably disagreeable rejoinder when the Countess appeared, in deep blue silk.

Lord Chalvington kissed her hand in the manner of a medieval courtier and offered his arm to lead her to the waiting carriage but he did not forget Lydia, who had stepped back into the shadows at the side of the hall.

"I'll tell you all about it tomorrow."

The party bound for the Assembly Rooms settled into their seats and the carriage began to move.

Emmeline, sitting beside her mother and opposite Lord Chalvington, was guiltily aware of the pleasure she had felt when he had kissed her hand for it was not so much the gesture, which was clearly a homage to her beauty and rank, as the appreciative expression on his face when he had beheld her, dressed for a ball. She was delighted with her step-daughter's appearance but could not help – or easily contain – the giddy delight of knowing that she was still the most desirable woman in the party; of course he could not be expected to appreciate his sister's looks but still there was no denying that she had had an effect upon him, which was not entirely – or perhaps even not at all – related to respect for a stepmother.

"I suppose it will be very provincial," Lady Fetcham said. "Nevertheless, it will serve as a rehearsal for London. I suppose you can dance, Alicia?"

"No."

"No? Lud, Emmeline, what have you been about that your daughter has not been taught to dance? And what is the use of that governess who, I must say, is not an amiable person?"

Emmeline, who had been subjected to the ministrations of a dancing master for several months before her launch, flushed with annoyance.

"I own I did not think to enquire precisely what Miss Westmacott was teaching the children, but, remember, Mama, I have not been here for long and for much of that time I was exceedingly unwell. In point of fact, I have recently begun to think more about the management of the children and have decided, subject of course to Maresfield's approval, to send Anthea to school – I thought to place her in my old seminary."

"Well, you could not do much better than that," Lady Fetcham said, mollified. "But, if I were you, I believe I would send the governess packing."

"It was Papa who engaged her – many years ago now," Lord Chalvington reminded them. "She has a difficult job – so many children, so many different ages – and both boys and girls."

"In that case she could do with an assistant – and of course you cannot be held responsible for someone your husband engaged long before he met you," the Baroness admitted, "but it seems to me that her priority should be preparing the girls for their entrance into Society; after all, the boys will go to school eventually. Can you play?" she asked Alicia, moving abruptly from the general to the particular.

"No – or only very badly – as was demonstrated the first night Lydia arrived. She can play – and sing – very prettily."

"I daresay she can dance too," the Baroness said darkly.

Chapter 15

"I should have given you a few lessons," Chalvington said, "but there was no time between the sudden decision to come out tonight and your spending the whole afternoon buying a dress."

"Could you have? Can you dance?" Alicia asked, surprised and disbelieving.

"Yes, of course. There were any number of balls when I was in the army: before and after every battle. I don't think you need to be too anxious: it is really not very difficult, all you have to do is copy everyone else – well, copy the women, I suppose."

"But if I do that, how can I talk to my partner?"

"You can't, but I should think that might be a good thing."

"Why? Are you convinced I will be rude to everyone?"

"Not completely, but, no, I wasn't even thinking that; I was thinking that, if you look at your and other people's feet all the time, you'll appear shy and many men like that. It makes them hope you'd be a biddable wife."

"Is that what they're thinking all the time – whether I would make a good wife? It is quite horrid. I might as well be a horse!"

"Yes, except that you wouldn't have any choice about your new owner if you were a horse, but I don't suppose Papa will be so cruel as to force you to marry someone if you don't like them above half."

"You told me you liked Papa before you married him," Alicia said to the Countess. "Do you still like him? I should think you must regret marrying him."

"Yes, of course I still like him – and, no, I don't regret my decision."

A silence fell in the carriage after this while most of those present wondered why in the world she had liked him and what possible reason there could be for continuing to do so.

"I suppose he was a good match," Alicia said at last.

"In some ways; the drawback was that he already had so many children," the Countess said sharply.

Alicia laughed at this. "Yes, it's a warning to me, isn't it? I don't think I'd marry a man who had lots of children even if I did like him."

"I'll wager you would," Chalvington said. "If you liked him enough."

"Well, I won't. I wouldn't want to be in Mama's shoes for anything!"

"I didn't know you had so much sympathy for me."

"No, I didn't; I didn't think about you beyond resenting you, but, now that people are talking about my marriage, I find I can't help looking at you and thinking that I do not, ever, want to end up in a similar situation."

"I never heard anything so ridiculous!" Lady Fetcham exclaimed. "What in the world has she to complain of? She has made an extraordinarily good match – to one of the foremost earls in the country, who has, in addition, one of the largest fortunes in England. She lives in a well-appointed house in an agreeable part of the country and has managed to give birth to a son within less than a year of marriage – an event which means that she is in the fortunate position of not being obliged to put up with her husband's attentions ever again if she does not wish to – and it seems he has little intention of bothering her again for that purpose. Lord, I would have considered myself uniquely blessed to have found myself in such a position."

"Was Papa so odious?" the Countess asked in a small voice.

"Not especially, but he was not without fault and, once I had succeeded in giving him an heir, I was delighted that he took himself off and left me to my own devices."

"I have not given my lord an heir," the Countess muttered. "He already had one – and several spares in case that one came to an untimely end."

"He still may," Chalvington reminded her, "but there are indeed several more so that I own I do not feel absolutely compelled to fulfil my duty."

There is no future worth thinking about for a woman other than marriage," Lady Fetcham opined, becoming anxious lest Alicia decide to defy convention.

"I should think I might as well cast myself into the river then," the girl said viciously.

"Oh, I don't think you should do that," her brother said lightly. "At least certainly not yet, for at this point in your life there is some hope that things will turn out well. Why, you may meet a man you love – and who will love you. I must say, this conversation and its emphasis on the general odiousness of men – and husbands in particular – is exceedingly unamusing for me. I *am* a man and I suppose one day I will be a husband. I like to think I will be able to make my wife happy – and, not entirely unnaturally, hope she will make me happy."

"You're always happy!" Alicia said.

"Not always, but most of the time and, although it may come as a surprise to you, it is by no means accidental or because I am uniquely blessed. In any event, I try to be cheerful."

"You have a good deal to be cheerful about," Alicia muttered, her general resentment returning.

"I know I do – and I count myself exceedingly fortunate – but, really, Alicia, you are not *un*fortunate. You are of good birth, you're reasonably good-looking, healthy and well-provided for – and now you are on the very brink of the most exciting and stimulating period of your life."

"And everything after that will be horrid," she concluded.

"Papa will not permit you to marry an unpleasant man," he said more soberly, perhaps understanding something of her fear. "He may be a little remiss in his attention to his family, but he is not a bad man, is he, Mama? Or cruel?"

"No."

"There you are then. I can only suggest you trust his judgment."

"Do you?"

"I? Well, I haven't asked him for his opinion on my choice of bride – not having made one yet – but I cannot fault him on his other decisions. It was kind of him to accede to my youthful demand to serve in the army in spite of the European situation being so exceedingly dangerous, as it was at the time."

"I think it was an excessively poor decision," the Baroness interrupted. "Fancy allowing you to join up at a time when it was almost inevitable that you would be killed. Did he not care what might happen to you? In my opinion, it was almost criminal to accede to such a request from a person who at the time was ill-qualified to make it."

"You would have refused?"

"Yes – and so would my husband, if he had been alive."

"If he had refused, I would still have gone but I would have lied to the recruiting officer about my name, my age and everything else. He would not have cared – they wanted as many men as possible – and, if I had joined under those circumstances, I don't doubt I would have been killed. By joining a crack regiment under Papa's influence, I found myself fighting but – at least to some extent – protected because of my rank."

"Well, I don't think he cares about females," Alicia said, failing to find anything else with which to argue in her brother's defence of their father.

"Of course he does, but I daresay he does not find it so easy to understand what they want. If I were you, I would acquaint him with your hopes and fears. How can he know if you do not tell him?"

Emmeline, listening to this eminently sensible advice, wondered why she had never tried this method and came to the conclusion that it was because she had not seen enough of her husband to be in a position to express such sentiments.

It had been a whirlwind courtship, begun when she first arrived in London and concluded when they married in August of that same year. He had swept her off on honeymoon to Scotland which, in August, was not particularly attractive: when it was not raining, the air was full of nasty little insects which bit her and brought up horrid, red, itching lumps all over her delicate skin. That was her first experience of becoming anxious lest his lordship recoil from her. He had not – at least not on that occasion. He had, instead, offered sympathy and the soothing lotion which the maids in that part of the country knew how to make to alleviate the discomforts inevitable upon spending time out of doors in fine weather.

She had been perfectly content with Scotland, although he had apologised for choosing it in preference to the more glamorous areas in Europe which were presently overrun with soldiers.

She had – almost – believed his protestations of love, which had continued in spite of the itchy, red rash which defaced her beauty, but she had been brought up from an early age to place enormous store upon her appearance and was convinced that its loss would lead inevitably to his rejection. Her mother's unrelenting pursuit of maintaining her own looks had convinced her that nothing much mattered besides beauty.

She had returned from Scotland – and as the year waned so did the attention of the midges – in an interesting condition. He, who had so many children already, probably knew before she did that his quiver was to be swelled again. He took her to Maresfield but did not stay long as there was still a good deal of uncertainty about the situation in Europe.

He had already taken several months' leave of absence, beginning in April after Boney was sent to Elba, during which they had met in London. Their marriage and subsequent honeymoon had obliged him to request an extension, but, by November, his colonel was beginning to agitate for his return to duty.

She was already feeling unwell when they arrived at Maresfield. Meeting his lordship's children, who all (even little Amory) seemed not only enormous but overpoweringly vigorous, had cast a damper upon her happiness, not helped by the weather, which was unremittingly grey and sodden, the garden almost obliterated beneath wind and rain and, on still days, obscured by impenetrable mist.

He had left her there, consigning her to the care of Nanny Macintosh, who had looked upon her shrinking, nauseated form with contempt. Parting from him on the day he returned to his regiment, she had a terrible presentiment that they would never meet again: either he would die - cut down in battle - or she would, most likely as a result of the child she was carrying.

As the months passed, they had exchanged letters, but he was not a man to wax sentimental on paper and, although he addressed her as his 'dearest' and although he sent her 'all his love', she was not reassured. Without his kisses, she grew increasingly to doubt the depth of his affection.

Jasper was born in early June and the Earl arrived a few days' later, having been unable to get away before. She did not know how he greeted his new son nor was able to observe his manner towards her for she was delirious with puerperal fever after a prolonged and difficult birth. She was indeed ignorant of his presence until he was about to leave again and, parting from him as he set off to join Wellington in crushing Napoleon once more, was certain that this would be their last meeting. She had clung to him with what little strength she had, weeping and wailing, and he, his face contorted with what she took to be disgust, had been forced to uncurl her fingers from his and almost run from the room.

She was still in bed when Napoleon was finally defeated a couple of weeks later but the Earl did not return to her side. He was unable to do so because he had been badly wounded and was brought home to London where he was tended by the most eminent doctors England could assemble.

She had not seen him since. Jasper was ten months old, but his father had not set eyes on him since that first meeting a few days after he was born.

By the time the carriage drew up outside the Assembly Rooms, the passengers had fallen silent, even Lord Chalvington's buoyancy affected by the gloom and irritation pervading the confined space.

The door was opened, the steps let down and Ambrose, casting a look of almost comical despair at the three women, jumped down first and held out his hand to assist his grandmother.

She took it without a word but even her rigid face cracked into a smile when she saw his.

"I daresay they'll come about," he said. "They're a little apprehensive."

"I can't see what there is to be apprehensive about in visiting a provincial Assembly Room," she said, adding *sotto voce*, "my daughter - I am sometimes afraid that the balance of her mind has been disturbed – by the terrible birth and her illness, you understand."

"Yes, of course, but I think she is most likely simply uneasy over whether my sister will conduct herself in an appropriate manner."

In the event the evening went better than anyone had dared hope.

They were greeted by the patrons, seats were found for them, drinks served and a succession of hopeful young gentlemen brought forward for Alicia's approval.

She was so unnerved by the whole business that she barely opened her mouth all evening – and thus horrified no one with her forthright opinions - but she stood up for most of the dances, her looks and breeding ensuring her a good deal of interest from everyone present.

Lord Chalvington, having seen her somewhat unsteadily launched upon the dance floor, took himself off to the card room, although he emerged later to stand up with a succession of pretty young women.

The Countess, seated with the dowagers beside her mother, endured the evening as best she could but was relieved when it came to an end.

The journey home was enlivened by the Baroness's animadversions on the excessive provinciality of the other patrons, the appalling taste of the ladies' gowns and the poor quality of the young gentlemen.

Alicia, who had enjoyed herself once she had become less anxious about where she put her feet and more certain that she would not want for partners, wilted beneath this diatribe.

"Will it be so much more sophisticated in London, Grandmama?" she asked, almost humbly.

"Good gracious, yes, child! That patroness – I cannot recall her name – but she would not be able to assume such airs and graces at Almack's, I promise you. Why, she is positively vulgar – her *hair*!"

"She was excessively kind," Alicia murmured, having been quite struck by the interest the despised lady had taken in her and the efforts she had made to introduce her to young gentlemen.

"She was flattered to have such a well-bred young woman attend; I don't suppose it is a common occurrence for an Earl's daughter to visit those Assembly Rooms."

"I suppose," Lord Chalvington said, feeling his sister's shame and discomfort as she shrank beside him, "that there are not so very many Earls' daughters anywhere – certainly not ones as handsome as Alicia. You will not want for partners at Almack's either, dear sister, I promise. It is in any event the most frightful place – full of pretentious people who spend their time elevating their noses to carefully graded degrees to persons they deem beneath them."

"Is it?" she asked tremulously. The evening's experience had been far more agreeable than she had expected, but her grandmother's criticism made her feel she was a country bumpkin for having enjoyed something which was clearly contemptible.

"Yes. It's run rather like a school where punishments are handed out almost arbitrarily to people the patronesses don't care for – or of whom they are jealous."

"Nonsense!" the Baroness exclaimed. "Have you been refused entry, Chalvington?"

"Good God, no! I am an Earl's son – and a well-breeched one at that. It's most unlikely they would refuse me entry, but I can't say that their fawning upon me when I turn up impresses me in the least."

"I daresay you find plenty of pretty girls there, though, do you not?" the Baroness asked slyly.

"Oh, yes, of course, there are any number but most of 'em don't have a word to say for themselves – too frightened of putting a foot wrong. I must say, I rather prefer the country girls who say what they think and aren't afraid of being barred from entry if they stand up for the waltz."

Chapter 16

Lydia was surprised to find that she felt bereft when the party left for the Assembly Rooms. She had not been at Maresfield for long and, apart from her daily rides with Lord Chalvington, had not so far found her sojourn either comfortable or comforting: the Countess was mostly sunk in gloom and, when she did rouse herself, was given to brusque remarks; since the arrival of her mother she had become even more morose and irritable.

This sense of abandonment was disturbing because she could not help but attach it to the absence of Chalvington; after all, the Countess and her mother, together with the irascible Alicia, having left the house for a few hours, ought to be a relief. She hoped she was not becoming dependent upon the young man and, if she was, she wondered why. Was it merely because, having lacked the presence of a brother all her life, she had taken to him immediately or was it – much more disturbingly – because she was beginning to develop a *tendre* for him? She knew that girls of her age frequently succumbed to unsuitable infatuations for handsome young men – just as boys such as Amos did for young women - but she had not seriously considered herself likely to fall victim to such an embarrassing affliction. Her father had been dead barely a month; it would be shameful if she were to have so far forgotten him that her heart could beat faster at the sight of another male. She reassured herself that it was simply that he, alone amongst this chaotic and disagreeable family, had shown what appeared to be genuine warmth and kindness towards her.

She would go upstairs to the schoolroom although, it now being well after the hour at which the children took supper, she supposed they would all be abed, or at least incarcerated in their rooms with books, but she might find Miss Westmacott wishful for some grown-up company.

In truth she did not warm much towards the governess but told herself sternly that the poor woman was almost certainly not at her best when trying to impose discipline. In fact, Miss Westmacott was the person who perhaps fascinated her more than any other member of the household for she combined a curious degree of haughtiness with suffering. Lydia had no difficulty in understanding the woman's torment, for managing such an ill-disciplined group of children day in, day out must be almost beyond endurance, but she wondered about the haughtiness. Was Miss Westmacott a scion of a noble family fallen upon hard times and forced to take a position as a governess? It seemed odd that she had not married for she was exceptionally good-looking.

She knocked but received no response. After a few moments, she knocked again and then opened the door a crack to call, "Are you there, Miss Westmacott?"

"I am; where else would I be?" came the irritated response.

"I do not wish to disturb you if you wish to be alone, but, now that the others have gone out, I was wondering if we might spend the evening together."

"You mean, I take it, that the more interesting people having abandoned you, you will put up with my company in preference to sitting by yourself?"

Lydia, unlike most people, had never been rejected by anyone until she came to Maresfield and, as a consequence, did not immediately assume that the governess disliked her or found her boring. She put the sharp tone down to the other woman's state of mind at that moment and, coming fully into the room but not yet shutting the door behind her, said, "In truth, I have not precisely chosen with whom to spend my time since I arrived, but assumed that politeness required me to attend her ladyship in preference to anyone else."

"Indeed? I own I thought you preferred Lord Chalvington's company to anyone else's."

Lydia blushed. "Is it your belief that I have been too much with him?"

"Not my belief – my observation."

"Oh! I daresay he may be quite tired of me; I will try in future to be less dependent upon him. I feel I should point out, however, that it is not I who suggests a ride every morning, it is he."

"I don't doubt it; like his father, he has an eye for a pretty face."

"I believe he is being kind and trying, with the best of intentions, to alleviate some of my uncertainty as well as my grief."

"Oh, your grief! You will fall back upon that as an excuse, will you?"

"No! Oh, I hope not! It would be abominable if I were to use it in that way. I did not mean that, only that Lord Chalvington is very kind."

"Huh!" Miss Westmacott exclaimed scornfully. "Men often seem kind when they are looking to seduce women. Do you think Lord Amos kind too? He has clearly formed an attachment to you."

"At the moment, but I am sure it will not last. I am not much acquainted with boys of his age, but I understand it is not uncommon for them to fancy themselves in love with an older woman."

"Is that what you think? You are scarcely two years older."

"That is true but, at his age, two years is a good deal."

"My lady Maresfield was your age – seventeen – when she met Lord Maresfield."

Lydia made no comment, not thinking that the two situations were much related to each other. She had by this time fully come into the room, shut the door and sat down in a chair on the other side of the fireplace from the governess.

"Have all the children retired for the night?" she asked, hoping to move the conversation away from relations between men and women of wildly differing ages, which, it seemed to her, would not advance their own amicability.

"Yes, thank Heaven! Were you hoping your admirer might be here?"

"No; I am relieved that he is not. I came to talk to you."

"Really! Whatever for? I am not an interesting person and cannot advance any of your ambitions."

"I do not know that I have any ambitions precisely and I hope that, if I had, I would not seek your company for such a purpose. I understand you have been here some time?" she tried in a further attempt to bring the conversation round to the governess who, she was convinced, suffered from a degree of isolation and perhaps even desolation.

"Approximately seventeen years. When I arrived, Ambrose – your Lord Chalvington – was three years old and Alicia was nearly one. The others have arrived since."

Lydia wondered at Anthea's insistence on remembering Miss Westmacott's arrival but supposed that she wanted to emphasise how much she disliked her.

"Were Anthea and Amos born after you came?"

The governess blinked. "Yes; she is sixteen and he's fifteen."

"Yes, of course. I daresay you did not expect the family to grow so large."

"I don't think I expected it not to – families are often large, especially in well-to-do households. Why do you want to know?"

"I do not particularly; I was simply endeavouring to make conversation."

"I see."

"So when you first arrived, I imagine there was only Ambrose in the schoolroom, although even he was very young – too young for lessons, surely? It must have been much easier."

"Looking back," the governess said, mollifying a trifle, "I suppose it must have been, although it seemed very difficult. Chalvington was always an agreeable child and, even then, did his best to help, but Lady Alicia, who was propelled into the schoolroom much too young in my opinion, was more or less unmanageable from the very beginning."

"Their mother was alive then, of course," Lydia murmured.

"Yes. Are you wondering but not quite liking to ask what sort of a woman she was?"

Miss Westmacott spoke mockingly, no doubt trying to make Lydia ashamed of her curiosity.

"I own I am," she admitted with a self-deprecatory little laugh.

This, it seemed, was the key to unlocking the governess's much-defended heart. She smiled with more genuine warmth and humanity than Lydia had yet seen.

"She was nothing like her ladyship in either appearance or character so far as I could tell – can tell. The present Lady Maresfield has not been here long and for most of that time she has either been expecting a happy event or recovering from it. It was a very difficult birth and she contracted a fever afterwards which nearly carried her off, but I have a sense that, underneath her despondency, there is a lively woman who is disappointed in how her marriage has turned out.

"The previous Lady Maresfield had, I suppose, already suffered all that disappointment and become inured to her life. She had, after all, been married for nearly four years when I first arrived. She was, in any event, a small, dark creature – not unlike you – and became increasingly worn down by childbearing. She was not a spirited woman and would have been wholly incapable of controlling Lady Alicia even if she had made any attempt to do so. She did not. She left it entirely to me and Nanny Macintosh."

"I would guess that Nanny Macintosh is quite strict," Lydia hazarded.

"She is strict with the girls," Miss Westmacott said, "but not at all with the boys, who she seems to think should be encouraged in every wildness they display. The girls, though, must be forced to sit still and not speak most of the time. Such a regime, when she was very young, had little effect upon Lady Alicia other than to make her resentful."

"I should imagine that she was glad to leave Nanny Macintosh's control for the schoolroom," Lydia suggested.

"You might think so but it's my belief that she takes most of her pleasure from making Lady Anthea miserable. In the schoolroom, at least at first, she was separated from her sister and had no one to provoke – except me."

Lydia laughed. "I don't suppose she got far with that."

"I have hardened in the years I have been here. I am ashamed to admit that at first I was wounded by her hostility and endeavoured to persuade her to like me. Of course, that was the worst thing I could possibly have done for she soon realised what good sport it was."

"I admire your tenacity. I believe I would have left."

"Do you? I had nowhere to go. Here, I received my bread and butter and, although Alicia was perfectly beastly almost from the moment I arrived, I had no trouble from her ladyship, who left everything to me."

"It must have been utterly miserable," Lydia said with feeling. She thought how lucky she was that, although she had lost her family and her home, she was not obliged to earn her living in the only way that respectable young women could.

"It was partially my own fault," the governess, who had become almost expansive under Lydia's gentle probing, admitted. "I had a Season – as Lady Alicia is about to – but I failed to marry and had, eventually, to look for a position."

"You must, though, have had any number of admirers," Lydia said gently for, even now that she was presumably aged somewhere between thirty and forty, Miss Westmacott was a handsome woman.

"Yes, but I did not care for any of them. I wish now that I had and I wish too that I had heeded my parents and taken the least disagreeable from amongst them for what they said was true: that a woman's life – if she has not sufficient money of her own – is hardly worth living unless she marries."

Lydia said, "Would you swap places with Lady Maresfield? I don't think she is any more happy than you."

"She is a fool!" the governess exclaimed with what seemed to Lydia to be quite disproportionate anger. "What has she to complain about? She has a high position, as much money as she can possibly desire – and she does not even have to endure her husband's presence!"

"I think she would give a great deal to have his presence."

"She is even more of a fool then! He …" Miss Westmacott was by this time so enraged that she could barely speak.

"Is he so very disagreeable?" Lydia asked.

"He is the most odious man who ever breathed!"

"But I am convinced that she holds him in strong affection."

"She is deluded. You will see, when you meet him, what a devil he is – and so will she."

"Good God! What is so unpleasant about him?"

"He thinks of nobody but himself and does not care two straws for her any more than he did for his first wife. He is a man who used, at one time, to be as handsome as your Lord Chalvington but, by dint of loose living, has ruined both his looks and his health. And yet, in spite of this, I understand he still keeps a number of mistresses, to none of whom he is faithful."

"But he fought at Waterloo – that was not so very long ago – was his health already ruined then?" Lydia asked, thinking that the governess's criticism was perhaps a trifle exaggerated.

"I suppose," was the contemptuous response, "that a man in his position would not be engaged in a great deal of actual fighting. I daresay he sent other people to do that."

"Yes, of course, I had not thought of that. But was he not badly wounded?"

"I believe so; that, at any rate, is the report we have received. None of us has seen him since – not even his wife."

"Well, unless she went to London – where I understand he has remained – she could not have done. You would surely be bound to see him if he came here."

"You think so? Unless I were to meet him by chance in the hall or on the stairs, why would I see him? He does not visit the schoolroom and would have no interest in enquiring of the governess how his children were progressing."

"I see. He does not sound prepossessing." Lydia was afraid that, having apparently lit Miss Westmacott's temper towards her employer, it was now moving inexorably back to her.

"Oh – *prepossessing*! But he is – or was – in spite of all his faults. They all want to save him!"

"Oh, I see! And yet clearly none of them has."

"It would be impossible to save him – he is thoroughly spoiled – by Nanny Macintosh!"

"I see, but has she not brought them all up? Lord Chalvington does not appear to be spoiled, although it is true that the others display a high degree of selfishness."

"And temper!"

"Oh dear – does Lord Maresfield also possess an ungovernable temper?"

"I am sure I cannot say! I have seen no evidence of such a thing. His children fall into rages because each one is so selfish that he – or she – will not give way to another, but *he* has his own way all the time – and always has had."

"Has he no brothers or sisters?"

"No brothers. He has one sister, who is a very model of unselfishness, although very likely her natural familial rage bubbles beneath. In any event, she is exceptionally well-behaved – almost unnaturally so. Don't forget that she was also brought up by Nanny Macintosh who has always been excessively severe with girls."

"I begin to feel quite nervous about meeting him," Lydia murmured, remembering that this fascinating insight into the disagreeable nature of a man who seemed to have incurred the governess's implacable hatred was exceedingly improper in view of the fact that the Earl was her guardian – and had been carefully chosen as such by her loving father. Did he, her father, know nothing of the Earl's unpleasant propensities?

"I shall be interested to hear what you think of him," the governess rather surprisingly said, implying, Lydia thought, that a certain friendship had developed between them and that her opinion would be of value.

"Yes; I don't know how long we will spend in London."

"The Season, I suppose; you will be back by August – and let us hope that Alicia will have found a husband by then."

"Do you think the children will behave better when she has left? I suppose the boys will be going back to school for the summer term soon."

"Yes – and apparently Anthea is to go too."

"But not immediately?"

"Perhaps not; I suppose it is more likely to be September. Have you been to London before?"

"No, never. But I do not expect it will make much difference as I am not likely to be going about much."

"You will not, though, be able to spend every morning riding alone with Chalvington."

"No; I own I shall miss that. Will he go back to Oxford?"

"I should imagine so – unless he cannot bear to be parted from you, in which case I daresay he will follow you to London."

Lydia laughed; it was intended to be an expression of her amusement at Miss Westmacott's peculiar insistence that the Viscount had conceived a *tendre* for her – or that she had for him – but it emerged as the sort of horrid simulated titter which she had heard the Countess utter when shamed.

She flushed and tried to cover it up by saying, "Surely he cannot please himself in that regard? If term has started, I am persuaded he will be obliged to present himself."

"Present himself perhaps but, I told you, the Maresfield men do as they please and Chalvington, although he seems to you to be so much more agreeable than either Amos or Adrian, is not above showing up for whatever they do to be marked as present and then sloping off again."

Lydia did not think that such behaviour was entirely incompatible with agreeability, but she said, "He told me his father particularly wished him to complete his studies at Oxford. If he does wander away, I am persuaded he would not be so foolish as to go to London."

This time it was Miss Westmacott's turn to utter a snort of spurious amusement. She said, "I don't suppose *he* would notice; he is most likely in his latest mistress's pocket most of the time, in a gambling hell or sleeping off his excesses."

"Surely he will not continue in that manner when his wife is in the house?"

"Or his ward?"

"I do not expect him to modify his behaviour for me," Lydia almost snapped. "If he had considered doing so, I imagine he would either have sent for me to go to London or come here to greet me himself."

"There!" the governess exclaimed, looking almost pleased for a moment. "You have already formed an unfavourable opinion of him. I suppose, though, that he must have written to my lady to inform her of the date of your arrival for she was waiting for you – and had told us all that you were expected."

127

Chapter 17

After this, Lydia, in spite of herself, grew more eager to go to London and meet her guardian. She told herself that, at least so far as she was concerned, life at Maresfield was perfectly pleasant but, apart from Lord Chalvington, no one else seemed to be content, much less happy.

The new terms for both the boys and the Viscount arrived before they had set off for the metropolis. The boys went first. On their last morning Sarah brought her mistress a passionate poem from Amos, expressing his joy in her presence, his admiration for her ravishing beauty and his utter desolation at being obliged to go away for nearly three months. His melancholy was only alleviated by his conviction that his hitherto lonely nights at school would be soothed by memories of her enchanting – if rarely directed at him – smile.

Lydia, reading it before breakfast, was aghast at the extent of the boy's rapture revealed in his composition and startled by what it revealed of a youth's mind. If it prompted hitherto unrecognised sentiments for a different Maresfield in her own breast, she did her best to suppress them, concluding somewhat hazily that boys were different from girls.

Sarah, seeing her flush as she read and noting her shaking hands and bowed head as she folded the missive, said, "Don't you be worrying about him, Miss; young men often have passions like that. He'll get over it."

"I don't doubt it, but I don't deserve it. I have tried to avoid him as much as possible and now feel that I have been unkind."

"The romantic interest for a boy that age is always unkind – whether she is in fact or not!" Sarah said placidly.

"Is it the same for girls? Will poor Alicia have to suffer the pangs of thwarted love before she finds the right man?" As she spoke, she was guiltily aware that she was using Alicia as an example in order to deflect whatever attention Sarah might have directed at her, for she was much afraid that her conscious looks might have given her away.

"Unfortunately, I don't think it is the same for girls - unless they're lucky enough to have a young man in close vicinity who is in point of fact out of reach," Sarah explained. "Girls amongst the Quality are kept so very close that they frequently marry their first love – and then find out that he's not quite what they thought at first."

"Like her ladyship," Lydia murmured.

It was not so much a question as a conclusion, for Lydia still thought that, although discussing such subjects in the abstract with her maid was acceptable, it would be wildly improper to apply any of their speculations to persons they knew – particularly one so far removed from the maid as the Countess.

But Sarah answered the question that had not been put. "Yes. Oftentimes the romantic interest is, like his lordship, much older than the girl. I hope you'll be careful, Miss."

"I shall not, just at present in any event, have the opportunity to develop a foolish infatuation as I shall be keeping to the house. In any event, I hope you will keep a close eye upon me, Sarah, and make certain I do nothing idiotic."

Lydia was beginning to relax as she perceived the dangerous moment of giving herself away to have passed. The next minute she was undeceived.

"Oh, I will, Miss, don't you worry. While we're on the subject, though, I've noticed Lord Chalvington's interest."

"Really? I assure you there is nothing romantic in it." Here she felt herself to be on firmer ground for, while Amos's declaration had alerted her to her own sentiments, she had perceived nothing of that nature in the Viscount's manner. "He has not written me poems praising my eyes or indeed said anything to make me think he does not view me as the sister he frequently calls me."

"No; he's too old for that sort of silliness, although he's not very old. He'll be going back to Oxford soon – and a good thing too, if you ask me."

"Why? There is nothing between us."

"No? But you are not the only woman in the household."

"The others are his sisters – or his former governess. You surely do not mean that there is anything between them?"

"No, I don't; she's too old for him. But there is the Countess, who is in fact younger than he."

"Her ladyship? Really, Sarah," Lydia sounded quite shocked – and she was, but not for the reason she hoped the maid would attribute to her reaction, "you are surely not implying there is aught between those two. Is that the gossip below stairs?"

"Yes; but they've all noticed he's transferred his interest to you now and they're speculating that may be the reason she's going to London."

"That's absurd – and a wicked lie, I am certain." But, as she spoke, Lydia knew that it was not. She had seen how the Countess's eyes rested upon the young man and she had felt the sting of what she had tried to convince herself was simply evidence of her ladyship's waspish tongue rather than jealousy. It was certainly time Chalvington returned to his studies and her ladyship to her husband.

They set off for London a few days later, barely an hour after the Viscount had ridden off to Oxford in a tearing hurry because it transpired that he should have presented himself the day before.

The two parties leaving at almost the same time meant that there was a great deal of coming and going, last-minute rushings-back to fetch something inadvertently left behind, cross words and general ill-temper and anxiety.

Several carriages jostled for position outside the front door: there were two, relatively modest vehicles, to convey the trunks and maids required by the feminine party, one to bear the precious burden of Lord Jasper and his attendants, and one, noticeably more luxuriously-accoutred than the others, to carry the Countess and her family - along with Lydia - to the metropolis. The last, which was still being hastily packed with his lordship's effects, including his valet, was to depart for Oxford, travelling respectfully behind Chalvington and his groom, who would, in any event, proceed mostly across country while the coach must necessarily keep to the road.

Chalvington, at last satisfied that everything he could possibly need for the next eight weeks had been safely stowed in the Oxford-bound coach and that Paterson, his valet, was comfortably ensconced inside, parted from Lydia with great affection but, she was convinced, absolutely no romantic sentiment.

"I'll miss our rides," he said, taking her hand as they stood in the hall. "When I've handed in a few essays and convinced my tutors that I'm a serious student, I'll come up to London and we'll take a turn in the Park."

"Can you do that without incurring censure?"

"Probably not, but, so long as it's not much more than a reprimand, I daresay it'll blow over. I'm not a boy after all, but some few years older than most of the students, which means I'm not subject to quite such strict rules."

"It would be delightful to ride in the Park with you, but I would not like you to run any risk of being sent down."

"Oh, I won't be sent down – rusticated perhaps – but who cares? *That* would enable me to spend the whole Season in London!"

"I should think your father would – and so would I if you were to be punished because you had absconded for such a trivial reason." As soon as she had spoken, she regretted it, fearing that she had taken his words too seriously when he was no doubt merely teasing, and anxious lest he jump back like a scalded cat.

He did not. He was still holding her hand and looked into her eyes before saying, "You have such exceedingly deep eyes and such absurdly abundant eyelashes that it is difficult to tell what you're thinking."

"Oh!" Now she did blush.

"There's no need to colour up," he said, backing away from what she was afraid he had been able to discern in her expression in spite of his remarks, "I didn't mean it as a flowery compliment; it was merely an observation."

"I cannot read you either," she admitted, becoming a little defensive. "I do not know when you are teasing – I think it is most of the time – but I cannot reliably tell."

"I would not jest about something of that nature. You have remarkable eyes – in a wholly enchanting face – but you must know that by now because my little brother has completely fallen under your spell and has no doubt waxed lyrical about them."

She blushed again, remembering the poem. "I daresay he will forget all about me now that he's gone back to school."

"Oh, I shouldn't think so for a moment. At school, there'll be nothing to take his mind off his love – and he'll enjoy telling his friends how exquisite you are!"

"Oh, pray don't be absurd – you are as bad as he!"

"I hope not! There's only one other thing I should warn you against and that's taking my sister too seriously and allowing yourself to become embroiled in her affairs. She has, if I am not mistaken, grown attached to you and will no doubt confide all her worries about her suitors – or lack of them – to you for she has little fondness for Mama."

"I daresay she will be too busy to have much time to spare for confidences," Lydia said. Alicia had not so far shown much inclination to confide in her but she had ceased to make unkind remarks and Lydia was aware that the girl, for all her abrasiveness, was anxious about the coming presentation and whether she would be a success – and aware

131

too that she had little time for the Countess, who, indeed, had little time for her.

He smiled. "You will be the still point in her life while everyone around her is going mad. Mama, although she thinks she will be taken up with escorting her to parties and so forth, will actually, I suspect, be more concerned about dealing with Papa; and Grandmama will be doing all she can to make things worse. You have my sympathy."

"Oh! Surely they will be out most of the time and, when they are in, will wish to rest."

"I doubt it. When they are in, they will wish to complain about everyone they have met while they were out."

She could not help laughing but she thought that she would miss his light-hearted understanding and feared that her trip to the Earl's lair in London with three volatile females might indeed prove wearisome.

The Countess appearing at this moment to bid her stepson *adieu* put an end to this discussion, somewhat to Lydia's relief because the more he spoke about how she would manage without him, the more she wondered whether she would be able to do so with any degree of sanguinity.

Her ladyship, on the verge of departure, seemed to have discarded her usual despondency for almost fluttering nervousness.

"Isn't it time you were leaving, Ambrose?" she asked. "It is a long ride to Oxford – and I can see Jem outside with your horse, which must be growing impatient."

"He will just have to contain himself," the young man said lightly. "I suppose I am permitted to bid my new sister *adieu*."

"Yes, of course. Lydia, you could assist me by going up to Alicia who is tying herself in knots over her packing."

"Of course. Goodbye, Ambrose."

It was only as she said this that she realised he was still holding her hand. As she withdrew it, he pressed her fingers and said, "Goodbye, Lydia."

An hour later the procession of coaches set off for London, the first one bearing the four women, the succeeding one Lord Jasper together with the nursery maid and Nanny Macintosh; the third carried the trunks and assorted maids.

Alicia and Lydia sat in the less comfortable seats opposite the Countess and her mother. The journey would take several hours and necessitate a number of changes when everyone could disembark for a few minutes and take some refreshment; nevertheless, it felt to Lydia like an almost unimaginable length of time to be incarcerated at close quarters with three women whose moods were as unpredictable and uncontrollable as those of cats.

She said nothing, determined not to provoke anyone, but endeavoured to fix an agreeable expression upon her face as she gazed out of the window. She was, however, conscious that the women opposite – the Countess and her mother – spent more time staring at her and Alicia than looking out of the window. They had been travelling for less than half an hour when the atmosphere turned stormy.

"He is going too fast," the Baroness said, "particularly when one cannot but notice how ill-maintained the road is just here. I'm sure I shall be bruised all over."

The Countess nodded and, no doubt in the interests of keeping the peace – even if it meant they would be forced to spend even longer in close proximity to each other – told Alicia to knock upon the dividing window and tell the coachman to proceed more slowly.

Alicia did not agree with her grandmother's concern about their speed and said, "We are positively dawdling, Grandmama; if we were to go much more slowly, I am sure we would not arrive before dark."

"I am afraid we will not arrive at all if we continue in this manner – swinging from side to side and almost bouncing when there is the smallest unevenness in the surface of the road. We will end in the ditch, mark my words."

"Oh, Merton is an excessively experienced driver," the Countess said. "And he has been this way countless times; I am persuaded he knows just how fast he should drive along this stretch."

"Are you defending Alicia's wholly unwarranted attack? Am I – at my age too – to have no say in the manner in which we bounce along this road?"

"I am not defending anyone – and I have asked Alicia to request Merton to drive more slowly, as you know very well, Mama, for you heard me issue the instruction. I am merely trying to reassure you that we are unlikely to come to any harm with the reins in Merton's hands. Alicia, pray do as I requested."

With an ill grace, Alicia banged upon the window, and receiving an interrogative look from the boy sitting beside the coachman, mouthed the order. The pace at which they were travelling slowed immediately and the four women reverted to uneasy silence. Lydia was put in mind of a somnolent volcano.

When they at length drew into a post house for the horses to be changed, Lady Fetcham, with a tut and a sigh, demanded refreshment and stalked inside without waiting for any of the others.

"This is intolerable," Alicia said. "Why in the world did you invite Grandmama to come with us?"

"I did not; I invited her to come to London but she either misread my letter or decided she would rather come to Maresfield and travel with us to London. In any event, I wished her to join us because I thought she would be able to help with your presentation; I am so very ignorant of such matters myself," the Countess explained placatingly.

"How can you be? It is but two years since you were launched yourself," Alicia exclaimed impatiently.

"Precisely. I do not know what one is supposed to do as the chaperone. I thought Mama would be an advantage."

"Well, you thought wrong – and I daresay even you must know that by this time."

The Countess flushed uncomfortably, confirming, Lydia thought as she scurried along behind, the accuracy of the observation.

"Pray hold your tongue, Alicia. I will not permit you to speak to me in that manner," her ladyship said, casting a look of strong dislike at her stepdaughter.

"But you agree with me, do you not?" the girl asked, now almost laughing with triumph.

"Mama is understandably anxious about the journey as well as worrying about all the things which must be organised when we arrive," Emmeline said weakly. "Pray do not pick a fight with either her or me. Lydia!"

The Countess turned irritably towards the younger girl, hoping no doubt to change the focus of attention.

"My lady?"

"Please walk with Alicia while I go ahead and try to head off Mama," she said, increasing her speed and leaving the two young women together.

"She wants you to stop me arguing," Alicia said, displeased. "Have you any ideas on how you can achieve that?"

"None at all," Lydia replied, wishing Lord Chalvington were with them.

"I hate that old woman," Alicia said. "And she is *not* my grandmother!"

"I suppose that is something to be thankful for," Lydia said lightly, "although, oddly enough, you bear a strong resemblance to each other."

This remark had a dramatic effect. Alicia stopped dead and stared, open-mouthed, at Lydia.

"I am not like that old witch!"

"Not to look at, no, and as a matter of fact she is neither old – indeed she is probably younger than your papa – nor do her features resemble those one generally associates with a witch, but you share a tendency to complain about the least little thing and to take any view anyone else expresses, which is contrary to your own, as a personal insult."

"Well! That is not mincing words, is it?"

"I was trying to be tactful!"

"You were not! You were trying to do what Emmeline wanted – draw my fire on to yourself. You have succeeded! All the same, I see no point in engaging in a fight with you; I have nothing against you except that you are a little bit like a mouse."

"I tremble in fear of your pouncing upon me!"

"Nonsense! You look like a little mouse but as a matter of fact I do not think you are frightened of anything, which is, I suppose why I can see no hope of amusement to be had by baiting you."

"Do you find it diverting to upset Lady Maresfield – and her mother? It is cruel to do so – and foolish too because Lady Fetcham is quite capable of refusing to go another yard – and then there will be nothing for it but to turn round and go back to Maresfield."

"She will not – cannot – do that!" Alicia looked so horrified by this possibility that Lydia was convinced that the girl was, in spite of appearances to the contrary, looking forward to her *début*.

"I would not be at all surprised if she did. Would not you, in similar circumstances, resort to cancelling the whole trip in order to have the last word?"

"Very likely."

"If you wish to go to London, I am persuaded it would be best to resist Lady Fetcham's provocation. Even if you spend the remainder of the journey in silence, there will be nothing much she can do other than needle you – and she will surely grow tired of that if you do not respond. Indeed, when we have eaten our nuncheon, I daresay – if no one speaks – she will fall asleep quite soon."

"Very well," Alicia conceded, adding rather surprisingly, "will you help me to contain myself? If you think I am about to speak, you must pinch me."

Lydia, touched by the other girl's request for help in what she knew was exceedingly difficult for her, acquiesced and the two young women followed their elders into a private room where they were regaled with such a substantial nuncheon that Lady Fetcham did indeed fall asleep soon after they set off again with a fresh set of horses.

Chapter 18

When the Countess and her companions reached the outskirts of London – having proceeded a little faster when the Baroness was safely asleep - Lady Fetcham, once more awake, felt it incumbent upon her to begin to yawn in an attempt to show how little excitement the dazzling attractions of the metropolis held for her.

Lady Maresfield became increasingly nervous, twisting her hands together and even, once or twice, tugging on a stray curl as though it were a bell pull with which she longed to summon aid.

The two young women, however, could hardly contain their excitement. They pressed their faces to the windows and, although Alicia had maintained almost complete silence ever since nuncheon – at least partly because she was at last beginning to understand that keeping her mouth closed prevented everyone else from criticising her – she immediately joined Lydia in pointing out all sorts of fascinating things, including absurdly dressed persons, that they noticed on one side of the carriage or the other.

The two older women looked at each other and shared a rare moment of understanding as they observed the childish antics of the young ones. Lady Fetcham seemed pleased to see Alicia behaving more like the sort of young woman she thought she ought to be so that, when the carriage eventually drew up outside the Earl's house, everyone was in an unusually good – and amicable – mood.

The door was opened, the steps let down and the Countess set her foot upon the pavements of London for the first time since her marriage. As she looked up at the house in which his family had lived, whilst in London, for several generations, her softened mood vanished to be replaced by a look of terror that would not have been inappropriate had she been approaching the scaffold.

An ancient butler, with whom she was not at all acquainted, was waiting on the doorstep to welcome his mistress and her companions into an elegant interior. At Lady Fetcham's request – *she* was not rendered almost incapable by her arrival in her son-in-law's abode – they were shown upstairs to their chambers immediately.

Emmeline, who had only visited the house briefly when she was the Earl's affianced bride, was shown into a vast and exceptionally fine chamber at the back of the house where her windows looked out upon a carefully tended garden. The windows were open, admitting a slight breeze which stirred the curtains and bore upon it the scent of the flowers blooming beneath. Even in her confused and agitated state, she was aware of a sense of tranquillity in the room, aided by the soft colours, the preponderance of silk in the furnishings and the sweetness of the scent.

Hot water was brought and her maid helped her to change her creased and travel-stained dress for a clean one, brushed and rearranged her hair and, with a few well-chosen words of encouragement, sent her down to greet her husband in as calm a mood as she could achieve.

She descended the stairs by herself and marvelled at their grace and beauty. She had not of course been upstairs on her previous visit; indeed, she had seen no part of the house but for a saloon, where she had been served ratafia accompanied by little macaroons in the presence of her betrothed, his sister and her mother. She had spent scarce half an hour in the house.

Reaching the hall, one of the footmen showed her into the same saloon where she found her mother, Alicia and Lydia. There was no sign of her husband.

"Apparently his lordship will be with us directly," Lady Fetcham informed her as the footman shut the door.

"Oh! I'm glad to see you have all found your way down and been offered refreshment," she said, observing the bottles and glasses upon a tray – as well as a plate of macaroons.

"Yes. I seem to recall we were served macaroons before."

"Yes, I remember that too."

Overcome with the awful anxiety about the moment her husband would walk through the door, she felt she could not sit waiting in what she kept reminding herself was her own saloon until the Earl chose to favour them with his presence.

"I think, if you are all quite comfortable, that I will leave you for a few minutes while I go upstairs and make sure Jasper is settled in the nursery."

With this, she turned on her heel and went out. She had no idea where the nursery was but supposed that the helpful footman would be able to direct her. Upon being requested to do so, he led her up several flights of stairs and opened the door of the nursery, saying, "I believe you will find Lord Jasper in here, my lady."

She went in and found, not only Lord Jasper and the nursemaid, but also her husband, on whose lap the baby was sitting.

138

Both baby and father looked extraordinarily pleased with each other; indeed, she had never seen her son look so happy although she recalled that, in their courting days, the Earl had – or so she had believed at the time – looked equally joyful. The child was cooing and wriggling with pleasure while gazing fixedly into his father's eyes and the man was smiling tenderly at the small eager face of his son. She knew that smile, although she had not seen it for a long time, but the sight of it, even directed at another, made her heart turn over.

"Oh!" she said again, falling back a step. "This is where you are!"

"I'm not certain whom you're addressing, my lady, but we are both here!" Lord Maresfield replied, the joy leaving his face instantly as though wiped by an unseen hand.

"You, my lord! I did not expect to find you here. I came up to see Jasper and make certain that he had everything he needed."

"I hope I know how to provide properly for my son – after all, it is not the first time I have faced such a challenge."

Put firmly in her place by this opening salvo, she, who still had very little idea of how to look after the child, found herself immediately on the back foot. Her husband had undermined her position quite as effectively as Nanny Macintosh did every time she saw her.

"I did not mean to question the provisions you had made for Jasper," she answered. "Of course, I am aware that you know just what to do for the best. I meant only that I did not expect to find you here."

"Did you not? I suppose I should have come down first to pay my respects to your mother and my daughter but could not resist coming first to see how Jasper did. He has grown a great deal – is indeed hardly recognisable."

"And me! Did you not think to pay your respects to me?" She heard the whining note in her voice and winced.

"I was not aware that I needed to do so or that you would either expect or desire it; you are not a guest."

He was not looking at her as he spoke but at the child, to whom he made little darting glances to keep him amused while he spoke to his wife.

He looked up now but not at her. His glance was at the nursemaid to whom he nodded in dismissal. "I will send for you when you are needed, Ann; in the meantime, I hope you will make yourself at home. I will engage to take care of my son."

"My lord; my lady." The girl curtsied and withdrew.

"What am I then?" Emmeline asked when the door had closed.

"What are you?" he repeated, apparently bemused. "My wife; the mistress of this house. How do you do, my lady? You look well." He held out his hand.

"I am better than when I last saw you, my lord," she replied coldly, ignoring the gesture.

He looked up again, clearly startled by her hostile tone.

"I did not mean that precisely. I meant that you look well – better than … well, certainly better than I. There could hardly not be an improvement from when I last saw you for then you were hovering on the very edge of mortality. Indeed, I daresay you do not recall the occasion for you had only just emerged from delirium when I left."

"I thought …," she began but stopped.

He kissed the top of the baby's head and she stared, mind and body in turmoil, at his bent head. He was the same and yet horribly different. The same smile, although it was not apparently available for her, the same effect upon her nerves – setting them jangling with such longing that she flushed with shame but, from what she could see of him, physically he was alarmingly different.

He had been, presumably still was, a tall man – a characteristic which all his children seemed to have inherited – but where, when she had first met him, he had been powerful with broad shoulders and strong legs, he now looked oddly shrunken as though his flesh had withered. He more closely resembled a skeleton than a healthy man. His cheeks, always lean, had fallen in so that, beneath the sharp cheekbones, hollows had appeared; his nose, once an impressive, almost hawk-like proboscis, now seemed not so much impressive as threatening, dominating the cadaverous face. Above, the large dark eyes, which most of his children had inherited along with the height and the chestnut hair, struck her as bleak and cold although their old tender warmth rekindled when he looked upon the child.

"What did you think?"

"To tell the truth, I did not know what to think. I have thought and thought, round and round in circles, but have come to no conclusion."

"How exceedingly distressing!" he said without much sympathy. "Was all this circular intellectual activity focused upon one subject – or did you range over a number of conundrums and fail to find an answer to any of them?"

She almost stamped her foot; she was finding it increasingly difficult not to behave like Alicia. She wanted to hit him or storm out of the room, slamming the door behind her. And yet, at the same time, she found herself fixed to the spot, as fascinated by him as she might have been by a snake. She feared, was indeed almost certain, that he would hurt her – although the wound was more likely to be to her sentiments than her person - but she could not step out of the way to safety.

"Why did you not …?"

He raised an eyebrow when she stopped.

"Come to Maresfield. Jasper is ten months old."

"I believe I told you – or someone else did, possibly Marianne – that I was badly wounded shortly after I left you. Everybody said, including of course Marianne, who always knows best, that the most skilled physicians were to be found in London. She was certain that I would die if I went down to Maresfield."

"Yes; she wrote. Are you still under the care of these brilliant doctors – and have they forbidden you to leave their aegis?"

"Do you think it an excessive length of time? I suppose it is, but, although I do not wish to argue with you – particularly within the first half-hour of seeing you again, I am afraid I must on this occasion contradict you for, as a matter of fact, I am indeed still subject to their ministrations. They are beginning to despair of me."

"Good God! What is wrong with you?"

"Do you really wish to know? Now? You have not asked before."

"I have not seen you."

"You could have written; indeed, Marianne has frequently expressed surprise that you have not come to London in all this time."

"You could have written too," she snapped. "I can see nothing amiss with your hands – or your arms."

He laughed, a short, bitter sound which made Jasper look up at his face anxiously.

"Is that all that is required to write a letter? Hands and arms? I see nothing amiss with yours either."

"I thought – when I heard nothing from you – that you did not wish to hear from me," she said.

"But you knew that I was ill."

"Yes, but later. It is near ten months since you visited – and you have barely set pen to paper since."

141

"Nor you, my dear. It seems that you consider me a neglectful husband; the truth is that I have an equally neglectful wife."

"I thought you regretted marrying me."

"Ditto."

She could feel the blood draining from her face and her heart falling from its accustomed place to lodge, fluttering, somewhere beneath her diaphragm.

She almost ran from the room. Perhaps the only difference with her exit and the one Alicia might have made in similar circumstances was that she did not slam the door – indeed she did not even shut it but fled, stumbling down the corridor towards the stairs.

Arriving a few minutes later in her own chamber, her heart hammering, her breath almost stopped, she rushed into the room and threw herself upon the bed, gasping and beginning to sob with great wracking shrieks interspersed with frantic breaths. So agitated was she that she did not notice the presence of her maid, who was still unpacking.

She felt a hand upon her shoulder and for one breathless moment hoped that it was the Earl's, that he had followed her to explain that she must have misunderstood, of course he did not regret marrying her – how could he when he loved her so?

Of course it was not he; it was Streeter, who, seeing the fleeting look of hope extinguished when she recognised who had touched her, needed little further explanation as to the cause of her mistress's distress.

"My lady, oh my lady, don't take on so!" she begged helplessly – and hopelessly – for no one knew better than Streeter either how much the Countess doted upon her husband or how bitterly hurt she was that he had failed to return to her side after Waterloo.

"How can I not when he has admitted that he wishes he had not married me?" her ladyship moaned between hiccoughing sobs.

"I daresay he didn't mean it," Streeter suggested without much hope.

"Why in the world would he have said it if he did not?"

"Perhaps you misunderstood, my lady."

"How could I have? He only said one word: 'ditto'. There cannot have been any other interpretation I could have put upon it."

"All the same, my lady, there may have been – perhaps he meant to say something else but was prevented by your reaction."

"I did not begin to scream immediately; the shock held me almost paralysed for a moment. I cannot stay here now; I must go home."

"Will you take Lady Alicia with you, my lady?"

"I do not see why she cannot stay here; he is her father."

"Yes, but he cannot present her himself – and I would doubt that Lady Fetcham would be prepared to remain without you."

"Nor he be likely to allow her to do so," Emmeline said, managing a sort of bitter laugh between her sobs.

"I think – forgive me for my seeming lack of sensibility – but I believe you should remain here and put a brave face upon it. You are not the first woman whose marriage has turned sour almost before it has matured – and will not be the last. Comfort yourself that you are married to him, he cannot – without good grounds – divorce you and you may as well try to enjoy being in London. From what I've gathered in the servants' hall – although of course I've barely visited it as yet – his lordship is still exceedingly unwell – horribly damaged by his wounds and experiences."

"He does not look to be, although he is very thin."

"I daresay his wounds are more internal than external."

"Perhaps. He seemed very pleased with Jasper."

"Well, that's a positive sign. Jasper is a charming little boy but not his lordship's first so that there is not perhaps quite the same infatuation with the infant as there sometimes is with a firstborn."

"No; clearly he was not so taken with him when he first met him for he has made no effort to see him again – until today – and that is only because I have brought him here."

"Nevertheless, you have, my lady, and you have gladdened his lordship's heart by doing so. If I were you, I would try not to refine too much upon what he just said to you. He may have meant almost anything."

Emmeline took the handkerchief her maid was holding out and blew her nose.

"You mean I should try to behave as though nothing has happened and as though we are an old married couple who have grown mutually tired of each other?"

"Something like that, yes, my lady."

"You do not think I should try to find the river and cast myself into it?"

"I assume you jest, my lady. No, certainly not. I think that would be premature."

"Very well. I cannot go down looking like this. Will you convey my apologies to Lady Fetcham and tell her I have the headache or something?"

"Of course – and I will send for some cucumber to lay on your eyelids and some cold water to make a compress."

Chapter 19

Lady Fetcham, having been almost solely responsible – with intermittent interjections from Lydia – for what passed for conversation amongst the trio left in the saloon, eventually ran out of flattering comments about every stick of furniture and every object which could conceivably be admired, including many entirely devoid of interest, and fell silent.

The clock on the mantelpiece struck four, indicating that they had been sitting there for nearly an hour and that it was the usual time when they sat down for dinner in the country. Of course, they all knew that dinner was taken much later in the metropolis but, having eaten all the macaroons and – in Lady Fetcham's case – already consumed too much wine, they began to agitate for more sustenance.

"What in the world can have happened to Emmeline?" she asked – wondered aloud perhaps - for there was no reason to suppose either of the others had any more information than she.

"I expect she is settling Jasper," Lydia offered.

"Faugh! Working him up, more like! I don't think I ever met a less competent mother!"

This sharp comment silenced Lydia for indulging in criticism of the Countess with her mother seemed to her to be grossly improper.

It had no such effect upon Alicia, who had been unusually silent while her step-grandmother's eyes had roved around the elegant apartment and passed judgment first upon the obviously valuable works of art and then, going over the same territory again with more finely tuned attention, on those which might perhaps have been placed in the second rung of worth. However, the Baroness raising the subject of something about which she felt she knew a good deal, she was immediately roused to speech – and opinion.

"Have I not said so all along?" she exclaimed. "Poor little Jasper hates seeing her – his little face screws up immediately and he begins to bawl. It is quite embarrassing to observe. And as a stepmother – well, I am sure I do not know how Papa could have brought himself to foist her upon us!"

Even Lady Fetcham looked shocked by this. "It's not your place to comment upon your father's choice of bride!" she snapped.

"We all know why he chose her!" Alicia continued, unabashed. Lady Fetcham disdaining to answer this, she continued, "I concede she is excessively pretty – or was – she has lost her looks since she had the baby – but I cannot see why he thought she would make a suitable wife, much less a mama to his motherless children."

"I should think it most unlikely he was thinking about his children when he chose her," Lady Fetcham pointed out witheringly.

"Oh, I'm certain he was not," Alicia agreed viciously. "He has never thought about us for one second! I suppose he has some new bit of fluff – and that's why he's abandoned her at Maresfield – along with us. Maresfield is a sort of rubbish emporium!"

"If that is the case, you may consider fortune to have favoured you now that my daughter has brought you to London. If you do not wish to go back at the end of the Season, I can only advise you to make yourself agreeable to any suitor who may express an interest in you. This is your chance to improve your situation – you must make the most of it."

This reminder of her likely fate if she persisted in making everyone she met dislike her clearly had an effect upon Alicia for she closed her mouth on whatever reply she had been preparing and adopted, instead, a mutinous pout.

"I wonder what time they eat their dinner here," the Baroness mused, observing this and, judging from her expression, taking credit for it. "I hope it will not be too late."

Neither Alicia nor Lydia had anything to say to this, neither being in a position to offer an answer.

"Miss Melway, would you ring the bell please," the Baroness said, her tone indicating that she considered Lydia to be the sort of inferior person who could be ordered about as though she were a poor relation.

Lydia did as she was bid and resumed her seat in the window where she had, until she had attracted Lady Fetcham's attention, begun to hope that she had succeeded in fading into the background.

The butler appeared.

"My lady?"

"Does his lordship know that we have arrived?"

"Oh, yes, my lady. I believe him to be with his son."

"His son? I thought he had gone to Oxford this morning."

"Not that son, Grandmama," Alicia said. "The baby."

"The *baby*? He cannot surely have been with him all this time. And where is her ladyship?"

"I believe she retired to her chamber, my lady."

"I see. What time does his lordship serve dinner, Blackstone? You are Blackstone, are you not?"

146

"Yes, my lady. His lordship generally takes dinner at about eight o'clock, my lady."

"Eight o'clock? I cannot wait that long. Whatever time does he retire for the night if he eats so very late?"

"Not usually before midnight, my lady." The butler spoke with punctilious courtesy but it seemed to Lydia that he was both surprised and appalled not only to be questioned on such a matter but, more importantly, to be obliged to listen to what was clearly disapproval of the hours the master of the house kept.

"Well, if we are to be forced to wait such an excessive length of time, I wonder if you could bring us some more refreshments and inform his lordship that his ward is waiting to be introduced to him."

"Yes, my lady." Blackstone bowed and withdrew.

Lydia waited with some trepidation for the appearance of his lordship, but he did not arrive. She wondered if that was because the butler had not considered it proper to issue his master with orders from his mother-in-law in his own house or whether it was because whatever he was or was not doing with his son seemed to him to be more important than greeting his new ward. She was both relieved and disappointed by this.

It was not long before Blackstone returned, preceded by a discreet knock upon the door so that no one supposed when it opened that the Earl would be upon the threshold.

"Refreshments have been laid out in the small dining room, my lady. Would you like me to escort you there?"

"Yes, please." The Baroness sounded gratified and Lydia found herself hoping that her success with issuing orders to the butler would not encourage her to think that she could control the rest of the household.

There was a cold collation laid out on the table in a small and pretty room at the back of the house which, Lydia guessed, was most likely full of sunshine in the morning and where nuncheon was probably taken. In the evening, with the curtains drawn and candles lit, it looked charming, its green walls both soft and warm and giving the impression, in the flickering candlelight, of an arbour. The meal laid out bore a startling resemblance to the sort of comestibles which they were accustomed to eat at noon, consisting of ham, cheese, fruit and bread, but there was in addition a tureen full of steaming soup which, when the three women were seated, the butler proceeded to ladle into beautiful porcelain bowls.

"Monsieur Mayeur, the chef, has not yet completed the preparations for dinner, my lady," Blackstone explained, "but expressed the hope that partaking of this humble repast would be acceptable for the time being."

Lady Fetcham, who had bridled as she observed the offering upon the table, was somewhat soothed by this explanation and went so far as to smile graciously upon the old man and permit him to fill her bowl.

When he had left, she pronounced the soup excellent and said she was looking forward to sampling a dinner created by such a gifted chef.

"It's bound to be excessively rich, I suppose," Alicia said. "Will it be wise for you to eat something confected by a Frenchman so late at night?"

"I am not in my dotage!"

"I did not say that you were, Grandmama," Alicia said in an unusually mollifying tone. "It was only that you yourself expressed anxiety about eating late."

"I suppose," Lady Fetcham conceded, leaning forward to help herself to some more soup, "that, now that we are in London, we will be obliged to alter our habits: we must rise later, eat later and retire later. It will be difficult but not impossible; after all, I have done it before."

They were still sitting at the table, by this time eating peaches and grapes, when the door opened and a man came in. He was clearly not a servant but, although he entered the room without either apology or explanation, Lydia did not at first realise that this was the Earl of Maresfield.

She knew that he was much the same age as her father, having been at school, Oxford and in the army with him, but she thought that this man looked much older. He supported himself on not one but two sticks, one on either side and leaned heavily upon them although it was apparent that he still had both legs – and indeed both arms. But, in spite of seeming to be whole in the most obvious sense of possessing all his limbs, it was clear that he was by no means whole in a subtle way. He was a very tall man, quite as tall as Lord Chalvington and, although his hair was receding from his temples, increasing the almost intimidating height of his brow, what remained was of a similar chestnut shade, although perhaps a little darker and finely laced with grey. He possessed the same large, dark eyes although, where his son's

148

sparkled with the sheer joy of life, the father's were deep pools, neither tranquil nor sparkling but, on the contrary, disturbingly full of indescribable pain.

She had heard a great many criticisms of the Earl from a variety of sources – although notably not from his eldest son – and had almost expected him to turn out to be a villain, a man whose evil nature had somehow escaped her father's notice in spite of their long association, but she had no doubt, as she saw him with her own eyes for the first time, that most of the dissatisfaction felt by his relatives or – in the case of the governess – employees resided in their breasts more than in his character.

He walked necessarily slowly, moving the sticks carefully forward to support his weight, but, reaching the table, took his mother-in-law's hand, kissed it and welcomed her to his house.

"I am sorry you have been forced to wait so long," he said in a voice that, lacking the joy and enthusiasm of his son, yet had the same timbre. "I am still not quite as strong as I was once and generally retire to bed for a time after nuncheon. When I rose, I was informed that you had arrived and went at once to greet my youngest boy whom I have not seen since he was a few days old. It was remiss of me not to receive you first and I can only hope that you will find it in your heart to forgive a father for wishing to see his son."

Thus appealed to, there was nothing Lady Fetcham could reasonably do but agree – and, further, to express a degree of understanding of his predicament.

He turned next to his daughter, taking her hand too and holding it in a firm clasp.

"I hope you will enjoy staying here for a while," he said. "Invitations have already arrived addressed to you so that I do not doubt you will find a great deal to entertain you in London."

"Papa," she said faintly.

She seemed, Lydia thought, to be quite overset by the sight of her father; whether this was because he looked so different from when she had seen him last or was on account of the man's extraordinary power, which filled the room and appeared to have rendered both of the usually excessively opinionated women almost tremulous and absurdly eager to please him, she was not certain.

When he turned the full force of his dark gaze upon her, she found herself similarly afflicted, her knees trembling and her own gaze unable to tear itself from his. He was, she thought, completely mesmerising, even in what was undoubtedly a much weakened state.

"You must, by a process of elimination, be my ward – Lydia," he said, holding out his hand.

She took it and felt it enclosed within the warmth of his. He might almost have been her father and, in spite of all she had heard of his deficiencies as a parent, she not only wished he was but understood immediately why her papa had chosen him as a substitute.

"Yes. I am Lydia Melway."

"Daughter of my dearest friend – a man I knew and loved from the time we were thirteen. I don't think you are much older than that now – oh, don't correct me, I know that you are seventeen, but to a man my age four years is very little. You are like him: not perhaps so much in feature but in your expression. You are, I believe, as resolute and brave as he."

Her mouth quivered and she blinked back tears. He, seeing this, apologised for distressing her.

She shook her head. "It is nothing – only that – that I understand now why he chose you – and I am immensely grateful that you accepted the commission."

"I could not very well refuse," he admitted, smiling at her. "He left you to me in his will. But I must apologise that I have allowed you to travel to Maresfield and to spend some time there with my family without my being there to greet you properly. As you can see, I am not altogether well, and my doctors have advised against such a long journey. Probably I should have ignored them; I have spent too long as an invalid; indeed, I am afraid I have become almost infantilised – I hardly dare do anything without their permission."

"Her ladyship made me welcome," Lydia murmured, so overcome in the presence of this man that she found herself hardly able to speak.

"Did she?" Now she saw for the first time something of what people complained about; the inflexion and the – so slight it was difficult to be sure it had taken place – raising of one eyebrow, which, subtly, cast opprobrium upon the absent Countess.

"She has been excessively kind – as has everyone," she reiterated more firmly.

"I wonder," he mused, "whether perhaps in my absence they have all undergone a sea-change. Everyone kind? I fear that, in trying to be polite – and perhaps not to cast aspersions on those present – you are straying from the truth. Did you meet my eldest, Chalvington?"

"Yes. He took me riding."

"Did he?" he repeated, but this time with an entirely different inflexion so that, instead of feeling irritated and rushing to defend the person he had criticised, she blushed.

"Yes. He showed me his new house too," she added, raising her chin defiantly and meeting the dark, amused eyes of her host.

"Ah! And did you like it?"

"Yes; I am persuaded it will be quite beautiful when it is finished."

"Did he tell you the story of his great-great-grandmother and great-great-grandfather?"

"Yes. I thought it very sad."

"If it is true, it is indeed sad, but not, I fear, unusual. People quarrel, grow apart, become determined to stand upon their pride but rarely seem to take into account the possibility of life – and their resentment – not continuing for ever. And then, I suppose, hope frustrated – for one has to assume that most people who have once loved each other always hope their affection will be magically reignited – can turn to bitterness."

"Do you think she was bitter?" She suspected that the Earl was speaking as much of his own marital difficulties as his great-grandparents'.

"You think it was bitterness which prevented her from moving to the house he had had built for her? I understood it as refusal to leave the place where she had lived with him – a sort of excessive sentimentality."

"No, I am certain that is why she stayed at Maresfield – to be close to what she remembered of their life together. I was thinking that it was bitterness which prevented her from recovering from his death and fulfilling his plan for her. Did she live long after he died?"

"Yes, as a matter of fact she did – fifteen years – and she never went anywhere again. Dear child," he went on, seeming to recollect his new ward's circumstances, "this is a macabre subject for one in your position but I will ask you one more question: would you have stayed in your own house if it had been possible?"

"You mean if I had not been turned out by the horrid heir? He is horrid, I promise. He hung around with his avaricious wife – well, perhaps that is unjust, but I could not help feeling that she was all but measuring the windows for new curtains while Papa was dying. Yes, of course I would and I took it very hard that I was obliged to leave almost before he was cold in his grave but ... do you know, now, I am

151

almost glad that I did leave because my life is so different with your family that I can barely recall my former one."

"And I daresay you will find London very different from Maresfield."

"I expect I shall, but I shall not, of course, be attending any parties or anything of that sort."

"No, I suppose you will not. That is a pity for, apart from its handsome buildings, the parties are for most people the main attraction of the metropolis."

"I shall look forward to hearing all about them from Alicia."

"Will you? I hope she will tell you for I believe part of the joy of going to parties is being able to tell someone all about them afterwards. We will see if we can find something to which you can go: a concert perhaps?"

"I would very much enjoy that, my lord, but I promise I will be perfectly happy remaining at home."

"Really?"

"She is very quiet," Alicia put in. "I don't think she will mind much but will she be permitted to ride in the Park, do you think?"

"I do not see why not. Persons in mourning cannot very well attend balls, I suppose – and the theatre would probably cause a frown on some faces – but a ride? Yes, I am certain there will be no prohibition on that – after all, you will need both exercise and fresh air."

"Although," Alicia said in a tone of such satisfaction that Lydia wondered if her father had tumbled headlong into the trap she had set by mentioning riding, "I am by no means certain Lydia will wish to ride without Ambrose to escort her."

"We will have to find someone else to go with her," he replied blandly. "There is your cousin, Alicia – he is in London at present and is, I think, a respectable enough fellow to be trusted with both you and Lydia."

"Cousin Gervase is in London?" Alicia asked, blushing.

"Oh yes; he is usually here. Cousin Gervase," the Earl explained to Lydia, "is my sister's son. He is a few years older than Alicia – and indeed slightly older than Ambrose too. My sister, Marianne, spends the majority of her time in London and has in any event been here ever since I was brought home, insisting that someone needs to keep an eye on me, apart from the myriad physicians she has engaged. Gervase is with her, although his father has grown bored with London and repaired to Shropshire, ostensibly to attend to their estate. Gervase is a somewhat idle young man but perfectly pleasant."

He turned to Lady Fetcham and enquired how she did, adding that it was exceedingly good of her to offer to help launch Alicia.

"I did not offer," she admitted. "Emmeline requested my help – which of course I was glad to give."

"Whatever the ins and outs of your arrival here, I am delighted to welcome you and hope that you will not find it too onerous dealing with my wife and daughter."

"Where is my daughter?" she asked, not apparently as enchanted by the Earl as the others.

"I am not altogether certain; I have seen her – in the nursery. I think she may have retired to her chamber for a short spell."

"Why? Were you unkind to her?"

"Good God, no! She does not look to be in the highest fettle and I daresay she is fatigued after the journey. I am sure she will reappear soon."

Chapter 20

It was not until just before dinner that the Countess emerged from her chamber. Her eyelids were swollen and her blue eyes dimmed beneath a sort of mist which made her blink frequently. She looked ten years older than when Lydia had first seen her.

She tottered into the saloon where the others were being entertained by their host with amusing stories about the more outlandish members of the *ton*. She was wearing a blue crepe dress of a hue so pale that it was almost grey. Lydia wondered whether she had searched her wardrobe for the gown most nearly resembling mourning for her expression, the marks left by the copious tears she had shed and the droop of her shoulders all spoke of bereavement.

"Ah, there you are, my dear," the Earl said, rising with difficulty to greet his wife. "We had begun to despair of your being able to join us for dinner."

"Despair?" she asked faintly. Her voice was hoarse and, having managed the one word, she swallowed convulsively as though something disagreeable were rising up her gorge.

"Indeed," he said softly. "You were always the most dazzling flower in the bunch."

Lydia thought that, while his ruined looks were mesmerising, it was his voice that made the heart beat faster and shivers run through one's frame. She could see that it had this effect upon his wife too for, for a moment so brief that it was almost imperceptible, her face brightened and something came into her eyes which betrayed her quickened pulse.

"No longer – withered now," she muttered almost beneath her breath.

"Not quite – wilting," he corrected. "Shall I ring for dinner?"

She nodded. "I will do so; pray sit down, my lord, you are not strong."

He ignored this instruction and remained upon his feet, waiting perhaps to go into dinner, but he permitted his wife to pull the bell.

"Is dinner ready?" my lord asked when Blackstone appeared.

Upon being assured that it was, he began to move towards the door, saying that he felt he should set off as it took him some time to cover the distance between the saloon and the dining room and he did not wish the dinner to be quite cold before they had sat down.

"Will you give me your arm, Lydia?" he asked, turning to her where she sat, as usual, on the periphery of the group.

"Of course, my lord." She rose and went to him, keeping her eyes averted from the suffering Countess.

"I think," he said as she arrived beside him, "that it is probably better if I continue on my sticks; you are too slight to support my weight, but will you walk beside me? I daresay," he went on, as they proceeded at a halting pace, "that you are accustomed to eat much earlier. I hope the refreshments Blackstone provided were sufficient."

"Oh, yes, thank you."

"I own I had expected Lady Fetcham to have retired to bed by this time." He spoke very low so that her ladyship, following with her daughter – Alicia was forced to bring up the rear by herself – would be unable to hear.

"I do not think she is in the habit of retiring early – only of eating early," she explained.

"She will have to re-accustom herself to London hours if she is to be much help in launching Alicia. How do you find my daughter? Will she 'take' do you think?"

"I know nothing about Society," Lydia replied truthfully. "She is a handsome young woman."

"Yes – handsome; unfortunately, all my children seem to take after me. It is all very well for the boys to do so but the girls turn out a little oversized. However, I don't doubt she will have some admirers; it is her character which concerns me most." He glanced down at her and added, "I can see you think that an outrageous comment coming from a man whose own character leaves much to be desired, but, once again, what – to some extent – enhances a man, diminishes a woman."

"She has been much looking forward to it," Lydia said feebly. She was beginning to wonder why the Maresfields seemed so bent on confiding the faulty dispositions of their closest relatives to someone who was little more than a stranger; she wished they would not for, in her eyes, not only was it improper but dangerous too. If she expressed sympathy for one member of the family *vis-à-vis* another and was then forced to listen to that one complaining about the other, she could see that in no time everyone would accuse her of betrayal.

"Do you offer that as cause for optimism?"

"I cannot say, my lord, since I do not know quite what you would consider a positive outcome."

"Oh, pray don't sit upon the fence, child! You have just spent some considerable time in the same house as my daughter and must have come to some conclusion as to the likelihood of her come-out proving successful."

"But what would be a successful outcome?" she asked, afraid that he might think her either deficient in intelligence or impertinent.

But he seemed to understand her difficulty for he said, "I am sorry; I should not have asked you such a question; clearly you cannot answer it. Now, I think, since you are – at least for a little while – by way of being a guest, you should sit here on my left, the position to my right naturally being reserved for Lady Fetcham."

The dinner was exquisite – displaying the sort of artistry which depends not only upon the finest ingredients but also upon the most delicate and precise timing - so that Lydia could perfectly understand why the genius in the kitchen had been unable to produce anything more complicated than cold cuts in what to him probably seemed like the middle of the afternoon. The soup, which had given an advance indication of the likely quality of the dinner, must have taken a deal of preparation.

After dinner, Lydia and Alicia were both put through their paces on the *pianoforte* and Lydia was prevailed upon to sing.

"I suppose *she* can't sing," Lady Fetcham whispered loudly to her daughter with a glance at Alicia, who was seating herself at the instrument to accompany Lydia.

"No, she does not care to do so," the Countess replied. She had survived sitting at the same table as her husband only because she had been placed some way from him, next to his daughter. Both women had felt rejected and both tried valiantly to conceal their disappointment, discovering in the process more understanding between them. It seemed that his lordship's new interest was his ward and, neither being inclined to consider her as a serious rival, they were able to achieve a miserable sort of connexion with each other.

"I'm sure I don't know what this generation is coming to," Lady Fetcham exclaimed, "doesn't *care* to? She must do as she is bid."

"Hush, Mama; Lydia is about to sing."

Lady Fetcham yawned, patted her mouth energetically and leaned back with a sigh.

Lydia and Alicia performed a song they had been desultorily practising together since Lydia's first night at Maresfield and managed to get through it with, if not precisely brilliance, at least competence.

"It's a good thing that child is in mourning," Lady Fetcham said, "for otherwise Alicia wouldn't stand up well to the competition. Of course, she's bound to become his lordship's latest discovery, so I suppose we'll have to put up with him behaving like a fool and her blushing and bridling. I wonder you stand for it, Emmeline."

"She is his ward – the daughter of his dearest friend," the Countess murmured pacifically.

"Faugh!" the Baroness said contemptuously. "You think that will stop either of them? He's already besotted – and now that he's so frail and looks so old it's positively *gênant*! As for her, well I don't trust her – she's undoubtedly out for the main chance. Only think how she set her cap at Chalvington!"

"Mama – pray, *pray* desist!" Emmeline begged.

"I want to hear you sing, Alicia," Lady Fetcham said as the two young women returned to their seats. "The ward can accompany you."

"I cannot sing!" Alicia said.

"All the more reason to practise!"

"I think we've had enough music for this evening," the Earl intervened lazily, "unless you particularly wish to sing, my dear."

"I wish I *could* sing," she retorted, "but, as I cannot, I most certainly do not wish to stand up and caterwaul."

"And, if you really make such a frightful noise as that, we do not wish to hear you. You must all be excessively fatigued after your long journey and will no doubt wish to retire in good time. In any event, I am going to the library now for, in truth, there is only so much time I can tolerate amongst my family, particularly now that I have become so frail."

"Why then did you have so many of us?" Alicia, who seemed to have recovered her spirit, snapped as he rose.

"Carelessness, I suppose," he replied. "Come," he added as she grew red and stood up in such a threatening manner that Lydia was afraid she might hit her father. "I was teasing. You must learn to take jesting in good part, my dear. Does not Ambrose tease you?"

"All the time, but he is not cruel like you, Papa."

"Is that what you think I am? No, no, I assure you I am quite devoted to you, dear child. You are my eldest daughter and I am exceedingly proud of you."

157

"Nonsense, Papa! How can you be when I cannot sing?"

"You have many other attributes of which I am growing prouder by the minute: for instance, your ability to stand up to me. I really don't think it is essential to be able to sing."

"Grandmama seems to think so."

"I doubt it. Unlike me, she doesn't take to people who stand up to her. Good night; I hope you will be comfortable here; don't hesitate to send for anything you require."

He kissed his daughter on the forehead, his mother-in-law on the fingers but took Lydia's hand and pressed it. As he passed his wife, he nodded at her and said, "It is a pleasure to find myself in the same house as you again, my love."

This declaration had an unexpectedly incendiary effect upon the Countess. Her face grew red, her eyes filled with tears and she exclaimed, "That is not what you said upstairs, my lord. Why can you not say what you mean instead of soft-soaping people when you wish to escape and abusing them for your own amusement when you have nothing better to do?"

"Lord!" he exclaimed, pausing beside her. "Have you been taking instruction from Alicia on how to stand up to me?"

"No, but I cannot bear it when you lie to me." The brief flame had already gone out and her manner was drooping and hopeless.

"I am not lying."

"Were you upstairs – lying?"

"No. As I recall, I said very little upstairs and had no intention of inflaming your temper. I believe you to have misread my words – and my intention. I repeat: I am glad to see you, here in my house, for the first time since we have been man and wife. I hope you will find it comfortable. Good night."

She could not bear to wish him likewise and shut her mouth mulishly.

"I daresay you are wise not to commit yourself to hoping that I will have a good night," he observed. "I sleep very badly these days."

When the door had closed behind him, no one found anything to say until Lady Fetcham suggested that Emmeline should retire too.

"You look excessively fatigued, my dear, and we will be busy tomorrow."

"Yes, Mama," Emmeline said meekly, rising and kissing her mother.

"Good night," she said vaguely in the direction of the two young women and followed her husband out.

"Tomorrow," Lady Fetcham said, "we will visit some dressmakers and milliners and see if we can outfit you properly. I daresay you will be able to entertain yourself," she added to Lydia.

"Yes, of course, my lady," Lydia replied. "I believe I will retire too."

She woke early the next morning to find that dawn had barely broken but, in spite of telling herself firmly that she could not rise so exceedingly early, she found it impossible to sleep any longer. She drew back the curtains, saw that it was to be a fine, sunny day and hoped that such auspicious weather might affect the rest of the party in a positive manner.

When Sarah came in answer to her bell, she apologised for getting up almost before it was light and requested that hot water be sent up.

"I suppose you can't expect to sleep for ever," Sarah said. "You went to bed almost before it was dark."

"I did not! Everyone else had retired except for Alicia and Lady Fetcham and I felt myself *de trop*. I understand they intend to spend the day shopping and, in spite of having assured them I would find plenty with which to occupy myself, I own I have few ideas. I suppose there is a music room somewhere where I could practise the *pianoforte* and, if his lordship does not spend all day there, I could visit the library."

"I got the impression that he does not rise much before noon so that I am sure it would be quite safe for you to go there now. I will ask downstairs for directions to a suitable place where you could take a walk later – when his lordship might be wanting his library himself. What will you wear today, Miss?"

"I have no idea; whatever is clean and available, I suppose. All my clothes are more or less identical in any event."

It was still too early for breakfast by the time she was dressed so she went down to the library immediately.

It was a delightful room – unsurprisingly full of books – but also furnished with several comfortable chairs and a number of elegant tables. She walked around, peering at the titles of the books and occasionally taking one out but hastily replacing it before she had read more than a few words. She thought that she had best ask his lordship if she might borrow one or two volumes before doing so and was about to leave the room and repair to the small dining room, where the footman had told her breakfast would be served within half an hour, when she heard the door knocker vigorously deployed. She took this to be an indication that someone outside wished to gain admittance with some urgency. She hesitated, wondering if she should retreat into the library again until the person had stated their business. She had no wish to be found loitering in the hall – or even passing through it – while the sort of conversation which she suspected the person outside might be about to embark upon with the footman was taking place.

She heard the front door open and voices in the hall and waited until silence had returned before venturing forth. Thinking herself safe from appearing to eavesdrop on whatever the importunate person might be demanding, she entered the hall to find several people there and the front door still ajar. An urgent colloquy was taking place between the butler, whose face seemed more lugubrious than usual, and the new arrival, a thin man of academic appearance. The reason she had assumed the hall to be empty was because these two were conducting their discussion in very low voices, clearly wishing to conceal the content from the two footmen, who hovered at the edges of the room.

It was too late to slink back to the library, so she continued, wishing she had stayed in her room with a book rather than creeping downstairs ridiculously early to look at the library. She would have to ask one of the footmen to show her the way to the small dining room.

As she walked past Blackstone, she heard him telling the academic gentleman that his lordship did not rise before noon and, on account of being unwell, could not be disturbed so early in the morning. Whatever the gentleman had to say, he must wait.

The academic gentleman did not take this decision well. He became quite animated and raised his voice so that Lydia could not help hearing him tell the butler that, however unwell his lordship might be, he had no doubt that he would wish to hear what he had to impart without delay. The matter was not one which would permit adjournment.

"I am sorry, sir," Blackstone repeated. "His lordship cannot be disturbed before noon."

"Very well; perhaps I could speak to her ladyship instead."

"She has not risen yet, sir, but may be up before his lordship. If you would like to wait, I can show you to a comfortable saloon."

It was at this point, when the thin gentleman was becoming increasingly agitated and irritated, that he noticed Lydia.

"Who is this?" he asked. "Is she a daughter of the house?"

Blackstone, glancing round and seeing the by now much embarrassed Lydia, gave a disappointing answer to the visitor.

"I am looking for the small dining room," Lydia said, feeling an explanation was expected for her presence in the hall.

"Jim will show you, Miss," Blackstone said, gesturing towards one of the footmen.

Chapter 21

Lydia was not, however, allowed to leave without the academic gentleman pouncing upon her.

"Miss Newick, I have something of the utmost importance to impart to Lord Maresfield concerning his son, Lord Chalvington."

"Chalvington?" she muttered faintly. "What about him?"

"I would prefer to unburden myself in private, Miss. Perhaps you could instruct your butler to permit us to withdraw to the saloon he mentioned."

"He is not my butler," Lydia said, coming to herself a little, "and I am not Miss Newick. I am Miss Melway, Lord Maresfield's ward. Who are you, sir?"

"William Woodham. I am Lord Chalvington's tutor. I wonder if I might have a word with you in private since I understand it is impossible for Lord Maresfield to rise before noon." This remark was delivered with a heavy coating of disapproval. "I have travelled overnight from Oxford and cannot wait until his lordship rises."

"No, of course not, but his lordship is not well – he was badly wounded during the war. Must you speak with him, sir?"

"I believe so, although, if her ladyship can see me, I suppose I will be obliged to be content with that."

"In that case, I suggest you permit Blackstone to direct you to a saloon where you can await her ladyship. It is still very early in the morning – I cannot think why I got up at such a ridiculous hour."

"I have driven all night," Mr Woodham explained, disdaining to comment upon Miss Melway's reasons for being about at such an hour.

"Oh, I see. Blackstone, I think it would be best if Mr Woodham were to be offered somewhere to wait for her ladyship in comfort. You must be fatigued, sir, and would no doubt welcome some refreshment."

"I have not come on a social visit," the thin man said sharply. "I have come to impart bad news about Lord Chalvington to his parents and own to being shocked that no one can spare me a minute to unburden myself."

"Bad news?" Lydia turned pale. "What has happened to him? Is he unwell?"

"He is excessively unwell – indeed he may already have gone to meet his Maker," the thin man snapped, forgetting in his agitation to lower his voice so that Blackstone and the two footmen must have heard his words.

"My God!" Lydia exclaimed. "I do not think, sir, that you should break such news to her ladyship without his lordship being present to support her; she is not strong and should, I am persuaded, be protected from the dangers inherent in receiving such a shocking communication."

"What the devil is the matter with this family?" the visitor exclaimed, considerably irritated.

Lydia, who had herself wondered the same thing, nodded sympathetically and said, "Since the war, sir ..."

Mr Woodham's thin cheeks flushed so that Lydia realised that not only had he not meant her to hear his comment but that she should have had the tact to pretend that she had not.

"Can we be private?" he asked.

"Of course, sir; come in here." She turned and addressed the butler as she opened the door of a small room she had never entered before. "Please inform his lordship that his presence is urgently required and that it is I who requests it."

Blackstone opened his mouth to argue but Lydia raised her chin and fixed him with a firm regard before which he visibly quailed.

"Shall I send refreshments, Miss?"

"Yes, please. Pray be seated, sir," she invited the academic gentleman.

He did as he was bid and, as she took a chair opposite, opened his mouth but closed it again when she held up her hand. She had, less than five minutes previously, demonstrated considerable authority over the butler in spite of her extreme youth and diminutive size; now it seemed she must exercise similar mastery over the unwelcome visitor.

"I am not the proper person in whom to confide your news, sir. I do not know how long it will take his lordship to rise from his bed and join us, but I beg you will be patient for just a little longer."

He nodded, but said, "I cannot delay for it will take me some hours to reach Oxford, and I must return as soon as possible."

"Of course. I gather, from what you have already said, that Lord Chalvington is unwell: I assume he is being attended by the best medical advisers to be found in Oxford?"

"Yes, Miss; of course, Miss, but, as his tutor, I still consider it imperative that I return to his side as soon as possible."

163

They fell into silence after this for it seemed, possibly to both but certainly to Lydia, that engaging in small talk would, in the circumstances, be inappropriate.

It was not long before coffee and cakes were brought in by Blackstone himself.

"I have roused his lordship, Miss, and delivered your message. He is rising now and has bid me reassure you that he will be downstairs as soon as he is able."

"Thank you."

Lydia, assuming the manners and demeanour of a countess, poured coffee for her unwanted guest, offered him the plate of cakes and sipped her own drink in what she hoped was a silence more sympathetic than resentful. She would infinitely have preferred to be eating her breakfast than drinking strong coffee from a small cup and eating cakes in the company of a man for whom she felt little warmth and who had, she felt certain, come to cause yet more distress and upheaval in an already disordered family. She was eaten up with curiosity and anxiety about Lord Chalvington. All the same, she was firmly of the opinion that it would be wholly improper to allow the man to confide in her. She was too young, not a blood relation and only recently admitted to the family.

"I notice that you are in mourning," Mr Woodham said as he took another cake.

"Yes; my father died a short time ago, since when I have become my lord's ward. I have not been a part of this family for long."

"I am sorry for your loss," he said formally, and she could not help thinking that he might be practising this well-used phrase for use later to the rest of the family.

She bowed her head in acknowledgment. Life was uncertain; people died at all stages of their lives, she supposed. Her mother had expired when Lydia was a very young child, since which miserable event two stepmothers and several infants had also been gathered to God's bosom, a catalogue of loss in her own family, which had culminated in the death which had changed her life for ever: her father's. The thought of the handsome, lively, charming Ambrose having joined – or being about to join - their company was too horrible to contemplate; he, more than anyone she had ever met, had embodied life and youth.

Mr Woodham began to revive a little and a degree of natural colour returned to his lean cheeks as he allowed his youthful hostess to

164

refill his coffee cup several times and to proffer the plate of cakes repeatedly. She, although she had not succeeded in reaching the small dining room to eat her breakfast, found she could not swallow more than the coffee for, the longer they were obliged to wait for the Earl to appear, the more the small amount of knowledge which Mr Woodham had imparted grew in her mind until she was certain that he was about to tell her guardian of his son's death.

It was probably no more than half an hour later that the Earl appeared, leaning heavily upon his sticks and looking, if it were possible, even more drawn and ill than he had the previous evening. She supposed that her message, which had dragged him from his bed several hours earlier than usual, must have filled his heart with dread.

Mr Woodham rose at once, stuffing the last of an exquisite little confection into his mouth, bowed and enquired in a voice somewhat stifled by cake, whether he had the honour of addressing his lordship, the Earl of Maresfield.

"Yes. Who are you, sir?"

"William Woodham, tutor to Lord Chalvington. I am sorry to be the bearer of distressing news, my lord."

"Is that why you sent for me?" the Earl asked Lydia, who had also risen and was preparing to leave the room.

"Yes."

"Must you go? I believe I would prefer it if you remained – if you can bear to do so."

"Of course – if that is what you would like, my lord."

She sat down again. The Earl sat down too. Mr Woodham remained upon his feet, perhaps not liking to sit without his lordship's permission.

"Sit down, man," the Earl said, discomfited by the tutor looming over him.

Mr Woodham did so. "My lord, I am sorry to tell you that your son, Lord Chalvington, suffered an accident yesterday on his way back to Oxford for the new term."

The Earl nodded but said nothing, which forced Mr Woodham to continue with what Lydia guessed was a prepared speech.

"He fell from his horse and was, so far as one can ascertain, gravely injured. In any event, he has lost consciousness and was still, several hours after he was brought to his rooms, senseless."

"Not apparently injured in any other way?" the Earl asked, frowning.

"No, my lord. The only obvious injury is to his head, although in truth that is not apparent either. His groom, who saw the fall, told us that it happened very suddenly when he was riding fast. He thought it looked as though the saddle might not have been properly buckled for he saw it slip sideways as the horse made a jump across a small stream. His lordship fell into the water and hit his head upon a boulder. He was immediately rendered senseless and the groom, dismounting in haste, pulled him clear of the water."

The Earl, whose complexion was already pale – possibly on account of his own frailty – had turned almost grey and the large eyes, which bore such a startling resemblance to those of several of his sons, seemed to have grown both larger and more haggard. She had heard his children complain of his lack of affection for them but the look upon his face as he listened to this grave news convinced her that they were mistaken. This was the face of a man who had received devastating information.

"You said he was still senseless when brought into his rooms; had he regained consciousness when you left?"

"No, my lord. We called several doctors, but no one could detect any sign that – that his lordship was still alive except that he continued to breathe. They all agreed that he seemed to have gone into a very deep sleep."

"Did they try to obtain a response from him by, for example, touching him with a sharp object?" the Earl asked. He knew that physicians did this sort of thing from his observation of how unconscious men were dealt with in field hospitals.

"I understand they did, sir."

"I see." The Earl evidently did not feel it necessary to press for the result of this test for he looked even more despondent as the tutor gave his answer.

"Has your carriage been sent to the stables?" he asked after a pause.

"I do not think so, my lord. So far as I know, it is waiting outside."

Maresfield nodded. "It had better be brought in and your horses attended to – it is a long way from Oxford. Have you been travelling all night?"

"Yes, my lord."

The Earl rose in his slow, unsteady manner and made his way, leaning upon his canes, to the bell pull beside the mantelpiece. Lydia, if

166

she had known his intention, could easily have performed this service for him but had had no inkling that his lordship, whilst clearly in the throes of suffering from the shock of Mr Woodham's announcement, would have been able to consider the other man's needs at such a time. From everything she had heard about the Earl, she would not have expected him to show such consideration for another in any circumstances, let alone the one in which he found himself.

When the butler appeared, he was instructed to arrange for the carriage standing outside the front door to be driven round to the back, the horses to be released from their harness and given refreshment, as well as the coachman.

"You cannot leave immediately with those horses," he said. "I see that my ward has looked after you, sir."

"Yes, yes, excellently, thank you, my lord, but I cannot tarry and must return with all haste."

"Of course – and I will come with you, or, rather, you should perhaps consider coming with me. I will order my carriage to be made ready in a moment and suggest you accompany me. Your own can be sent back when both horses and driver are rested.

"Lydia, will you go to my lady and tell her what has happened? She may like to come too as I know she is attached to Chalvington. I do not think we need to take Alicia or Lady Fetcham; indeed, if we leave them here together, they can proceed with whatever preparations her ladyship feels necessary for Alicia's presentation."

"Yes, my lord." Lydia rose but, before she had left the room, his lordship's voice arrested her again.

"I would like you to come too, if that is not too much trouble for you. From what my wife has told me, she finds your presence a comfort and I am much afraid that she will need that in the next few days. Will you consent to accompany us?"

"Of course, my lord, if that is what you wish. Would you like me to rouse her ladyship and tell her that you wish to speak with her, or shall I tell her something of the content of what you will say?"

"I hesitate to place such a burden upon one so young – and so recently bereaved – as you, my dear child, but, yes, I think the news may be more palatable, more easily assimilated perhaps, if it is broken to her by you rather than me."

Lydia went at once. Not knowing where her ladyship's chamber was, she repaired to her own room and sent for Sarah, of whom she asked directions.

The maid said, "I don't think her ladyship has risen yet; is it so urgent that you must speak to her while she is still in her bed?"

"It is his lordship's wish that I do so," she said in a far more distant voice than that with which she usually addressed her servant.

"What? Is he risen? I understood he never appeared before midday. What has happened, Miss? You look distraught."

"It is Lord Chalvington; he has been thrown by his horse and is unconscious. It is his tutor who has come up to London to inform his lordship."

"Oh, Lord!" Sarah exclaimed, horrified. "And he wants you to tell her ladyship?"

Lydia nodded.

"That is a heavy burden to place upon such young shoulders," Sarah murmured disapprovingly. "It makes me think that what the servants are saying about his lordship and her ladyship not having much to say to one another may be true."

"I don't know," Lydia said. "I think his lordship is worried about how her ladyship will take the news and believes I will be better placed to console her – or perhaps to wipe her tears."

"Because they have become estranged," Sarah concluded.

"Is that what they're saying downstairs? I don't think either of us should pay any heed to such nonsense."

"No, Miss," Sarah said, chastened.

"His lordship wants me to accompany him and Mr Woodham – and possibly her ladyship too – to Oxford so perhaps you could pack a few things for me. I don't suppose he will wish to delay his departure for long."

"Good Lord! I thought his lordship was too ill to go anywhere."

"Apparently not," Lydia said, more coldly than she had ever spoken to Sarah before. "He is infirm, certainly, but there is no sign that he is otherwise unwell."

"No, Miss, but, pardon my mentioning gossip to you again: the reason he has not visited Maresfield for so long has been given as his being unwell."

"Do you know where her ladyship's chamber is?" Lydia asked, determined not to engage in speculation about her guardian and his wife.

"No, Miss, but I can find out."

"So can I," Lydia said, afraid that her maid seeking the location of the Countess's room might add fuel to the gossip.

168

She went downstairs again and sought help from one of the footmen.

Chapter 22

By the time Lydia knocked upon her ladyship's door, it was past eight and she hoped that she would find the Countess already up – or at least awake.

Bidden to enter, she opened the door and saw her ladyship sitting up in bed with a cup of hot chocolate in her hands. She did not look much rested – indeed Lydia suspected that she had passed a good deal of the night weeping for her face was pale and puffy and her eyes red.

"Lydia! What are you doing here?" she asked, startled. She had no doubt been expecting her maid.

"I am sorry to disturb you. His lordship requests your presence downstairs – in the blue saloon."

"His lordship? What – has he risen already? It is scarce dawn."

This was an exaggeration, but it was nevertheless true that his lordship had been dragged from his bed several hours before his usual time for leaving it.

"It was I who requested his presence downstairs," Lydia said gently.

"You? Why, in God's name? Has there been an accident? A fire? A burglary?"

The Countess seemed both annoyed and fired up by the various possibilities she envisaged as having been instrumental in parting her husband from his rest.

Lydia was relieved that the subject of an accident had already been raised although the need to approach the subject subtly seemed to have vanished with the news that the Earl was up. Almost, it looked as though such a radical change from his accustomed routine was shock enough to overset her ladyship.

"Yes, I am afraid there has been an accident." She paused, hoping to allow the narrowing of the catalogue of disasters to prepare her ladyship for the next piece of information.

"To whom? Not to Jasper? Oh, pray tell me it is not Jasper!"

"No, my lady. So far as I know, Jasper is quite well. It – it was a riding accident." Once more she tried to approach the awful revelation of who had been hurt by gradual degrees.

"Riding? Who …?" And then, quite suddenly, as though struck by a bolt of lightning, the Countess knew.

"Not Ambrose?" she cried, her face, if it were possible, becoming even more pale.

"Yes, I am afraid so. He took a fall on his way to Oxford yesterday."

"How bad is he? Not bad, surely?"

"I am afraid he is not good," Lydia temporised, feeling as though she were holding back a tidal wave with one finger.

"Not dead? Oh, not dead?"

"No."

"Thank God! But, but how do we know? Who told you this?"

"His tutor, Mr Woodham. He has driven from Oxford overnight. He is downstairs with his lordship."

"Who? Ambrose?"

"No, Mr Woodham. Ambrose is in Oxford. My lady – Emmeline – his lordship wishes to speak to you – I think he is intending to travel to Oxford almost immediately."

"What?" The Countess seemed quite distracted. Lydia had taken the cup of chocolate from her when her hands had begun to shake and the liquid to tilt alarmingly from one side to the other.

"Will you – he wanted me to break the news to you – but I think you should join him in the blue saloon where he can tell you more – and where Mr Woodham can explain."

"I cannot – I am not dressed! Will he die? Oh, Lydia, pray tell me he will not die – I do not think I could bear it!"

"I do not know."

"What?" the Countess took refuge in her preferred exclamation, one which asked a question but also, in the tone in which it was uttered, expressed such horror, such a desperate wish to deny what was becoming increasingly clear, that Lydia could not be in much doubt about her ladyship's sentiments towards her stepson.

She had suspected, during the short time she had spent at Maresfield, that her ladyship's youthful passion, no doubt originally awakened by her husband, had been transferred to the handsome and cheerful young man – and she was not surprised, particularly now that she had seen for herself what a close resemblance the youth bore to his father. Emmeline had fallen in love with the father but, frustrated by his absence and suspecting him of indifference, it was not surprising that, thrown together with the son, whose age so nearly matched her own, she should have re-assigned her feelings in favour of the Viscount.

"He had not regained his senses when Mr Woodham left," Lydia explained.

"But why did he fall off? He is a first-rate rider!"

"Even excellent riders sometimes fall," Lydia said. She had not liked the idea that the fall had been precipitated by a loosely fastened girth for that indicated either extreme carelessness on the part of the groom or malice by someone presently unknown. She was afraid that, if she mentioned this apparent cause of the accident, her ladyship would start down another variation of the 'what?' route which Lydia was afraid would, when she thought about it afterwards, make her realise that she had given herself away.

She was beginning to think it fortunate that his lordship had sent her to break the news and, following that thought, wondered if he had more than an inkling about his wife's affections and wished to spare her shame – and perhaps himself pain. Lydia was already beginning to view the Earl much as her father had done – as a good and reliable man. It did not particularly surprise her that the rest of his family, except Ambrose, had misjudged him for it seemed to her that they were all, in one way or another, unusually ready to perceive slights where none were intended.

"I will leave you to dress," she said.

Returning to the blue saloon, she found Mr Woodham alone. He had been furnished with more cake, coffee and a bottle of wine, into which he had already made considerable inroads.

"His lordship has gone to oversee the packing of an overnight bag, Miss," the man said, rising and bowing.

"Ah! Have you everything you need, sir?"

"Yes, thank you."

"Her ladyship will be down directly," Lydia told him, hoping that his lordship's attention to his packing would soon be completed and wishing that she had not returned to the saloon without first ascertaining whether the Earl was there. On the other hand, she did not feel it right to leave the Countess to encounter the now rather red-faced academic by herself.

"You told me that you are his lordship's ward," he began.

"Yes."

"I suppose Lord Chalvington is by way of being a brother to you, then?"

"I suppose so. I have not known him long."

"Oh, indeed?" The gentleman refilled his glass and, no doubt concluding that, if that was the case, she would be less horrified by the thought of the young man's imminent demise than anyone else in his

172

family, continued, "I'm sorry to say that it doesn't look good at present. There are no discernible marks upon Lord Chalvington, but his condition gives one cause for considerable anxiety. It's my belief he will never regain consciousness. His appearance is moribund. I suspect he took a hard knock upon a sensitive part of his skull which has penetrated his brain. It has obviously been a blow to his lordship. Has he other sons?"

Lydia stared at the man, appalled at his insensibility and, suspecting that his sudden loquaciousness was prompted by the wine, tried by means of the rigidity of her features to deter him from any further confidences.

He did not, unfortunately, appear to notice her disapproval for he continued, "I daresay he was going too fast – young men are much inclined to such foolishness – and probably was not as familiar with the terrain as he would have been in his home county. In any event, it seems he took a heavy fall at an awkward spot. I should think his lordship will want to punish the groom for not having buckled the girth properly, but it seems to me that the young man should have checked himself before setting off on what was, after all, quite a long journey."

Lydia said nothing, but Mr Woodham did not appear to notice – or certainly did not refine upon her absence of encouragement – for he went on, "So many young men destroy themselves in a similar manner. He was late of course – should have been back a couple of days earlier but thought he could get away with it, I suppose. I daresay he was paying court to some local beauty and couldn't tear himself away. He has – had – quite a reputation in Oxford, but then young men like him – well-breeched, Quality and, not to put too fine a point upon it, handsome, generally do acquire a good many female admirers. Of course, they burn the candle at both ends too: seduction, gambling, drinking and riding too fast – driving too fast too. He should have come in the carriage with his baggage but, no, they never want to be restricted in that way unless they drive themselves and then they're a danger to everyone else on the road."

He stopped abruptly, perhaps suddenly becoming conscious of his listener's increasing horror.

"You are shocked!"

"Yes. What subject do you teach, sir?"

"Latin. He was good enough at the language – well taught at school, I suppose - but his essays were always late. He should have known better than to ride as though the Furies were pursuing him because he wasn't a boy."

"No; he fought for his country at Waterloo."

"Huh!" the older man exclaimed disparagingly. "I don't doubt he enjoyed that – rushing into battle and coming away without a scratch. I imagine his father made sure he was well behind the front line!"

"You do not seem to have much opinion of him," Lydia hazarded.

The tutor poured the last of the wine into his glass and drank it noisily. Lydia winced.

"He was no worse than any other," Mr Woodham conceded. "But he'd never make a scholar."

"I don't suppose it would have been of much use if he had; his future was – is – mapped out for him. He is to run a large estate."

"*Was*! It'll be the next one now – I suppose there are a number of sons?"

The door opened as he was speaking, and the Countess came into the room. She had dressed but her hair, although pinned up, made no attempt to look becoming: it was scraped back uncompromisingly and confined to the back of her head with a number of pins but no ribbon – or cap. Her face was still pale and her eyes red but her hair, oddly, shone – touched to gold by shafts of sunlight coming in at the window. She looked, Lydia thought, like a suffering angel moments before martyrdom. She knew what was coming.

"Your ladyship?" the tutor said, rising at once and bowing so deeply that Lydia thought he was about to snap in two.

"Mr Woodham?" she responded, extending a hand which trembled.

He took it, seemed hardly to know what to do with it and, after holding it for a moment, dropped it.

She looked at Lydia, who murmured, "Shall I leave you, my lady?"

"No, pray do not. What have you to say, Mr Woodham? Is my son dead?"

Mr Woodham raised his eyebrows for, in spite of looking exceedingly drawn, the Countess was clearly of a similar age to the man's pupil.

"He was not when I left Oxford," he replied carefully.

"Then let us hope he will not be by the time we reach him," her ladyship responded. "My husband has, I understand, offered to carry you with us while your own horses rest. I believe we will be ready to leave directly."

Emmeline had come downstairs more prepared for bad news than Lydia had expected. She had also taken some considerable time to appear. This was because her husband had come to her room shortly after Lydia had left it.

Lydia having more or less instructed her to dress, she had rung the bell for her maid but the person who knocked upon her door a few minutes later was the Earl.

Having been invited to enter, he had come in, taken one look at her face and understood, not only that the terrible news had already been communicated to her by Lydia, but also something of the shock and grief with which she was wrestling.

"I see Lydia has told you of Ambrose's accident," he said gently.

She nodded. "Pray tell me all. Will you sit down, my lord?"

He did and gestured to her to join him in the other chair arranged before the fire.

"I am not yet dressed," she murmured, embarrassed and ashamed to be found in her nightclothes by her husband.

"I can see that. I dressed in haste when informed of the arrival of Ambrose's tutor. What has Lydia told you?"

Emmeline repeated what the girl had said before falling silent and beginning to shake.

There was another knock upon the door, which opened, after a moment, to reveal the maid who, surprised to see the Earl, made to retreat. His lordship prevented her, saying, "Your mistress has received a shock and is not ready to be dressed yet, which is, I daresay, why she sent for you. Will you, instead, fetch some coffee, brandy and something sustaining to eat? There has been considerable call upon cake this morning – if you can find any more in the kitchen, I feel that would be just the ticket in the circumstances."

The maid curtseyed and withdrew.

"Shall we wait for the brandy before I fill in the gaps which Lydia left?"

"No; no, I want to know now. I cannot bear to wait, not knowing."

"I don't think any of us know a great deal," he said, still gently. "Mr Woodham, the tutor, has more knowledge than we but even he is ignorant of the latest situation."

She nodded, but said, "Will he die?"

175

"I don't know; I own the prognosis does not precisely fill one with optimism."

He told her then all he knew. While he was speaking the maid returned with the refreshments. When she had placed the tray upon a table, the Earl dismissed her, telling her that he would ring again when her ladyship was ready to dress.

Alone once more, he poured brandy into a glass and leaned forward to give it to his wife.

"I cannot drink brandy at this hour of the morning!" she declared, flinging herself back in her chair as though about to be attacked.

"It will steady your nerves," he told her and she, always subject to his will and mesmerised by the intensity in his eyes, took it obediently and applied her lips to the glass.

He watched her carefully, saw that she did not tilt the receptacle to allow any of the liquid to enter her mouth, and said, "Drink it, my dear. There is no need to down the entirety – a sip will likely suffice. It will do no harm and may do you good."

"I think I'm going to die!" she exclaimed dramatically.

"No, you're not – or not just yet!" he responded harshly, "but Ambrose may."

Tears started to her eyes, whether in response to the severity of his tone or the thought of the Viscount expiring neither could have said, but she did as she was bid and almost immediately a faint flush of colour rose in her cheeks.

"There! That is better. Now you should eat some cake and drink some coffee. It is no use your killing yourself – it will not help him to survive. You know he was late back for the start of the Trinity term? I must suppose he could not bear to leave!"

"Was he? I did not know."

"Mr Woodham seemed to think he must have been hurrying – because he was late – and offered an explanation for his tardy departure from home."

"I can't see what he would know!" she exclaimed, the colour increasing rapidly in her cheeks. "And I think it outrageous that he should speculate in such a manner."

"People are bound to though, are they not? I suppose I should have been there to lend respectability to the set-up, but I own I preferred to keep away!"

"What in Heaven's name are you implying?"

"Do you really wish me to put it into plain words?"

176

"Definitely."

"Do you deny that you have transferred your affections from me to my son? It does not surprise me – you are of an age and he is – was – a better man than I ever was."

Chapter 23

The colour that had mantled her cheeks for a few moments drained away, leaving her looking more her husband's age than his son's.

"I have grown fond of Ambrose but there is nothing between us of an improper nature. Indeed, since Lydia arrived, I rather think he has developed a *tendre* for her; if he chose not to go back to Oxford at the right time, it was most likely on account of her."

"I see; well, we cannot ask him now, can we – and I understand why you wish to deny it. I have asked Morrison to pack a valise for me and intend to go to Oxford as soon as the horses have been harnessed. I have suggested the tutor return with me; his carriage can be sent back later. Do you wish to accompany me? I have heard it said that the voice of a person to whom one is attached can rouse the insensate."

"You had better take Lydia then!" she snapped.

"I have already invited her. Will you allow her to steal a march upon you, my dear?" This last was spoken in a sarcastic tone.

"I cannot see that it matters," she responded dully, her brief display of passion subsiding.

"Have you given up on him already? I suppose I should not be surprised: you gave up on me pretty quickly."

He rose but, when he reached the door, delivered a parting shot.

"You had better stay here then and escort Alicia round the fashionable salons while my son and I bid farewell to each other."

After he had gone, she began to cry again. She knew that there was more than a grain of truth in his accusation: she had begun to experience wholly improper sentiments towards her stepson but they were of fairly recent inception. She did not see how the Earl could have detected anything untoward because she had not met the young man until after Waterloo – and she had not seen her husband since she had given birth to Jasper – some few months earlier. Had someone – presumably one of the servants – communicated his or her suspicions to the Earl? She did not think she had far to look, for Pelmartin's disapproval and dislike of her was almost palpable.

Since the birth and the long period of recovery, Chalvington, unwounded, had spent a considerable amount of time at Maresfield, and this was, she had to assume, the period when Pelmartin had felt it necessary to warn his lordship of what was going on. Looking back, she realised that it was during this period that she had begun to care for Ambrose. At first, she had merely been grateful for his kindness, his concern for her health, the gentle and courteous way he helped her in those first, shaky days when she left her bed.

He had spent a great deal of time with her, reading to her, playing the *pianoforte* and frequently accompanying himself in a song. It was unusual for a man of his background to play, but his mother had been an excellent pianist and he had been accustomed to sit by her feet as a small child. Both he and she had been soothed by her playing.

She knew this only because, when she had questioned his unusual tenderness, he had confided that he had, for many years, comforted his mother in this manner. After Amos and Adrian's arrival, she had been particularly low and he, while not understanding the reasons for his mother's dejection, had hit, more or less by chance, upon a method of consoling her, and indeed, giving her a reason for living.

It was thus not perhaps surprising that, finding himself once more alone with a woman in whom his father appeared to have lost interest, he did his best to offer her succour. The difference of course was that this time she was not his mother and he was not a boy.

She was by no means certain that Ambrose felt the same way; indeed the fact that he had immediately taken Lydia under his wing made her think that very likely he had a natural connexion with females and, perceiving another one whose life had taken a distressing turn, had rushed to the rescue – and Lydia was free. But then, very likely he also had a string of conquests in Oxford, for what woman would be able to resist him if he exerted himself to appear more in the guise of a lover than a cavalier?

Her husband's parting shot rankled, implying, as it did, that she had a preference for fashionable parties to attending her stepson's deathbed. She wanted desperately to see Ambrose but at the same time she feared doing so lest she give herself away and lest she find herself unable to cope with the horror. She had, in addition, no wish to travel in a closed carriage with the Earl for she did not doubt that he would amuse himself with sarcastic barbs, although the presence of Lydia and the tutor might deflect these a little.

When Streeter appeared in answer to her summons, she told her something of what had transpired, washed and dressed hurriedly, instructed the maid to pack a small valise and went downstairs.

As she opened the door into the blue saloon, she observed that her husband was not present and that only Lydia was there, looking uncomfortable in the presence of the tutor, whose last words had been audible as she went in.

She took an instant dislike to him, perceiving from the ugly flush on his cheekbones and the empty wine bottle that he was partially inebriated, and said, "It does not matter how many sons one has – each is equally precious and cannot be lost without desolation."

The flush rose higher – and lower – for she could see his neck, around his neckcloth, was burning too.

"My lady!" he said, rising to his feet and bowing.

"My husband has told me everything you have communicated to him," she said coldly, sitting down and drawing her skirts closer as though to protect herself from contamination.

"Yes, my lady! I understand he is intending to set forth for Oxford within the hour. I hope we will find Lord Chalvington beginning to recover."

"Do you think that likely?" she asked but, giving him no time to reply, turned at once to Lydia, saying, "Have you consented to come with us?"

"Yes – if that is what you wish, ma'am."

The Countess managed a wan smile and said, "In that case you had better go and eat your breakfast and instruct your maid to pack a valise. I will inform Alicia and my mother of our plans."

She rose again, nodded at the tutor, said, "I trust you will not object if I leave you for there are a number of things to do before we can be on our way," and swept Lydia out of the room.

"What a horrid man!" she said a moment or two before she closed the door.

"Yes, quite ghastly!"

"Have you been sitting there all the time he has been drinking wine? He's half-cut. I suppose it was Maresfield who furnished him with it. I can't think why; he should surely have known better. I've heard that these people – tutors, academics – are often inclined to over-imbibe."

"Most of it; I cannot help but agree that it might have been wiser to leave him with coffee. Will you leave Alicia and Lady Fetcham here?"

"I suppose so. Mama can continue with Alicia's launch and, in truth, they will probably manage better without me."

"I am persuaded they will not."

The two women, by mutual consent, made their way to the small dining room where, as expected, they found both Lady Fetcham and Alicia. The two were deep in conversation about the dressmakers they planned to visit that morning.

While Lydia helped herself to breakfast, Lady Maresfield told her mother and Alicia what had happened.

Lady Fetcham looked irritated, suspecting no doubt that she would be called upon to do more than she had originally intended and that she might be left to deal with Alicia by herself. While she enjoyed social events and had been looking forward to launching another girl on to the Marriage Mart, she had not realised quite how difficult it might prove to manage this one. The thought of being left alone with a girl who gave every sign of being far more troublesome than her own daughter had proved filled her with dread.

Alicia's reaction was a surprise. Considered thoroughly self-centred, the expectation had been that she would complain about the ruination of her chances of a good come-out. She did not. She uttered one loud, horrified scream and then, having looked round desperately at the faces surrounding her, seeking perhaps for any chink in their own horror to reassure her and failing to find it, she spoke in a curiously squeaky voice, as though something was impeding her breath..

"Ambrose! Oh, he cannot be badly hurt! Are you trying to tell me he's going to die? Pray, pray, say that he is not!"

"We cannot tell," the Countess responded gently. "That is partly why your father and I have decided to go to Oxford immediately."

"Without me? Oh, you cannot! I want to see him! Can I come too? Is Lydia going?"

"Yes, but Lydia is not about to be presented. I made sure you would prefer to stay here with Mama and continue with the arrangements."

"How could you think such a thing when my brother is lying in Oxford? I want to come too."

"I cannot see that you would be much help," Lady Fetcham put in, "and there will surely be quite enough people there without you. Your brother is insensible – your presence will be of no benefit to him and will very likely only distress you. You had much better stay here. In any event, your father will have the last word on the subject. Where is he?" This last question was directed at the Countess.

"Making arrangements. I think we will be ready to go very shortly. Alicia …"

The plea was issued without much hope of being heard. It was not, for Alicia had, in response to her grandmother's summary dismissal of her request, descended – or perhaps ascended would be a more accurate description – into nothing short of hysteria. She was screaming at the top of her voice whilst drumming her heels upon the floor and her fists upon the table so that the crockery jumped and shuddered and Lydia's recently poured cup of coffee spilled into the saucer.

Lydia, who had never seen such a display of temper in her life, had turned pale and put a restraining hand upon the girl's arm, murmuring some soothing platitude at the same time.

Alicia turned upon her, jumping up with her own cup in her hand and confronting the other girl. "How dare you speak to me so? What the devil do you know about it? You haven't got a brother!"

"No; I did not mean to upset you, Alicia, I only wanted …"

She did not finish the sentence for Alicia dashed the coffee into her face with a curse, hurled the cup into the wall and prepared to storm out of the room.

Lady Fetcham, with one horrified glance at her daughter, jumped up and followed the girl to the door where she took her arm to prevent her from leaving the room and administered a hard slap upon her face.

Meanwhile, the Countess had begun to mop up Lydia, dabbing at her with a napkin and asking whether she had been hurt, was the coffee hot and so on.

"Yes," Lydia answered, "but not too hot! I am not hurt! I am sorry I intervened; I meant only to try to calm her."

"I know, I know, my dear," the Countess said, trying in her turn to soothe Lydia, who, although not inclined to hysteria, had nevertheless begun to cry.

Meanwhile, at the door, Alicia had been shocked into momentary silence by the slap.

"You had better go to your room," Lady Fetcham said sternly. "No doubt your father will deal with you – if he has time before he sets off."

"Are you hoping he will beat me?" Alicia asked, recovering slightly.

"I'm sure I don't hope for anything except that he will prevent you from behaving like an overgrown baby," her ladyship retorted, opening the door and indicating her wish for the girl to go through it.

The way, however, was blocked by the Earl. He had completed his arrangements for the care of Mr Woodham's horses and carriage, ordered his own to be made ready, had his valise packed and was ready to depart. Arriving outside the breakfast parlour, already in his greatcoat, where Blackstone had informed him his womenfolk were to be found, he was assailed by the sound of high-pitched female voices so that, when the door opened in front of him and he was confronted by the stony face of his mother-in-law and the burning one of his daughter, he was already more or less prepared for what he would find inside.

"Papa!" Alicia cried, raising her tear-stained face to his.

"Why, whatever is the matter?" he asked in a paternal tone, possibly adopted in the interests of gaining time for his wife suspected that he had a pretty good idea.

"They – they will not let me come with you to Ambrose," she sobbed, exchanging the raging virago for a tearful supplicant. "I do not want to be left behind."

"Really?" he enquired, raising his eyebrows. "Why not?"

"Because he's my brother and I – I am attached to him. I want to be with him."

"From what I can gather," her father said, "he will not know whether you are there or not, but, if you so earnestly desire to accompany us, of course you may. Go upstairs, wash your face, pack a valise and be down in the hall within ten minutes or you will be left behind and, since we will have left, there will be no one, apart from your grandmother, at whom to direct your temper."

"Really, Papa? May I truly come?" she asked, brightening.

"Yes; but I will not wait above ten minutes for you."

He stood aside so that she could run out of the room and allowed his gaze to rest upon his mother-in-law's angry face. "Did you say she could not come? I think it will do no one any good to leave her here in a rage; if he is to die, I believe her immediate knowledge of it, and the opportunity to bid him farewell – whether he is aware of it or not – will be of some benefit to her later."

"Mama thought there would be enough people travelling and that it would be better to leave her here," Emmeline said, deeming it her duty to intervene on behalf of her parent. "She has been kind enough to offer to stay with her."

The Earl acknowledged the rebuke with a lift of the eyebrow and said in a more emollient tone, "I am sure you were thinking of everybody's good, ma'am, and I am of course sensible of the extreme kindness of your offer, but, as I say, I think she had much better come. What will you do? You are, of course, very welcome to come too if you would like, but I think, in view of the extent of my son's injury and the likely outcome, that launching Alicia just now — or even in a few weeks' time - is probably unwise. She will have to wait for a more propitious moment."

The Baroness, softened by his approach, agreed. "She is nearly eighteen, my lord, and there is little time to be lost; all the same, I have observed her conduct to be excessively childish and believe that it is possible that she will have matured sufficiently to achieve success next year. I only hope she will not be too disappointed."

"Disappointment is a fact of life," he replied shortly. "The sooner she becomes accustomed to such reverses of fortune, the better. Will you come with us, ma'am?"

"No, my lord. I am grateful for the offer, but I do not think my presence at such a time will be of much benefit. I shall, of course, hold myself ready to do anything you require. I believe I will go home but feel it incumbent upon me to write to all the kind people who have already sent us invitations to inform them of our decision. I will not of course mention Lord Chalvington."

"Thank you for your understanding. Pray make yourself at home here until you are ready to leave. Forgive me for running away, but I think the ten minutes I promised Alicia are almost up and I would not want to keep her waiting."

He left the room and the Countess rose, kissed her mother and apologised for their hasty departure.

"Come, Lydia."

"Good-bye, my lady," Lydia said meekly to the Baroness.

"Good-bye, dear child," she responded with a surprising degree of warmth. "I shall be relying upon you to effect a change in Alicia's manner before next year."

Chapter 24

It was rather more than ten minutes later that the Earl's carriage pulled out into the streets of London. There were five people sitting uneasily inside: his lordship, his wife, his daughter, his ward and Mr Woodham. None of the travellers was overweight, indeed most of them were on the thin side of normal but it was, nevertheless, a tight fit. The Earl and his wife sat on the comfortable side with Mr Woodham squeezed between them like a bony bolster and the two girls sat opposite.

Lydia wondered whether it would have been, at least for the duration of the journey, more comfortable if the Baroness had come with them, for nobody supposed that it would not have been necessary to use a second carriage if there had been a round half dozen of them.

Nobody spoke, and everyone gazed out of the window in order, presumably, not to look at anyone else and not to feel obliged to converse. The only person for whom this was difficult was Mr Woodham, who had to decide which window to turn his head towards or, if he could not do that, must stare straight ahead between the two young women and fix his gaze upon the coachman's back.

The Countess, who had passed a restless and largely sleepless night, soon fell asleep, rocked by the motion of the carriage. She leaned her head against the side, and it was not long before Lydia, who was sitting opposite her, saw her eyelids droop and close. She was pleased to observe this for she thought her ladyship had been looking ready to drop earlier. Asleep, her extreme youth reasserted itself and the lines of care and distress were miraculously extinguished.

His lordship, who had presumably been woken much before his usual hour for rising, seemed almost to age before her eyes, the lines and shadows on his face deepening with every mile that brought them closer to his ailing son. She reflected that Chalvington's likening of the Earl's children to vegetables, left to grow by themselves untended by their progenitor, seemed to have been proved tragically incorrect for it was obvious that he cared deeply about the young man.

Alicia, beside her, fidgeted and sighed. She had behaved in a similar fashion during their journey to London, but this time she did not speak, silenced perhaps by the rebarbative presence of the tutor or by the soreness of her throat after her bout of unrestrained screaming.

"Do you find our faces more interesting than the scenery outside?" the Earl asked after some considerable time had passed and Lydia, growing bored of the interminable trees and hedges, had glanced surreptitiously at her guardian.

"Yes; the scenery is of course beautiful but – I am sorry, I should not have been staring at you."

"No. Mr Woodham and I are not pretty but my wife – now that she has ceased to agitate and has become peaceful – is quite lovely."

"Yes." She assumed the Earl was remembering how his wife looked when she was asleep for, with Mr Woodham in the way, he could not in fact see her.

"Have you ever visited Oxford before?" he asked in a conversational tone.

"No, but then I have not been anywhere very much. I had never been to London before either."

"It is unfortunate that circumstances have denied you your visit now, but there will be time enough for you to go there again. Oxford is a handsome city and a great deal more compact than London."

"But we will surely not be visiting the sights?" Alicia asked, affecting shock at this evidence of her father's apparent indifference to the reason for their journey.

"Perhaps not, but I do not think we can all hang around Ambrose's bed all the time. I believe it would be perfectly in order for you to walk into the town, perhaps go down to the river, which is particularly charming."

Lydia remembered the river at Maresfield and how she and Ambrose had thrown twigs into it, not just on that first occasion when he had likened her life to that of a twig carelessly cast into an unpredictable current, but on several subsequent occasions too. She thought that, as she continued to meander down the stream by fits and starts, he, so strong and certain of his direction, had fallen foul of an unexpected, and potentially far more unyielding, obstacle than the patch of waterlilies into which her twig had blundered. He was only partially submerged as yet – so far as she knew – but could he, even at this stage, be rescued? She wished she could swim – metaphorically – but feared that she was ill-equipped to help him.

Alicia looked unconvinced by this promised treat. She nodded at the tutor, still sitting upright but now with his eyes closed and his mouth open, and said, "I don't like him."

The Earl frowned, glanced at the man beside him, and said, "It is not required that you should."

"Do you?"

"I have not thought about it one way or the other. This is not the time or place to discuss your sentiments for a man with whom you are unacquainted."

"He smells of wine," she said, with a little shudder of disgust.

"He drove all the way from Oxford last night to apprise us of the news and must have been exhausted by the time he arrived. It is not surprising that he imbibed a little too much a little too early – no doubt he needed refreshment."

"Did he order it for himself?"

"No; I ordered it."

"You did?"

"I own I did not expect him to finish the bottle within half an hour," the Earl admitted with a little humorous twitch of his lips.

Alicia, with a satisfied grunt at having managed to elicit this admission, turned to Lydia beside her.

"Do you like him?"

"No; but, although it looks as though he's fast asleep, I do not think you can be certain of it. Pray let us talk of something else."

"What else is there to talk of? I cannot bear to contemplate what has happened to Ambrose and I cannot sustain any interest in dreaming about what the streets of Oxford may have to offer."

"In that case, I suggest you refrain from talking altogether," the Earl said.

Alicia looked annoyed but she was sufficiently overawed by her father not to argue – as she would certainly have done if it had been the Countess who had made the suggestion.

Silence descended upon the carriage after this, broken only by the snores of Mr Woodham. These were so varied – in length, volume, degree of *vibrato* and frequency of pauses – that Lydia was once again put in mind of Lord Chalvington who would, she was certain, have enjoyed composing a humorous musical comment. She decided that she would try to essay one herself in the hope that she would be able to entertain her new friend when he came to his senses.

Everyone woke up, Mr Woodham with a loud snort, when they stopped to change the horses. The Countess surfaced from sleep with the same grace – and rather better temper – than her infant son generally displayed. She stirred, opened her eyes, stretched – in a thoroughly well-mannered and restrained fashion – and looked round.

"Are you feeling better, my dear?" the Earl enquired.

"A little – I wish you would not call me your dear when I know I am not," she added, becoming a little sulky.

"Don't be petulant," he advised. "Would you like to disembark for some refreshment? I have already sent the others inside."

She blinked and looked around the carriage, now empty save for her husband.

"Where is Mr Woodham?"

"Gone inside. It was a wonder you were not woken by his snoring – I have never heard anything so loud or so varied – almost a symphony, although *not* harmonious."

"I did not hear him, for which circumstance I am profoundly grateful for I think him a horrid man. And you made him drunk! How could you?"

"I did not mean to do so! I promise I did not force the liquor down his throat!"

"You should not have made it available. I suppose I must have gone to sleep before he did. I own I am surprised Alicia put up with it – I would have expected her to kick him."

He laughed. "I told her to be quiet, but perhaps I should have permitted her to kick him. Apart from you, we have all endured the most frightful journey so far, our ears assaulted by his snoring and our noses by his foetid breath. I own I wish I had not invited him to travel with us."

"I wish you had not either. He sat far too close to me; did you not notice that I kept trying to move away?"

"No; I was trying to avoid him on my side! Odd, really, because he is cadaverously thin – I cannot conceive how he managed to spread himself across the seat in both directions. I will make him sit in the window during the next stage so that it will be I pressed up against you – or would that disgust you even more?"

She flushed. "Of course it would not; you are my husband."

"Indeed, but I suppose that does not mean that you are bound to wish to be pressed against me."

"If it is to be a choice between you and Mr Woodham, I have no hesitation in choosing you, my lord. At least I am – or was – familiar with you and I suppose, once, I chose to be close to you."

"No more?" he asked, raising the familiar eyebrow and fixing his dark gaze upon her blue one.

She flushed even more deeply, the colour this time extending across her neck and chest.

"I did not mean that."

"What did you mean?"

"I was trying to hold on to my pride."

"Ah! You seem to be under the impression I have rejected you – I have not. I have been exceedingly unwell and, when I last saw you, you were very ill indeed. I made sure you did not wish me to approach you."

"No," she uttered in a strangled voice.

"Come then, shall we go in? Will you take my hand?"

As he spoke, he was climbing carefully out of the carriage, presumably intending to offer his hand when he reached the ground, but she leaned forward and touched his arm.

"Will you, rather, lean upon me, my lord? I can see that it is hard for you to walk."

He gave her a twisted smile but consented, asking after a moment, "Am I too heavy, my lady?"

"Of course not."

Her voice shook as she spoke and he said, "Things are different between us now."

"Must they be?"

"I am afraid so."

"Will you not recover a little more, my lord, with time?"

"Perhaps. My doctors say that I will eventually, although I will never be as I was. Both my legs were shattered – crushed beneath my horse, which was killed - and mended, in the first instance, crooked. Recently, they have been broken again and re-set."

"My God! That must have been excessively painful."

"Yes. I think they are straighter now but are still very much bound up – to keep them straight – and I have been told not to walk far."

"And perhaps not to bend them?"

"Indeed. That is why going up stairs and sitting down and getting up again are difficult. I have been sleeping downstairs and generally do not go up – except of course for yesterday when I went up – very slowly - to greet my little son."

189

"He could have been brought down! Why did you not send for him?"

"I don't know. I daresay it was foolish. The thing is that I get despondent about the slow progress and about the limited number of things I can do. I daresay I have always seemed old to you, Lina, but I am not – not really. I am only two and forty."

"You are not old!" she said at once, her heart thawing as he called her by the old pet name he had adopted when they were first married.

"More than twice as old as you – and now I look three times as old."

"I don't think I look very young either," she murmured.

"No," he agreed with the twisted smile. "You do not. I have wondered whether you have quite recovered from Jasper's birth and your extreme illness afterwards. Or is it my family that has aged you? I can see that Alicia is as petulant and ill-behaved as ever."

"I miss you, my lord," she said, so quietly that he could only just catch the words.

"Do you? I thought you were content with Ambrose."

"What do you mean?"

"What I say: I did not want to be in the way - a doddering old fool playing the master."

"You are the master; why do you let Ambrose usurp you?"

"I thought it would make you happy."

"What? Why?"

"I don't think you need a detailed explanation: you know as well as I do that I cannot be what I was – probably never will be – and he is – was - young and able," he added on a low note.

She was too much shocked to think of a reply.

"How do you get on with Miss Westmacott?" he asked as they reached the door of the post house.

His question reminded her of her plans for Anthea, but she was too much distressed to mention them now – and in any event there was no time for more confidences as they could see the others already seated at a table.

Nobody wanted to eat much although only Alicia had taken breakfast; the others had nibbled on cake and drunk too much coffee to feel anything but agitated and fatigued and it was not long before they made their way back to the waiting carriage, now equipped with a fresh set of horses.

They arrived in Oxford during the late afternoon. On this part of the journey the two young women fell asleep as well as Mr Woodham, who had been moved into the corner seat and was able to lean his head against the side of the carriage. The Earl sat in the centre and thus protected his wife from close contact with the tutor. She did not think it was comfortable for him there as he had nothing against which to brace himself when the vehicle lurched.

"We might almost be alone," he observed, nodding at the sleepers. "I asked you about Miss Westmacott. Have you any comments?"

"I own I do not like her," she said slowly. "And, which is surely far more important, I do not think she maintains discipline properly – or indeed instructs her pupils adequately."

"I thought she would be bound to," he said. "Evidently I was wrong. Is she kind to them?"

"She may be – I really do not know. The children do not like me, particularly Alicia and Anthea, and are as rude as they can be without Miss Westmacott ever seeing fit to intervene. That is one of the reasons I thought it was time Alicia was married. I have it in mind to send Anthea to school in the autumn – and Amabel next year - for I feel they would receive more discipline there and would, moreover, have the company of other girls of their own age. Amabel is still very young but I believe it would be advisable to send her as soon as possible– in order to avoid her turning out like the other two."

"Are they so very bad? And disagreeable to you? Why did you not say so before?"

"I have not seen you."

"You could have written. What about the boys?"

"The two little ones are like wild animals but Amos and Adrian – now that they are at school – have become noticeably more civilised. Amos has conceived an infatuation for Lydia."

"Indeed? I had not realised how old he is – remiss of me, I know. She must be glad to have escaped his attentions."

"Yes, I think so, but she has handled it well. In truth, I think Ambrose is – was – taken with her too."

"I hadn't thought of that, but then I suppose I did not think him free. How has she reacted to that?"

"She enjoys his company. I do not believe there is more to it than that – at least not on her part – but then she is very newly in mourning and has not, in any event, been with us for long. They spent every morning riding together – alone – at his instigation and then in the evening they performed duets. She has a pretty voice and plays well – as does he. Sometimes he sang and sometimes she did."

"It sounds delightful. Did you enjoy listening to them?"

"Yes. Alicia, unfortunately, can neither play nor sing – for which I hold Miss Westmacott responsible."

"Perhaps she lacks natural talent."

"Who – Miss Westmacott or Alicia?"

He grinned. "Both, perhaps. Alicia's mother played and sang charmingly and I understand it was she who taught Ambrose. It seems odd that she did not extend the same attention to Alicia. But tell me more about Miss Westmacott."

"I thought you knew about her; it was you who sent her to us."

"Yes, but that doesn't mean that I was familiar with her teaching abilities. You say the little boys are wild – what precisely do you mean by that?"

"They fight like puppies, mostly in a fairly good-natured way, but they heed no one, neither Miss Westmacott nor me. Lydia spent some time in the nursery in the afternoons, during which time Amos fell in love with her, but I think she managed the little boys quite well; she did not complain of them, in any event, and neither did she visit the nursery less frequently. She may even have become friendly with Miss Westmacott, although I doubt it, for the governess is not a warm person."

He frowned and said, after a moment, "Are you thinking that she could be dismissed once they are all at school except Albert and Amory?"

"Amory will need a governess for some time," she said, although she had dreamed of dispensing with Miss Westmacott's malign presence.

"I suppose a tutor could be engaged instead. There is, after all, Nanny Macintosh to provide female influence. Would you like me to give her notice?"

"Yes," she said without hesitation. "We could no doubt find a replacement governess instead of a tutor."

"If all the girls are either married or at school, I see no need for a governess. The boys will receive more discipline from a tutor and he will be better qualified to prepare them for school as well. I will see what I can do."

"Thank you," she said with such heartfelt gratitude that the colour rose in his cheeks.

192

The party was deposited at a hotel where, as soon as chambers had been allocated, the Earl left them to go on alone with the tutor to his son's rooms.

The three women, annoyed at being left behind and having nothing to say to one another after their mutual and spontaneous expression of relief that Mr Woodham had been removed, gathered in their private parlour for refreshments which none of them wanted. It was time for dinner in the country, but not in London, so that nobody was quite sure when it was generally taken in Oxford. The Countess in any event thought they should wait until his lordship returned. She suggested a short walk through the town as none of them had ever visited it before, although all had connexions with it through their menfolk's attendance at the university.

Alicia refused to contemplate leaving the hotel in case the Earl should return with news of Ambrose, so the trio sat and fidgeted together in the private parlour to which they had been shown.

In the event it was not long before his lordship returned – without the tutor. As he came in, they all scanned his face and, having done so, hardly needed to hear what he had to say before drawing the conclusion that there was certainly no improvement in the young man's condition – and possibly some deterioration.

"He is still unconscious," he said without preamble. "He is attended by two physicians and a nurse, none of whom has left his room since he was brought to it. They have not been able to observe any change."

"He has not got worse?" the Countess asked, clutching at a straw of hope.

"They say not. He looks peaceful – perfectly still, very pale and quite unblemished."

It was decided that he would take the Countess back immediately, after which they would all have dinner. He saw no purpose in the two girls visiting until the morrow. Alicia attempted to say that she saw a good deal of purpose, but her father was tired, anxious and in no mood to argue. He told her, without embellishment or even softening of his tone, that she should be guided by him and do as she was bid. Alicia, never having submitted to anyone's orders before, nevertheless quailed before her father and put up no further fight.

Emmeline, as they travelled the short distance in the carriage to Lord Chalvington's college, where his rooms were, glanced at her husband. He was, not surprisingly, looking even more fatigued than he had when he received the news. His mouth was set in a thin line, which she suspected was an indication of his determination to hold on to whatever he was feeling. She did not think that her making a trite remark would be of the least comfort to him – indeed suspected that it might finally break him - and therefore kept her own counsel.

When they arrived, he led the way up a long flight of stone steps which she thought must be excessively painful for him to negotiate. He was obliged to climb one step at a time and lean heavily upon the banister, more or less hauling himself up by the strength in his arms. She followed, unspeaking.

He knocked upon the door, which was opened by a nurse, clad in a neat grey gown together with an almost dazzlingly white apron. Her hair was concealed beneath an equally white headdress so that she had an air, not only of gravity, but also of extreme hygiene and almost religious austerity. She dropped a brief curtsey to his lordship, another to her ladyship and led them to their son's bedside.

"Nothing has changed, my lord, since you were last here," she said.

The two doctors were also in the room, standing beside the window in low conversation with each other but, upon seeing the Earl again, both converged upon him and his wife.

"My wife," the Earl said.

The physicians bowed, looked immensely grave and invited her ladyship to sit upon a chair beside Lord Chalvington. She shook her head and gestured towards her husband who was, she murmured humbly, more in need of rest than she. Another chair was brought and the pair sat down.

Ambrose was as his father had described him: pale, still and unblemished. He looked as though he was made of marble. Emmeline realised that she had never seen him so still or indeed with the soft gaze of his dark eyes absent. Instead, two curved lines of black eyelashes lay upon his porcelain cheeks; she thought he had never looked so young;

but for his length, which could be discerned beneath the blankets, he might have been scarcely older than her son, although of course the bones of his face were more evident, but the flawless skin bore a startling resemblance to Jasper's.

She took his hand; it was warm but inert, lying unresponsive in hers; it would not have done so two days ago – the long, slender fingers would have pressed hers and the exquisite mouth would have twitched into its easy, loving smile. She saw that, in spite of his comatose condition, his beard was continuing to grow.

"Is Paterson here?" she asked.

"I believe so," the Earl answered, following the direction of her eyes. "Do you think he should be shaved?"

"It seems a trivial matter but – I don't know, my lord, you know such things better than I."

"I'm not sure I know my son better. You have seen far more of him recently."

"I have known him for less than two years," she reminded him.

"I will ask the physicians whether it would be advisable or not; what do you think of him?"

"He looks so young."

"He is older than you."

"But looks so much younger. Dear Ambrose, pray rouse yourself," she pleaded. "Your papa, in spite of suffering exquisite pain, has come all the way to see you: I really think the least you can do is open your eyes and smile at him."

One of the doctors, approaching the bed, heard her and said, "Yes, my lady, you do well to talk to him. There is a belief that people, even when they are unconscious, can sometimes hear the voices of those to whom they are attached. You might be able to rouse him."

"Do you think he will wake up?"

"It is difficult to tell. The longer he remains comatose, the less likely it is. As you can see, there are no obvious marks upon him. It is as though he is simply asleep, but we know that he fell from his horse and that he hit his head upon a rock. On the other hand, his unconsciousness may be as a result of the violence – the speed – with which he fell. He was galloping, I understand, and, at the moment when he lost his seat, was in point of fact jumping across a small stream. His injury may be on account of his brain having been, as it were, shaken inside his head."

They remained for some half an hour before the Earl took his wife's hand and drew her away.

"We must go back to the others and eat our dinner," he said gently.

"Will he not be hungry?" she asked, rising and preparing to leave. "He was always so excessively hungry – I used to think he could have eaten dinner twice without noticing that he had done so."

"We will feed him a little sugared water, my lady, so that he does not lose too much of his strength," the doctor said.

"He is not in pain," the Earl said, as they drove back to the hotel.

"No, but he's not happy either," she replied.

While Lord and Lady Maresfield were out, the two young women were thrown together without anyone to divert them one from the other. Alicia rebutted Lydia's suggestion that they take the projected walk. She could not, she insisted, put herself out of reach of receiving the latest news on her brother as soon as it was available.

"We do not need to go out for more than half an hour," Lydia said. "It will be at least that length of time before they get back – more likely an hour, I should imagine."

"Well, I do not want to go out," Alicia snapped. "You can go if you like; it's a pity you left your maid in London, but I expect you can ask for one of the hotel servants to accompany you."

"I would rather go out with you," Lydia said mendaciously. She did not like spending any time with Alicia, whose hostility was almost palpable.

"I'm persuaded that's not true; you don't have to be polite – I'm not civil to you!"

"No, indeed you are not, but I don't think that is sufficient reason for me to insult you."

"No doubt you don't! You are so excessively well brought-up, are you not, and always so very proper? Everyone already holds you in affection – even Papa looks upon you with tenderness and approval – and Ambrose ..." Alicia's voice was suspended by sudden choking sobs.

Lydia did not speak for she could think of nothing that would help the other to bear what they were all convinced was to be the permanent loss of Lord Chalvington and, in truth, she was not certain that she would be able to master her own voice.

196

"Why do you not speak?" Alicia demanded, raising her head from the scrap of lace into which she had sunk it.

"I cannot think of anything to say that would be of the least use. I am not a member of your family and have known none of you for long. Also, I never had a brother – nor a sister."

"You might have become my sister in time," Alicia said, sniffing and, when she did not receive the response she had expected, made her meaning plainer. "Ambrose was in love with you."

She got a reaction then. Lydia's mouth fell open. "I am certain he was not. He was simply being kind and endeavouring to welcome me to your family."

"What – riding with you every day, singing with you every evening, smiling at you as though you were an angel? He was wildly in love with you – and *Mama* was jealous!"

"It sounds as though you were too," Lydia said, trembling at her own temerity.

"Jealous? I am not in love with my brother," Alicia exclaimed with a little pout of disgust. "But Mama is with her son – and Papa knows it."

"He is not in point of fact her son," Lydia contradicted. "I cannot say whether I believe her to have been in love with him; certainly, she was - is -attached to him and enjoys his company, but then ... the rest of you are so unkind to her." She was beginning to find choosing the right tense for any discussion concerning Lord Chalvington increasingly difficult. So far as she knew, he was still alive – and yet, horribly, not alive.

"She's a year older than I – two years younger than Ambrose – why the devil should we accept her as a mother? In any event, she does not even wish to be a mother – she doesn't care for her own son."

"I don't think you should jump to such a conclusion," Lydia murmured although she had in fact drawn the same one herself. "Do you wish to be a mother?" she added, taking the argument to Alicia in an attempt to prevent her spiteful attacks upon the Countess, who, it seemed to Lydia, was an excessively unhappy woman; whether that was because she had discovered, too late, that she preferred her stepson to her husband or whether it was because she believed her husband no longer loved her – or whether, perhaps, it was because she hated herself for not loving her own child – she did not know. What she could not help noticing, however, was that Alicia was also

197

extraordinarily unhappy but, instead of falling into a mood of despondency like the Countess, directed her misery outwards towards others whom she did her best to wound, hoping perhaps that someone else's pain would alleviate her own.

"Good God, no!" Alicia replied at once. "But I suppose, if I marry, it will be inevitable."

"Not necessarily. Do you wish to marry?"

"Of course; what else is there to do, as Grandmama said – become a governess?"

"I don't think you'd have the patience and, in any event, whoever heard of a child addressing his governess as 'my lady'?"

Alicia gave a hollow laugh. "I suppose I would have to pretend to be Miss Newick. I hate Miss Westmacott too," she added hopefully, as though an expansion of her field of hatred might soften Lydia's attitude.

"I own I do not like her a great deal myself," Lydia admitted. She found she preferred to criticise the governess than the Countess if passing judgment on other people was the only sort of conversation possible with Alicia.

"Do you not? Do you know, I find that a comfort? You are so very perfect and so exceedingly charitable towards everyone that you make me feel positively sinful. Why do you not like her?"

"She is hard, I think, and unsympathetic. How long has she been with you?"

"Oh, practically for ever. Indeed, I do not remember a time when she was not with us. Mama did not like her either; it was apparently Papa who engaged her. I heard Mama begging him to send her away once and he refused."

Lydia frowned. She thought it odd that it had been the Earl who had brought Miss Westmacott into the house and even odder that he had not sent her away when his wife complained.

"She was horrid to Mama too, when she was alive, so that it is not only the present Countess who suffers," Alicia went on.

"Well, since you dislike her so cordially, I'm surprised that you follow her lead in attacking poor Emmeline," Lydia said tartly.

Alicia flushed with annoyance. "Just because I hate her does not mean that I am bound to love Emmeline."

"Of course not. The thing is that I feel a good deal of sympathy for Emmeline but very little for Miss Westmacott, although her position is far less to be envied than Emmeline's."

"I suppose she is poorer, but otherwise I don't see that there is great deal to choose between their situations. It's my belief that she's jealous of Emmeline – and was jealous of Mama too."

"Why – because she wanted to be a countess – or was it more to do with her holding a candle for your papa?"

"Do you think she does?" Alicia sounded both surprised and shocked.

"She gave every indication of disliking him extremely," Lydia said, remembering her conversation with the governess. "On the other hand, so excessive was her distaste for him, and so vitriolic her description of him, that I own I suspected she might once have felt differently."

Alicia stared at her, both mouth and eyes wide open so that Lydia realised that the other girl had never thought about either her father as a man or the governess as a woman.

She said, "She is closer to him in age than Emmeline and has been with you since she was quite a young woman. I do not believe it is unknown for a governess to harbour romantic feelings towards her employer's husband."

"But it was he who engaged her!"

"Precisely."

"Do you mean what I think you mean?" Alicia asked, still so surprised that her cheeks had flushed with excitement.

"I am probably quite wrong," Lydia said in a damping tone, afraid that she had given Alicia more fuel to feed her habit of spiteful gossip. "No doubt I have been reading too many romantic novels."

"If you're right, she probably hoped that, when Mama died, he would turn to her; instead of which he brought in Emmeline who, for all her faults and her sappy ways, is excessively pretty."

"I should imagine Miss Westmacott was very pretty when she was younger and before she became so embittered," Lydia said.

"Yes; she probably was; she is still handsome. Do you think Papa engaged her because he was having a *liaison* with her and, now that he has grown tired of her, does not want to spend much time at Maresfield?"

Lydia nodded reluctantly. "Pray do not let anyone know of what we have been speaking. Will you come for a walk with me now – to blow away the remnants of our disagreeable imaginings?"

Alicia, feeling more charitable towards Lydia after such a satisfying interlude, nodded. "Yes, all right. Of course I will not say anything –

199

to whom would I say it in any event? I hope I am not so stupid as to speak of such things to either Papa or Emmeline. I might have discussed it with Ambrose, who was much older than I when Miss Westmacott first came and who might remember something suspicious in her manner then."

The two young women put on their bonnets and pelisses – for it was still quite cold as the sun grew lower – and sallied forth into the street outside. Neither of them knew the town and had no idea which way to go but the doorman suggested they turn left and continue for a little way when they would come to the river.

They followed his advice, having nothing better to do, and soon saw the gleam of water ahead. They turned on to a path which ran alongside and walked for some way. It was exceedingly pretty and was, Lydia remarked, a much bigger river than the one which she had visited many times with Lord Chalvington. There was a good deal of greenery bordering it and signs of a large amount of weed in the water so that she could not help thinking a twig would not have much chance of travelling any great distance before it would meet an obstacle. This naturally led to her thinking about the impediment which had felled him while she, who had been so much more conscious of meeting a hazard and being unable to circumnavigate it, was still floating onward. She remembered too his comments about being the eldest son and how lightly he had taken his position, saying that his father had such an over-abundance of sons that his breaking his neck would barely register with the Earl. She did not think this had proved to be the case for Maresfield, who, so far as she could see, was utterly devastated by his son's accident.

Chapter 26

The two young women returned from their walk at much the same time as the Earl and Countess were disembarking from their carriage.

Lydia, reading their expressions, did not need to ask how Chalvington did.

"You have been out?" the Countess asked unnecessarily as the two parties entered the hall together.

"Yes. Lydia more or less forced me; I own I was not eager," Alicia admitted but, to her ladyship's surprise, this was not uttered in the usual sullen tone but, on the contrary, with an almost affectionate glance in the other's direction.

"We found the river," Lydia said, trying to maintain a semblance of normality.

"How was Ambrose?" Alicia, less good at reading other people's demeanours, asked.

"Unchanged," her father replied, leading the way into their private set of rooms. "We will have to decide what to do."

"What do you mean?"

"His physicians say that he may never regain his senses and, that even if he does, it may not be for some considerable time. The fact that he has been 'out' for so long does not bode well for the future."

"Will he die?"

"It is more than probable. No, no, pray do not take on so," as Alicia began to cry. "We must face the facts, which are that he has been unconscious for more than a day and a night, as a consequence of which the physicians think he is increasingly unlikely to wake up. If he does, he may not be as he was."

"What do you mean?"

"He may not recognise us – or be able to speak, or indeed walk."

"*What?*" Alicia shrieked.

Lydia made no sound but the physical sensation of her heart falling from its accustomed place and leaving a gaping hole where it had once resided, almost felled her. Her throat felt dry; it was as though her life were draining from her.

"I have been thinking about it as we drove back," the Earl went on, "and I have come to the conclusion that we should take him home to Maresfield where he can be looked after in the best possible way. I am intending to invite one of the physicians and the nurse to accompany us. I will then engage, with their advice, a couple of replacement medical people if these two do not wish to remain at Maresfield."

While he was speaking, his wife was looking quite as surprised as Alicia, although she controlled whatever degree of hysteria was threatening to overtake her rather better. She supposed that his lordship had not thought of discussing the move with his wife, possibly because she was not the young man's mother.

"Will not the journey make him worse?" she asked now.

"I don't see that he can be much worse," the Earl replied on a low note. "I am hoping that, on the contrary, the jolting may wake him."

"Is that what the doctor thinks?"

"He admitted that he does not think anything we can or cannot do will affect him now," his lordship confessed, sitting down stiffly.

"Oh, my God!" Alicia exclaimed. "You mean – he means – he is as good as dead? Can I go to see him before you have him thrown into a carriage and delivered to Maresfield like a parcel?"

"I am not proposing throwing him into a carriage; on the contrary, I have every intention of making sure that he is as comfortable as possible. But, yes, you may visit him in the morning if that is what you wish."

After this, the rest of the evening was more or less as miserable as it could be. It occurred to Lydia that, dressed as she was in unrelieved black, she must present as a horrid sort of harbinger of doom and hoped that her crow-like appearance would not add to the general air of mourning. It seemed to her that her arrival at Maresfield, wreathed in grief and never far from tears, might easily be interpreted by irrational persons as a triggering factor in the calamity which seemed set to engulf the family. She found herself thankful that, during the time she and Alicia had been alone, there had been a softening of the other girl's attitude towards her; that, indeed, she had become an object of comfort rather than desolation.

"Can I not go tonight?" Alicia asked after they had chased their dinner around their plates and sent it back to the kitchen almost untouched. "He may be dead in the morning."

"I think it would be better not," the Earl began but was interrupted by his wife.

"Let her go, my lord; she wishes to see him and will not rest until she has. I will go with her."

"I would prefer to go with Lydia," Alicia said, although not unkindly. "Will you come with me, Lydia?"

"Of course, if you will permit it, my lord."

He bowed his head and ordered the carriage.

As they travelled, Alicia sat unusually still, almost as though frozen. At last she said, "He has always been there."

"Yes."

"Do you think he will die?"

"I don't know; I haven't seen him yet, but I suppose that, if the doctors say he will, it is most likely."

"Will you sing to him?" Alicia asked. "He liked to hear you sing."

"He liked to sing with me," Lydia said. "And I must suppose there will be no *pianoforte* in his room. I will be obliged to sing unaccompanied."

"There will be one at Maresfield – or at least we will be able to have one taken upstairs."

It was only a short journey from the hotel to the Viscount's rooms and they were soon being led up the stairs by the porter.

"Oh, Ambrose!" Alicia exclaimed as they were shown into his room.

She ran across and flung herself on top of him, kissing his face in transports of emotion, an exhibition which rather surprised Lydia. It seemed that Alicia, in spite of – or perhaps because of – her general air of hating everything, in fact loved her brother passionately. She wondered if the girl's habitual sullenness had been adopted in order to conceal an excess of sensibility.

"How handsome he is!" she exclaimed, sitting back at last and turning to Lydia, who stood a little way away.

"Indeed," Lydia agreed, looking sadly upon the still face of the young man. He was almost unrecognisable in his stupor for she had never seen him asleep - or indeed in any state where he was not lively and aware.

"Speak to him!" Alicia exhorted.

Lydia approached the bed and took his hand. It lay unmoving in hers: warm, but entirely without animation.

"I wish you will wake up," she said. "You are causing your family unspeakable grief."

"Not you?" Alicia asked accusingly. "Does it not grieve you to see him so passive?"

"Yes, it does – very much. Ambrose, my dear lord, do you not think it is time to wake up?"

"Sing to him!" Alicia ordered.

"Perhaps you should sing."

"You mean because my caterwauling would wake the dead?"

Lydia laughed. "Why, yes! Has he not said as much?"

"Yes, oh yes, he has never spared my feelings. Very well. Hold on, Lydia, sit down and put your hands over your ears."

"Lydia will provide an accompaniment by tapping her foot," Alicia explained to her brother, "and I will sing. Pray listen; if you do not like it, I beg you will stop me."

She raised her eyebrows at Lydia, who nodded.

"Do you remember Mama used to sing 'Bobby Shafto's Gone to Sea' when we were children?" Alicia asked.

Lydia began to tap upon the floor and Alicia launched into the popular song. She did not sing it well, but it was easier and more light-hearted than the sort of offering she was expected to provide after dinner. Ambrose did not attempt to prevent her from singing but Lydia, watching his face as her foot moved, thought she saw a ghostly tremor pass across it.

"He heard – you did hear, did you not?" Alicia exclaimed, seeing it too. "Will you sing it now, Lydia, although I am not certain I can maintain the rhythm?"

Lydia began, along with Alicia's uncertain accompaniment, matching her words to the other girl's tapping foot, just as she had when they had performed in the drawing room that first evening – and this time both were certain that his lordship's lips twitched slightly.

"You haven't got yellow hair any more," Alicia told him, "but you did have when Mama used to sing it. She never did after Amos was born. You were her Bobby, weren't you? Silver buckles at your knee – she used to dress you with them – do you remember? But it's better that Lydia sings it for she can sing, like Mama, and you could marry her, couldn't you? You couldn't marry me because I'm your sister."

She was gabbling but she was so convinced that she had seen him smile that she was determined to provoke him into doing so again.

"Did you want to go to sea when you were a little boy?" Lydia asked him. "You could have drifted down the river like one of those twigs and boarded a boat when you got to the sea. I expect you would have had a girl in every port."

"He joined the army instead," Alicia said. "He looked very handsome in red."

Thinking of it, she was suddenly overcome with despair again and burst into tears, flinging herself passionately across his body and beginning to shake him.

The nurse, who had been standing at the other side of the room, intervened.

"You mustn't do that, my lady; you might injure him."

"What harm could I do that has not already been done?" she cried, raising a face that was already red and swollen.

"We are hoping that, with a little more time, he may recover," one of the doctors, approaching behind the nurse, said.

"Are you? Are you truly hoping that? Papa wants to take him home – will that hurt him?"

"Not if we are careful."

"Shall we sing again?" Lydia asked. "It may have been my imagination, but I am sure I saw his lips quiver."

"So did I – I know they did!" Alicia agreed.

But neither of them could discern any change in the young man's face again so that they were forced to bid him *adieu* and go back to the hotel in a disappointed mood. They found that the Countess had already retired to bed and the Earl was waiting only for their return before he too took himself off.

"I have arranged for us all to travel back to Maresfield tomorrow," he said. "We will go very slowly so that Ambrose will not be jolted. I have ordered several more carriages and instructed that one is to be prepared so that he may lie still. Nurse Robinson and the physician, who is, I believe, called Dr Marley, will travel with him."

"We sang to him," Alicia told her father, "and I am sure that he smiled when Lydia sang. He did not when I did, but I did not expect that. I hoped it would rouse him to beg me to desist."

He laughed. "You shall sing to him every day when we get home," he promised.

"Will you come too, Papa?"

"Of course."

The next morning the Earl had already been taken to his son's side by the time the two young women appeared in the parlour. The Countess was sitting at a small desk under the window engaged in writing a letter to Nanny Macintosh, requesting her to return to Maresfield as soon as possible with Jasper.

"Have you told her what has happened to Ambrose?" Alicia asked.

"She will already know for everyone in London will be perfectly aware of why we all dashed off so incontinently. I have told her that there has been no change in him but that that, at least, means he is no worse."

Lydia did not think this was altogether true for no change in a person who has no consciousness did not bode well for his ever returning to his senses, but she did not say so because she had the impression that her ladyship was already suffering quite enough from the initial blow. She thought the Countess an exceedingly unhappy woman, teetering uncertainly on the edge of collapse, and it was her opinion that the last couple of days in her husband's company had not improved her mood.

The Earl did not return from his son's bedside until the young man had been loaded into his specially adapted carriage and the two medical attendants seated beside him. He waved them off and went back to the hotel where his wife requested that he frank the letter to Nanny Macintosh.

"Of course," he said at once, doing so, "but, now that we have decided to take Ambrose home, you and Alicia could return to London. I daresay your mother will not have left yet."

This suggestion did not meet with approval from either the Countess or Alicia. Emmeline looked distraught, fearing, Lydia suspected, that she was to be sent away from Chalvington's side and expected to tear around London during the fashionable Season without being able to say good-bye to him; Alicia, never able to control her sentiments or 'put a sock in it' as her brother might have described it, fired up immediately and refused point blank to be despatched to the metropolis while her brother was dying.

"Very well," his lordship agreed. "We will leave in half an hour; pray be ready."

The journey to Maresfield, although unpleasant and undertaken in a spirit of impenetrable gloom, was not quite so ghastly as the one from London had been – although it was longer.

They fitted more comfortably into the carriage, having left Mr Woodham in his own rooms, and they were no longer on tenterhooks about what they would find when they arrived for they did not expect to see any material change in the patient.

They soon overtook the vehicle which was carrying Lord Chalvington, a circumstance which struck many of them as horridly symbolic. When a young person on the upward trajectory of his life expires, there is all too soon a disagreeable sense of overtaking him in those younger. Alicia obviously felt this for she exclaimed in distress.

"It will be useful for us to get there before him," her father explained, "for it will give us time to prepare for his arrival."

"Yes, but he would hate to be travelling so slowly," she argued. "He would take it as positively insulting to be overtaken by the family carriage."

"If he had not been travelling so fast when he fell, I daresay he would not need to move so slowly now," her father said unwisely.

"It sounds as though you're glad you can beat him," Alicia snapped. "I suppose you didn't much like your son outdistancing you recently."

"That's enough, Alicia," the Countess said weakly.

"No, it's not – he was taking everything you had, wasn't he?" She did not quite have the temerity to mention her father's wife but cast such a meaningful glance at her that nobody could be in any doubt what she meant.

"I suppose," the Earl said, not apparently particularly annoyed by this, "that it is in the nature of the young to overtake their parents at some point. It may be difficult for you to believe, Alicia, but most of us are in point of fact quite pleased to cede our places to our children."

"Unless of course they died when we were small," Alicia muttered.

"Indeed; it is excessively sad when they do, but, again, it is in the nature of things that this sometimes happens."

"Well, I wish Mama was still alive," Alicia went on with an air of defiance, as though, Lydia thought, she suspected her father had not mourned his first wife but swiftly taken the opportunity to replace her.

There was a general murmur of assent to this, no one wishing to encourage her to continue with her criticism and everyone desirous of fixing the sentiment securely to the loss of a beloved mother rather than the acquisition of a substitute.

Although they had started after Lord Chalvington's vehicle and had soon overtaken it, they did so again later because they paused for nuncheon for more than half an hour; shortly after they had re-embarked, they saw it again ahead of them.

"Oh, must we pass him again?" Alicia exclaimed. "I was trying to forget him."

"It is like the fable of the Hare and the Tortoise," the Earl said. "Strange that Ambrose should become the tortoise."

"It is horrid!"

"Do you think we will, in the end, arrive first?" the Countess asked.

"I own I had assumed we would, but we will need to find an inn in which to spend the night before it gets dark. They will continue all night because Dr Marley will not want to unload Ambrose."

"I don't want to stop again. Can we not drive all night too?" Alicia asked.

"I don't think your father is well enough to undertake such a long journey without a pause," the Countess demurred.

"I do not mind," the Earl replied, much to everyone's surprise. "I will put the matter to Cooper at the next change."

It was another few hours before they stopped again and, the others having been ushered into another post house to recruit their forces with some refreshment, his lordship spoke to the coachman. He had, Lydia thought, become noticeably less infirm since the news of Ambrose's accident and she wondered if being obliged to take charge and deal with the consequences had perhaps roused him from his despondency. She did not mention it to Alicia because she thought it would only add grist to her belief that her father had been rejuvenated by his son's infirmity.

The Countess, on the other hand, seemed to have sunk further into gloom; she had hardly spoken since they set off and walked into the inn with the air of a barely animated doll.

Apparently, Cooper had fallen in readily with the scheme to continue all night without hesitation, saying that he and the under-groom could take turns at driving while the other took forty winks.

His lordship decided that they should eat their dinner immediately and set off, fresh, on the remainder of the journey afterwards. A perfectly adequate repast was served but nobody felt particularly hungry since they had spent almost the entire day sitting in the carriage and were, in any event, so disheartened that any pleasure they might have derived from their dinner seemed almost insulting to poor Ambrose.

The Countess picked at her food, Alicia pronounced it inedible and it was left to Lydia and the Earl to plough through what they had ordered with determination.

His lordship attempted to make conversation but, since only Lydia seemed to understand the necessity of talking of trivial matters as they ate, it soon turned into a dialogue between the two.

She asked him about Waterloo and the battles preceding it and received more information than her father had ever given her. He spoke of her parent with great affection and retailed a number of stories from their shared past which brought her beloved father to the front of her mind again. Speaking of his boyhood and youth, the Earl too began to grow more lively so that, by the time they rose and went back out to the carriage, she had begun to understand what had made the youthful Countess fall in love with him.

Chapter 27

It was a long night and those who had fallen asleep before they stopped for dinner were unable – although not for want of trying - to return to a slumber which was necessarily far less comfortable than if they had been in their beds. No longer able to stare idly out of the windows and thus be rocked and soothed into rest, they were confronted with nothing but darkness. The moon was thin and seemed to have decided to take refuge behind clouds; the stars were likewise concealed; there was thus nothing to look at to divert their minds from revolving pointlessly and depressingly around the reason for their journey, an exercise which led inevitably to the even more forlorn prospect of the future.

The Countess, sitting beside her husband, tried to turn her mind from his eldest son to his youngest, hoping that, by focussing upon the baby, who was healthy, she could alleviate some small portion of the pain in her heart. She had begun to feel more affection for Jasper recently. Thinking of him, it was inevitable that she would begin to dwell upon the memory of her husband sitting in the nursery with the baby. Her conviction that he was indifferent to his children had suffered a succession of blows since then for, not only had he obviously been delighted by the baby, but he was also clearly devastated by what had befallen Ambrose.

She felt unable to offer him the comfort he needed because she was so certain that he not only no longer loved her but positively despised her. She was also wary of even mentioning Chalvington because he seemed so convinced that she had transferred her affections to him.

In fact, sitting there in the dark with nothing to do but ruminate in a hopeless manner, she realised, with a sudden blinding flash that the extraordinary thing about the accident was that, shocked and anxious though she was about the young man, she knew that she was no more in love with him than she was with the man in the moon. Her thoughts about him and the likelihood of his death were not for a lover, they were for a son – a man barely more than a boy cut off in his prime and, more than that, the son of the man she did love, still loved, with all her heart.

She sat beside the Earl and, although she almost cowered in her corner of the carriage, determined not to make demands upon him and fearful of falling asleep and inadvertently leaning against him, her heart reached out to him with painful longing.

Alicia and Lydia opposite, young and healthy and with hearts presumably undivided over their concern for Ambrose, eventually fell asleep, each leaning back in her own corner. Emmeline had noticed, even in her own misery, that the pair seemed to have reached some sort of an understanding where Alicia had come almost to rely upon Lydia. The tiresome girl had become less hostile and, although still much given to arguing every point with her father, had quite ceased to show contempt for Lydia; indeed, she seemed to have developed a deep need for the other girl. If only the circumstances had been different, she would have almost begun to hope that she was at last growing up. It was, she guessed, the good sense and maturity of the younger girl which had enabled her to settle down and be less wary or afraid of losing her own place. The atmosphere at Maresfield was inclined to be heavy with barely-suppressed anger and aggression as though, in spite of its vast size, everyone feared losing ground if they did not constantly fight off any competition.

As the night wore on, the temperature dropped so that, although spring was well advanced, it became extremely chilly inside the carriage. She leaned forward and picked up the rug, which had slipped to the floor, and wrapped it more securely around Lydia, who was sitting opposite her.

"Are you cold?" Maresfield asked quietly.

"I was afraid Lydia might be."

"Yes, but I wondered if you were too. It has grown almost wintry in here."

"I own I am a little. You, my lord?"

He reached across in the dark and found her hand. His was warm but she knew hers was cold for she had begun to shiver.

"You are almost freezing," he said. "Why did you not mention it?" He took both her hands in both of his and held them firmly, a move which caused her heart to beat faster and warmth to suffuse her body – although, unfortunately, it did not reach her hands, which remained icy.

"I thought you were all asleep."

"They are. It is easy to sleep when you're young. It is a long time since I found it easy, even in a bed. I should think it must be time to change the horses soon – we seem to have been going for ever; I will ask for another hot brick when we stop. I'm beginning to think we should have spent the night in that last inn after all."

"We do not want Ambrose to arrive before us though, do we? Suppose they do not know what has happened at Maresfield – it would be the most frightful shock for them."

"It was a frightful shock for us; they will get over it. In any event, I should not think there is anyone there who cares for him half so much as we do."

"I own I was surprised to see how much affected Alicia is. I had not thought her capable of thinking of anyone but herself."

He gave a soft laugh and said, "I believe she is learning, led by the example of my new ward. What do you think of her, Lina?"

"Lydia? I like her – enormously. She seems a steady sort of female. Ambrose called her 'resolute'."

"Did he? He was always perceptive, even as a boy. I think it came of being his mama's companion when the others were so very young and she was alone. I have not been a good husband, have I? I was a poor one to her – worse even than you think – and I am not proving much better to you, although I have not betrayed you with another woman."

"Have you not? But then you have been so exceedingly ill – how could you have done?"

He laughed again, very softly and with some degree of embarrassment.

"Do you think I would have if I could have?" he asked, removing one of his hands from hers and flicking her cheek lightly with one finger.

"Without a doubt."

"What in the world has led you to think such a thing? Did you not believe what I said before we were married – or indeed after, during our too brief honeymoon?"

"Yes, at the time I did, which only shows what a fool I was. Now I realise that you were simply fired with initial enthusiasm which, as it did with your previous wife, dissipated like mist in the sun when you had been away from me for a time. Or was it – have you always in point of fact had another interest in London?"

"Good God, no! You were my interest. I did not rush away from Maresfield – or you – because I wished to leave but because I had to go into battle. I begged for the few days' leave of absence which enabled me to see Jasper shortly after he was born but you – very likely you

212

barely remember that – you were so very ill at the time. I thought you would die, and I considered refusing to go back – deserting in effect. I wrote to Wellington to beg for longer with you, but he refused, saying that I would be home very soon in any event for he intended to deal with Boney without delay - once and for all."

"But why have you not come to Maresfield since? It is months since Jasper was born and the war finished."

"Why did you not come to London once you were well enough – which I believe you to have been for several months now?"

"You did not invite me."

"Why should I have done? You are my wife – you can – indeed some would say, should – be in any house where I am. It did not occur to me to issue you with an invitation. If such things were necessary, why did you not invite me to Maresfield?"

"Because it is not my house, it is yours."

"Did I not promise to share everything which I own with you?"

"Yes – in the marriage vows – but I have never thought of Maresfield as mine."

"I am beginning to wonder if you think of me as yours."

"Of course not; people do not own other people."

"Do they not? Do not husbands own wives and wives husbands? Do you not refer to me as 'my husband'?"

"Yes," she murmured, the words making her heart beat fast again and her limbs dissolve; she was glad that she was sitting down and that it was dark for she could feel herself blushing like a girl.

He was still holding her hands and she tried now to withdraw them. He let her, but said, "Have we been at cross-purposes all this time? But you, unless I am much mistaken, have fallen in love with Ambrose; he is younger, handsomer and vastly more agreeable than I."

"You are mistaken. He is all those things," she agreed, her voice warming as she heard the despair in his, "but people do not fall in love with other people because of their relative youth, good looks or agreeableness – although perhaps they should give more consideration to the latter."

"No, they do not," he agreed. "The devil alone knows why we fall in love with the people we do."

"In any event," she pursued, regaining a little of her spirit now that she knew he could neither get up and leave the room nor see her embarrassment, "I am married to you; what would have come of my falling in love with him?"

213

"A few hours of amusement, I suppose."

She thought of the Viscount and how, to her shame, she had dreamed of just such a thing; she was well aware that, if he had ever suggested it or made a move towards her, she might have been unable to resist the lure. He had seemed so like Maresfield and yet so deliciously different: so cheerful, so young, his skin so smooth, his eyes so bright and without that cynical shadow which so often crept across her husband's gaze. It would have been such wicked, sinful pleasure and she had longed for it; the more she had yearned and dreamed and imagined, the more she had become convinced that the Earl had never loved her, never would love her and, indeed, had almost certainly grown tired of her – as he had of innumerable women.

It was, she thought now, the sheer joy which blazed from Chalvington that lit the room whenever he was in it; it had warmed her heart, made her skin glow and her pulse quicken; when his eyes had dwelled upon her face, hers had drowned in his; when he called her 'Mama', she had believed he wished to remind her of their connexion, to warn her off, but now she wondered if it was not done so much for that reason as to dangle the tempting fruit before her; he was, without doubt, much given to teasing.

She had known nothing of such earthly rapture before she married; she had begun to suspect, when she met Maresfield, that this was the secret of the sort of relations between the sexes which led inexorably to jealousy, infidelity, violence, murder even – in short all manner of wickedness which in the moment of surrender seemed a small price to pay for those all too brief moments of gratification, moments which must be sought with increasing desperation if one were not to fall into the most deadly despondency. Once married, she had discovered that this was indeed the case but, safe in the knowledge that their relations were not only permitted but indeed encouraged by Society, she had thought herself in Paradise.

Had she ever imagined that it would end? That the gates would be closed and locked against her until Chalvington, riding up on his black horse, had shown her that it was still there, albeit now only attainable by sinful means? Why had she thought that, why had she reacted to Chalvington's youth and beauty in such an improper way? Was it because she had tasted the fruit but had it snatched from her before she had sated her appetite? Or was it perhaps because he bore such a startling and unsettling resemblance to his father?

She knew now, sitting beside her husband, that whatever she had felt for Chalvington, whatever she had been tempted to enjoy with him, was but a pale imitation of what she felt for her husband. It was him she wanted, him she remembered and him for whom she had mourned. She would miss Ambrose, she would mourn him as a son but the fire he had lit in her blood was only a reflection of that which had dimmed during her husband's absence, but which, she now realised, needed only a little prod to blaze into life once more.

"You know more of such things than I," she said at last. "Is the brief amusement worth the days, months, years of regret?"

"No, probably not, but the thing is, you see, that, even knowing that, it is so hard – so almost impossible to resist them. I know that, from bitter experience – long before I met you – and, because of that, I can understand – or I thought I did – how irresistible such lures can be. I did not want to be a killjoy, to deny you what I knew would inflame you, give you memories which, while painful, would still, most likely, enhance your life. But I could not have let you – have stood back – if I had been at Maresfield, if I had seen your eyes gleam when you looked at him – and so I kept away. I thought I was giving you what you wanted – and what I had taken away by marrying you when you were so young. And I thought," he added so low that she was not sure she had heard, "that I deserved to be cuckolded."

"With your own son?" she exclaimed, horrified.

"He – or another – but my son was there, and I knew that I could trust him not to ill-treat you."

"Do you think I am so stupid that I would have picked a bad man if you had allowed me to choose?"

"You might have done; I cannot, could not, tell. I have chosen bad women in the past – one in particular. It is alarmingly easy to do."

"What did she do – this bad woman?" she asked, curious because his voice had taken on such a bitter note that she almost shuddered.

"She made a fool of me and I – ashamed and labouring under a sense of almost intolerable guilt – allowed her to exact a terrible price."

"Good God! Where is she now, this evil person? Has she suffered the retribution she deserved?"

"Oddly enough, although that was not my intention, I believe she has – and does every day."

She did not ask for the bad woman's name for she did not suppose that it would mean anything to her, but she realised that her husband laboured still under this burden of shame and guilt. Why, she

215

wondered, had he not mentioned it before they married? Had he been afraid that she would back out of the contract if she knew to what depths he had sunk? She did not think she would have done – could have done – for she was so in thrall to him that she believed she would have found some justification for going ahead. All the same, it seemed to her that if he had confessed what clearly still haunted him, and if she had been given the chance to forgive him, they might have been able to begin on a more honest note and might not have grown so far apart that the distance had become unbridgeable.

There was no time for more for the carriage slowed and a few minutes later turned in to the courtyard of a post house. The Earl knocked upon the window and requested hot bricks be fetched while the horses were being changed.

Neither of the other two woke although both stirred and, when the brick were brought, the Earl ordered them to be placed under each of his passengers' feet. The cold ones were taken away in exchange.

"I would do it myself," he confided to his wife when the door had once more been shut, "but, as you may have observed, I cannot easily bend."

"There is no reason why you should do it; I could have done it myself."

He had ordered several and placed one between him and the Countess.

"Let us hope that this will save your fingers," he said.

"Thank you."

The carriage moved off again and they continued through the night. She did not sleep for what he had told her seemed to have driven all thought of rest from her head but he, having partially cleared his conscience, fell asleep soon after the journey resumed.

All three woke with the dawn, sighed, stretched and blinked.

"Are we nearly there?" Alicia asked.

Chapter 28

"I should think we must be," her father answered.

She nodded and Emmeline saw the young face, which had been relaxed in slumber, become creased with worry again.

When they next stopped, everyone disembarked and went inside the inn to bespeak breakfast. They were all stiff but his lordship, so much more afflicted than anyone else, could barely get himself out of the carriage and had to be helped by both the groom and the under-groom.

"We will be home before nuncheon," he said as coffee was brought to the table.

"Do you think Ambrose will have arrived yet?" Alicia asked.

"I hope not for the whole point of our travelling all night was to enable us to prepare the household for him. How do you feel, Lydia?"

She smiled. "I, my lord? I am quite well, although a little stiff. But you, you look to be in great pain, sir."

"I own I am a little, but the morning is always bad until my muscles have eased. Lina?"

"I was much better once we had those extra bricks."

"Did you sleep or were you forced to listen to the rest of us all night?"

"You did not make any noise."

"Well, that is a relief. I was afraid I must have snored or even shouted. I don't generally sleep well and am often woken by nightmares but last night, oddly, in spite of the discomfort, I slept soundly."

"I'm glad. Now that you're awake, you look a little better, my lord."

"Really? I must have looked positively atrocious before."

The carriage turned in at the gates of Maresfield a couple of hours later, reminding Lydia of the first time she had been driven towards the house with Sarah beside her.

She knew something of what lay ahead now; she knew who lived there and how quarrelsome most of the family was, although it seemed to her that Alicia had mellowed. But, as the house that was Chalvington's appeared amongst the trees on her right, she thought of its owner and how proudly he had shown her round it and how the woman for whom it had originally been built had never lived there; she feared that he never would either. It hit her then: the loss of the man who had made her time at Maresfield so joyous in spite of the rawness of her grief for her father and her own home; he had made her smile - often. She had smiled when she thought of him; for a moment, she felt her lips curving before the awful reality wiped her remembered pleasure, leaving behind a dawning realisation that, without having been aware of it, the *tendre* which she had reluctantly acknowledged, was in fact far more serious: she had fallen head over heels in love with him.

It was a sober party which climbed out of the carriage when it drew up outside the wide steps. The door was opened by one of the familiar footmen; Pelmartin was presumably elsewhere for they had not been expected, had sent no word of the accident or of their plans. Indeed, they had had no plans until they had reached Oxford and seen how gravely ill Lord Chalvington was.

The footman bowed, turned briefly to say something to his colleague – presumably to fetch Pelmartin – and went down the steps himself to help his master climb painfully up to the open door of his ancestral home.

The women, escorted by the groom, followed, their faces pale and drawn. If the unexpectedness of their arrival had not been enough to alert the menservants to something of the nature of the reason for their return, their faces would have done. If the person leading the party had not been his lordship, the assumption would probably have been that it was the Earl who had suffered some terrible reverse.

Pelmartin, appearing at the top of the steps somewhat out of breath, hurried down and, pushing the footman out of the way, assisted his master himself. Once in the hall, the Earl made for the small saloon on the left, requesting Pelmartin follow him.

The butler tried to delay receiving the news as though by doing so he could protect the household from its dread effects. He offered refreshment and hovered about his master with a footstool, rugs and cushions.

"You may send wine when I have told you what I must," the Earl said. "There is not much time before the other carriages arrive and I wish you to be aware of what brings us back to Maresfield – and to issue instructions to the rest of the staff."

The man bowed and ceased his efforts although he remained standing in front of his lordship with a pair of cushions in his hands as though preparing to soften whatever blow was about to be delivered.

The Earl broke the news and, no doubt relieved that his servant did not burst into tears, fall down in a faint or otherwise give any indication of suffering from strong emotion, told him what must be done immediately to prepare for Lord Chalvington's arrival.

The butler bowed again, put down the cushions and retreated to carry out his orders while the Earl, alone for almost the first time since he had received the bad news, closed his eyes and lay back in his chair with a sigh.

He did not remain alone for long; almost before the sigh left his lips, he felt a pair of cool hands cover his, opened his eyes and saw his wife.

"Do you wish to be alone?" she asked.

"I thought I did; now I know that I do not. This is a sad day."

"Yes, but all is not necessarily lost: he may recover."

"It is increasingly unlikely. Pray do not attempt to offer me false hope; I am as capable of seeing and understanding the reality as you."

"More so, I should imagine."

"It is not the homecoming of which I dreamed."

"Did you dream of coming home? To me?"

"Of course, but I was too afraid of what I might find to be able to carry it out. I confess, since Waterloo, all my courage – what little I ever possessed – seems to have deserted me. I find it increasingly difficult to face the possibility of loss; so many of my friends died in the war, including Lydia's father."

"Were you close to him?"

"We were together, more or less, ever since we were thirteen. He shared my time at school and at Oxford, and then we joined up together. He was a brave soldier and a kind and loyal friend. I'm touched – and honoured - that he left me his daughter. My children were left to Ambrose. If I had died before he reached his majority, my cousin would have been obliged to act as 'regent' until Ambrose was of an age to take over the estate himself. Now …"

"Ambrose may still recover; I do not think you should abandon hope."

"I cannot bear not to; hope is such a cruel mistress and, when she dies, there is nothing left at all. He was hardly hurt in the war, barely scratched. I made sure he would outlive me."

"Did you arrange for him to be kept from the front line?"

"I tried to, but it was not easy; he defied my wishes; his commanding officer had a high opinion of him – said he would have made Field Marshal if he had stayed."

"But, in spite of that, you encouraged him to sell out."

"Yes. It is, I suppose, all part of my loss of courage; my fear for him grew monstrously out of proportion for, as so many have pointed out, there is little danger now; indeed, with hindsight, one can see that there would have been less danger in the army than in civilian life where it is only too easy for a young man to fall in love and, reluctant to leave his beloved, try to ride too fast on dangerous terrain."

"Do you really think that was what he was doing?"

"That is what that exceedingly unpleasant tutor said, was it not? That he was late for the start of the new term? Was it you he was so unwilling to leave?"

She shook her head. Her own petty concerns and misplaced attraction to her stepson having faded, she saw more clearly what – or, rather, who – had delayed him.

"I think it was Lydia. They have been as close as peas in a pod ever since she arrived: riding, laughing, playing and singing together; all with apparent innocence; nevertheless, I'm convinced it was she for whom his eyes had brightened."

As she spoke, he was watching her intently, although she thought he was trying to conceal the fact.

"And she? What, in your opinion, was her opinion of him?"

"It's hard to say; she is still in deep mourning and not, therefore, I imagine, thinking about romantic entanglements; nevertheless, it was clear that she took a great deal of pleasure in his company, so much so that Mama voiced her disapproval. She did not think someone in her position should be laughing so much."

"I have hardly seen her laugh – even before we received the news about Ambrose, she was not precisely laughing but then, of course, he was not with us in London. I would have liked her as a daughter-in-law; would you?"

"I have not thought about it," she returned, although this was untrue. "I believe I was so much focussed upon Amos and his infatuation that I did not spare a thought for what Ambrose might have been feeling."

"*Amos?*" His lordship's tone was not only surprised but disdainful. "He is only a boy."

"He is a bare two years her junior. It was her seventeenth birthday the day she arrived."

The Earl did not speak although his face betrayed a variety of emotions, so many and so varied that Emmeline was unable to read them.

She reflected that, if Ambrose died, Amos would be Lord Chalvington and, eventually, Earl of Maresfield but, in view of her husband's grief at his eldest son's injury and his contemptuous dismissal of Amos as not old enough to fall in love, she did not like to point this out.

"He has matured since he met her," she murmured.

"Who has? Amos?"

"Yes. You think it ridiculous that he should be showing an interest in females, my lord, but, were not you at his age?"

"I can't remember. Yes, it is ridiculous – and disrespectful of a girl who has so recently been bereaved."

"He cannot help feeling the way he does!" she exclaimed, surprised at her own reaction and at the way she appeared to be coming to one of her stepsons' defence. "And Ambrose felt the same way. She seems to be an extraordinarily appealing young woman."

"She is everything a man could hope for – at least so far as I can tell without knowing her particularly well. She is pretty, modest and kind; she seems not only to have tamed Amos – if what you say is true – but Alicia as well."

"Oddly enough, I believe she has. My lord, would you like me to speak to Miss Westmacott – warn her of what has happened so that she can prepare the children?"

"What? Why – because Amos will be the heir if Ambrose dies?" His lordship's tone was so sharp that she shivered.

"No, because the children need to be informed – all of them. In any event, neither Amos nor Adrian is here. They went back to school a few days before we left for London."

He started. "Good God, I must be losing my wits – of course they're at school. That's something to be thankful for, I suppose, for I own I would find it hard to deal with Amos's excitement at what he will no doubt hope will be his imminent elevation. Ring the bell, and we will send for Miss Westmacott and give her the news together."

"Have you instructed Pelmartin to prepare Ambrose's chamber?" she asked as they waited for the butler to answer the summons.

"Yes; I told him as I came in, but we had best mention it again – as well as the fact that he will need to arrange accommodation for the physician and nurse."

When Pelmartin appeared, he told his master that Lord Chalvington's room was nearly ready and expressed the hope that his lordship would be as comfortable as possible.

"I don't suppose he has any knowledge of whether he is comfortable or not," the Earl said in a despondent tone. "He will be accompanied by a doctor and a nurse, one of whom will be with him all the time, but I suppose they will each need a chamber for those moments when they are resting. Would you ask Miss Westmacott to join us here as soon as possible?"

The butler bowed and withdrew to carry out his lordship's bidding. It was some considerable time – near half an hour – before Miss Westmacott entered the room.

Emmeline thought she looked nervous; she had tidied her hair but there was a tell-tale sheen of perspiration on her upper lip and she wobbled as she curtsied to the Earl, almost tripping over her own feet as she went down. The Countess wondered if she was expecting to be dismissed when *she* was greeted with a glance of unconcealed loathing accompanying what could only be described as an insultingly cursory bob.

The Earl noticed and raised an eyebrow, which Miss Westmacott, watching him carefully, clearly noted for the colour rushed into her cheeks. He did not invite her to sit down so that she was forced to remain standing, her hands clasped together in front of her, the fingers laced so tightly that her knuckles showed white.

"I expect you're surprised to see us," he said coolly.

She inclined her head and licked her lips but did not reply.

"My son has suffered a serious accident," he went on.

Her face paled and her bottom lip trembled. She caught it between her teeth as though afraid that it might run away if she did not secure it, but she did not look at his lordship, keeping her head down and her eyes veiled.

"I suppose you're wondering which son," he pursued. "He was injured on his way to his educational establishment."

"You mean …?" she asked, the lip now trembling so much that she could hardly form the words. Her head snapped back and her eyes, blazing with some strong emotion which Emmeline could not read, flew to the Earl's face for a moment before being lowered again.

For a moment he said nothing while she tried – and failed – to conceal her apprehension.

"Did you think I meant one of the schoolboys?"

"I ... I did not know whom you meant, my lord."

"I have – had – so many sons, have I not? I meant Lord Chalvington, who was on his way – on horseback – to Oxford when he fell."

"Ohh!" she exclaimed on a long note, the colour rushing back into her face as though a tap had been turned on.

"He is very badly injured – insensible. His medical advisers think him unlikely to recover."

"Oh, oh!"

"Yes. It seems the girth was not properly tightened – or had somehow come loose while he rode. He was effectively tipped out of the saddle. He fell near Oxford and hit his head on a rock."

"Oh!"

"He is being brought back to this house as we speak and will be nursed here – so far as he can be – until he either comes to himself or loses what remains of his life."

"How ...?" She rallied. "Have you dismissed his groom, my lord?"

"Not yet. I have not spoken to the man other than to hear his account of the accident which, as I say, he put down to a difficulty with the girth. One would assume it was he who failed to tighten it sufficiently. At the moment – and ever since I was informed of the accident – I have been too taken up with the event itself to make any attempt to deal with the perpetrator, although I daresay I will be informed that it was an accident or an oversight or some such. When I have leisure – which I daresay I will have while we all await the outcome – I will leave no stone unturned in my investigation to discover where the fault lies.

"I sent for you because he, Chalvington, will arrive at any moment and my wife thought it best if you were to be given the facts so that you may inform the other children and prepare them for what is to come.

"I think it would be best, at present, not to write to the schoolboys; we may as well leave them in ignorance for as long as possible."

"Yes, my lord. You wish me to tell the other children?"

"Yes; that is what I said."

"Am I …? Should I prepare them for the worst, my lord?"

"Tell them he is going to die, do you mean?"

She nodded. She was still nervous and unable to meet the Earl's gaze, but her lip was no longer trembling.

"I would like you to tell them what I have told you: he fell from his horse, hit his head and has lost his senses. We do not know any more than that at present. I will leave you to decide whether to put a pessimistic or optimistic slant upon the matter."

"My lord …," the Countess interrupted.

"Yes? Do you not agree with my orders?"

"It is only that – some of the children are very young – I – it's my belief they should not be frightened if it is possible to avoid that. Anthea is probably old enough to be given a more honest assessment of the situation but the others …"

"Very well. You hear what her ladyship says, Miss Westmacott?"

"Yes, my lord. Would you like me to speak to Lady Anthea by herself?"

The Earl looked at his wife.

She said, "Yes, I think that would be a good idea. Tell the others only that he is very ill and emphasise that she should not worry them unnecessarily. We do not want her to tell them tactlessly. They all love Ambrose," she added to her husband.

"Everyone does," he said flatly. "I do myself."

Chapter 29

Upon arrival, while the Earl and Countess went into the small saloon, Lydia and Alicia went upstairs. Unaware of what his lordship planned to tell the children and with no fixed intention of any sort other than to find a place where the noise and bustle could be relied upon to preclude thought, they went with one accord to the schoolroom.

Miss Westmacott was engaged in an arithmetic lesson but ceased speaking as soon as she saw the two young women.

"I did not expect you, my lady," she said to Alicia with the irritated air of someone who believed she had successfully ejected a particularly aggressive wasp only to find, when she turned round, that it had darted back before she had been able to secure the window.

Whatever Alicia might have been about to reply was lost in the immediate chaos of the children jumping up, delighted to have been interrupted in the tedious repetition of their times tables. One or two knocked over their chairs in their excitement, which fell with a series of loud bangs. Ignoring this, they hurled themselves with every sign of enthusiasm at the new arrivals. Only Anthea, who had been enjoying being the senior child while her elder sister was absent, looked displeased and failed to rise, although she did when Lydia enquired how she did.

"It has been very quiet," she admitted, "without the boys or Alicia. There have been hardly any disagreements. As a matter of fact," she added, with a little self-conscious smile, "it has been excessively boring. Why have you come home so early? Did Grandmama send you away when you damaged the *pianoforte*?" she added to her sister.

"No one sent me away," Alicia snapped. "And it would not be up to Grandmama to do any such thing for we were in Papa's house."

"Was he agreeable?" Anthea asked curiously. "What did you think of him, Lydia?"

"I thought him charming," Lydia murmured.

"Really? Perhaps he was to you; I understand he can be and that most women like him – rather too well indeed – but he is not very appealing to his family. He doesn't care about us, you see," she added with a little nod.

"He ..," Lydia began, about to explain that she believed there to have been a general misunderstanding about the Earl's attachment to his family, it being abundantly clear that he fairly doted upon Ambrose,

225

but she was interrupted by Pelmartin, who, entering the room in his usual lugubrious fashion, told the governess she was to report to her master in the blue saloon immediately.

While the children had been talking, Miss Westmacott had retreated to the window where she was watching the siblings' greeting, her expression impossible to read. Pelmartin's arrival and the message he conveyed evidently had a strong effect upon her for, although always pale in complexion, she grew almost white while drops of perspiration began to form on her upper lip. It seemed to Lydia that she was positively terrified, presumably because she feared that his lordship, encouraged by his wife, had come to Maresfield for the express purpose of dismissing her.

She left the room in Pelmartin's wake, not even pausing to consign the care of the smaller children to Lydia and Alicia.

"Has he come to sack her?" Anthea asked, having formed a fairly accurate assessment of her stepmother's intentions for the governess.

Alicia frowned. "I don't think so; I don't know. We haven't come back because of her at all; we've come because Ambrose has been hurt – he fell off his horse on the way to Oxford - and is insensible. He is being brought back as we speak."

"What?" Anthea asked, shocked.

"Ambrose?" Amabel exclaimed, beginning to cry.

The two little boys looked confused and upset, presumably made apprehensive by their sisters' behaviour, and screwed up their faces preparatory to following Amabel's lead.

Lydia went to the boys, drawing them down to sit with her on a sofa while Alicia was besieged by her sisters asking questions.

"Is he going to die?" Albert asked, always preoccupied with death.

"We don't know," Lydia told him. "We are hoping not. There is a doctor and a nurse with him so that he will have every care possible."

"Can I see him?" Albert asked. "Has he cracked his head open?"

"No; there is no sign of any injury, so far as we can tell. I believe it is his brain – inside his head – which has been hurt."

"Oh!" the boy exclaimed. "Will he be a lunatic?"

"I should not think so. I expect," she went on, frantically trying to cobble together a coherent and soothing narrative in her head, "that his brain is just resting while it gets better."

"Do brains do that – get better?"

"I don't really know but I don't see why not; everything else gets better – with time."

"No, it doesn't. Mama didn't get better. She died – and our new mama nearly died too after Jasper was born. Is he here?"

"Jasper?" Lydia almost sighed with relief that they seemed to have left the perilous subject of Lord Chalvington's prognosis. "No; he did not come with us to Oxford – we went there to see Ambrose – but I believe he and Nanny Macintosh have been sent for now."

"Aren't you going back to London?" Anthea asked, having been listening with half an ear.

"Not at the moment, I don't think; I do not know for certain; I daresay Mama will be able to tell you."

"But what about Alicia's come-out?"

"I think it may have to be postponed for a year."

This suggestion not unnaturally infuriated Anthea who, probably correctly, assumed that Alicia's launch being delayed would lead inevitably to her own also being held back.

"Oh! Are you not disappointed, Alicia?"

"No, not particularly. I am more worried about Ambrose."

This, it seemed to Lydia, was a perfectly proper sentiment. It struck her that Alicia's brief trip to London, followed by the journey to Oxford and home again had had a remarkably maturing effect upon her.

"There's a carriage – several – coming up the drive now," Amabel informed them. Shocked by the news and perhaps trying to avoid hearing too much about it, she had retreated to the window where, if anyone outside had been looking up, they would have been able to see her little face pressed to the window.

Everyone immediately crowded around, including Alicia and Lydia, and were thus able to see Pelmartin appear upon the steps, the carriage door open and, after several extra men had been drafted in to help, the inert form of a man wrapped in blankets brought out and carried inside with the care which might usually have been afforded to a particularly precious object. The whole was overseen by a serious-looking man with a doctor's bag in his hand and a nurse in a grey uniform. All these people hurried inside after the cavalcade carrying the patient, whose face could not be seen.

"I think he's already dead," Albert said.

"Shut up!" Amabel screamed, putting her hands over her ears.

"Not listening won't make it any less true!" the boy told her with a scornful look.

227

"All the same it is not the right thing to say in the circumstances," Lydia said, taking the boy's hand and leading him away before Amabel, who had raised her arm, could hit him.

"Was that Ambrose?" Amory asked, following them and leaning against Lydia's knee when she sat down.

"Yes; they are taking him up to his room."

"I want to see him."

"I'm sure you'll be able to, but you must let them settle him comfortably first," Lydia said, her eyes meeting Alicia's above his head.

"If he dies," Anthea said, "it will mean Amos becoming Lord Chalvington. That'll make him and Adrian fight even more because Adrian will be furious. I wouldn't be surprised if one of them killed the other."

"Pray do not exaggerate," Lydia said sharply.

"Well, he will," Anthea said, adding viciously, "I don't suppose you'll care though because they're both in love with you so, whoever gets the Viscountcy and - in time – the Earldom, you can still be Lady Chalvington."

"Hold your tongue! That is a horrid thing to say – and a horrid thing to think too!" This, surprisingly, was Alicia. "You are a nasty vicious little beast," she added in case her sister had any doubts about her own character.

"I'm only saying what everyone else is thinking," Anthea pointed out. "In fact, I wouldn't be surprised if it was her arriving that made Amos do it."

"Do what?"

"Arrange for the 'accident', which I don't suppose was accidental. Amos would have stopped at nothing to get what he wanted. I expect he was afraid Ambrose would snap her up before he got home for the holidays again."

"How could he have done any such thing?" Alicia asked. "He had already gone back to school before Ambrose even set off."

"I don't know; I don't know how it happened, but I wouldn't be surprised if he engineered the whole thing. Now he's just sitting at school waiting to be told he's the new Lord Chalvington."

"That will do!" Lydia exclaimed, standing up and confronting the two girls, who appeared to be sizing each other up preparatory to engaging in some sort of a catfight. Lydia did not know whether they did this kind of thing, but she was horrified by what Anthea had suggested. She had not considered Amos to be dangerous although she acknowledged that she had not perhaps taken his infatuation as seriously as she should. In any event, she did not see how he could have done what his sister was suggesting from the confines of school – unless, of course, he had absconded, crept back under cover of darkness and interfered with Ambrose's saddle before he set off; but, surely, the groom would have checked. Also, if he had run away from school, she supposed the headmaster would have been in touch with his father. Taken up with the frequent disagreements between the brothers, she had not noticed how bitterly Anthea resented the boy who came after her – and who was barely a year younger. She must have been a small baby when he was born. Had she hated him ever since? She resolved to ask Nanny Macintosh about the relations between them.

"Tell her she's being absurd!" Alicia urged.

"I do think you must be mistaken," Lydia said to Anthea. "I do not see how he could have done anything from school – why it is miles and miles away!"

"They only left the day before," Anthea said, "and very likely he had already partially cut through the girth so that it did not last very long."

"I am certain the groom would have noticed," Lydia said gently. "It was an accident, Anthea."

"Oh, you would say so!" the girl exclaimed. "If you've lost Ambrose, you won't want to lose Amos too! In fact, now I come to think of it, I don't suppose it was Amos at all, it was probably you. Did you go out there to say good-bye to him? While he was gazing into your eyes, you probably cut it yourself."

Lydia almost laughed. "I don't possess a knife and, even if I did, I wouldn't have the strength to cut through a leather girth – they are quite thick, you know – particularly while I was saying good-bye! Be reasonable, Anthea! Your brother is badly hurt: is it really so important that somebody else should have been behind his injury? I do not see how it can have been anything but an accident! But, if you are so anxious about it, why do you not speak to your papa, tell him what you have told us and ask his opinion?"

"Because he won't listen to me; he only cared about Ambrose."

"If that is true, which I do not believe, he will care if someone tried to hurt him. Tell him your fears and let him decide what to do."

As she was speaking, the door opened to admit Miss Westmacott. Lydia was not certain whether the Earl had given her notice or whether he had merely told her of Ambrose's condition, but her expression was anxious, her lips held firmly together.

"What are you two doing here?" she asked, looking from Lydia to Alicia and back again.

"Looking after the children," Alicia said. "Have you been sacked?"

"Of course not, but I do have some sad news to convey to the children. Since I assume you already know, I suggest you leave me to speak to them on my own."

"We know too," Anthea said. "They've told us: Ambrose is hurt and has been brought back here to die. We saw him being carried in. And," she added spitefully, "we'd rather talk to our sisters than to you for they were with him."

"When he fell?" Miss Westmacott asked quickly, her eyes darting between Alicia and Lydia.

"No, of course not; we were in London. She means we have seen him since the accident. We think he smiled," Alicia went on, "so that it is probably only a matter of time before he opens his eyes and starts talking."

"Did he? Did he truly smile?" Amabel asked.

"We are not certain," Lydia said, "but we think he may have done."

"Can I go and see him?" the little girl asked.

"Not yet; I think you should let him be settled first, but I am sure you will be able to soon."

It was not until the afternoon that Nanny Macintosh's party returned with Lord Jasper and Sarah. The children were glad to see her for, although she had been a strict disciplinarian when they were small enough to be in the nursery, she had also been a loving and steady presence.

She came into the schoolroom where it was apparent that, no matter how bad the news or how dire the future looked, nothing seemed to have had much effect upon the usual fidgeting and quarrelling. Miss Westmacott was endeavouring to get them to put on their coats and hats to go outside for their usual walk. Nobody wanted to go and, although they did not have the nerve to refuse outright, they found endless excuses not to be ready: losing their boots, mislaying their hats, suffering from a tummy ache and so on.

Nanny Macintosh had no sympathy with such behaviour and told them that a brisk walk would do them good – Lord Ambrose would still be here when they got back.

"Will he still be alive?" Albert asked.

"Yes, of course he will," Nanny replied. She was not interested in excuses and was of the belief that children should do as they were told while grown-ups, although obliged in principle to tell the truth as often as possible, should not feel bound to stick too rigidly to it if circumstances dictated otherwise. In her opinion, a great deal of unnecessary anxiety could be avoided if children were told only what they needed to know; Lord Ambrose was still alive – in a manner of speaking – at the moment and if, later, it turned out that he was not, that would be quite soon enough to inform the children.

Her firm manner had the desired effect. Everyone laid their hands upon their shoes and hats and found their tummy ache improved and, a bare quarter hour later, were ready to sally forth.

"I want Lydia to come with us," Albert said. Lydia had gone to her room to speak to Sarah as soon as the nursery party arrived.

Nanny Macintosh was not very interested in what children wanted either; her main focus was usually on what they needed at that precise moment and it was clear to her that Lydia's presence on the walk was unnecessary.

"She is otherwise occupied," she said firmly. "As she is neither your nursemaid nor your governess, she is sometimes engaged on other matters, none of which need concern you."

"I wish she was our governess," he said boldly.

"What nonsense!" Nanny Macintosh said. "I wonder you allow them to be so impertinent, Miss Westmacott."

"I cannot prevent them," the governess muttered.

"Of course you can – or you could if you would only set your mind to it. Go along, children: you will feel much better for some fresh air!"

She shooed them out of the room, although Alicia, who was sitting in her favourite place in the window, did not go with them.

"I expect you're disappointed to have had to leave London so soon," Nanny said with a surprising degree of sympathy.

"Not really."

"I can see you're anxious about your brother; no good worrying though – best to get on with it!"

"What can I get on with?"

"You could try comforting your mama – and perhaps your papa too. He's still extremely unwell – can hardly walk - and I gather he's plagued with nightmares. Go and show him that daughters can be useful too."

Alicia gave a bitter laugh. "If he'd thought that, I don't suppose he would have married again – she's young enough to be his daughter. Obviously, the ones he had weren't good enough."

"Don't be idiotic," Nanny snapped, reverting to her usual manner. "Wives perform quite a different function."

"Pray don't tell me about it," Alicia besought. "Although I can't see how she can do that when they've been living in different houses."

"No doubt," Nanny said darkly, "you'll find out all about what wives do – and the function you're referring to is by no means the only one – when you're married."

"I don't see how you can know; you've never been married," Alicia muttered.

"Indeed," Nanny agreed cordially. "So that's something you'll know that I never will. Now, be off with you and see what you can do to comfort your parents."

Chapter 30

Lydia, having greeted Sarah and given her a carefully-worded report on Lord Chalvington's condition, left her room and wandered off down the corridor. She did not altogether admit to herself that she was thinking of visiting Lord Chalvington but the fact that she did not go up the flight of stairs which would have taken her back to the schoolroom was perhaps more indicative of her intentions than she was prepared to admit, even to herself.

It was not long before she came to his chamber. She had known more or less where it was for he had told her soon after she arrived, explaining that, if she became hopelessly lost or despairing, she could call upon him to set her on the right path. She was not, at present, lost, but she was despairing. Not entirely certain which door would take her into his presence, she was both relieved and delighted to observe that there was a servant standing rigidly in front of one; this was surely his and, now that she had got this far and had been seen by the servant, there seemed to be nothing for it but to attempt to visit him.

She did not make any sort of enquiry as she approached, considering that such a question would undermine her authority, but stated simply that she had come to visit his lordship. The servant, who had, like everyone else in the servants' hall, noticed and speculated upon the closeness of the pair before they left Maresfield, did not demur but immediately stood back so that she could open the door.

She knocked softly and went inside. It was a large room with windows which she suspected would have let in a great deal of light if the heavy curtains had not been partially drawn across, rendering the chamber exceedingly dim. She could see the form of the patient in the bed with the nurse sitting beside him; the doctor was by the window, reading something or other – possibly a medical paper – by the sliver of light filtering between the curtains.

Both looked up as she came in but neither, once they had ascertained who it was, made any attempt to drive her away.

"How did he take the journey?" she enquired softly, approaching the bed.

"There was no change. We took it slowly so that he was subject to as little jolting as possible and he is quite comfortable now. I have given him some sugared water and he is sleeping now," the nurse said.

"Sleeping? Do you mean that he was awake earlier?"

"No, no, he was not awake."

"May I sit with him?"

"Of course, Miss." The nurse readily rose for she had seen Lydia in Oxford and drawn her own conclusions as to the sort of person she was and the likely effect she might have upon the patient.

"If you like," Lydia said, exceedingly bold, although she spoke still in a soft and considerate manner, "you can go downstairs and take some refreshment – or perhaps walk outside a little. The sun is out, and I am sure it would do you good to have some fresh air. There is a man outside the door who will show you where the servants' hall is."

"Thank you, Miss; very thoughtful," the nurse said at once, but she looked to the doctor in the window for permission to leave. He, putting his paper down, nodded and the nurse left.

"What do you think of him?" Lydia asked the physician.

The man looked at her and, having made his own assessment, said, "If he does not regain his senses in the next twenty-four hours, I am not hopeful of his ever doing so."

She nodded. "Is there anything I can do to help rouse him?"

"Speak to him, remind him of some of your recent conversations, ask his opinion – and touch him: hold his hand, perhaps kiss him – if that is something you have done before."

She blushed. "We were not on those terms."

The doctor grinned. "In that case you might shock him into waking! I believe I too will go downstairs for a moment or two."

He left the room and Lydia sat down in the chair recently vacated by the nurse.

"I wish you will wake up, Ambrose," she said in a practical manner, "although it being so dark I daresay you think it's night. I will draw the curtains – neither of them told me not to and it's my belief you like fresh air. I'm going to open the window too and, if you don't like it, pray tell me so by one means or another. You could frown or sigh or – or say something for I am sure you are still there and probably listening to everything people are saying about you."

She rose, went to the window, pulled back one of the curtains and opened the window, at which the sun, having been shining determinedly upon the glass for some time, burst into the room along with a gentle breeze which, while it did not succeed in stirring the heavy curtains, did disturb her hair.

"I could almost pretend I was riding," she said, returning to the bed. "Can you feel it, Ambrose – the breeze? It is not far off summer and, since it is your last term, I must suppose you to have examinations

234

to sit in a month or two. Are you trying to avoid them? Pray do not! I am sure nobody would care a jot if you fail, but I promise everybody cares a great deal if you do not even sit them."

She looked down at his porcelain skin and thought that, in the few days since he had been unable to eat his dinner – a man who was always hungry – he had lost an appreciable amount of weight. His cheeks, the skin as smooth as silk, had grown leaner and the fine bones more prominent. He was, she thought, quite beautiful in a way that, when he had been conscious - smiling, laughing and talking - she had barely noticed. Looking at the innocent curve of the two rows of eyelashes, she was reminded of little Jasper: just so did he sleep, his skin paling until he resembled a marble effigy.

"You look very young," she said. "I wonder if I do when I am asleep. Do you know, since your accident, I have been feeling quite dreadfully old; it is partly, I suppose, because I have become aware that I have already outlived a whole lot of people whom I loved. I never would have expected that my little twig would travel further than yours – it cannot be right that it will. I suppose yours has got caught somewhere but I daresay you're hoping that the breeze will dislodge it and send it on its way again."

Her breath caught in her throat and, mindful of the doctor's suggestion, she bent and kissed his cheek, just below the bone, above where his beard had already begun to grow, where the skin was as soft and delicate as a rose petal. Emboldened by her own temerity, she kissed his lips. How soft they were and how cool! When she pressed a little harder, they seemed to yield and she found her own mouth over his open one; seizing the opportunity, she blew a tiny portion of her own breath into his partially open mouth.

He sighed; she was sure he did.

"I told you to sigh if you did not like my drawing the curtains and opening the window, but you did nothing. Are you now sighing because you wish I would leave you alone?"

She sat back and took his hand again.

"Why did you fall off?" she asked. "You are such a good rider. I might have fallen off, but I never would have expected you to do so."

"What?"

She was not sure at first whether she had imagined his reply and peered closely at his lips to see if they showed any sign of having recently formed a word. But there was nothing.

"Did you speak? Ambrose, if you did, pray say something more so that I can be sure!"

There was at first no response, so she said, "You fell off your horse – do you remember doing so?"

"Did I? Don't remember; saddle must have slipped." The words were indistinct, but this time she saw his lips moving.

"Why did you not check it properly?" she asked, hardly daring to believe he had spoken. His eyes were still closed but she was sure she saw the lines of eyelashes flutter.

"Left it to Jem, I s'pose. Stupid."

"No, not stupid; after all, what do you pay him for if not to do that sort of thing?"

"Won't be paid now," he said and, although the words were still faint and only partially complete, she was startled and delighted to discover how coherent they were. It seemed that he perfectly understood what she had said and was not only able to answer intelligently but also think of another person – a characteristic for which he had always been notable.

"Where is he?" he went on when she did not immediately reply.

"I don't know; do you wish to speak to him?"

"Yes. Will you fetch him?"

"Of course, but, before I do, will you open your eyes?"

She saw the eyelashes flutter again and discerned the dark glint of his eyes beneath them.

"Hard to open eyes – eyelids so heavy. Easier to speak – odd that. Lydia – can you find Jem before they send him away?" His voice was already firmer, his tone insistent.

"I'll call the doctor and nurse first," she said and rang the bell. "We are at Maresfield," she told him. "You were brought back earlier today. Did you know that?"

"I became aware, I think, of motion. Brought back? Where was I? Were you with me?"

"No; you were on your way to Oxford. Do you not remember that?"

"No."

The door opened to admit both doctor and nurse.

"He has regained his senses," Lydia announced.

"Good God! I thought he might if we left you alone together," the doctor said enigmatically, hastening to the bed.

Lydia rose and ceded her place to him.

"He has asked me to find his groom," she said, "so I will leave him with you."

"Yes. My word!"

The doctor, in spite of saying that he had expected his lordship to wake, was displaying signs of extreme surprise. He peered at his patient, picked up his wrist to take his pulse, although the nurse was already doing that on the other side of the bed, lifted his eyelids, listened to his heart and, in short, carried out a medical examination.

"How did you rouse him?" he asked Lydia, who had reached the door and was about to set off in search of the groom.

"I kept asking him questions. I think what prompted him to reply was when I queried his having fallen off his horse – I believe he took that as a criticism and could not allow me to get away with it."

The doctor laughed. "You see, you would not have been so outspoken if anyone else had been present. I believe you have saved his life, Miss."

"Oh no, I think that would be an exaggeration, sir. It is you who has saved him. Should I announce his return downstairs?"

The doctor frowned. "Not yet, I think. Leave that to me. I will not mention your hand in the matter for it might arouse disagreeable questions."

She blushed. "I will have to tell the groom because his lordship wishes to speak to him."

"Yes, yes, of course, but you can surely do so in confidence."

"Very well."

She went to her room and sent for Sarah for it seemed to her that her maid could more readily ascertain the whereabouts of the groom. If she were to go downstairs and start looking for him, speculation would mount as to her motives.

When the maid arrived, she asked her, emphasising the secrecy the doctor had requested, whether Jem, his lordship's groom, was still on the premises.

Sarah, amazed and delighted at the news of Chalvington's likely recovery, said she thought he had taken refuge in the stables; he had not, apparently, been dismissed yet and had, indeed, only arrived from Oxford a short time ago.

Lydia told her to seek him out and ask him to meet her at the gate into the meadow where she and his lordship had been used to ride every day.

When she reached the gate, she saw that Jem was already there, on horseback, with the horse she generally road, Nerys.

"I thought you wished to ride, Miss," he said, looking a little put-out to see her not dressed for riding.

"What an excellent idea; it would have looked far less peculiar for you to be accompanying me on a ride than if anybody were to notice us talking by the gate, but I would have to go and change and I believe I should give you his lordship's message without delay."

"His lordship's message?" he asked, immediately looking anxious.

She, realising that he must be thinking she had been deputed to tell him something – most likely to be gone immediately – by the Earl, said, "Lord Chalvington."

"My lord Chalvington?" he repeated.

"Yes; he has regained his senses and requested me to fetch you. He does not remember much of the accident – indeed, he did not seem to know where it took place – and wishes to question you about it."

"He ...? Thank God! I was afraid he would – would not ..."

"Quite so. He is with the doctor now, who requested that we do not, just at present, tell the rest of the family that he is so much improved. He wishes to speak to you first," she added, thinking that it sounded exceedingly odd that his lordship should want to conceal his recovery from his family.

"Yes, of course, Miss. Shall I go up now – when I have taken the horses back?"

"I think you had better come with me as I don't suppose you know where his chamber is and anyone you meet in the house may try to send you away."

Thus it was that Lydia, feeling distinctly furtive, led Jem into the house through a side door, up the stairs and along the corridor towards Lord Chalvington's room.

They did not meet anyone until, passing the stairs up to the second floor, they encountered Miss Westmacott. She was alone and was wearing her hat and coat so that it looked as though either the schoolroom party had not yet left for their walk or had already returned from it.

Lydia, who was on the look-out for an encounter of some sort, heard the footsteps before she saw who it was and tried to pull Jem behind a curtain but he, no doubt even more nervous than she,

238

stumbled, grabbed a portion of the curtain to steady himself and thus revealed their attempt to conceal themselves.

Miss Westmacott, whose presence on the turn of the stairs was much more readily explained and bore no whiff of impropriety, seemed to be even more horrified by the encounter than either Lydia or Jem. She jumped, uttered a small shriek and also stumbled, falling backwards on to the step above.

Jem, unsure whether he should be defending Miss Melway from a nameless threat – although most probably it was one of misunderstanding rather than violence – or running away, stood uncertainly a step or two behind.

Lydia, finding an unexpected seam of courage and aware that what she was doing might be a trifle secretive but was, in spite of that, nothing of which to be ashamed, adopted a manner modelled on that of the Baroness. She stepped forward, leaning solicitously towards the fallen woman and offered her hand to help her regain her feet.

"Miss Westmacott? So sorry to have startled you – were you going out?" Not receiving an immediate answer, and seeing the haughty woman discomposed, she moved into a higher gear, "Where are the children?"

Miss Westmacott, disdaining the proffered hand, rose to her feet, girded herself with propriety and launched her own attack, "What are you doing skulking about behind a curtain with a groom, Miss Melway?"

This was the question to which Lydia, ever since she had led Jem into the house by a side entrance, had been frantically seeking an answer. She saw no alternative but to tell a portion of the truth for she did not doubt that the governess would somehow manage to put about the fact that she had found the new ward, still dressed from head to toe in mourning, hiding behind a curtain on the first floor with an outside servant.

"I am taking him to see Lord Chalvington in the hope that a familiar voice may rouse him, although I do not see that it is any business of yours," she said untruthfully, disdaining to defend herself against the other woman's implication.

"Does Lord Maresfield know of this plan?"

"He has not the least objection."

"You haven't asked him, have you? You're carrying out this absurd – and no doubt dangerous – experiment off your own bat, are you not? Who the devil do you think you are to take such matters into your own hands?"

"And who, pray, do you think you are, Miss Westmacott, to question my actions?" Lydia asked, raising her chin and attempting to stare the governess down, although in point of fact the employee was several inches taller.

Miss Westmacott turned a fiery red, understanding that Lydia had successfully, if meanly, pulled rank.

For a moment the two women stared at each other but Lydia, in spite of being smaller, probably less than half the other woman's age and caught in what most people would have considered a compromising situation, had the advantage, especially since Miss Westmacott was perfectly aware that her position in the household was already shaky.

Lydia, sensing victory, stepped back to allow the governess to continue down the stairs.

"I hope you enjoy your walk," she said cordially. "It is a lovely day."

When the governess was out of sight, Lydia, with a nod at Jem, proceeded on her way down the corridor towards Lord Chalvington's room.

Jem, who had been about to utter a "Whew!", closed his mouth and followed meekly.

Chapter 31

Neither the Earl nor the Countess, once more alone when the governess had gone, spoke.

He, slumped miserably in his chair, stared past her out of the window into a garden that was full of burgeoning spring plants. Everything outside looked hopeful while everything – and everybody - inside seemed to be mired in despair.

She, sitting opposite him, was denied the sight of the garden and, if she was not to stare at him, must focus upon one of the many portraits adorning the walls. She had never found any of these old-fashioned persons inspiring – and she had spent many hours alone in this room after the birth of her son. She tried not to look at her husband, fearing that he would take exception to her attention, but her gaze kept returning to his face.

At last he said, "Do you find much to fascinate you in my features?"

"Yes, my lord."

"You do? Good Lord, what, in Heaven's name?"

"You are my husband."

"Indeed; even I know that. I suppose you find me much changed?"

"You have begun to be more recognisable since we received the news about Ambrose."

"Ah. Is that, do you think, merely because it is so long since we have met – and we knew each other so imperfectly – that you had forgotten what I looked like but are beginning at last to be able to recognise me?"

"No," she said impatiently, unsure whether his bitterness was directed at her or at himself. "I think it is because, now that you are thinking about Ambrose – and realising, perhaps, how much you care for him, you have begun to leave behind the self-pitying person I found in London."

"Good God! Pray do not attempt to spare my feelings! Is that what you thought?"

She nodded.

"Why did you not say so? I had no idea I had become such a pitiful wretch. Is it then your opinion that my reawakened affection for my son has had a beneficial effect upon my face? I own my legs are not much improved by the softening of my hardened heart, but perhaps it is only a matter of time before they too are affected by my new lease of life. In any event, no one else has any sympathy for me so I suppose I may be permitted to extend some to myself."

"Permitted, yes, but self-pity should not, to my mind, be encouraged. You are, after all, alive and, although not in particularly good trim, better than many others," she pointed out.

"Indeed – and when I think of my poor friend, Melway, I realise how fortunate I am – not only to be alive but to have been willed his daughter. His loss is my gain in that respect."

"You already have daughters," she reminded him repressively.

"Yes, but they are not half so amiable as his. I don't know how he achieved it but suspect it has something to do with his own character and perhaps also to his devotion to his wife – her mother. I have not been either a good husband or a good father."

"You could make amends now."

"Really? Where shall I start – with wife or children?"

"It is too late to repair whatever damage you did to your first wife, which is, I suspect, the source of your difficulties with your children, but I think you could begin by expressing an interest in your living – conscious – progeny."

"I stand corrected. Chalvington was by far the most agreeable amongst them so that I find myself wondering whether the Almighty has seen fit to punish me by removing him."

"You do not really think that, do you – that God would deprive Ambrose of life merely to punish you?"

"He would certainly be a jealous God if that were so; no, I am sure He has better things to do than try to reform me. How do you suggest I go about softening my children's attitude?"

"Show interest," she repeated. "They are convinced that you do not care whether they live or die."

"I own I had not realised that I did," he admitted.

"And even now I suspect you think that it is only Ambrose who matters to you."

"I always liked him, but you will say that is only because he is my heir. Good God!" he suddenly exclaimed as a terrible thought struck him.

"What?"

"I have just realised that, unless I take drastic steps, Amos will step into his shoes if Ambrose dies."

"Is Amos so very bad? He has conceived a rather ridiculous infatuation for Lydia but then I rather think Ambrose had too – only, because he is older, one called it love."

"I know Amos no better than any of the others so cannot make a judgment of his character; it is not that which exercises me so much as his position."

"Second sons have inherited before," she suggested tentatively.

"And then there is my treatment of my wife," he went on, casting her a look of horror and abandoning the subject of his heir.

"The first one or the second?" This time she managed to inject an edge of humour.

He did not respond to it, saying, "As I said, it is too late to right the wrongs I did the first one, although I rather think I may have to confess them to the second. Is it too late for us to find happiness, do you think?"

She started, blinked and blushed. Without warning, he had veered towards the personal – and the immediate.

"No; is that what you wish, my lord? Do you truly think it possible – now?"

"I hope it is, but I am very much afraid it may be too late – will, I should imagine, almost certainly be when you have heard the whole about the way I behaved towards poor Clarissa."

"You did not ...? What in the world did you do that most men in your position do not?" she asked, wondering if he had beaten his first wife or locked her in a dungeon as well as betraying her with any number of other women.

"I neither beat, starved nor incarcerated her," he said, reading her mind. "I was, however, unfaithful - on occasions too numerous to catalogue. I have not, since I met you, had the smallest desire to stray from your side."

"You can hardly claim to have cleaved to it, surely?"

"I suppose you mean since Jasper was born?"

"Yes."

"Some of that time I spent in a field hospital, the rest I have spent in London, surrounded by medical advisers. As you see, I can still only walk with difficulty."

"Nobody has suggested you should have travelled to Maresfield on foot," she responded tartly.

"The eminence of my physicians has however precluded their leaving London. I could not expect such highly qualified and universally respected men to quit the metropolis, even for a day or two."

"That is a paltry excuse! How often do your doctors examine you?"

"Every day."

"So what will happen to you now? It is already more than two days since you were in London – will they have visited only to find their patient fled? And why, in any event, do they need to see you every day?"

"Because it is not only my legs – my walking – which is at fault. I received a wound to my abdomen – the one indeed which unseated me – which has unaccountably flared up again and become both swollen and painful. I suppose it never healed properly inside, although at first it appeared to mend quite well. In any event, the physicians have taken to examining it every day, fearful that the new swelling indicates something foetid inside which may yet carry me off."

"So is there a danger that it may grow worse now that you have left their aegis? Can you not ask Dr Marley to see to it?"

"I can see you think I am exaggerating. Do you wish to see it?"

"No, of course I do not, but ..."

He had already stood up, undid his trousers and pulled his shirt free as she spoke. She stared in horror as, wincing with pain, he lifted it to expose his chest, across which she saw he was heavily bandaged. He undid the pin which held the dressing in place and commenced unwinding the cloth.

She jumped up and laid her hand over his.

"Pray, pray do not – not here."

"Where then?"

"Has Dr Marley dressed it since you left London?"

"No. I suppose it is time that he did."

"Yes, but not here, my lord. What if someone should come in?"

"And find me undressing in front of my wife?"

"No – not that – undressing, unwrapping a serious wound – pray, pray do not."

She picked up the pin which he had laid on a table beside his chair and, leaning forward, attempted to secure the bandage again.

"Go upstairs!" she commanded. "Send for Dr Marley."

"He is busy with Ambrose."

"Nonsense. Nothing is likely to have changed in the last half hour – and, in any event, he can leave the nurse to watch him. Come, come with me; let us go upstairs and send for him now."

He appeared to heed her for he allowed her to fix the pin and, when she had done so, let his shirt fall again before fumbling with his trouser buttons.

"Let me," she said, noticing how white his face had become.

He let his hands drop and she, with shaking fingers, applied herself to the buttons.

"Have you ever dressed anyone before?" he asked, amused.

"No, I don't believe I have."

"Very likely not even yourself?"

"Not often. Buttons are difficult, are they not?"

"A certain amount of dexterity, together with carefully focussed force, is required, I think. You see, it would be no good if they were too easy: they might come undone by mistake."

She looked up, her face flushed from a combination of effort, frustration and embarrassment.

He met her eyes, his own with something of the old teasing light restored, and said, "I keep forgetting how very young and inexperienced you are in every respect."

"I am sorry. There, I have done one!"

"So you have! Now that you have the knack, I daresay you will be able to do the others in no time."

When she had completed the task, she prevented him from sitting down again, saying, "You must go upstairs and send for the doctor to look at your dressing. Come, we will go together."

"Give me my canes then or shall I lean upon you?"

"Of course you can." She offered her shoulder, but he disdained it, holding out his hands for the sticks.

They made their way slowly out of the saloon and into the hall before beginning upon the stairs.

The Earl, as they passed the footmen, told them to request the doctor attend him in his own chamber.

"I presume the bed is made up?" he asked, as the man bowed and began to make his way towards the door into the servants' quarters.

"I am afraid I do not know, my lord. I will send someone to prepare the chamber."

"Thank you. I daresay whoever is deputed to do it will get there before we do."

"May I assist your lordship?" the other footman asked as his colleague disappeared.

"No; I believe I can manage with my wife beside me."

It took them a very long time to climb the stairs although the treads were neither deep nor narrow, but his lordship was in a great deal of pain.

When they reached his chamber, they found a maid warming the sheets, another placing a steaming jug of hot water on the washstand and a third on her knees lighting the fire.

"The doctor has been sent for," he was told.

"Thank you."

He did not avail himself of the bed but sat down in one of the chairs before the fire whose youthful flames were bright and long but not yet warm.

"Would you like me to shut the window, sir?" the maid with the warming pan enquired.

"No; the country air is invigorating."

The maids finished their tasks and slid out of the room, leaving the married couple alone.

"I am sorry," she said into the silence. "I was unaware of the extent of your injuries."

He shrugged, but said, "You thought the worst of me."

She bowed her head. "Why did you not tell me the extent of them?"

"I did not want you to take pity on me."

"So preferred to indulge in self-pity rather than admit weakness."

"Yes; was that so very silly – or unusual?"

"No," she said after a moment of thought. "Not unusual, but silly – yes, although understandable."

There was a knock upon the door and, upon being invited to enter, the doctor came in.

"Would you like me to leave you?" Emmeline asked.

"No; now that you have some inkling of my condition and now that you have admitted to despising me, you might as well stay."

"I did not say I despised you."

"You said I was silly – is that not the same thing?"

"Not in the least."

He shrugged again and she thought how like his daughter he looked now that he had become sullen. He might have been a half-

246

grown boy although the lines of pain in his face made him appear preternaturally old.

She withdrew to the window while he told the doctor about his injuries, how long he had suffered from them and how he had acquired them.

Dr Marley, looking grave, requested that his lordship extend himself upon his bed so that he could take a proper look. After a careful examination and a good many probing questions, he said, probably unaware that the Earl had been under the long-term care of several eminent London physicians, that he thought the stitches should be removed, the whole cleaned, packed with boracic powder and left uncovered for as great a portion of the day and night as possible.

"It has become septic," he said, with a disapproving look as though the Earl's previous medical advisers had failed to adhere to the most basic principles of medical hygiene.

"It was redressed every day until my son's accident when I left London somewhat precipitately. I'm afraid I have ignored it since and – having travelled all night – had not even looked at it until just now."

"It does not seem to me that the infection is so recent," the doctor said. "On the contrary, I believe it has been festering for some time. If you will permit, my lord, I will request the presence of Nurse Robinson immediately so that we can, together, do our best to prevent it from spreading any further."

"What about my son? He should not be left by himself while you attend to me."

"He will come to no harm for a little while, my lord, and it's my belief that, if we do not do something to alleviate the risk of such a noxious wound killing you, he will wake up to find he is Lord Maresfield. I will go now to fetch Nurse Robinson, as well as my instruments, so that we can see to your complaint at once."

"Will he wake up?" the Earl asked, diverted.

"I sincerely hope so."

The doctor, by now bolstered by his knowledge of his own expertise and perhaps desirous of flexing his medical muscles on a patient who had a rather more readily treatable complaint than the one for whom he had been engaged, had become almost authoritarian, so much so that the Earl, rarely willing to subject himself to anyone else's decisions, submitted.

"Would you like me to sit with Ambrose while Dr Marley attends to you?" Emmeline asked when the doctor had bustled out of the room, promising to return within a few minutes.

"Yes; I do not wish you, in any event, to be present while he saws me open as I don't doubt there is something repulsive inside which is likely to smell abominable as soon as he exposes it to the air."

"I would rather stay with you."

"Would you? Whatever for?"

"To offer what comfort I can, I suppose, while Dr Marley hurts you – for I am sure whatever he is planning to do will be painful. If you truly think Ambrose should not be left alone for even a short time, we can ask Lydia if she will sit with him."

"I don't think she should be asked to do that. Ring the bell – I will send Paterson."

"I am persuaded she will be happy to do so; in any event, if she is reluctant to sit with him on her own, she can ask Alicia to join her."

"Very well; ring the bell."

The Earl's valet came in answer to the summons, failed to hide his surprise at finding the married couple alone together and was despatched with the message.

"His lordship is quite peaceful," the doctor said, returning with the nurse in tow. He did not disclose that the young man had come to his senses nor that he was lying in his bed with Miss Melway in attendance. The time for such a disclosure was not, in his professional opinion, now for he was certain that the news would galvanise the Earl into rising from his bed without waiting for his own treatment and thus put himself in grave danger.

More hot water was brought together with piles of torn sheets – and a request was sent to the valet, as well as Chalvington's man, to return for, the physician explained, the procedure would cause his lordship such exquisite agony that he might require the strength of two men to hold him down.

Chapter 32

Lydia led the groom to Chalvington's door. There was no longer a man standing outside but, when they went inside, the nurse was there, sitting beside the patient. She rose when she saw who it was, curtsied and withdrew.

"Ambrose," Lydia said, approaching the bed, "I have brought Jem."

The eyelashes fluttered, half rose and revealed a gleaming portion of his lordship's orbs.

"You need not stay if you prefer to go," he said. Although he was still lying prone in his bed, his voice – and even his manner – were so much restored to what they had been that it was hard to believe she had thought him almost lost such a short time ago.

"Do you wish me to stay, my lord?"

"I wish to have you always by my side but will contain my disappointment if you have something else to do."

"What could I have to do that is more important than you?"

"I own I cannot immediately think of anything. Come closer, Jem. You see that I have recovered my senses in a manner of speaking, although I own I cannot recall anything of what has laid me so low. I am hoping you will be able to enlighten me."

"Oh, my lord," Jem mumbled, stumbling closer and standing respectfully beside his master.

"Perhaps you could sit down; I find your looming over me disconcerting. Now, please tell me precisely what happened. I gather from Miss Melway, who is the only person to whom I have spoken since returning to Maresfield – indeed it was she who told me where I was for I don't suppose I would otherwise have known – that I took a tumble from Adonis. How in the world did that happen? Was there a snare – or a creeper or something of that nature which caused him to stumble? And is he unhurt?"

Lydia, who was sitting on the other side of the bed, noted that his lordship had not only recovered his senses but also a good deal of his understanding and wit. He seemed, already, to be making light of an event which had cast the rest of his family into unimaginable anxiety.

"I don't know how it happened, my lord, but it must have been my fault. We were crossing one of those fields not far from Oxford when you jumped a stream. It was then you fell, but it wasn't because Adonis stumbled or because you were going too fast – although you

249

were, begging your lordship's pardon. I was just behind, and I saw the saddle slip sideways as Adonis gathered himself for the jump. You wasn't expecting it, my lord – especially since we'd already gone a good long way from here – so that it took you by surprise."

"Why did it slip?"

"I can't have buckled it properly, my lord."

"You say we weren't far from Oxford – I don't remember it at all, you see. Why did it not happen before – we'd gone a good way, as you say?"

"I don't know that, my lord, because you had jumped several gates and one or two streams. It must have got looser, I suppose."

"How could it have done so unless the leather was worn?"

"I think it was, my lord. When I inspected it afterwards, I saw that it was very thin in one place – almost fraying. I'm wondering if, it perhaps having been a bit slack to start with, it worked looser as you rode so that that jump put an extra bit of stress on it which caused it to snap."

"Snap? So it wasn't that the saddle slipped and tipped me out, it was that the whole thing fell off, along with me?"

"Yes, my lord, I think it must have been. When you fell, I didn't look at it because I was attending to you. You hit your head on a boulder at the edge of the stream and were knocked senseless. I expect you'd have been all right if you'd just fallen on the ground. I thought you were dead, my lord."

"Yes, I'm sure you did, but I'm not, so now we need to work out why it happened – and make sure it doesn't do so again. Where is the saddle?"

Jem flushed uncomfortably.

"I brought it back here, my lord. I only got back a few hours ago. It's in the stables."

"Has anyone else looked at it?"

"I don't know, my lord. I rode back, leading Adonis. I put it on him, using a spare strap because it would have been hard to bring it back loose."

"Yes, of course. Did you say the original one is broken?"

"Yes, my lord."

"Where is it?"

"I threw it away. It weren't no use."

"No; except as evidence. Where did you put it?"

"In a pile of odd bits and pieces of broken bridles and stirrups – and the remains of old saddles – I put it there."

"Been there a long time, do you think – the pile?"

"Oh, yes, my lord – years, I should say. I s'pose they don't know what to do with it all – and maybe sometimes they find a bit that can be useful for something or other."

Jem was growing a little more relaxed for Chalvington's manner, although probing, was neither hostile nor accusatory, although Lydia did wonder what he was seeking to ascertain and what he intended to do with Jem. When he had first appeared, the groom had looked terrified as well as guilty and had shambled along behind her with his head hanging. Their encounter with Miss Westmacott on the stairs had further unnerved him, although there had been a moment – when the governess had looked almost ready to hit her – when he had advanced as though ready to defend her.

"Yes, I expect they do. When you took it off, what did you think had caused it to fray so badly in such a short time? After all, you noticed nothing amiss when you put the saddle on – and surely you would have done?"

"Yes; I can't believe I didn't. I've thought about it a lot since and the only thing I can come up with is that, when we did set off, we did so in quite a hurry, so that perhaps I put it on carelessly."

"Yes, but it wasn't your carelessness that made it fray – or break. If I understand you aright, it was not that you failed to do up the buckle but that the strap itself had deteriorated."

"That was what it looked like. In fact, when I took it off, it didn't look like the usual strap – it looked much older, a bit like the ones in the pile of discarded stuff at the College. I wondered how I didn't notice when I buckled it up. I'm so sorry, my lord, I – I almost killed you."

"Well, luckily you did not – and the whole thing seems odd. Were you in a hurry the day we left here?"

"Yes, because there had been a bit of an upset in the stable the night before. One of the doors hadn't been bolted properly and Jephtha had got out. Luckily, he hadn't gone far – he was grazing in the field next to the stable. Mackenzie was afraid someone had got in and wanted me to check all the horses - and all the tackle as well. By the time I'd done that, you were ready to leave so I s'pose I did saddle him up a bit fast."

"Did anyone else go out that morning – before we did?"

"Miss Westmacott went for her usual early morning ride but no one else did."

"Miss Westmacott? I didn't know she rode at all."

"Oh, she always has, my lord, but she goes out very early – long before anyone else is up really; I s'pose that's because she's busy all day. She once said she was used to ride a lot as a child but that employers don't like governesses using their horses."

Lord Chalvington made no comment upon this assertion but Jem, perhaps feeling that some further explanation was required, added, "Apparently his lordship, Lord Maresfield, gave her permission to ride any of the horses when she first came. I wasn't here then."

The Viscount asked which horse she generally favoured.

"Oh, she usually takes Minerva; she says Nerys is too small."

Chalvington made no comment on this piece of information so that a short silence fell between the two men. It was broken by Jem, who asked deferentially if there was anything else he could do for his lordship.

"Yes; I don't suppose you'll like it because you've only just got here, but I'd like you to go back to Oxford and see if you can find the broken strap. I find myself fascinated by your story and would like to have a look at it."

"Of course, my lord. Shall I go now?"

"I believe you should, you know, for it might turn out that the pile of useless bits of leather may finally be cleared away any day now."

"Very well, my lord."

The groom rose, bowed, retreated a step or two before pausing and asking, even more humbly, "Do you still wish me to work for you, my lord?"

"Yes, I think so; I'll make my mind up when I've had a look at the strap."

"Yes, my lord; thank you, my lord; I will leave immediately."

"Are you still there, Lydia?" Ambrose asked as the door closed upon the groom.

"Yes. What do you think happened?"

She rose from her seat in the window and returned to his bedside.

"I've no idea! The last thing I remember was saying good-bye to you in the hall. Was there anyone else there?"

"The footmen, I suppose. And Emmeline."

"Yes, of course, she would be. Did she say good-bye to me?"

"I should think she must have done, but I was not there when she did. She came into the hall as we were speaking and more or less told you to be on your way. She sent me upstairs to find Alicia for some reason which I have forgot. I don't know what she did or said then – or indeed what you did or said."

He frowned. "I seem to remember that you and I were indulging in a little romantic interlude – what did I say to you?"

She laughed. "You swore undying love."

He blinked and blushed. "Did I? I own I don't remember that and I am sure I would because, in truth, I was thinking it but did not quite have the audacity to voice it."

"I'm sorry; no, you said no such thing – I was teasing."

For a moment he looked almost vexed. "You should not tease a man with no memory or try to implant false ones in his head! Did I make you an offer?"

It was her turn to blush. "No, of course you did not! She, Emmeline, came down the stairs, saw us together and jumped to an erroneous conclusion. You were holding my hands – and you had been for some time – but you said nothing untoward. Indeed, when Emmeline approached, she accused you of taking too long to get going – she said your horse would be impatient – and you said, 'I am only bidding my new sister *adieu*' or some such."

He was frowning even more by this time so that she was afraid she must have overtaxed his feeble strength and made to withdraw.

"No, no, pray don't go now or take fright! I need to remember what happened and you are the only person who can help me."

"No, I'm not; I daresay Emmeline could. She spoke to you after I did."

"Yes, but I think it was what I said to you – or you said to me that was important. From what you say, it sounds as though she was quite annoyed; was she?"

"Yes," she said slowly. "I think she was and, as I went up the stairs, I felt uncomfortable. I don't think she was annoyed with you, but with me. I didn't know you were setting off late and I was a little surprised that she took such exception to our saying good-bye to each other."

"I wish I could remember what she said when you had gone. You see, I don't remember your going; the last thing I remember is holding your hand and speculating about whether you would be able to go on without me – an absurd notion, in any event."

253

"You don't remember mounting your horse?"

"No; and I don't remember anything about the ride either. I suppose I galloped off at full tilt in my usual manner and I suppose Jem followed me. The next thing I knew was you holding my hand again just now – half an hour ago."

"Don't you remember waking up?"

"I thought you kissed me – did I dream that?"

"The doctor suggested it."

"Good God! What the devil possessed the man? He told you to kiss me – and you did? Was he watching to see if you did it right?"

"I don't suppose I did; I've never kissed anyone before – or at least, of course I have, but not like that!"

"Like what?"

"Oh, I wish you would stop interrogating me! The doctor told me to talk to you and suggested I kiss you. I said we had not been on those terms but, when he and the nurse left the room, I did. I wouldn't have done if they'd been there."

"Will you do it again?"

"No."

"Why not? Was it very disagreeable?"

"It was embarrassing and now you've made me feel horridly ashamed of taking advantage of you."

"But you didn't; from what you've just said, I believe you did it in the interest of my health. In any event, that was what brought me back from whatever far shade I was locked inside. Did you do it on sufferance – just because the doctor had ordered it?"

"I'm sure I don't know why he did; it was a most peculiar suggestion and then – then – he left the room, taking the nurse with him."

"Most improper, but you did what you had been told, and I suppose he didn't think I posed much threat."

"No, but I did."

"Dear me! I don't recall feeling threatened! Will you repeat the action so that I can make a proper judgment about it?"

"What will you do if you realise how disagreeable it was to be on the receiving end of – of it?"

"I suppose I'll have to throw you out and tell you never to darken my door again. I'll be obliged to issue orders that you are to be barred from entering my room. Is it such a terrible thought? Did you have to grit your teeth and clench your fists to kiss me but resolved to do it, even

254

if it should prove to be unpleasant, in order to bring me back to consciousness? What an unselfish girl you are, to be sure!"

"I suppose," she said, lifting her chin and fixing him with a stern gaze, "that I felt sufficiently grateful to your family for taking me in to try my best to help them in their hour of need. You cannot conceive how devastated they all are! Your father, in spite of being exceedingly unwell – and increasingly in pain if his face is anything to go by – has accompanied you all the way, as has your mama, and even Alicia has been rendered almost hysterical at the thought that you might never regain consciousness!"

"Good Lord! What about you – what did you feel?"

"I was naturally very concerned about you," she replied stiffly, a response which made him suddenly utter something resembling one of his whoops of laughter.

"Do they know you are here now?"

"No," she admitted, abashed. "Neither do they know that you have regained your senses."

"Do you know, I think I will pretend I haven't and see how many of them come to visit – and what they say when they're here? Or is it already too late? Has the doctor gone to tell my father that I have returned to Earth?"

"No, I don't think so. Indeed, it was he who asked me not to disclose your near-miraculous recovery."

"Really? Why? Surely he will wish to take some credit for it?"

"He might – indeed, I am sure he will – but in the first instance I believe he was afraid you might disappear again, as it were."

"Ah! Perhaps I can deceive him too."

"Do you not think it unkind to keep them in ignorance? They are so very anxious I own I would like to see them rejoice."

"Well, unless the doctor is proved right and I fade away again, you will be able to in due course. Indulge me – say nothing to anyone for the time being."

"Shall I go about with a long face when inside I am entirely joyous? It will be difficult."

"Will it? Are you joyous?"

"Of course."

"Have you heard from your lover?"

"My what? I do not have one."

"I thought you told me Lord Dorman was taking an interest in you."

"Yes, he did, but I have heard nothing from him so must suppose that his interest has waned – or perhaps he never had any and was merely being polite. It is so hard to tell what people really think – and feel."

"Do you know what I think?"

"No; and I own I am so startled to find you once more capable of thought that I cannot begin to guess at what is going on in your head."

"Or my heart? Can you not read what is going on there?"

"By no means. Your thoughts are, to some degree, communicated through your speech and your expression but your heart – by what means does it communicate?"

"The same way – through the self-same channels – my words, my tone and my expression. Are they all so blank or so distorted that you cannot decipher the meaning?"

"Yes; the heart is not an organ with which I am familiar. I believe it speaks in a language I do not understand."

"Nonsense! I have just told you it uses the same means of communication. It's my belief you're refusing to listen to it."

"I am afraid I must ask you to translate what it is saying. Can you," she asked, giving herself away, "read mine?"

"I am certain our hearts can read each other."

Chapter 33

While Lord Chalvington and Lydia were playing a sort of game which both were both enjoying, the Earl and his Countess were playing another sort of game, this time both less joyful and more complicated.

He was being operated upon by the doctor, with his valet as well as Chalvington's, together with the nurse, in close attendance, and was concentrating upon not uttering the merest squeak of complaint. This must have been extraordinarily taxing because, having strenuously refused to have the pain dulled with brandy, he was in full possession of his senses while the physician sliced open his flesh.

She, meanwhile, was equally determined not to flinch from the distressing sight of Dr Marley bending over her husband with a sharp knife in his hand. Having refused to be banished from the room, she had consented to retire to the window seat, from which she could not discern a great deal of what was going on and where her husband, prone upon his bed, could not see her. Because of this, she felt it incumbent upon her to speak from time to time in a soothing manner. Thus, their game consisted of him pretending nothing much was happening, a charade in which she readily joined by speaking as though he were a small child having nothing more serious than a splinter removed.

"I'm persuaded it will soon be done," she said, unaware that her voice, laden as it was with sympathetic pain and anxiety, was anything but soothing.

"You will be all the better once it is over," she continued, trying to convince herself as much as him.

She had been horrified by the sight of the angry swelling when the doctor unpeeled the bandages and was now berating herself for having misjudged him: he was exceedingly unwell. Her assumption that he had been indulging in all sorts of nameless forms of loose living while she was out of the way at Maresfield had clearly been far from the truth.

It had been bad enough seeing him hobbling about like an old man and noticing the new lines on his face but, seeing the ill-healed wound, she realised that this was most likely the reason why he had recovered so incompletely in the months since Waterloo.

She suspected that he had stayed away – and refrained from inviting her to London – because he did not wish her to see him in such a weakened and vulnerable state; it was, she thought, his pride which had nearly killed her love and almost thrown her into his son's arms, and pride which might still lead to his death.

"There!" the doctor said at last. "All, done, my lord. It will be tender for some time, but I think I've managed to cut away everything that was infected."

"How much have you taken away?" the Earl asked, essaying humour. "Am I a fraction of what I was?"

The doctor, perceiving the anxiety behind the question, said, "Nothing that you will miss, my lord. The wound, as I said before, was much infected; it should heal well now and, once it has, you will be precisely as you were before it was inflicted. May I ask what it is that impedes your walking?"

"Both my legs were broken when my horse fell upon me and healed crooked so that I could barely walk at all. The physicians in London broke them again recently and have bound them up with splints to keep them straight. They seem to be taking a long time to mend."

"Dear me! I should imagine the wound has so weakened you that your constitution has taken a blow; once that heals – and with plenty of rest and good food – I am convinced you will soon begin to see some improvement there too. I will take a look later. I think you have had enough of my ministrations for the time being. I will come back and see how you're doing in an hour or so. Come, Nurse, we will leave his lordship to rest."

When the medical advisers and the valets had left, Emmeline returned to her husband's side.

"Do you feel a little better, my lord?" she asked tenderly, sitting down in the chair beside the bed.

"No; in truth, I feel a good deal worse. The operation was exceedingly painful."

"I daresay you would like to sleep – and I believe it would be beneficial, but perhaps you should take a little sustenance first. Shall I send for a drink or something to eat?"

"A drink, yes, please."

She leaned across the bed and tugged the bell. It was Morrison, the valet, who came in answer and took his lordship's order for watered wine.

When it was brought, Emmeline poured it and lifted her husband's head on to an additional pillow so that he was able to drink it. He looked very pale and seemed too fatigued even to speak so that, when he had swallowed the best part of a glassful, she took the pillow away, drew up the blankets and prepared to leave him, but he reached out a hand and grasped her wrist.

"Will you stay with me?"

"Yes, of course."

She sat down again but did not speak. He raised her hand to his lips and, having kissed it, laid his cheek upon it and closed his eyes. In a moment he was asleep.

It was some considerable time before the doctor, having completed his operation upon the Earl, returned to Lord Chalvington's bedside, accompanied as always by the nurse.

The Viscount and Lydia had progressed from trying to provoke each other into declaring their sentiments to speculating upon Amos's probable disappointment at being baulked of stepping into his lordship's shoes.

"I don't believe he has been told that they almost became vacant," she said.

"No; I've not been at death's door quite long enough for anyone to have recalled him from school – or even written to him. I believe Miss Westmacott corresponds with him frequently but, since even she knew nothing about it until earlier today, I suppose, if she has written, he would not have received it yet."

"Do you think I should ask Pelmartin not to ask your papa to frank the letter just yet?"

"I shouldn't think Pelmartin would produce the letter very quickly for, as soon as Papa reads the direction, he will know what it's about."

"Do you think he'll take exception to it?"

"If what you say is true – and neither exaggeration nor fantasy on your part in order to make me believe Papa cares about me – I imagine he will be less than eager to have the possibility of my demise committed to paper."

"I have no doubt your papa has been distraught at the prospect of losing you. He is not at all well and is, in my opinion, in a great deal of pain, but he has not spared himself in chasing after you and bringing you home."

"Why then has he not come to see me? I have been here for hours and nobody has visited me but you?"

"I don't think you can be certain of that; after all, you were not in possession of your senses until recently."

"Did he come before I regained them?"

"I don't think so, but he must have been feeling quite dreadfully fatigued after the journey."

"Perhaps. And what about my mama? She has not been either."

"Have you been waiting for her?"

He grinned. "Of course. I cannot, in the circumstances, do aught but wait."

"But do you particularly wish her to sit beside your bed?"

"Are you afraid I might want her more than you?"

"I am persuaded you must – after all, she is your mama."

He uttered a bitter laugh, so unlike his usual cheerful response, that she almost wondered whether his character had changed during the period of his insensibility.

"It has been difficult living in this house with her and without my father," he acknowledged. "She misses him and it's my belief she has been exceedingly lonely. She is still very young, and I own I feel sorry for her. I have wanted to comfort her – have tried to do so – but cannot pretend to be indifferent to the power of either her beauty or her melancholy. She is not my mother, although I am supposed to think of her and address her as such, but it is difficult to muzzle what I am certain are perfectly natural sentiments when my father has been absent for such a long time."

"It sounds as though you have fallen in love with her." Lydia hoped that he might interpret her desolate tone as indicating her understanding of his dilemma rather than alerting him to her own breaking heart.

"There was a time when I believed I had – and I am fairly certain she felt the same. I tried to keep away as much as possible but knew that, without either me or Papa, her misery would deepen."

"She is certainly excessively sad. It was the first thing I noticed about her and the second was that, when you appeared, her demeanour brightened. You speak of how you have striven to resist her; I am certain she has wrestled with the same conflict; she winces every time you call her 'mama'."

"I am aware of it. And then you came."

"Yes, and I saw at once how strained relations were between all the grown-ups. She was miserable, bullied by Alicia and Anthea, disliked and undermined by Miss Westmacott and more than half in love with you, a situation which added guilt and fear to what must already have seemed an almost unendurable burden of loneliness and heartbreak. She

260

thinks – thought – your father no longer felt affection for her and was certain – with, in truth, good reason - that nobody else did, except of course you. I don't think it's surprising that you should have fallen in love with each other."

It was not easy for Lydia to say this for, although she had suspected it from the moment she saw the pair together, she had denied it to herself – just as she suspected the Countess did. It seemed that Lord Chalvington, the most straightforward member of the family, had been more honest with himself, although the circumstances had prevented him from voicing it to anyone else before; she wondered why he had chosen her as a *confidante* and supposed it must be because she was so quiet and dull.

"She threw us together," he said, ruminatively. "I believe she noticed my manner towards you from the beginning. I saw her face as we came into the saloon together that first evening and knew that she was jealous and - at the same time - ashamed of her sentiments. She could have forbidden us to ride together or insisted upon a groom always accompanying us, or she could have made it difficult by asking you to help in the schoolroom; she did not. She positively encouraged us to spend every morning alone with each other."

She nodded. There was a lump in her throat, and her heart, in spite of her valiant efforts to control it, was no longer able to maintain its usual position. It seemed to have slipped its anchor and slid from its accustomed place, leaving behind a painful hollow. All that joy beside the river, all the long talks and teasing games with twigs, all that had been nothing more than a charade invented by a pair of guilty would-be lovers in a vain attempt to break away from each other. She had been used by both as a diversion.

Suddenly she could not bear to sit beside him any longer. A few minutes ago, when he had been speaking of how their hearts communicated with each other, she had read his words as a declaration of love but was now convinced that it was no such thing. He thought of her as a sister; he had always called her that: 'my new sister'. But then there had been that nonsense about her kissing him when he was insensible; again, she had interpreted his teasing as flirtation but, if he had truly wanted to kiss her when he was conscious, would he not have said so? Perhaps he had believed her to be as light-hearted as he in the matter, but she was not.

She pressed his hand in an attempt to conceal the reason for her rapid departure and rose.

"I think you should sleep now. Are you still determined to pretend to be unconscious for a little while longer?"

"Yes, I want to see what they do. Must you go?"

"I believe I must. Where, I wonder is Dr Marley and the nurse? Will you be all right if I leave you alone?"

"Of course. Will you come back soon?"

"Of course," she replied, her echoing of his words underlining the closeness of which she had hoped so much but which she was now convinced was merely sibling affection. She detached her fingers from his almost with impatience. She could hardly wait to be gone, to break the cord of which only she seemed to be aware. "I expect your father will come up soon."

"And my mother?" he asked, teasing again and watching her closely from under half-closed eyelids.

"She too, but I expect she will come with your father."

"Perhaps. No doubt I shall soon find out. Can you try to keep Alicia away? I'm afraid she'll shake me and I'll inadvertently let out a cry of protest."

"If you do, you'll just have to let her into the secret."

"It wouldn't remain a secret for long. Do you think me cruel to extend their period of anxiety unnecessarily?"

"I don't understand why you wish to do it."

"To see what they truly feel about me."

She flushed and made to leave once more.

"I wonder," he said as she reached the door, "whether anyone else will kiss me."

"I wouldn't have done if the doctor hadn't told me to," she snapped and went out before he could find another reason to detain her.

There was no one in the corridor when she emerged. She wondered idly what the doctor and nurse were doing for they had been gone for some considerable time but, since she was determined to root Lord Chalvington and his state of health from her mind, she shook herself and set off with determination for the schoolroom where she found the usual people, including Alicia, still apparently waiting to go out for their afternoon walk, although most of them had discarded – and apparently instantly mislaid - the coats, hats and gloves which Nanny Macintosh had succeeded in making them wear.

"Where have you been all this time?" that damsel asked, speaking rudely above Miss Westmacott's rather dreary repetition of the importance of always knowing where one's outer clothing was to be found.

"Nowhere much," she said untruthfully.

"I'll wager you've been sitting with Ambrose," Alicia said, "but are ashamed to admit it. Is he still the same?"

"I believe so," she said untruthfully, soothing her conscience by reflecting that he was unaltered since the previous occasion on which she had seen him.

"Did you sing to him?"

"No. Are you going out for a walk with the children? Will you wait for me while I fetch my hat and coat?"

"We'll never get out at this rate," Miss Westmacott, who had removed her coat since Lydia had met her at the turn of the stairs, said sharply. She picked it up from the chair on which she had laid it and put it on again, saying, "I believe I won't wait for you; as I am the only one ready to go out, I'll do so at once and wait for you in the sunshine. I'm heartily sick of importuning everybody to put on their outdoor clothes. No doubt you'll have more success than I, Miss Melway."

With which, she turned and flounced out of the room.

"She's getting worse!" Alicia said. "I wonder if Papa gave her notice; if so, she won't care what she does now."

"Is she really leaving?" Amabel asked.

"I don't know," Lydia replied. "Not so far as I know. Come along, everyone, pray put on your boots and whatever else you're accustomed to wear for your walk. I'll go and fetch mine and shall expect you all to be booted and buttoned into your coats, with your hats upon your heads, by the time I return. Will you watch them, Alicia, and chivy them into obedience?"

"I suppose I shall have to, but pray don't be long."

Chapter 34

The Countess, sitting beside her husband as he lay somewhere between sleep and waking, reflected that their roles appeared to have been reversed for she had gained the impression that, the extent of his illness having been at last revealed, his pride had been excised at the same time as the infected flesh. He had requested she remain with him so that, for the first time in her life, she felt herself to be a grown-up person who could provide comfort for another.

All through her childhood, and even more acutely during her come-out, she had perceived herself as, at best, a diversion; at worst, a burden. She was the eldest of her family and supposed that, being female, she must have been a disappointment when she was born. She was not only of no use but, because provision must be made for her future, expensive. She had proved to be less of a millstone than had originally been feared on account of her beauty; she would be relatively easy to dispose of when the time came, although of course a dowry must be provided and she must be meticulously trained in the proper ways of her rank in order to attract a good offer.

But, with that emphasis upon her appearance and her manners, she had gained the impression that she was little more than an ornament – a valuable one which must be carefully protected, but nevertheless a decorative object rather than a useful one. She had done everything she should and married a man who had been highly prized for his wealth as well as his position. She had gone on to fulfil everyone's expectations – although in this case they were superfluous – by giving birth to a son within a year of marriage.

Afterwards she had been discarded. Her beauty fading and her value consequently diminished, she had been abandoned with neither friends nor entertainment and had languished in despairing contemplation of the remaining decades ahead of her. Nobody, except her stepson – whose proximity and likeness to her husband had both stimulated and unnerved her - had appeared to either want or need her, nobody had loved or even liked her; even her son preferred his nurse and her husband had seemed to prefer almost anybody.

She watched his still face and saw him slip almost imperceptibly from repose into sleep; his breathing grew slower and she saw the lines which pain had carved into his countenance relax; the frown vanished and the beautiful mouth lost its pinched look and softened into the shape she remembered.

To watch another sleeping is to experience an overwhelming sense of their trust. She had never held her son until he slept, never seen his features relax nor his skin grow pale, never seen his little lips part nor heard his regular breaths as he lay in her arms; perhaps, if she had, she would have fallen in love with him as deeply as she had with her husband. She had seen *him* sleep before and had known that swelling of the heart that she felt now; only this time it came as an unexpected gift, a revelation of how deeply and absolutely she loved him. She did not know whether he loved her, but she did know that he trusted her enough to fall asleep beneath her gaze and her heart opened to him.

He slept for a long time and she sat beside him, almost without stirring, until the sky darkened and evening came on. Nobody disturbed them and, when they did, it was a shock to both for she, as the sun grew lower and her back grew stiff from sitting so long in one position, had lain down beside him and, lulled and reassured by his regular breathing, fallen asleep as well.

Lydia went to fetch her boots, pelisse and bonnet, walking rapidly back along the corridor she had so recently traversed, down the stairs and along the passage towards her room.

For all her valiant efforts to fix her mind upon the forthcoming walk, she was still horridly conscious of the hollow in the middle of her chest and, as she came in sight of Lord Chalvington's door, increased her pace with the intention of getting past it as quickly as possible.

In spite of this, her steps dragged as she drew closer and she could barely prevent herself from pausing, from putting her hand upon the door knob and turning it. The man who had originally been stationed outside was still absent and she supposed that by now the doctor and nurse must have returned. She wondered if Lord Maresfield was there – or the Countess. She did not wish to meet the Countess just at present, certainly not if she was unaccompanied by her husband.

As she stood, almost paralysed with the desire to see the man she loved, she heard what sounded like a scuffle inside the room, followed by his lordship's raised voice and what was clearly a feminine scream.

"What the devil do you think you're doing?" his lordship shouted.

The other responded with a small, outraged scream.

Lydia stood rooted to the spot; what was going on? Had the Countess woken him or perhaps kissed him when he had not been expecting it? The sounds of scuffle continued. To the embarrassed listener, it sounded as though something akin to a fight was taking place;

265

did that mean that he had taken exception to her advances? Or had she taken exception to his and, fighting him off, angered him? Was Chalvington, who had always seemed so gentle, not above forcing his attentions upon an unwilling woman?

What should she do?

"Let me go!" the female voice screamed.

"Do you know I don't think I will – at least not until you've explained yourself?" came his lordship's reply, now in a more familiar, half-amused tone.

"I merely came to see you," was the reply, "and thought to make you more comfortable. It's not my fault I tripped over something."

It was not the Countess's voice; it was Miss Westmacott's.

Had Chalvington been conducting an *affaire* with her too? She was some years older than he but was an exceptionally handsome woman and, recalling the rumours she had heard about his father's frequent dalliances as well as having the evidence of his flirtatious manner with her, Lydia did not think it impossible that he had been engaged in a *liaison* with the governess. She had believed his hints at having conceived a *tendre* for her; no doubt the governess had believed his declarations of love too.

She wondered what she should do. Should she go in and try to save Miss Westmacott from whatever Lord Chalvington was doing or should she hurry off down the corridor and pretend she had heard nothing? She had at least an answer to her question about whether the doctor or nurse had returned for it seemed unlikely that he would have made a pass at Miss Westmacott if there had been anyone else present. Had she gone in, stared at his apparently unconscious face and as a consequence tempted him to try to pull her into the bed with him?

"What?" he asked, disbelieving but still amused. "What did you trip over?"

"The pillow; it was on the floor."

"It was not, it was under my head – that is, until you put it over my face."

"I did not mean to. I intended to raise your head and insert it underneath for it was lolling dreadfully. I thought you would be uncomfortable."

"You lie. You pulled it out. Why did you want to suffocate me?"

Lydia gasped and held her breath.

"I did not; I swear I did not; why should I want to do any such thing?"

The governess was trying to sound amused, teasing, but her voice was unnaturally high, which Lydia thought betrayed her anxiety.

"I can't imagine – that's why I'm asking you. Did you also damage the girth on my saddle?"

"No!" This time her voice was so high it almost hurt the ear. "How could I have done that?" she added.

"Lord knows! I don't remember much of what happened; the last thing I recall was bidding Lydia goodbye – and taking such a long time about it that her ladyship grew impatient. What were you doing at the time?"

"I don't know when it was, but I was probably upstairs with the children."

"Why are you not with them now?" he asked, momentarily diverted.

"They would dilly-dally, as they always do whenever they're asked to do anything, so I left them with your Miss Melway."

"She's not my Miss Melway. Has she been engaged as a governess's assistant?"

"I don't see why she can't do something to help," Miss Westmacott exclaimed on a whine. "Why is she so important that she cannot be expected to pull her weight?"

"She is not an employee, as I've pointed out to you before. I might ask, why are you so desirous of lowering her rank?"

"Her rank? Who is she? Mine is as high as hers."

"It may have been once but, as soon as you took a position as a governess, I am afraid it sank. Why did you?"

"I had no portion; what else was I to do?"

"Could you not have married like everyone else?"

"Why should I if I did not wish to?"

"No reason at all, except that, by refusing to do so, and unfortunately not being possessed of a fortune, you were obliged to earn your own living. It was a decision you took a long time ago for reasons which I daresay seemed persuasive at the time but which, it seems to me, you have since had cause to regret. Why have you not left us, in any event, since you appear to find my siblings so troublesome? And why do you want to suffocate me?"

"I don't – I didn't. Let me go! You're hurting me."

"Nonsense – I'm holding your wrist with quite remarkable gentleness. You wanted to kill me! If I could reach the bell without

267

dragging you on to the bed, I would summon Paterson. Attempted murder is a serious offence."

"Why were you pretending to be senseless?"

"I wanted to see who would visit me and what they would say as they hung over my unconscious form. How lucky I did, *n'est-ce-pas*?"

"Who has visited you? Her ladyship?"

"Not so far as I know, nor my devoted papa neither. I hope he has not been taken ill himself; he is not, you know, in very fine fettle at all, but I daresay you do not care about that any longer, do you?"

"What do you mean?"

"I seem to remember there was once a good deal of gossip about you and him. Of course, I was only a child and Mama was still alive, but the general opinion was that he had installed his mistress in the family home. Was it that, being asked to look after his children, which made you so malevolent? Did you hope he would marry you when Mama died? No wonder you do your best to undermine poor Emmeline. You must have been appalled when you failed to win the prize you had waited for so patiently."

"Poor Emmeline!" she almost screeched so that Lydia was afraid she would be heard all down the corridor and perhaps even in the room below. "Poor Emmeline who's your mistress? Why should I feel sorry for her?"

"I don't know; it's an interesting question: are you wondering whether sympathy would be wasted on a woman fortunate enough to be my mistress? Would that, in your opinion, be such a paradisiacal position that envy would be the only natural response? But think of the dilemma with which she must wrestle every day – married to one man and mistress to his son! Does such a position not prompt pity?"

"No! It's repugnant! And what of dear little Lydia? Is she your mistress too? That little mouse! She should be flattered!"

"I don't believe she would be and, for your information – because I don't suppose we will exchange another word after today – she is not my mistress and never will be – and neither is her ladyship, who, likewise, will never be in that position. She is married to my father and, unlike you, Miss Westmacott, both she and I hold to our principles. She is a good woman."

"Have you failed to seduce her? And little Lydia? I suppose she's too dull for you."

"The way you're speaking I find myself wondering if you've wished for that position too. I don't doubt it would have amused you to

268

make love to both the father and the son. But why did you want to kill me? Sheer bitterness at not having been the recipient of my attentions? Come, Miss Westmacott, you must have grown quite desperate immured here with my father's latest wife and his children, but without him on hand to amuse you."

"How dare you?"

"Easily."

Lydia, increasingly appalled by what she was hearing, but reluctant to leave before everything had been revealed – although, in truth, it did not seem to her that there could be much more - stood trembling outside the door. She had entirely forgotten that she had left Alicia in charge of the children.

"Oh!" The exclamation was followed by the sound of another scuffle, this time embellished with thumps as well as screams.

It was when she heard a crash as of a heavy object hitting the ground that she ran into the room.

She saw Lord Chalvington no longer lying passively in his bed but wrestling vigorously with Miss Westmacott. She had evidently found a new weapon for the hand that was not in his lordship's possession was brandishing a heavy silver candlestick which, having listened to the recent argument, Lydia had no doubt she meant to bring down upon the patient's head if only she could control its weight sufficiently to apply it accurately. On the floor by the bed lay the remains of a china chamberpot, whose smashing must have been the noise that had propelled Lydia into the room.

"What is going on?" she asked in a tone which she was only too aware resembled a governess's when faced with unruly children engaged in a pillow fight.

"What the …?" Miss Westmacott exclaimed, turning, horrified, towards the speaker.

"Do you require assistance, my lord?" Lydia asked in a cold tone. She had heard too much – and jumped to too many conclusions – to feel much sympathy for him; on the other hand, she could not, even hating him as she did, stand by and allow someone to murder him.

"God, yes! She's a very tigress! Ring the bell – I daresay Paterson will answer it. Where is my doctor – and the nurse? Have they left?"

"Not so far as I know; perhaps they're taking a rest."

"Perhaps. No one, apart from my assailant, has come in since you left."

"Ha!" the governess shrieked. "I suppose she was in your bed!"

"I most certainly was not!" Lydia exclaimed, losing some of her carefully acquired air of *sangfroid*.

"I told you she was not my mistress," his lordship said.

"Nor ever like to be!" Lydia added bitterly.

"Did you hear that? Have you been standing outside the door for some time? Why the devil didn't you come in to save me before? This woman tried to suffocate me, thinking, no doubt, that I was already unconscious and that it would be a matter of a moment to put a definitive end to me."

"I did not like to," she admitted, embarrassed.

"Why not? Were you waiting to hear something else? It is said that eavesdroppers never hear any good of themselves although I don't think I've said anything unpleasant about you. I did indeed state that you would never be my mistress, but I don't suppose you troubled to consider why I said that — or what I meant by it. You just assumed I wouldn't stoop to make love to a person Miss Westmacott described as a mouse."

"I didn't hear everything," she muttered.

"I suppose what brought you in was her dropping the chamberpot on the floor. I think I must be holding her better hand because, fortunately, she doesn't seem to be very adroit with the other. Ah, thank God you're here, Paterson!"

The door opened to admit the valet, who took one look at the scene and strode across the room to take hold of the governess, who was struggling frantically to be free.

"Are you unhurt, my lord?" he enquired solicitously.

"Yes, but it's a wonder I am. This woman tried to suffocate me and, having failed in that endeavour, has tried to smash my head with a chamber pot and a candlestick. Please take her away, lock her up somewhere and inform the magistrate."

Chapter 35

When the Earl opened his eyes, it took him a moment to realise that, not only had he slept for several hours without a nightmare, but that his wife was lying beside him.

"Lina," he murmured tentatively.

"My lord," she replied, sitting up.

"Oh, pray do not move; I have slept better than I have for almost as long as I can remember. It is dark; what has happened to the day?"

"You have slept it away and I am persuaded it has done you a power of good. You already look better."

"Do I? But then it's dark so I suppose you can barely make out my features. What time is it?"

"I don't know. Shall I light a candle?"

"Yes. Did we have dinner?"

"No; you have been asleep ever since the doctor did his work."

"Good Lord! What has everybody else done? Have Alicia and Lydia had their dinner and what has happened to Ambrose?"

"I don't know. I've not left your side and no one has disturbed us."

"Didn't like to, I suppose. Lina: there is something which I must confess – as I hinted earlier."

"You can tell me after dinner."

"I would prefer to tell you now – before I lose my nerve again. Since no one has reminded us about dinner, one must assume that Alicia and Lydia have eaten theirs – and, since no one has disturbed us, one must also assume that there has been no change in Ambrose. Will you give me a little more of your time while I confess to perhaps the most idiotic thing I have ever done, the consequences of which may end by driving you away and altering my family history for ever?"

She nodded. She had by this time lit several candles and drawn the curtains.

"Shall I light the fire again?"

"No, leave it; pray do not seek to divert me. I daresay you have no more desire to hear what I have to say than I to say it, but I *will* tell you. I meant to – intended to – before we married and should have done so but lacked the courage; I was afraid I would lose you. Now that I have lost you, I may as well confess all. The doctor has eased my physical pain; I believe my confession may ease my heart – although I fear you will never forgive me."

"From what you say, I take it you committed this appalling sin before you married me?"

She had returned to his side, but not to the bed; she pulled up a chair and sat down while he pulled himself up into a semi-recumbent position, trying not to grimace as his movement dragged on the new wound. She rose again and busied herself with gathering several spare pillows and inserting them behind him.

"Sit down," he said at last. "I am quite comfortable. Pray cease fidgeting and listen to what I have to say. Yes, my idiocy took place long before I met you, but that doesn't alter the fact that I married you under false pretences."

Was he about to confess that he had at the time of their nuptials already been married to another and that their marriage was therefore bigamous? Did he wish to return to his lawful wife? If not, she did not think that she would much care if it turned out that she was not in point of fact married to him. If he wanted to remain with her, that would be enough for her; if he did not, she did not see that it would make much difference whether they had ever been man and wife or not. She knew that she would never marry another – or even love another.

"I was married to Clarissa at the time. We wed when we were far too young and Ambrose was born when I was just the age he is now – one-and-twenty. At first, we were happy – or I thought we were - but it was not long before we - both, I think - began to realise that we had little in common and that what we had originally shared had weakened as we grew up.

"I am ashamed to say that in my discontent I left her here and went back to London where I conducted myself in a manner that I should undoubtedly have outgrown before I married. I did all the sort of foolish, ill-considered things that young men do, including running through a whole catalogue of women, most of them married but one or two not.

"It was one of these who turned out to be my nemesis. She was eighteen – not much younger than I – and in London for her first Season. She must have known I was already married and had left my wife in the country but she – I was going to say, threw herself at me - but I daresay that would be unfair. We flirted all that spring, but it was not until August, when nearly everyone had left the metropolis, that we became lovers. Nobody knew – or, at least, I have no reason to suppose they did because I never heard a whisper of a scandal concerning her –

but by Christmas she was in an interesting – and devastating – condition."

He paused but Emmeline said nothing. This was all a long time ago and, while she dreaded the *dénouement*, she did not think it was that unusual. Indeed, she found herself filled with pity for the poor girl for there was no doubt that she must have been ruined. She hoped his lordship had provided for her financially.

"You do not say anything," he muttered.

"I have not heard the whole so feel I'm not yet in a position to pass judgment."

"Lord, how careful and considered you are!" he exclaimed, almost irritated.

"Did Clarissa know about it?" she asked when he did not resume the narrative.

"No – not until I was forced to tell her. I had left her here, as I have you, so that she knew nothing of what was going on in London.

"The young woman I ruined did not take her fall from respectability with any degree of either humility or shame. She was furious. She threatened to tell the whole world that I had forced her into my bed – than which nothing could have been further from the truth – and demanded that I not only support her and the child financially – which I had always intended to do in any event – but that I somehow arrange matters so that she could retain her good name. What would you have done in similar circumstances?"

"I? Heaven, I don't know. I own my sympathies are with the young woman, although I do wonder what I would have done. I don't think I would have threatened you, but it's impossible to guess what one is likely to do in such a situation."

"I sense an absence of sympathy for me," he said with some bitterness.

"You are right," she admitted. "No doubt you will cite your youth in mitigation, but you knew then, perhaps not quite as well as you do now, but you did know, that making love to a woman frequently results in conception. You should have known better; when I was introduced to the *ton*, I was very carefully watched and guarded and I knew perfectly well that if I were to transgress in that particular manner – and especially if it were to result in a child – I would be cast out – ruined. She must have known that too – and yet she found you so irresistible that she gambled with the whole of her future life."

"Is that so incomprehensible to you?"

273

"No, it is not. I suppose that, by the time you met me, you had learned the lesson – or perhaps you didn't find me so irresistible – for you never attempted to seduce me."

"Are you hurt by that? Do you take it as proof of my indifference? Pray don't be idiotic, Lina. By the time I met you, I was widowed and therefore free to marry you, something I determined to do from the moment we met. I fell in love with you."

"Not with her?"

"No. Would I have done if I had been widowed then? I don't think so. She was beautiful, lively, but, as I hinted before, she knew perfectly well that I was married and yet made no attempt to repel my advances, which, in the circumstances, plainly stemmed from no respectable intentions. In point of fact, I do not think she fell in love with me."

"Why in Heaven's name did she get into your bed in that case?" she asked, shocked.

"I can only suppose I was too fascinating," he replied, self-mocking.

"It doesn't sound as if she put up much – or indeed any - resistance. All the same, I do feel sorry for her. What did you do? And what did her parents do?"

"She hadn't told her parents by the time we agreed on a solution – and, so far as I know, they are still ignorant. She was convinced that they would cast her out and she would be ruined. I believed her and, unable to think of anything else and – I own – worn down by her increasingly threatening outbursts, I gave way and brought her, as she demanded, into my own household."

"What? Is she still here?"

"Yes."

"Good God! Who is she?" But she did not need to ask the question because she knew her identity.

He, seeing her dawning realisation in her face, said nothing, and she continued, "I have wanted to lay her off ever since I arrived. Would you in the end have allowed me to sack her? And what, in God's name, did poor Clarissa have to say on the matter?"

"I didn't ask her opinion and neither did I tell her the truth. I said that the poor girl was in an interesting – to tell truth unfortunate – condition, that her lover had abandoned her and that I believed she would make an excellent governess."

"She cannot have been happy about it. Did she not enact you a Cheltenham Tragedy?"

"No; Clarissa was not that sort of person; Miss Westmacott is; she wore me out with her melodramatics so that, weakly, I gave in. Once she was installed, I became reluctant to spend time here."

"I see; so, it's not so much that you didn't wish to see your wife, more that you didn't wish to see the governess," she said drily.

"Yes. I tried to persuade Clarissa to come to London more frequently, but she wouldn't leave the children."

"What happened to Miss Westmacott's infant?"

"He is here, masquerading as one of Clarissa's children."

"What? Do you mean that nobody knows that he is – was – not Clarissa's? She knew – how in Heaven's name did she endure that?"

"I don't know. She treated him no differently from her own and no one except his mother, Pelmartin and I ever knew any different – except of course for Nanny Macintosh."

"Which one is he?"

"Amos."

"I see."

She was silent while she thought about this and the ramifications of the governess's illegitimate child being on the verge of becoming the heir. When she spoke, it was with considerable bitterness.

"No wonder you're confessing this now. If Ambrose dies, he'll inherit unless you reveal the truth about his birth. I suppose you don't care for that; or is it that you don't like his mother?"

"You make it sound very sordid."

"It is. You treated Clarissa shabbily and you've hoodwinked me. I suppose your mistress hoped you would make her your Countess when Clarissa died?"

She was beginning to grow angry on both her own and the dead Clarissa's behalf.

"No wonder she hates me – and no wonder Pelmartin and Nanny Macintosh treat me with contempt. I'm just another goose who's been drawn into this despicable deceit because I couldn't hold out against a powerful and corrupt man. On what terms are you and she now? Is she still your mistress?"

"No; she has not been for many years – not, in fact, since she came here, several months before Amos's birth."

"Of course; I'm sure I don't know why I asked for I have ample evidence that you lose interest in a woman's charms when she has a baby."

"What? If that were so, how do you explain why Clarissa had so many children?"

"I suppose you were doing your duty by your name at that stage," she retorted coldly, adding, "You have not been near me since some time before Jasper was born."

"I went to war and then I was wounded. Are you still questioning my sentiments towards you? Why the devil do you think I married you?"

"What, you mean because you could have made an honest woman of Miss Westmacott but chose me instead? I cannot begin to imagine why you did but am certain you regret it now as much as I."

"Ah! You admit you wish you were free? May I enquire why?"

They matched each other for contemptuous tone and angry, frowning faces. She was horrified by what she had heard and felt more belittled and undermined even than she had when she had assumed him to have remained in London to be near his numerous lights of love.

He, having expected and hoped for understanding and, perhaps ultimately, forgiveness, was disappointed. He had, in a sense, laid his entire fortune on an unwise wager and lost.

"I am disgusted, horrified and, indeed, positively outraged by what I have heard: to foist your mistress and her bastard on to your wife in such a way that she was forced to pretend the child was hers and to suffer its horrid mother's presence, not only in the house, but also as a preceptress for her own children – it is ... Of what did she die?"

"She had puerperal fever – as you did – after Amory was born but, unlike you, she never properly recovered. He was less than a year when she died."

"Are you sure that's what killed her? It could not have been despair?"

"Are you asking if she took her own life?"

"Yes – or whether the interloper took it. Was Ambrose a soldier at the time?"

"Yes. Are you implying that she hoped he would be killed?" The Earl's voice was no longer bitter but, on the contrary, more alert than she had heard it since he had galvanised them all into setting off for Oxford.

"I'm certain she did – but then, frustratingly, you married me. She must have been furious."

"But she cannot have expected me to marry her then – we had had nothing to do with each other for years."

"I should think she did expect it all the same. What will you do if Ambrose dies?"

"God knows! What can I do? It would be the *scandale de nos jours* and it would be devastating for Amos if he were to be obliged to make way for Adrian."

"With whom he fights all the time already – or at least did until he turned his attention to making love to Lydia. Are you in fact certain he is yours?"

He stared at her, his eyes opening wide, so that she did not think it had ever occurred to him that Miss Westmacott might have double-crossed him.

"He looks like me," he said weakly.

"You mean the hair? They all have that hair – and so does Miss Westmacott. His is a little more Titian – like hers - and his eyes are grey."

"Jasper's are blue."

"Yes, like mine. Miss Westmacott does not have grey eyes – and neither do you."

"My God!" he exclaimed, passing a hand across his face. "I never thought of that! I seem to have been a most complete idiot."

"You were young," she said, almost sympathetically, "and in a blue funk. Do you recall her having several other admirers?"

"Of course she did, she was a beautiful woman – but one in particular? Yes, I believe she did, now you put it to me. The Duke of Tallent. He was much older than either of us – at least forty, I should say – and not married so that everyone assumed he must at last be looking for a bride. He made a dead set at her and I'm sure she was flattered and, thinking she had it in the bag, may have succumbed to his blandishments. He was known to be a rake. Then, when he cried off or in any event made it clear that she was not to be his future Duchess, she turned to another man to whom she had extended her favours. I suppose she had no others who were single."

"Lud! Shocked as I am at what she's done to you – and to Clarissa in particular – I cannot help but pity her: she had high hopes of becoming a Duchess, didn't wait for the ring and found herself in the devil of a predicament. She must have been frantic and, casting around for a way out, hit upon the most tender-hearted man she could find amongst her lovers, browbeat him into submission and ended by becoming a governess. Did she, I wonder, only succumb to your charms after failing to bring Tallent up to scratch?"

Chapter 36

She did not know what made her say something so cruel; afterwards, she wondered if she had wanted to hurt him; certainly it did, for it was immediately apparent that it had never crossed the Earl's mind that he might have been double-crossed. Superimposed upon his guilt about the past and his present terror that he was, as it were, throwing himself over a cliff, she saw his face register raw shock.

"Good God! Do you know, I never thought of that!"

"No; I daresay you were too much engaged in casting around desperately for a solution and castigating yourself for behaving like an idiot to wonder if the whole thing was a tissue of lies. It's not my intention to cast further aspersions upon Miss Westmacott's character, which we have already shredded, but I do find myself wondering about the accuracy of her conjecture, at least as expressed to you, regarding the paternity of her child."

Having delivered herself of this facer, she waited while his lordship assimilated the awful ramifications of her suggestion. She observed the shock develop into shame – presumably of his own foolishness – and, finally, anger. But, eventually, this too faded from an initial blaze which had made her briefly thankful that Miss Westmacott was not in the room to a more contained, if no less powerful, indignation. When he spoke, his voice was controlled, his expression pensive.

"I believe you may be right; our *affaire* was not of long duration – indeed consisted of only a couple of occasions - and her announcement about finding herself in an interesting condition, accompanied by copious tears and melodramatic language, took place shortly afterwards – probably, in hindsight, a little too shortly. I did not question it; I had dallied with a female I assumed to be a respectable *débutante* and believed I must pay for what I had done. I was a fool; it never occurred to me that she would have yielded to Tallent – after all, he was unmarried and to all intents and purposes pursuing her in a respectable fashion – although in point of fact he had an appalling reputation with well-brought-up females and would never have married a girl who had allowed him to seduce her; it would have convinced him that she was not to be trusted as a wife."

"Perhaps he did not so much seduce as force her."

"You seem determined to take her part."

"I do not mean to; I dislike her, have always done so – and she detests me – but I have to admit I admire her resourcefulness. Leaving

279

aside the immorality and duplicity of her actions, she did the best she could in horrible circumstances and, while she certainly exacted a heavy price from both you and Clarissa, she paid one too. The punishment she would have received from Society if she had admitted the truth would have been extreme; she would have been ruined; I hate to think what would have become of her."

His lips twisted in a bitter smile.

"And what is your opinion of the men?

"Disgraceful."

Once again, he seemed to allow time for the harshness of her verdict to penetrate because it was some minutes before he went on.

"What I did to Clarissa was unforgiveable. My only excuse is that I was weak and foolish. I am sorry. You have married a dishonourable and contemptible man. I can only say that I will do – or not do – whatever you think best for everyone, including Amos."

"If Ambrose survives, I do not think you have to do anything just at the moment, but I believe Amos should in the end be told something of the circumstances of his conception and the uncertainty regarding his paternity. In addition, if you feel as strongly as you appear to about a boy of unproven pedigree inheriting the Earldom, you must come clean about the identity of his mother and the sundry men who may have fathered him. Does Ambrose know? He must have been about five when Miss Westmacott arrived. Was Amos born here?"

"Yes. In point of fact, her arrival and the ages of Clarissa's children at the time have been subject to a degree of shuffling. Miss Westmacott came here when Ambrose was two and gave birth to Amos at much the same time as Alicia was born."

"So Ambrose would be unlikely to remember and Alicia would be entirely ignorant of what happened."

"Yes."

"And poor, deceived Amos is not fifteen but much the same age as Alicia – nearly eighteen. No wonder he is so impatient – he's two years older than he thinks he is – and no wonder he's fallen in love with Lydia, who is, in point of fact younger than he."

"Yes; now you point it out, Amos has always been older than he – or almost everybody else thinks. In addition, he was born several weeks early – or so I was led to believe."

"It doesn't surprise me. He's obviously always been precocious." She spoke sarcastically.

"I will sack Miss Westmacott," the Earl said.

"Can you? Will she not refuse to go?"

"I'll have to pay her off. You had already told me, before you knew anything of this, that you would like me to dispense with her services and I don't think you can be expected to put up with her now that you have the full picture. What I am wondering though is whether you can put up with me?"

"I'm not sure," she replied honestly. "I own I am disgusted by the story – and appalled by the consequences which, even if Ambrose lives, are extensive; a solution of some sort must be contrived."

He nodded and said dully, "I will await your decision; in the meantime, I believe I must see how Ambrose is progressing. Will you ring the bell for Morrison?"

She leaned across the bed, but said, "I don't think you should get up just yet, my lord."

"I will do as I wish, except so far as you are concerned, where I have agreed to do your bidding. I will not extend that power to allowing you to decide whether I get up or not."

She shrugged and moved away as Morrison knocked and entered the room.

When Miss Westmacott had been dragged, sullen but with her lips firmly closed, from Lord Chalvington's room, Lydia rose.

"Alicia is waiting for me with the children," she said. "We were to meet Miss Westmacott outside for our usual walk."

"You will not find her in a good temper," he warned. "You have been either here or standing outside the door for some time. What in the world will she be supposing has happened to you?"

"I expect she thinks I've absconded. She may think I'm waiting outside with Miss Westmacott."

"She will be even more irate if she's gone out and found neither of you. I'm surprised she hasn't come looking for you."

"She may have, but I don't suppose she would think of coming here."

"Why not? I thought everyone believed us to be close."

"Well, they were wrong, were they not?"

"I hope not. Lydia …"

He stretched out his hand, but she ignored it.

"Why are you angry with me?"

"I'm not, but I cannot leave Alicia any longer."

281

"You are. Is it because you've been listening outside the door and, not perhaps having heard every word, have jumped to the wrong conclusion?"

"I doubt it. What might I have thought?"

"Ah!" His infectious grin spread across his face. "What did you think?"

"I thought …" She stopped.

"Would you like me to help you?"

She nodded.

"Did you think you heard me declaring that I was in love with Emmeline? And did that wound you – make you fear that I was not in love with you?"

"Why in the world should you be in love with me?" she asked angrily, flushing.

"I've no idea for love knows no reason, but I think it may be because you are the prettiest girl I ever saw and have the most steadfast yet gentle character of any person I have ever met. I have loved you ever since I stumbled upon you in the hall ages ago.

"I never loved Emmeline – not like that, in any event. She is a beautiful woman and I own I was attracted to her; I am also attached to her as to a relative, but I am not – and never have been - in love with her. Perhaps I might have thought I was until I discovered what being in love really is – and that was when I met you."

"Oh!"

"Do you think you could ever return my sentiments? I know it is too soon after the death of your father, but can you give me hope that one day – perhaps not too far distant – you may reciprocate something of what I feel?"

"Oh!" she said again as her heart swelled and almost burst with joy.

"Is that all you can say?"

"Yes – no – you've taken me by surprise."

"I understand women always say that, but I also understand it's rarely the case. You must know how much I value you, what pleasure your company gives me – why, it was your voice, your kiss, which revived me."

"Like Sleeping Beauty?"

"Exactly like that. So now I am yours. Will you have me?"

"Yes, oh yes, indeed I will."

"Then will you kiss me again?"

"Should I? What about Alicia?"

"The devil take Alicia. Come here."

Unable to resist obeying his lordship – for when patients are convalescing it is generally accepted that their every desire, no matter how trivial or exacting, must be immediately fulfilled – she complied.

The pair were still entwined upon Lord Chalvington's bed when the door opened to admit the Earl.

"What the devil ...?" he exclaimed, seeing the son whom he had thought to be on the very edge of mortality, engaged in an exchange of endearments with his ward.

Apart from the fact that the two young people were alone in a bedchamber, it was clear that only kisses – although perhaps a good many of them – had been given and received. Lydia was fully dressed and lay upon the coverlet, his lordship – in his nightshirt – was beneath the blankets but the pair lay closely entwined with her head upon his shoulder.

But, whether it was the sight of a young couple obviously in love in what, if it were to get about, would certainly be considered a compromising situation, or whether it was seeing – and hearing – his son fully awake and in possession of his senses – which had the greater effect upon the Earl's state of mind it would have been hard to say.

His wife having left him in the hands of his valet, the Earl had dressed and walked carefully along the corridor to his son's room. He half-expected to find his wife there but she was not and, whatever he had feared about his son's sentiments towards his stepmother, he saw that either he had been mistaken – as seemed likely since it appeared that he had got almost everything wrong for a number of years – or the object of the young man's attachment had undergone a transformation.

Lydia sat up when she heard her guardian's voice, but it was noticeable that she did not appear ashamed, although her blush indicated that she was embarrassed.

"My lord!" she said.

"I see my son has recovered," the Earl observed drily.

"Yes; is it not wonderful?"

"Indeed it is. Did he revive under your kisses, Lydia?"

"Not precisely ..." she began.

"As a matter of fact I did," Chalvington interrupted. "She tells me the doctor suggested it; I wonder if the medical profession often uses such apparently unscientific methods so successfully. In any event, it has had a most wonderful effect. I am not feeling quite as strong as ever, which is why you find me still in my bed."

"Oh, is that why? I rather thought there might have been a different reason. Dearest boy, I am utterly delighted to see you so well – and indeed to see you so happy. Has my wife visited you yet?"

"Not since I regained my senses. Papa, pray forgive me for not sending word to you at once. I own I have practised a little deception; I wanted to hear what people would say when they hung over my bed lamenting my imminent demise. I have in fact been in possession of my senses for some little time now and have spoken to Jem about the accident – of which I recall nothing. I've sent him back to Oxford to collect the damaged saddle for I am at a loss to understand how it can have slipped in the way it apparently did, and reluctant to believe that he is at fault."

"Yes," the Earl said gravely.

Lord Chalvington raised an eyebrow, evidently surprised by his father's cynical acceptance of the incomprehensibly broken girth.

"It was fortunate I did embark upon the ruse," Chalvington continued, "for it was not long after I had begun it – and I own I was growing bored, Lydia having gone off to take a walk with the children – when I did receive a visitor. It was not Mama, nor Alicia. The person who came into my room shortly after Lydia left approached my bed with some stealth and, barely pausing to ascertain whether I was still insensible, removed the pillow from beneath my head and placed it – with considerable force – over my face."

He paused to watch the effect of this narrative and was surprised to see his father's face settle into yet deeper lines and increased gravity.

"Do you want to know who it was – and what I did about it?" Ambrose asked.

"I can see you fought off the attack successfully. Where is the would-be assassin now?"

"After quite a scuffle, I was eventually rescued by Lydia, who always seems to be in the right place at the right time. She summoned Paterson, who has taken the miscreant into custody and is, I trust, even now informing the magistrate. Do you not wish to know the person's identity?"

"Unfortunately, I think I can guess."

"Really? Who do you think it is?"

"If I told you that – and I was wrong – I would be doing the person a grave disservice. I think you must tell me."

284

"Miss Westmacott."

The Earl uttered such a groan that both the young people wondered if he had suffered an unfortunate medical event but, after a moment, he nodded.

"As I thought."

"Good God!" Chalvington exclaimed. "Did you know she was a murderess – or likely to turn into one – when you engaged her? She seems an odd choice of governess to have the care of your children."

"Of course not, but I am afraid I have practised a truly appalling deception upon you – for years."

With which, the Earl retailed all that he had confessed to his wife.

His listeners, not having quite the same sense of betrayal that the Countess had suffered, heard him out in silence, even Lord Chalvington refraining from interjecting humorous remarks.

When he had done, Ambrose said, "Well, I think we should be glad Amos is safely locked up at school at the moment. I suppose you will have to tell him of his presumed parentage in due course. I should think the most distressing aspect will be the identity of his mother – I assume he doesn't know."

The Earl nodded, his face so marked with regret and sorrow that neither of the young people liked to expand upon the boy's likely reception of the laying-bare of this lamentable imbroglio.

"Poor Amos!" Lydia said.

"No wonder he was in love with you," Ambrose said, recovering his humour slightly. "He's not such an infant after all, is he? Indeed, he's older than you. Do you prefer him to me?"

"No."

"Thank God!"

Lydia left father and son together, saying that she really should relieve Alicia of her care of the children but assuring them both that she would say nothing either of Ambrose's recovery or of the attempted murder, let alone Amos's unfortunate parentage.

She found Alicia playing games with the children and, surprisingly, less irate than she had expected.

"Where in the world have you been?" she asked.

"I'm sorry; I went in to see Ambrose and then I met your father and have been speaking to him," Lydia said, suppressing a long space of time between her first action and her last.

"Well, you have been a very long time – and you still haven't put on your outdoor clothes. And where is Miss Westmacott? I'm surprised she hasn't come back wondering where we are."

"I daresay she's pleased to be relieved of her duties," Lydia said.

"Perhaps Papa has already sent her packing."

"Perhaps. Do you still want to go out?"

"I never wanted to, but by all means let us go at once because I should think it must be nearly time for the children's supper. See, I have got them all be-coated, behatted and shod – have I not done well? We will go down and wait outside for you."

Lydia was so overjoyed to be greeted pleasantly by Alicia and relieved that she was not to undergo a more intense inquisition on her whereabouts that she almost ran down the corridor to fetch her outdoor clothes.

They did not find Miss Westmacott outside, but they did find the Countess. She had evidently been for a walk herself for her cheeks were pink but, in spite of this positive sign, she did not look particularly happy. She also enquired as to the whereabouts of the governess but, receiving an ambiguous answer, asked if they would mind her accompanying them.

"Not at all," Lydia replied at once as Alicia looked both surprised and displeased.

"Has there been any change in Ambrose?" Alicia asked.

Lydia, grateful that the question had been directed at a person who could, in all truth, declare that, so far as she knew, there had not, remained silent.

"Will Papa send for Amos and Adrian?" Alicia asked.

"I shouldn't think so – why should he?" the Countess asked sharply.

"Well, if he's going to die …" Alicia said.

"I do not think you should be speculating on what will happen if he does not come to his senses," her ladyship returned, clearly irritated.

But, when they returned from their walk, which was necessarily a short one, they found the Earl awaiting them. His face was so grave that everyone – except Lydia – immediately assumed he had bad news. It seemed he had for he requested they take the children upstairs and hand them over to Nanny Macintosh, who would oversee their supper and put them to bed. When they had done that, he would expect them in the blue saloon where he had something of importance to impart.

The Countess and Alicia turned pale.

"Ambrose?" they asked in unison.

"There is no need for anxiety on that score," he told them tersely and turned away before they could question him further.

Chapter 37

When they entered the saloon half an hour later it was to find Lord Chalvington, resplendent in a silk dressing gown, sitting in a chair beside the fire.

"Ambrose!" Alicia cried. "Am I imagining this?"

She flew to his side and embraced him.

The Countess, closely watched by her husband, also exclaimed but did not rush to his side.

"When did you regain your senses?" she asked. "And are you certain it is wise to leave your bed so soon?"

"I am being very careful," he assured her. "Papa wanted us all together because he has something to tell us and doesn't wish to have to say it several times."

They all obediently sat down, were furnished with glasses of wine and prepared to listen to the Earl as he explained what had happened since Ambrose had been brought home, together with something of the history of the governess's long tenure of her position. He did not mention any suspicions he might have concerning the broken girth, perhaps thinking that Miss Westmacott's behaviour with the pillow was sufficient cause for consigning her to the care of the law without voicing any additional and - at present – uncertain conjectures regarding the cause of his son's accident.

Alicia, who had known no part of the story until now, listened with her mouth repeatedly falling open in astonishment, but she did not interrupt more than once or twice.

The Countess, who knew most of the story, took the news of Miss Westmacott's latest iniquity with equanimity. She was not surprised for, during her first walk, alone, she had thought a great deal about what she had heard and about the various protagonists.

When the Earl came to the part of the story where he had entered his son's room to find him and Lydia in each other's arms, the Countess looked delighted and exclaimed with genuine pleasure at the prospect of welcoming Lydia to an even closer position within the family, a response which, judging from his expression, set the Earl's anxious heart at rest.

It was not until after dinner, which Ambrose had not only attended but for which he had dressed appropriately, that the Earl and Countess found themselves alone again.

"Well, it seems I won't have to sack her after all," he said drily. "No doubt the magistrate will make certain she does not return here. What do you wish to do about engaging another?"

"I suppose we should advertise – unless you know of a suitable candidate."

"I'm surprised you would trust me with such a task after the last time," he said.

"You are considerably older and – I hope – wiser. Do you have any mistresses in interesting conditions who are looking for a position?"

"I have no mistresses."

"I suppose," she said slowly, "we can choose a governess together."

"Will it be, do you think, the first of many tasks we can perform together?"

"Will you stay here?"

"If you will have me."

"I do not think I could bear to be without you," she said on a quaver.

"I know I would find it heart-breaking to be without you, but I do not want you to take me back out of a sense of duty."

She shook her head. "I have never really understood duty; all I know is that I love you more than all the world, whatever your faults, and that I don't feel able to stand upon my dignity and send you away; such an action would punish me quite as much as you. If you wish to come back, pray, pray, do so."

"My dearest love, will you kiss me?" he asked, holding out his hand.

She took it and fell into his arms.

Printed in Great Britain
by Amazon